Presidential LIABILITY

~

CHRIS TAYLOR

Library of Congress Control Number:		2012901142
ISBN:	Hardcover	978-1-4691-5545-6
	Softcover	978-1-4691-5544-9
	Ebook	978-1-4691-5546-3

This book was printed in the United States of America.

To order additional copies of this book, contact:
Xlibris Corporation
1-888-795-4274
www.Xlibris.com
Orders@Xlibris.com
107803

DEDICATION

This book is dedicated to the two people that make me the happiest man on earth, my wife Alison and my son Benjamin. I love you both.

ACKNOWLEDGMENTS

I want to thank everyone that helped make this book possible. First, I want to thank Alison and Benjamin for being patient with me while I wrote it. I am grateful for your support and encouragement. Mom, Dad, Don, and Kate thank you for reading the early drafts and responding with enthusiasm. Finally, thanks to Thomas Maul, one of my favorite authors, for pushing me to write the book and for giving advice throughout.

CHAPTER 1

New York City
Upper East Side

The couple left the small mosque and entered their vehicle for their rendezvous in Canada. What they planned would surely bring the United States to her knees. Just a few more days and their mission would begin. After the attack they would be number one on America's Most Wanted list, vacated since the death of Osama bin Laden. The American president would be begging for their mercy, and they would become the hero of their people in the Middle East.

The Middle Eastern couple placed their small bag in the backseat of the car knowing that their trunk would be full of more important material. They left the city traveling at low speeds, frustrating drivers along the way. They did not care about speed. They were in no hurry, and they were too focused to be bothered by the middle fingers and other obscene gestures directed their way. "They curse us now," he said to his wife, "but soon they will respect us."

They reached the outskirts of the city and never looked back. The mosque the couple built together would continue to promote their philosophies, they were sure of that. Leaving their hard work behind was the difficult part. They devoted their lives to making it a success and risked their lives spreading radical Islamic teachings in the facility's basement.

They knew that the U.S. government was suspicious of them, but the couple was good at covering their tracks. They had given generously to local charities and ran a legit mosque on the main floor. The vast majority of the congregation did not realize what was being planned below ground level.

Over the last few months, the couple noticed the familiar vehicles of the federal government lurking around the streets of the mosque. The watchfulness of the CIA forced the group to expedite their plans. Now was the time to act.

~ ~ ~

The White House
The Residency

The president of the United States received his wake-up call at his customary time of 6:00 a.m., and he and his wife climbed out of their bed to prepare for their morning workout. President William Seaborne and his wife, Ann, took advantage of every minute they had to spend together. Since moving into the White House, they had become accustomed to working long hours while the president had business dinners and other functions almost every night.

They left their bedroom on the second floor and went through the West Sitting Hall. The room was decorated in yellows and was used for many occasions—from family parties to entertaining visiting heads of state. The couple proceeded up the private stairs to the third floor. At the end of the beautiful Center Hall was their workout area. Located next to the music room, the workout room was converted from an old bedroom; and it included an elliptical machine, a bench press with an attached squat machine, and dumbbells.

The president asked his wife, "Are you ready for your trip?"

"I am heading out in a couple of hours," Ann responded. "It will be great to see Charlie! It has been almost two months."

Charlie was a senior at Youngstown State University in Youngstown, Ohio. He was a prelaw / political science major and was in the process of researching law schools. YSU was a small urban school of about fourteen thousand students. Charlie could have gone to Ivy League schools—his parents had pushed for Harvard—but he wanted to go to school where his father went many years before.

"Make sure that you tell him I wish I could be there. I have too much on my plate right now to make it to Youngstown. Has he said anything about his choice of law schools?"

"He is waiting for Lindsey to hear back from Boston College and Ohio State. He will decide from there. Apparently he wants to go where she goes, and we both know she is not going to get into the caliber of schools that Charlie will. I am not sure how I feel about him waiting for her. Anyway, I just hope she gets into a school near Boston so Charlie will go to Harvard."

Ann Seaborne did not think much of Lindsey because she was not as driven as Charlie nor was she politically connected. They would have chosen someone with a better family background. Her parents were decent people, but both barely graduated from high school and lived in Youngstown their entire lives.

"I know how you feel about her," the president said. "Charlie will make a good decision. He is a smart and competent boy."

"Nonetheless, I still do not have to like it. Tonight I will meet them both for dinner, and afterward I have a speech at Liberty High School. Tomorrow I will be able to spend the day with them; we will probably go to Mill Creek Park. That park is the only good thing about Youngstown. Then I will be back late tomorrow night."

Ann was giving a speech about drunk driving. Each first lady usually picked a major topic of focus while in the White House. Nancy Reagan supported "Just Say No," Hillary Clinton focused on health care, Laura Bush on literacy, and Michele Obama on childhood obesity. Ann took on the issue of drunk driving since her brother was killed by a drunk driver when he was learning to drive. She worked for prevention and harsher penalties for offenders.

Ann was sweating on the treadmill as the president finished up his bench presses.

The president sat up on the bench snatched a towel and wiped the sweat from his face. He looked at his wife and smiled.

"You are still are a very attractive lady. Possibly the most beautiful first lady to ever live in the White House," William said.

"I doubt that! What about Jackie Kennedy? I do not see people running to copy my haircut or putting me on the cover of every fashion magazine in the country."

"The country does not know what it is missing," William said, trying to flatter her.

"Well, thank you anyway. What about that new intern you hired? What is her name? Jessica? She is cute, is she not?" Ann said, playing along with her husband.

"Are you jealous of a twenty-two-year-old intern that will be stuck working around the clock for the next year? She has nothing on you."

"Well, I would hope not. With a man your age, it would be disgusting."

"Bill Clinton got away with it. Who knows, maybe I can pull it off too?" William joked.

Ann gave her husband a soft punch to the stomach.

"I think that there is a rule that the first lady is the only person that can hit the president and get away with it," she said.

"Is that right? Let's just go ask," William responded while gesturing to the door.

The couple went into the hallway and saw a Secret Service agent standing guard. The residence was the only place where the president was able to be left mostly alone, but the Secret Service still had a presence. They had agents posted at both ends of the hallway so they could respond to emergencies.

"Stuart, I was wondering if there was something you could help us out with."

"Of course, sir. What would that be?" the agent asked.

"The first lady seems to believe that she can hit the president, is that true?"

Stuart smiled and said, "I think that is true, sir. In fact, we might even look away."

"I think I need to talk to your supervisor," the president responded with a smile of his own.

"Yes, sir, Mr. President," Stuart said.

"Have a good day, son."

William took Ann by the hand as they headed back to their room. Ann was pleased that her husband was in such a good mood. He was usually a serious man, but since becoming president he joked around even less.

Ann also did not play around much like this either. Many people who knew her thought she was stuck-up possibly because she liked nice things and expected only to be in the company of the privileged. Truthfully, William probably would not have run for president if she had not pushed him.

The agents assigned to protect the first couple did not get along well with the first lady; she often treated them like peasants and did not give them the respect to look them in the eye when she talked to them. She treated them like glorified bellboys, always asking them to take her luggage and fetch her belongings. The president, on the other hand, was adored by the Secret Service agents. He worked hard to know all of their names and to learn about their families. He would do small gestures such as giving them leftover food from parties and making sure he recognized birthdays with cake and a personally signed card. He also held a Christmas party at the White House in which he invited only the Secret Service agents and their families, all paid for out of his pocket.

The president was generous, but he did set high expectations. He expected all employees to be at work on time and work long hours, and he demanded that everyone gave 100 percent to support him. Many staffers wore down and went on to pursue other ventures, but those who stayed knew that they were working for a great man, making the time away from their families more meaningful.

~ ~ ~

After a relaxing breakfast with the first lady, the president headed to the Oval Office where he received the Presidential Daily Brief (PDB). The director of the Central Intelligence Agency, Thomas Host, led the meeting.

"Good morning, Mr. President," Host said.

Thomas Host was a short man with a full head of gray hair. He was not fat, but he had a large potbelly that automatically got him signed up to dress as Santa Claus at every holiday party in Washington. Looking at him, a person would never believe that he was the powerful director of the Central Intelligence Agency. His sloppy appearance did not give his intellect justice. He had a brilliant mind and was the best analyst in the CIA, which helped him climb the management ladder throughout his career. Many insiders were upset when Seaborne nominated him for the job because Host was never in the field. Most who held the position at least served in the military. Despite his lack of experience, the president knew that Host would earn the respect of everyone around him; and Seaborne was right. Host's practical and analytical mind allowed him to make solid decisions.

"What is the update on the terrorist cell in New York?" the president asked, as he took his seat behind the *Resolute* desk.

The Farah terrorist cell was gaining strength in New York City. They hid in a small mosque and used the basement to spread their anti-American sentiment. This activity was relatively normal in the U.S., but there was proof that they had recently acquired explosive materials. They had connections to the Taliban in Afghanistan, and it was believed that they had recently smuggled bomb material over the Canadian-American border. The problem was that no one knew where the material went.

After taking a deep breath Host replied, "No new information, but we are trying to get someone on the inside. Bruce Maul is heading up the team. We also have surveillance on the building, and we are recording everyone that goes in and out. We feel the material is just a scare tactic that is being used to excite their base. Maul tells me that we will have some progress by the end of the week."

Vice President Aaron Sewell added, "We are not too concerned about the situation. As far as we can tell it is just a small cell with no real power or motivation to cause too many problems. I think we should shift our focus to the Iranians. They are getting closer to having the technology required for building nuclear weapons, and the Nuclear Emergency Search Team is getting worried. Our biggest concern is keeping those weapons out of terrorists' hands."

The Nuclear Emergency Search Team was a specially trained team of about one thousand members that worked on locating nuclear weapons. Funded by the Department of Energy, the team was made up of both government and civilian employees and was a well-armed group who was ready and willing to fight themselves out of any situation in order to track down nuclear weapons.

Vice President Sewell was the secretary of defense before joining President Seaborne on the presidential ticket. Seaborne chose him because of his experience in foreign policy and military affairs, something Seaborne lacked and therefore relied heavily on Sewell's advice.

"With all due respect, Mr. Vice President, Iran has zero nuclear weapons," Host said. "While I agree that we need to keep an eye on Iran, we have more pressing issues in places such as North Korea that has about a dozen nuclear weapons and Pakistan that has around ninety-four."

Host leaned forward and looked at the president and said, "When it comes to Iran, sir, I am more concerned about the biological weapons. They were opposed to destroying diseases like small pox when the issue went before the United Nations. Why would they do that? Because Iran knows those pathogens are cheaper and easier to create and they are relatively easy to transport. If they manufacture small pox, they could do much harm, especially in the United States. In my opinion, it is a waste of resources when it comes to looking for nuclear arms in Iran."

The vice president defended himself and countered, "Can I remind you, Mr. Director, that if Iran can get their hands on nuclear material, they pose a real danger to Israel, our very close ally. There are many people in the Middle East that would pay top dollar to use that material against Israel, and we would need to come to Israel's defense in turn getting us involved in another war that our citizens want no part of."

"Host, investigate Iran's biological weapons, but do not get distracted and lose focus on their building of nuclear weapons," the president said.

"Yes, sir, but just for the record, I think we need to be more concerned with the biological weapons," Host said.

"Keep an eye on Iran and keep me updated on the cell in New York. Anything else?" the president asked.

After no response, the president added, "Good. Thank you for your time. Let's get to work."

He looked at his chief of staff, Don Austin, and asked, "What's next?"

As the group left the Oval Office, Austin and the president's top political advisor and deputy chief of staff, Brad Wilder, took the chairs on each side of the president's desk.

"Sir, I am a little worried about the terrorist cell. We do not know where the weapons are headed. I think that we need to spend more time and effort trying to track them down," Austin said.

Wilder chimed in, "Sir, we need to keep this quiet for now. If word gets out, we will have chaos."

The president thought for a moment and said, "Get Maul on the phone. I want to talk to him directly."

"Yes, sir." Changing topics, Austin said, "Mrs. Seaborne is expected to leave the White House in two hours for Ohio. She will land at the Youngstown-Warren Region Airport where the motorcade will be ready to pick her up. She will be staying at her favorite hotel, the Spread Eagle Tavern and Inn."

The chief of staff stood and stated, "Mr. President, you need to go meet with the winners of the Proud To Be an American Essay Contest in five minutes in the East Room. After that, we will call Maul."

The Proud To Be an American Essay Contest was a nationwide competition to see which high school students could write the best essay on why America was such a great country. This contest was Seaborne's idea; he wanted to see high school students write more and show pride in their country.

~ ~ ~

The East Room was full of thirty of the top writers. The president entered the room with a thunderous applause. The students and their parents were undoubtedly having an experience of a lifetime. They each had a gourmet lunch, received a certificate, and had a picture taken with the president.

Seaborne spoke for about five minutes then waited in line to greet each award recipient. As he stood there, he could not help but to think of Iran. That was the problem with being the president; they always had a million important decisions to make, and most of them were life-or-death decisions.

He did enjoy events like this where he got to meet everyday citizens. However, all he could think about was all the other places he needed to be right now. For each of the thirty students, Seaborne faked a smile, shook their hands, and posed for the picture.

CHAPTER 2

Erie, Pennsylvania
Interstate 90

Aahil Farah was driving his rented blue sedan on the New York highway. A couple of hours earlier he crossed the United States and Canada border and was headed west on Interstate 90. He was about five foot ten and one hundred and seventy-five pounds with black hair and a dark complexion. With him was his wife, Taybah, a petite woman about five foot two and one hundred and fifteen pounds. Both wore typical American styles in exchange for their regular clothing. In most circumstances Taybah would have had her body covered with the exception of her eyes and hands, but the exemption was made because they were on a mission.

When they pulled up to the guardhouse a short time earlier, the American Border Patrol officer asked, "What country are you a citizen of?"

Aahil answered calmly and collectively, "The United States."

"What were you doing in Canada, and how long were you there?"

"We only spent a couple of hours in Canada. We were at a friend's wedding in New York, and being from Florida we have never been to Canada before, so we came up here for the experience. We had lunch at a restaurant and are headed back to Florida for a game this Sunday. We have Miami season tickets, even though they are the worst team in the division this year. Like they say, it is easy to support a winning team, but a true fan will support a team even when they are down for years."

"I have been a true Buffalo fan all my life, and I know exactly what you mean," said the officer. "If they win five games a season, I am happy."

The officer looked in the backseat and saw that they had two child seats and Miami stickers in the back window. The guard was at the end of his shift and had dealt with people complaining to him all day about the wait to get over the border. "We are only coming from Canada!" was a common phrase throughout his day. Little did these people know how much contraband crossed the border every day, from prescription drugs to high-powered weapons.

The officer was not in the mood for a fight and had to get to his son's football practice. He ran the couple's passports, and they came up without any hits. To avoid the headache, the officer passed the American passports back to the smiling couple and said, "Have a great day and have a safe trip back to Florida."

The guard had just let them through with a trunk full of fertilizer mixture similar to what was used in the Oklahoma City bombing.

~ ~ ~

The couple continued on I-90 in order to get to Casalnuovo di Napoli Pizzeria in Erie. The pizzeria was a small restaurant off of Peach Street and was known to have the best pizza in town. The Stizza family started the small chain two decades before and named it after their hometown in Italy. Casalnuovo di Napoli was a beautiful city of about fifty thousand people on the west coast of the peninsula, northeast of Naples.

This particular branch, one of four locations, was also known by gangsters as a source to acquire weapons. Fred Ferrari owned the restaurant and had long connections to the mob. Ferrari was a large man, about six foot three and two hundred ninety-five pounds, and wore flashy gold jewelry. His father was a captain in the Erie mafia, the Pali family; so when Ferrari went to purchase the branch, the Stizzas felt they had no choice but to sell it to him. They also turned the other way when suspicious activities were rumored there. Some even said they had late-night poker games after the doors were locked and thousands of dollars was gambled in one sitting. One late poker game almost led to a gunfight before Ferrari was able to control the situation by making threats with a gun of his own.

When Ferrari took control, his first priority was to add a storage closet in the back of the store. The addition was larger than needed, but since Ferrari had a habit of overdoing everything, not too many people thought much about it. The front of the room was used to store extra supplies, but there was a false wall in the back. Behind it was where he made most of his money—selling illegal weapons. Most weapons were gathered from the local kids that made up the little gangs of Erie. They would burglarize houses, steal guns and other valuables, and then sell the weapons to Ferrari. Gangs and other mob families passing through would help add more military-style weapons to the cache. Surprisingly, he was able to build a pretty large collection of weapons. Ferrari would then sell the weapons to his connected friends and members of the area crime families. He even sold to larger gangs as far away as Los Angeles.

Today, he was expecting a different type of customer. He received a call earlier in the week from a connection in New York City. Although he was not too keen on helping a radical Muslim organization because he considered himself a patriot, the contact had promised large profits, so he placed his personal feelings aside.

~ ~ ~

As Aahil and Taybah pulled onto Peach Street, they were amazed by the ability of how a small-town gangster could garner such a supply of weapons. They pulled into the parking lot of Casalnuovo di Napoli Pizzeria and entered the store as they were greeted by one of the passing waitresses who told them to have a seat anywhere. The couple chose a small table in the back and waited for their menus. When the waitress arrived, they asked if they could see Fred, as if they were old pals from high school. The waitress said she would pass the message on.

Fred came out of the kitchen a few minutes later and gave Aahil a hug as if they had known each other for years. After a few pleasantries were exchanged, Fred invited them to his office in the back under the guise to catch up. They sat in the little office and began to talk business. Fred agreed to sell the couple his entire supply of AK-47s and M16s. When the cash was exchanged, Fred told Aahil to drive around and park next to the dumpster. Fred had the dumpster placed next to the storage room to help conceal movement in or out of the storage closet. Aahil took out the car seats and threw them in the dumpster, and the old cardboard boxes that stored the guns were loaded in the backseat of the sedan. A passerby would only suspect that the couple just went shopping at a bulk store and needed to buy plastic cups and paper plates for a weekend get-together.

The Farahs were soon on I-90 heading west, not too far from their next destination, where they would meet up with the rest of the group.

CHRIS TAYLOR

~ ~ ~

Washington DC
The White House

After the appearance with the essay winners, the president went to his private office on the second floor of the residency. Next to the Yellow Oval Room was the Treaty Room, and this room had long served as the president's private office. The Treaty Room was Seaborne's favorite room in the White House; it was historic and a place where he could get away from the busy Oval Office. Every modern president used it as an office, and George W. Bush spent many late evenings here preparing for the next day's agenda. President Seaborne chose to have the *Resolute* desk in the Oval Office; therefore the beautiful Treaty Table was used as his desk. The table was used by Ulysses S. Grant for his cabinet meetings before it was converted to a desk. The room was decorated with fine American art, and the president's favorite piece was the grandfather clock directly behind the desk.

Seaborne was of average height and had a full head of gray hair. When he took office, his hair was brown; but like all presidents, it quickly changed colors, which he denied had anything to do with the stress of his job. He was a little overweight, being a stress eater; and since becoming president, it seemed like he was always snacking on something, which added weight despite his workout routine. The president was known as a no-nonsense guy and expected answers when asking questions.

He dreamed of becoming president for as long as he could remember. When William was just an infant, his dad came back from a business trip to Washington DC and gave him a "Future President" onesie. When he was sixteen, William found a picture of himself wearing it as a baby and thought how cool it would be to become president but never imagined it could happen to him.

William was born and raised in Youngstown and school was always a breeze for him as he easily became the Valedictorian of his class. He decided to stay close to home and attend Youngstown State University when his father became ill with colon cancer. Every day his father pushed him to go away and pursue an Ivy League school, but William refused and instead received a full scholarship at YSU. He worked nights throughout college to help pay the family's medical bills.

His dad died his senior year and William quickly enrolled into Harvard Law School. He left partly to make his father proud and partly to get out of Youngstown and all the reminders of his dad.

Growing up in Youngstown had made him tough, as most boys there were. Many attribute that quality to the hard work that Youngstown men did every day in the mills. Fathers would pass down the work ethic to their children. Besides the Youngstown mills, football was always a popular sport, and the area produced many great coaches including Bob Stoops and Bo Pelini.

The president picked up the phone and said, "Hi, Bruce, how are you?"

"Just fine, Mr. President. It is great to talk to you again."

"What the hell is going on with the Farah cell? I don't want a bullshit answer either."

"Sir, we have lost track of the Farah cell. The main players anyway. Our surveillance has not seen Aahil or his wife in three days. The second in command, Maali, is also gone. We have a feeling that they are on the run. We are hoping for the best, but I am concerned about their whereabouts. They are small but have the means to gather weapons. What they lack in size they make up for in resourcefulness."

"The vice president does not seem too worried about the cell."

"Sir, with all due respect to the vice president, he has not been following them like I have. I know their full potential. They have a lot of motivation to cause some damage. There is reason to believe that they have been sighted coming into the United States from Canada this morning. We have a computer program that matches all pictures of people crossing, and they came up as a possible hit."

"Then why the hell didn't we stop them? If they had them they should have been stopped!"

"The program does not work in real time and even if it did, we would not have any probable cause for arrest. It is used for intelligence only. Even then, the cameras are not of high quality, and we only have an 82 percent match. Good enough to convince me, but not a judge."

"What would they be doing in Canada?" the president asked concerned.

"My only guess would be that they were buying explosives. It is fairly easy to get guns here, but explosives are another story. Getting explosives would be easier there, that is the only reason I see them going to Canada."

The president was silent for a minute then asked, "Any idea where they are headed?"

"No, but I will keep an eye on the situation and will run around-the-clock surveillance on them. They have to turn up sooner or later."

"Okay. I want to know the minute something comes up, you hear me? The very minute," the president yelled into the phone.

"Of course, sir, you will be my first call."

The president hung up the phone and wondered why Sewell was not as concerned as Maul was. Was he trying to hide something? He hit the intercom on his phone, and when his secretary picked up he demanded to talk to Sewell.

"Mr. President, you wanted to speak to me?" the vice president asked.

"I just got off the phone with Maul, and he seems very worried about the Farahs. Are you hiding something?"

"Sir, we just don't know enough to be worried yet. Maul is a good agent, but sometimes he can get overly anxious, which can cause a lot of problems."

"Maul said the Farahs could have been spotted coming across the border, possibly with explosives. Make sure he has everything he needs to track them. Call Host and tell him the same thing."

"Yes, sir, I will call him right now."

The president knew that Sewell and Maul did not get along. When you have two extremely alpha males in the same room they rarely did. Seaborne would just add this to the list of things to be worried about for the day.

~ ~ ~

Down the hall from the Oval Office was the Vice President's office. The office in the West Wing was often used by most vice presidents as a ceremonial office, but Sewell wanted to be right in the middle of things. He loved the power and the ability to always be on the minds of everyone in the building. He felt that the office in the old executive office building (OEOB) took him too far from the epicenter, thus he could not be a major player in the administration.

His office was large and had a magnificent desk at the far end of the room. On the other end of the room there were two large yellow couches and two yellow chairs that sat in front of the fireplace. The chairs and couches were staged to make a meeting more informal, but in reality no one could relax in the West Wing.

As the president had ordered, he picked up the phone and called Thomas Host at the CIA.

"Hi, Mr. Vice President, what can I help you with?"

"Thomas, the president has asked me to call you. He is still concerned with the Farah cell, and Maul thinks it is more serious than originally thought. He wants you to give Maul all the resources necessary to track them down."

Host said, "Sir, Maul is looking too much into this. The Farahs are just a small group with little following. They have the capabilities of acquiring weapons and explosives but aren't experienced enough to do anything with them. We will appease the president and let Maul track them, but, at the end of the day, it will be a waste of time."

Both Host and Sewell agreed that the president was a smart and honest man, but they believed that his lack of a military background was his downfall. Sewell joined Seaborne on the ticket to help his chances at the presidency eight years later, so for now he would bide his time.

Host continued, "I talked to Maul today; and he believes that the Farahs crossed the border this morning, and he can use his time to track them down. It won't take much; Maul likes to work alone, and all he needs is some computer support at headquarters. He has orders to call me with anything new."

"The president wants updates; if anything comes up let me know. We should spend most of our time on the Iranians. The Israelis are nervous about the situation and as our biggest ally, we need to pay attention."

"Yes, sir, talk to you soon," Host ended the conversation.

Host also wanted to move up the ladder, so he would keep the vice president close to his vest.

CHAPTER 3

Youngstown, Ohio
Victory Aviation

The first lady landed in the early afternoon at the Youngstown-Warren Regional Airport. The airport was relatively small with no major airlines flying in or out. The plane was met by a crew from Victory Aviation, the airport's only fixed-base operator or FBO. Her arrival did not draw a large crowd, and she was met with her limousine and was taken south on Belmont Avenue for the twenty-minute ride to the YSU campus. She did not have much security; her limo was sandwiched between two typical black SUVs with an Ohio Highway Patrol car leading the way.

As they pulled onto Fifth Avenue, the first lady turned to her top aide, Kate Jenner, and said, "I love coming onto campus and seeing Stambaugh Stadium. It is a great symbol of this school."

Stambaugh Stadium was the home of the Penguins, who were a member of the Division 1 Football Championship Series, formally Division 1AA, and had great success. Under local hero and former Ohio State Head Coach Jim Tressel, the Penguins won three national championships in the 1990s. The university also claimed the star of TV's *Modern Family* Ed O'Neill and ESPN's Ron Jaworski as its most famous graduates. The small school mostly served the Youngstown area but had seen a rise in applications since the first son enrolled there.

The beautiful one-hundred-and-forty-five-acre campus was in an urban setting with trees and flowers lining the sidewalks and was surrounded by the brick buildings. On the edge of campus sat the modern education and business buildings that were the most utilized areas of the campus.

The motorcade turned left onto Spring Street behind Kilcawley Center and the bookstore. The first lady wanted to stop in the bookstore to shake hands and take pictures with the students under the suggestion of Brad Wilder. He wanted to get as many votes as he could from northeast Ohio, which was traditionally a democratic area. The Republican president knew that he could win Ohio if he got the following of his hometown. "Ohio is an important swing state, which often means the presidency," Wilder often said. But it wouldn't be easy; Youngstown might have elected Democrat Jim Traficant from prison if Congress wouldn't have kicked him out. No one could remember the last time a Republican came close in an election, let alone win a political office, from the area.

After the library, the first lady walked across the picturesque campus to the Cafaro House, Charlie Seaborne's dorm. Charlie met her by the front door.

"Hey, Mom. You were all over the news shaking hands at the library. Looks like you got some good press."

Charlie was six foot and was an attractive young man who never had any trouble with finding a girlfriend. Ann remembers chasing away girls when he was in middle school. His short brown hair and bright blue eyes got him a lot of attention, along with his imposing athletic look from frequently working out and playing pickup basketball whenever he got the chance.

"I'm just trying to get some votes for your father. He wants this area bad next year, and you know Brad never lets an opportunity slip to campaign. Wow, I see that you haven't shaved in a while."

Charlie rubbed his chin and felt his newly grown beard. Proud of how thick it had grown, he said, "I thought I needed a change. Do you like it?"

"I can't say I do," the first lady said with a disapproving look. "Can't you at least trim it? It looks trashy."

"Maybe sometime soon."

"Where is Lindsey?"

"She is writing a paper on the Vietnam War. She will be over in a little bit. Come on up to my room and relax for a minute. I don't want to have a conversation in front of the entire dorm." Other residents of the dorm started to gather and were gawking at the first lady.

They got in the elevator and headed to the second floor. Charlie's room was close to the stairs in case of an emergency if he needed to be evacuated. The rooms to the left and right of his were being used by the Secret Service agents in his detail. These rooms allowed them to monitor the hallway and the building, and they always had someone posted outside Charlie's door. His window was made of bulletproof glass to prevent an attack from outside.

When they arrived at the room, Ann said, "How has the protection been? Are they giving you more room now?"

Charlie had complained to his parents that the Secret Service had been too oppressive. The agency had promised to back off a little bit, meaning that instead of sitting in the classroom, they would sit right outside the door. They still followed him everywhere, including romantic dinners and frat parties. Most first children often complained of the protection because it vastly limited their freedom.

"It is getting a little better," Charlie said, sounding annoyed. "They are still all around."

"I know how hard it can be with them tracking you everywhere, but we both know it is for your own good. Try to pretend they are not there."

"Easier said than done."

Ann looked around her son's room. It was a little messy and crowded, just like every other college student, she thought. On his desk was his textbook for the Constitutional Law course he was taking this fall. On the bookshelves were the books of some of his favorite authors, including Brad Meltzer, Vince Flynn, and John Grisham.

"I hope you are not spending too much time reading novels instead of studying."

"No, I only read in my spare time or just before I go to sleep. Bob and I swap books when we can." Charlie started to laugh, "Did you hear about Bob? We were out drinking the other night at a sorority house"—he stopped to let out a loud laugh—"and after about six shots and a bunch of beer we were on our way out. He stopped to say hi to a group of girls but instead fell down a set of stairs and broke his right ankle! The entire house saw it. Ha-ha! We won't be going back there any time soon."

Ann was not impressed. "What would have happened if someone caught you on tape and put it on YouTube? That would have been played on every news station in the world! You are the first son of this country, and you need to be more careful. You will embarrass your father and the nation!" Ann felt the skin of her face getting warm and knew she needed to calm down before she ruined the night.

"I know, Mom. We were just out having a little fun."

"Charlie, just look at all the time the princes of England have been in the news or the Bush twins getting caught partying. You just need to be careful."

"I'm not out there dressed like a Nazi like Prince Harry. It was just a few beers."

Trying to change the subject, Ann said, "Why don't you give Lindsey a call? We need to get going to dinner, so I can make it to the high school on time."

"Sounds good. When are you and Dad ever going to warm up to her? She is a great girl. I know her family is not political and are working class, but that could be a good thing. They will never interfere with Dad's career. I really love her, Mom; I want you guys to give her a chance."

"We can talk about this later, sweetie. Just give her a call."

Charlie reluctantly listened to his mother and picked up the phone to call Lindsey.

~ ~ ~

Ann, Charlie, and Lindsey decided to go to dinner at the Golden Dawn restaurant. It was an old and small restaurant but it was almost a historic place in Youngstown. A couple could have a great meal for fewer than twenty dollars, including drinks. The owner was in his eighties and didn't believe in raising his prices, which kept his customers loyal. The Golden Dawn was decorated in pictures of past athletic teams of the Ursuline High School Fighting Irish. The pride of Ursuline sports was its football team, which had won several state championships in the last decade. The Secret Service sent an advance team to sweep the building. Once word got out, the Golden Dawn had people out the door all the way to Wick Street.

The first lady drove in her motorcade, while Charlie and Lindsey drove in their own car. The first son was able to drive his own vehicle but was closely followed by a Suburban, as is typical of all first children. To some extent, it was the only sense of freedom they got. Many presidents' children used this as a perfect chance to escape and tried to evade the detail, including the Bush twins.

They sat in the back of the restaurant and quickly looked over their menus even though they knew what they wanted. The ladies ordered the rigatoni with meatballs, and Charlie ordered the Jumbo, which was a big burger and fries for less than four dollars.

"I always love coming here," Charlie said.

"Me too, Charlie," Lindsey added. "My parents and I have been coming here for years."

"I'm not so sure this is my favorite place," Ann stated. "Is there not a fancier place around?"

Charlie and Lindsey ignored the comment and an uncomfortable silence went over the table. Charlie continued the conversation, "When are you going to finally accept Lindsey and I, Mom? We see a future in each other."

Ann was slightly embarrassed and horrified that her son would bring up the topic now. "I don't think this is the . . ."

She was cut off by Charlie. "Then when? You always blow me off."

Frustrated she said, "Your father and I just want to wait until after college. There are so many people out there for both of you. You two are just too young. Give it a couple of years of grad school then we will talk."

That was not the answer Charlie was looking for. "You are going to have to accept it one way or another. It will be a lot easier for everyone if you just accepted it."

Their food was served, and they ate the first couple of bites in silence.

Finally, Ann felt the need to break the tension, "So Lindsey, any new word on grad school?"

"Not yet, Mrs. Seaborne. My top choice is Boston College; they have a great history program there." Lindsey had aspirations to become a history professor, specializing in American history. She was a petite girl about five foot four with shoulder-length brown hair and brown eyes. She was a very beautiful girl especially when she was dressed up. Charlie swore that she could stop a crowd in its tracks.

"I will have my fingers crossed for you. Boston is truly a beautiful city," Ann responded with a smile.

As they finished up their meal, Kate paid the bill while Charlie and Ann walked around and greeted the patrons, and Lindsey respectively waited by the door. They shook hands and smiled like they had done a million times. Charlie was used to this; it was fun having everyone running after you all the time. But reality proved to be annoying, sometimes he fake-smiled so much his cheeks hurt.

When they left, the parties got into their separate cars—the first lady headed to Liberty High School and the kids to a local party at Rust Belt Brewing Company. They would meet up again in the morning to tour Mill Creek Park and visit some local high schools.

~ ~ ~

Youngstown, Ohio
West Side

As the first lady was getting into her limo, the Farahs arrived across town at an old house they rented in a largely abandoned part on the west side. The city was hit hard by outsourcing, just like most cities in the rust belt. Old timers could tell stories of when everyone in Youngstown had a great-paying job and factories lined the streets. The downtown area was full of stores, restaurants, and theaters that made for the perfect night out. Now, the city looked almost abandoned, and there was no worry of traffic jams on the main strip. The city had recently done a good job in bringing back the life to the downtown area with more bars and restaurants opening up; but with the emigration of young people leaving the city, they have a lot of work to do. The main problem Youngstown had was that most people after graduating from YSU left the area to find better jobs, leaving behind a void of skilled workers. Until high-paying jobs come back to Youngstown, this would be a continuing trend.

They were met at the front door by Maali, who was running things while Aahil was away. There were a total of eight people in the group, all with the same mission.

"Hello, how are you my friend?" Maali asked of Aahil. They spoke only English so they could better blend when out in public.

"Do we have everything ready? I want no mistakes tomorrow." He looked into the front room, and the other five were sitting on the couches watching TV. Aahil hated television. He believed that it would be the downfall of the Americans because they spent too much time in front of the "idiot box."

"What are you fools doing?! We have a mission to prepare for. Get off your asses and get the weapons out of the car." After hearing Aahil's words they jumped quickly to comply. Aahil turned to Maali and continued his rant, "How can you let them be so lazy! We are not here to watch television; we are here to serve Allah."

"I am just trying to let them relax for a minute. We have been working all day and have completed the checklist you have sent us. We are ready." Maali calmed him down and continued, "We got word today that they will be visiting several high schools in the afternoon, including Poland High School. As they are coming out we will attack. Their security forces are not very large, and we have enough explosives and firepower to stun them. We have the vans ready in the garage. Taybah will drive the lead van, and you and I will capture the first son and head out. The others will have a vehicle waiting and have an escape route planned. I assure you that it will go flawlessly."

"It better because we have a lot riding on this. Have them unload the weapons from my car and finish getting the vehicles ready. Then make sure they get a good night's sleep. If I hear the television on once tonight, I swear I will blow it up." Aahil and Taybah headed up the stairs to get a good night's sleep. They would have a long day in the morning.

~ ~ ~

Youngstown, Ohio
Near the Youngstown State Campus

"I don't think you should drive home," the bartender said.

"I'll be fine. It is not a long drive anyway," replied Scott.

"I can call you a cab. It won't cost too much," the bartender offered.

"No, thank you." Scott pulled out a fifty-dollar bill and set it on the bar. "Keep the change. I'll see you next time."

Scott Morgan got in his truck and began driving home at eleven thirty. Lynyrd Skynyrd's "Saturday Night Special" played from his greatest-hits CD in the background. He got in a fight with his wife, Tracy, earlier in the afternoon and decided that he would just drink his problems away. She was mad because he spent their much needed money on a new PlayStation 3. He said he could play online for free with all of his friends, but she knew it was only another excuse to drink. He worked for a local HVAC company and Tracy worked as a nursing assistant at the Northside Hospital. He drove a 1978 green-and-white Ford F-150 that was his pride and joy. He was a little upset with the bartender suggesting that he could not drive home, but like most things in life he shrugged it off and concentrated on the road.

After realizing that he was drunker than he thought, he said out loud to himself, "Come on, Scott, you are almost there." He was praying that he would not get pulled over, as it would be his third DUI, and he would more than likely face jail time if he was pulled over. He imagined what Tracy would say then.

He was getting ready to pass through an intersection; he looked up and noticed that the light was red. A red 2010 Mustang flew through the intersection, and he instinctively hit his brakes. It was not in time, however, as he slammed into a big black Suburban that followed the

Mustang. Scott's front end was smashed, and the side of the large SUV was badly damaged.

Scott glanced through the broken window and saw the Mustang screech to a stop. The two men in the Suburban were wearing suits and were both moving, a sign that they were fine. Trying to save himself the DUI, he started the engine and drove the badly damaged truck home and prepared for another fight with Tracy.

~ ~ ~

Charlie's heart was pounding in his chest as he hit the brakes and the car came to a quick halt. Charlie and Lindsey were just leaving the Rust Belt Brewery at the Old B&O Station, just down the street from the YSU campus. He was there to celebrate his friend's birthday, and although he was at a brewery, he did not have more than two beers for the evening. His mother's word about drinking and driving had sunk in over the years, and even though the Secret Service was the most reliable designated driver in the world, he enjoyed his freedom more than being intoxicated. By now his mom would be sound asleep at the Spread Eagle, and he wanted to get home early so they could meet the next day.

"Oh my god, Charlie, what just happened?" Lindsey asked in a panic.

"They just got hit behind us," Charlie responded winded. Charlie then had a thought.

"You know this could be our best opportunity," he said.

"What are you talking about?"

"Let's go. Let's just take off and go south so we can have some freedom. This is our only chance to get away for a while." Lindsey was quiet for a second, which made Charlie get more anxious. "Come on, Lindsey!"

"Screw it, let's go!" Lindsey started to have a knot in the pit of her stomach.

As they pulled away, Lindsey was thinking about how bad of an idea it was to leave. She had to finish her paper on the POWs of the Vietnam War, and what would her parents think? *Too late now,* she thought.

"We need to ditch the car. Do you have any ideas?" Charlie interrupted her thoughts.

Lindsey thought for a moment and remembered that her friend's dad from high school owned a small used-car lot.

"My friend Mandy owns a car lot in North Jackson, and I have been there a thousand times. I can get us in and grab a set of keys in no time," she said.

"We can ditch the Mustang on the way out of town. What about going to Florida?"

"Great. I need a tan."

Charlie pointed the Mustang west and headed down Mahoning Avenue toward North Jackson.

CHAPTER 4

Youngstown, Ohio
Fifth Avenue

Rich Maxwell and Ray Turner were taken by complete surprise when the 1978 F-150 plowed into the side of their vehicle. Rich was Charlie's lead agent, but he and Ray had developed a very close relationship. They trusted each other extensively, both on a professional level and a personal level. Their families spent a lot of time together, and their wives had become best friends. The wives figured it was because they were the only ones that could understand the lifestyle of being married to Secret Service agents. Their husbands were constantly on the road, working on weekends, and they had to live in one of the least desirable cities that were available in the Secret Service.

Ray was behind the wheel and immediately took out his firearm. "Rich, are you okay?"

Rich yelled back, "I'm fine. Are we under attack?!" Rich had suffered a broken collar bone, but he put the pain behind him.

Both men went through a lot of training for this very moment. Their first priority was to get to the first son. Lindsey was an afterthought. When George W. Bush was president, he went to visit a friend for dinner. The Secret Service sent an advanced detail and picked a small closet where the president could be taken into if the house came under attack. After looking into the closet, Bush's friend said, "It looks like there is only enough room for maybe two people in there." The agent replied, "Enough for an agent and the president. If we are under attack that is all we need." Bush's friend understood that if they were ever under attack, he and everyone else at the party, including the first lady, were left to fend for themselves. The same theory applied to this situation, Charlie was the only objective.

Both men looked up and saw the truck reversing, then speeding off, but not before Ray was able to get a bullet off. Not knowing if they were still under attack, they turned their attention to Charlie's red Mustang in front of them. What the agents saw next was the scariest of all: the car took off.

Rich yelled to Ray, "Go!" The agents' vehicle was too badly damaged, and it did not move. "What the hell? Get this car moving!" Rich yelled.

"It won't move!" Ray responded.

Rich took his radio in his hand and made the hardest call of his life, "Attention all agents; Jamin has lost his protection. I repeat Jamin is on his own."

All members under the surveillance of the Secret Service are given code names. Charlie got his because Benjamin Franklin was his favorite historical figure, and he liked to listen to music. Jamin comes from the end of Ben*jamin*.

The FBI dispatcher responded in disbelief, "Do I hear you correctly Agent Maxwell? Jamin is no longer under Secret Service protection?"

"That's correct. We have been rammed by a late model 1970s pickup truck, and Jamin has left our area. We must consider this as a possible attack. Call all available units to the intersection of Fifth Avenue and Wood Street. You also need to call Washington immediately."

"Did you see what direction they were headed?" the dispatcher responded.

"They went north on Fifth."

"10-4. Backup is on the way."

~ ~ ~

Washington DC
Secret Service Headquarters

Barbara Harper was the director of the Secret Service and was in the office when the crash occurred. She worked long hours and she was married twice, but the job got in the way of both marriages. For this reason, she thought it was better just to work. Being a female in this job was tough, and she had to prove her worth, more so than a man ever would. She was in her office when she received the phone call. Her office was on the top floor and decorated with pictures of her with all of the world leaders that she had protected over the years. It bothered her sometimes that she did not have any pictures of children, or at this point in her life, grandchildren, to hang on the walls.

When her intercom beeped she jumped a little in her chair, startled as it broke the silence.

"Ms. Harper, you have an urgent call from Youngstown," her assistant said.

When she heard the key phrase "urgent call" she knew she was in for a long night.

She snatched the receiver and said, "This is Harper."

She could sense the panic in the voice of the caller. "Ms. Harper, this is Jennifer Martinez. We have a situation."

Jennifer Martinez was a Hispanic woman who was very diligent at her work, and it helped her ascend quickly through the ranks of the service. She was waiting for her next promotion, the lead on the president's detail. Most in the agency believed that she would one day be the next director. When Martinez first got the call, she was a little ashamed that the first thing she thought about was the possibility of not moving up. While she was not at the scene, the responsibility ultimately was on her shoulders.

Martinez continued, "Agents Turner and Maxwell were following Jamin when a green-and-white 1970s Ford F-150 collided with their vehicle. The agents on scene took a shot at the truck as it sped away. Their first reaction was to stop the vehicle." She was watching her words, making sure that everything came out perfectly. "As they turned their attention back to the Mustang it was already heading down Fifth Avenue. The agent's vehicle was too badly damaged to pursue. At this moment," she hesitated before saying, "Jamin is missing. We have not ruled out the possibility of an attack. We have all agents on the streets now, as well as the Ohio Highway Patrol and the Youngstown Police Department. Choppers have been scrambled and will be in the air in minutes."

The Secret Service kept a pair of helicopters at the Youngstown airport for a situation just like this. Since the first lady was in town, the agency had people at the airport on standby.

Harper's blood pressure immediately jumped as she screamed into the phone, "You better find him and now!" Realizing that yelling would get her nowhere she calmed down and said, "What makes you think this could be an attack?"

"We don't have anything solid yet. For all we know, while the agents were firing their weapons at the truck, someone could have gotten behind the wheel, or somehow forced the first son into their control. We understand that Jamin's first response might be to get out of the area, but he should have checked in by now. He knows all of the safe houses in the area."

"That is of great concern. I am going to call the White House, you keep me up to date, and I don't want to miss a detail! Martinez, make sure that everyone keeps this quiet, we don't want the press getting a hold of this yet."

The director hung up the phone, took a deep breath and looked through her phone book for the chief of staff's cell phone number.

"Hello," Austin answered after the first ring.

"Don, this is Barb. We have a situation. I need you, the deputy chief of staff, vice president, CIA director, and the secretary of defense in the Situation Room now. I will explain the details when we get there." The group made up what the director called the Emergency Response Team, which was the most important people needed in the event a protectee was missing.

"On my way, Barb. I will make the calls now."

Harper knew the chief of staff would understand how dire the situation was once she called the group to the Situation Room. Normally, she would take orders from the chief of staff, but in times of emergencies, she was in charge of the president's and first family's life, and no one, including the president, would tell her no. She was just hoping she wasn't the one who was going to tell the president that his son was missing.

~ ~ ~

North Jackson, Ohio
Route 45

"Where is the dealership at, Lindsey?" Charlie asked.

"Right down here on Route 45," she said as she squinted to gain a better view of "Bush's Quality Auto" sign. It was a small dealership that only dealt with used cars. The office building was only about 1,600 square feet and was in dire need of updating, but the locals still shopped there because of the service. "There it is, on the right. Pull in the back."

Charlie turned off the lights and pulled behind the small building. North Jackson was made up of mostly farms and a few restaurants, so Lindsey wasn't afraid of too much traffic.

They looked around the lot to see what car they wanted to take. They wanted something small that would not draw too much attention. Charlie noticed a black 1998 Ford Taurus and told Lindsey to get the keys.

Lindsey went to a window next to the back door.

"Mandy's dad was always too cheap to put in a good alarm system. They only have the doors wired, so if we go through a window we should be fine."

She grabbed her jacket and wrapped it around her elbow and broke the glass. Charlie thought that it was ironic that they broke the pane that displayed the alarm sticker. She reached up and unlocked the window and climbed in. Charlie was surprised that Lindsey was so efficient at breaking in.

Lindsey looked back and asked, "Why do you look so surprised? Look around you; we didn't have much to do in this town, so sometimes we got ourselves into trouble. Wait right here, and I will grab the keys."

Three minutes later Lindsey was back with the keys and a license plate.

She told Charlie, "I got the keys and figured that we wouldn't get too far without a plate." The license plate was one that the dealer used for test drives.

Charlie was secretly impressed and attracted to the side of Lindsey that he was discovering. He gathered his composure and responded, "That will have to do. Get what you need out of the car, and we will get going."

"What about your Mustang? You are just going to leave it here?"

"They will be on to us soon anyway, why waste time trying to ditch the car? It is well enough hidden now and won't be found until the workers get here in the morning. By that time we will be three states away."

Lindsey collected her purse from the car while Charlie took his CD collection, which mostly consisted of alternative and rock music.

Standing next to the Taurus Lindsey started having second thoughts. She asked, "Charlie, what are we doing? This is dumb. We have no clothes, no idea where we are going, no money, we have class tomorrow, and we are running from the U.S. Secret Service! We should go back. For all we know Rich and Ray are really hurt."

Rich and Ray liked to take the night shift when Charlie was out on the town, and consequently Lindsey got to know them well. They were friendly enough, but their job did not allow them to get too close, even so Lindsey was still genuinely concerned for their well-being.

"I'm sure they are fine," Charlie said starting to get a little annoyed. "Look, this is our only chance for a taste of real freedom. We won't be gone long, and we can think of it as a little vacation. You know I have plenty of money in my bank account. We can buy enough clothes for the week and hit some nice hotels. We will pay in cash with no questions asked."

Lindsey considered the idea. "Your parents put that money in your account for school. They will be pissed when they find out you took from it, especially if the money is used for me. This situation is just getting worse."

"They won't stay mad at us for too long, and they will just refill the account. You know my mom can't hold a grudge against her little boy."

Charlie walked to the back of the Taurus and put the magnetic plate on. He knew he wouldn't get too far with an out-of-state dealer's plate as he went south, but it would have to do for now. Plus, the Secret Service will know what make and model to search for therefore he knew at some point he would need to get a new ride. But for now he needed to get Lindsey in the car before they lost their chance. He knew that the best way to get her moving was to get in the driver's seat and start the car. As he started the ignition, Lindsey got into the passenger seat and leaned over holding her stomach.

"What's wrong," Charlie asked.

"Just nervous. We better get going before I change my mind." She was feeling guilty from breaking into her friend's dealership, running away without telling her parents, and leaving her school work behind.

Charlie put the car in gear and pulled onto Route 45. He asked, "Is there an ATM here?"

"Go to the center of North Jackson. Keep going this way, and it is where forty-five crosses Mahoning Avenue. How much money are you going to pull out?"

"I was thinking a couple of thousand. That should be enough to pay for food, hotels, gas, and clothes for a couple of days."

When they arrived at the bank, Charlie got out of the car and walked to the ATM. He put his card in the machine and typed in his PIN. When it requested the amount needed, Charlie typed "$3,000." The computer beeped and flashed a message that the maximum amount was $300.

"Shit," he said to himself. He completed his $300 transaction and went back to the car. He was not looking forward to asking Lindsey to use her card too.

"The ATM maxes out at $300. I need you to withdraw some money; I will reimburse you when we get back." She was too quiet and he added, "This is it. We need to go now or back to YSU and finish out the year with no new adventures. And we will still hear about this whole thing from my parents anyway."

He pulled her close and kissed her on the forehead. "Please."

"Fine."

With the newly acquired $600 they got from the machine, and the $250 combined they had in their wallets, they would only have enough money to last a few days. Without access to credit cards, and the need for hotel rooms, new clothes, food, and gas they would need a new idea to get more cash.

"Charlie, what are we going to do about money? We are going to need more than $850," Lindsey asked.

"I know the right person who will help us. We will be there by morning," Charlie responded.

Charlie decided to get gas before he got on to I-76 because he knew it would be the last time he could use his credit card because the Secret Service would be tracking it. He figured since he used his ATM card anyway, they would already know he was in the area.

While he was filling the car, Charlie remembered that the Secret Service could track their cell phones. *Great*, he thought sarcastically, *more good news to break to her.*

He leaned into to the window and said, "I need your cell phone."

"Why?"

"The Secret Service can track us using the GPS systems in them. I will throw them in the trash, and the Secret Service will be here soon to retrieve them. I will buy a new one on the road."

Lindsey went into her purse and pulled out her iPhone and handed it to Charlie. Charlie put both phones in the trash. He was sure the Secret Service would pick them up soon.

A few minutes later Charlie was back in the car, and they were headed south. Charlie pulled out a Blink-182 CD while Lindsey reclined the seat and put her feet on the dash. Charlie tapped to the music as he merged with traffic, and Lindsey closed her eyes wondering if this adventure would be worth it.

CHAPTER 5

Hanover, Ohio
Spread Eagle Tavern and Inn

The first lady had just gone to bed and began reading a new romantic novel. She knew that it was an easy read, but she enjoyed them, and it took her mind off the everyday stress that came with being the first lady. The speech at Liberty High School went well, and she drew a large crowd; for that Brad Wilder would be pleased. She loved the historic Spread Eagle Tavern and Inn. It had been there since the early nineteenth century, and she was staying in her favorite room, the Washington Room. She was looking forward to spending time with Charlie tomorrow, and Mill Creek Park was a wonderful way to spend the day. Mill Creek Park was arguably the most beautiful place in Youngstown. It had a large rose garden, trails, and a large skating rink in the winter.

Ann started to nod off a little as she was reading the book; she tried to convince herself that she could stay awake, even if it was just for a couple more pages. But her fatigue finally took over, and the book fell to her chest.

The next thing she remembered was the door of her room being busted open as she was swarmed by Secret Service agents.

"What is going on?!" she demanded.

"There is a situation. We need to leave the building now."

Still trying to wake up, she argued, "But I am in my night clothes! You can't expect me to go out like this." The first lady was wearing a night gown that was not too reveling, but she did not want anyone seeing her in it except her husband.

As she was finishing her statement, one of the agents took her by the arm and pulled her through the room's small door. Ann was surprised she didn't break an ankle as she was dragged down the stairs to the waiting motorcade. As she was thrown into the right side of the limo, Kate entered the left side, she too still barefoot and in her pajamas. The motorcade sped from the hotel and was soon joined by three Hanover police cruisers. It was a small town and Ann thought that it had to be all the cars they had on patrol that night. One joined the highway patrol car in the front, while the other two fell behind.

"I demand to know an answer right now!" she yelled.

"Ma'am, just remain calm. We have a threat and as soon as I know more details I will let you know. Right now we are headed back to the airport and will soon be in the air for Washington."

"But I have full schedule tomorrow!"

"That is not my area, ma'am," the agent responded without elaborating any more.

She looked at Kate for guidance, but all Kate could muster was, "We will be in the air soon. I will work on the schedule as soon as I get my things brought to me. Don't worry, everything will be fine."

Ann's face drained of blood, and she looked like a ghost. "Oh my god, is Charlie okay? What about the president? Please give me some answers. *Now!*"

The agent turned to her and said, "Honestly, I am not sure yet myself. We were just told to evacuate you as soon as possible. I will keep you informed by letting you know as soon as I find anything out." The agent lied to the first lady because if he told her that her son was missing, he would not have been able to get her on the plane.

The first lady looked out the window and prayed that Charlie was not in danger.

~ ~ ~

Washington DC
The White House

It seemed like everyone got to the White House at the same time, with Barbara Harper being the last to arrive. She was amazed by how fast the group could get to the White House, but they were helped out by police escorts. As soon as she got off the phone with Don Austin, she called the Washington DC Metro Police Department to have cruisers lead the way for the members of the Emergency Response Team.

The White House was placed under lockdown, meaning no one was allowed in or out with the exception of essential people. Since it was late at night, it was not a big inconvenience. The decision was made to not wake the president because he was already in a secure location. Agents were posted outside his door to move in if needed.

The White House Situation Room was a large area in the basement of the West Wing that was used for the country's most sensitive issues. It was updated in 2006 under the Bush administration in order to advance its confidential communication system. The room featured secure video rooms, a live feed directly to Air Force One, windows with frosted glass for confidential meetings, and a system to prevent unauthorized cell phone use. The main conference area had a large wooden table with three large screens on the wall where important images, maps, and live teleconferences could be projected. The president's seat was reserved at the top of the table facing toward the large monitors on the wall.

After passing clearance, Harper walked into the room and sat at a chair in middle of the table. The chief of staff was to her right, and the deputy chief of staff was to her left. Directly across from her was the CIA director, the secretary of defense, the secretary of Homeland Security, and the vice president. If the president were in the room, the chief of staff would be on his direct left and the vice president to his right.

Harper started the meeting. "Good evening and thank you for coming in so late. We have a situation in Youngstown." Harper could see them trying to think who was missing, the first lady or the first son, and secretly wondering who would be worse to lose.

"Earlier tonight Jamin was driving down Fifth Avenue toward his dorm. He was being closely followed by his two primary agents, Maxwell and Turner. As they were crossing the intersection of Wood Street and Fifth Avenue, an unknown vehicle crashed into the agents' Suburban. The agents were able to fire a shot at the truck, but the F-150 got away." She paused to take a deep breath before continuing, "As the agents moved their focus to Jamin's car, it drove off. At this point, we have to assume that he has been kidnapped. We have patrols looking for his vehicle as we speak."

Brad Wilder was the first to speak up. "The news doesn't have this, right? I mean, we need to be careful of who gets this information. Losing the first son will be horrible politically." As the top political advisor in the White House, his first concern was the political impact of any situation. Most resented this, but everyone knew that it was a necessary evil in the world of politics, and when it came down to it, they all wanted to keep their jobs for another four years.

Sewell intervened, "More importantly we need to protect Charlie. If any would-be terrorists, foreign or domestic, finds out that he is on the run, we will have some real big problems. For now, no press. Make the site look like a normal accident, and you need to make sure that all who are involved know that this is a sensitive situation. Hell, most cops get off on the idea of being involved in a top-secret case."

"We have contacted the agents protecting the first lady, and so far it is quiet," Harper said. "She is awake and on the road to the airport where she will be escorted on her plane to come back to Washington. Her motorcade has been expanded to three more patrol cars in addition to the motorcade already in place. Host, what are your people saying?"

"Right now, Barb, we have no intel on the ground. The Farah Cell is making me nervous though."

"For god's sake, Host, I thought you said they weren't a threat, and now you are telling me they could be involved!" Sewell was irate at the implication because he was made to look inept to the president.

"Mr. Vice President, we followed strict protocol in consideration to the cell," Host responded in his defense. "I talked to Maul on the way over here, and he is tracking the Farah group west on I-90. He is actually pretty close to Youngstown. He should be there in about an hour and a half and will be able to tell us if this is connected to a terrorist group, specifically the Farahs."

"We have all our agents and the area police departments looking for the green-and-white truck. We have told them it was associated with a drinking and driving incident, so we don't need to worry about journalist monitoring the scanners," Harper said.

Often members of the media would sit at home and listen to police scanners to help them catch a good news story for the next day.

"Now, Don, this is your area. Who is going to tell the president?" Harper asked.

"I'll do it," Austin responded. "I have worked with him very closely over the last few years. Plus, as chief of staff I am becoming used to delivering bad news to him."

"I want to be there too," Sewell added.

"Thanks for the support, sir." Austin turned to an aide and ordered, "Have the butler call the president and wake him up. Make him aware that we are headed there right now." Turning back to the group Austin added, "He is going to be pissed."

~ ~ ~

The White House
The Residency

The president had a large bedroom on the second floor of the residency. The room had white wallpaper and green butterflies that had been there since Nancy Reagan had installed it in the early 1980s. The bed stood across from a large fireplace and a desk and chair were placed perpendicular to the bed.

The president was sound asleep, peacefully unaware of the situation. He was startled when the phone rang and rushed to pick up the receiver.

"Hello?" He knew a call at this hour meant it was urgent. His first thought was the Iranians had caused some trouble.

The butler said, "Sir, Mr. Austin asked me to call and let you know that he and the vice president are on their way up. They have just left the Situation Room and will arrive momentarily."

"Damn it," he said under his breath. "Have the kitchen brew some coffee; this is going to be a long night."

He hung up the receiver on his nightstand and climbed out of bed to put on a bath robe and slippers. Just as he was dressed he heard a knock on the door. "Come in," he yelled.

Both the vice president and the chief of staff were visiting the president's bedroom for the first time. This was the one area where the president had complete privacy. They would not have entered the room if Mrs. Seaborne was in the room, but she was on an airplane somewhere above Pennsylvania.

"Mr. President, we have a situation that needs your immediate attention," Austin said.

"Just get on with it," the president responded bitterly.

"Sir, an hour and a half ago Charlie was on his way home from the Rust Belt Brewery and was being followed by the agents. A green-and-white pickup truck ran a red light and slammed into the agents' vehicle."

"Oh, god," the president got out before he found a chair in front of the fireplace and sat down.

Austin continued, "The truck backed up and the agents were able to fire a shot at it but were unable to slow it down. The agents then turned their attention to Charlie's vehicle, and it took off down the street. All we know at this point is Charlie is missing, and we have every resource at our disposal trying to track him down. We need to assume that he and Lindsey have been kidnapped, but we cannot be certain."

The president sat silent for a moment to let the news sink in. The worst fear of any parent was losing a child to a kidnapping, but for the president of the United States, it meant so much more. His son could be a target of a terrorist, and the president could be forced to pick between a terrorist's demands or his own son's life.

"What about my wife, is she all right?" the president asked.

"Yes, sir, as we speak she is in the back of her limo and on the way back to her Boeing 757 aircraft at the Youngstown airport. We have added more security to her detail, and we are treating her protection with the highest priority."

There was a knock at the door, and the men noticed a butler holding a tray with a coffee carafe, hazelnut creamer, and a cup for the president. The butler asked the other two men, "Would you like cups as well?"

The president answered for them, "That will not be necessary; they will be leaving soon. But make sure that every pot is on in the West Wing."

"Yes, Mr. President," he responded as he put the tray on the end of the table and left the room.

The president poured some creamer in the cup and followed it with coffee.

He thought for a minute and said, "There better be a good reason I am just hearing about this now. My son has been missing for an hour and a half. What the hell is wrong with you?"

The vice president spoke up for the first time, "Mr. President, our first priority was to assemble the Emergency Response Team, and we needed clear heads to assess the situation. With you in the room, people would have been more worried about upsetting you instead of making the best analysis. There was nothing you could have done that would have changed the situation. If the circumstance needed your direct involvement, I assure you that we would have waked you up."

The president, clearly upset, said, "If this ever happens again, you all will be looking for new jobs." Changing his tone to sincerity, he asked, "How are the agents?"

"One broke his collar bone when he hit the door and otherwise suffered some minor injuries. It could have been much worse."

"Good. I am going to get dressed, and I will meet you in the Oval Office in ten minutes. Make sure the Emergency Response Team is there with a complete update."

The president dressed in a pair of khakis and a button-down shirt and appreciated his first cup of coffee that would be the first of many that day. He thought about Charlie and wondered where he could be. He hoped that he was just being dumb and went for a little joy ride without his protection, but Charlie was more responsible than that. He was also prepping to tell his wife that her only child was missing. With that thought, the president took a long sip of his coffee and prepared himself mentally for the lack of sleep he would get in the next few nights.

CHAPTER 6

Allen Kinsey worked for the Secret Service and the Department of Homeland Security since its establishment in 2002. He graduated with a computer science degree from the University of Wisconsin, which had one of the best computer science programs in the country. He was always a computer whiz, and many people around him thought he was a geek, but he was still goofy enough to make people laugh. At thirty-three years old, he was still single and never really had a long-term girlfriend, which he blamed on his demanding job. He was a computer technician for the Secret Service, and his job was to clear and secure the service's intelligence software.

Even though Kinsey made $70,000 a year, he had no extra money. He was heavily in debt from his student loans, was a little too careless with credit cards for the last two years, and his big city rent was taxing on his bank account. When he was first hired by the Secret Service, he was excited for the opportunity to serve his country. After a couple of years he began to dream about all the money the free enterprise would bring, but every time he went back to Wisconsin, his grandmother introduced him to her church friends as the grandson who protected the president. He would wait his time to make her proud, then he would move on to earn the big paycheck he knew he always wanted.

His thinking changed when he was at a local bar, Ray's Hot Spot Bar and Grill in downtown Washington. He was standing at the bar ordering the next round for a couple of buddies when he was approached by an attractive woman. She was wearing a white sundress that looked perfect with her dark brown skin color and long silky black hair. The conversation started when she bumped into him as he ordered a round of Yuengling for the group.

"I am so sorry," the woman said.

"No worries," he said back with a polite smile.

"You know, I am new in town. I just came here from a little town in Utah. Is this normally a fun place to hang out? It is kinda dead tonight."

"No, this is about it," Kinsey said. "It is a cool place to hang out and drink cheap beer. Other bars are more upscale, but they can be pricey, and it is so loud you can barely hear yourself think let alone have a conversation."

"How long have you lived in DC?" she asked.

"About ten years. I work for the Secret Service."

"I didn't know I was standing next to a special agent." She smiled.

Kinsey was a little embarrassed and said, "No, no. Nothing like that. I am an information technology specialist."

"That sounds pretty complicated," she said flirtatiously. She gave him a sexy smile and elbowed him in the side.

Kinsey smiled and felt his face begin to blush a little. "No, it is not so bad. I maintain the data network equipment, develop backup procedures, and update and write software for the intelligence department of the agency. I also help the computer system run and am on standby if one of the computers shuts down when it concerns a protectee."

"Well, it sounds complicated to me. I can hardly turn on my computer."

"Can I buy you a drink?" Kinsey asked awkwardly.

"Sure. I will take a vodka and cranberry."

The couple went to a table in the back and Kinsey received thumbs up from his friends behind her back, mildly upset they did not get their beers. They talked for almost an hour, mostly about how to get around the city.

"I had a great time tonight, but it is time for me to get home." She paused and looked in his eyes and placed her hand on his arm. "I still don't feel safe around town, and I hadn't expected to stay here this late. I know it is a lot to ask, but will you take me back to my apartment? It is only two blocks away."

Kinsey's smile spoke louder than words, even though he had tried to contain his happiness. It had been a long time since he was asked to a woman's house, even if it was just to take her home. "It would be my pleasure."

They left the bar and headed south and soon were standing in front of her apartment building.

"I normally don't do this, but would you like to come up?" she asked. "It would be nice to continue our conversation. I have a bottle of wine we can share."

"That sounds great! You lead the way."

They took the elevator to the fifth floor, and her apartment was the second to the last on the right. She reached into her purse and fumbled for her keys. When she found the right one she opened the door and led him in.

"Make yourself comfortable on the couch while I get the wine," she said while eying him up and down.

He was looking around the sparsely furnished apartment when a man came out of the bedroom. It startled Kinsey, and he wasn't sure how to respond. Aahil pulled his Glock 45 from his pocket and demanded that he sit.

"I don't understand what you want. Just leave, and we won't make a big deal out of this," Kinsey pleaded.

"Ha-ha. Have a seat, you idiot," Aahil commanded.

Kinsey complied and Taybah came out of the kitchen holding a glass of water.

Kinsey was doing his best to hold his composure and said to her, "Stay calm, this man is robbing your house. Just stay calm and everything will be all right."

She said to him, "As long as you listen to us, you are correct, everything will be fine."

"What the hell is going on here?" he yelled. Kinsey thought for a minute and said, "Look, mister, if she is your girlfriend, I am sorry. I had no idea."

Aahil hit him across the head and demanded, "Shut up! Now we must talk business."

Kinsey reached up and touched his head and felt a little blood. He sat down as he was told, thinking about his luck. He finally went home with a beautiful girl then gets himself caught in a horrible position.

Aahil spoke again, "I have a proposition for you and you would be very wise in complying. You have something that I want, and I am willing to pay you good money for it."

Kinsey spoke up, "I don't have anything. I have trouble even paying my rent!"

"I want information, Kinsey. You can get me that information. You see, we have been following you around for a while. We have watched you leave your apartment in the morning and have seen you go home at night. We even know the bars you frequent. What I want is information on Charlie Seaborne. That's all you need to do. Tell me where he is going to be, when he will be there, and how he will be protected. That's all. For your work, I will pay you a lot of money."

"I can't betray my country and no amount of money will make me change my mind!"

Aahil reached in his pocket and pulled out a silencer. After screwing it on, he pointed the gun at Kinsey and fired a shot that missed him just to the right. "I am a very good shot. What do you think about helping me now?"

"You won't shoot me! I work for the Department of Homeland Security! They will do anything to track you down. I can't even leave the country without giving them my itinerary."

When federal employees with security sensitive positions leave the country for any reason, they had to give their itinerary to their organization. If a hotel was taken siege in a foreign country, the government checked the database to see if any employees were in danger. The goal was to protect the information, not the person.

Aahil fired another round, this one to the left of Kinsey. "I do not care about that. Your government will never find me. You have one more chance before this bullet is in your leg." He raised his gun and pointed it at Kinsey's knee.

"Okay, okay. Just don't shoot me," Kinsey said in a panic. "What do you want me to do?"

"We have purchased a pay-as-you-go cell phone. Here is the number." He handed the phone to Kinsey. "We programmed the number as 'Billy' in your phone. We will send you a text when we want to meet for a drink at the bar where you met my wife earlier tonight. She will meet you there to give you your orders. We will follow the same process to retrieve the information that we are seeking. For your troubles we will pay you three thousand dollars a month. This money will be paid in cash, just don't be a fool and spend it lavishly. Your agency will be looking at that. Put the money away in your freezer or under your bed. You can take it out for things like buying your friends drinks, but no new cars, better apartment, etc. Do you understand?"

Kinsey was quiet for a minute. To get a faster response, Aahil again raised his gun at Kinsey's knee.

"Yes, I understand. What kind of information do you want exactly?" Kinsey responded nervously.

"Just where the first son will be and his protection for given events. Rather easy." He reached into his pocket and pulled out a brown envelope. "Here, this is a down payment for your trouble tonight. It is fifty thousand dollars. That plus the three thousand a month should buy your cooperation."

Aahil held up a small video camera while Taybah joined Kinsey on the couch. Aahil filmed Taybah handing Kinsey the brown envelope filled with cash.

"This video is my insurance policy," Aahil said. "You screw up; I send it to every Secret Service agent in the country. Do not break this arrangement, or I will be very upset. Now, get out!"

Kinsey took the envelope and ran to the door. He was disappointed that he cracked so easily. But then again, he did not have a high tolerance for pain. The extra fifty thousand dollars would mean he could pay off his loans and apartment bills and could still have more spending money. He was certain that the government would not find out if he spent money on a new computer. He could also buy all the games and programs he wanted without the government knowing.

~ ~ ~

Present Day
Washington DC

Kinsey did not see the Farahs very often. They made good on their agreement of three thousand dollars a month, and they had not asked for much information in return. The drops, as Kinsey liked to call them, were quick and easy. They would meet at Ray's Hot Spot Bar and Grill, and the envelope was exchanged.

He thought about his last contact with the terrorists. Two weeks ago, Aahil had called Kinsey and told him to meet at Ray's. Taybah gave him an envelope with orders to focus on the day the first lady went to Youngstown. The instructions were to give the time and locations of where Charlie and the first lady would be in Youngstown on the full day of her visit.

"You will come here two days before her trip," Taybah said. "You will see an associate of mine. He will come to you; just have a seat in the back. You will give him the protection details for her trip. After that we will leave you alone, and you will never hear from us again. When you make the drop you will be given a ten-thousand-dollar bonus." She stood up and leaned on the table. "Thank you for your help."

As she walked out of the bar, he admired her backside. He chugged the rest of his beer and went home. On his walk back to his apartment, he came to the realization for the first time that his work would do some actual harm. When the time came, he passed the information over as he was instructed and received the bonus he was promised. Before the drop, it was just notes on a piece of paper. Now they were ready to do something horrible, and he helped them do it.

He did not give it too much thought because he enjoyed the extra income. He used his money wisely, not spending too much to make it look obvious, but he had nicer clothes and spent more time out buying rounds of drinks. He had hid the money in an old coffee can in his closet, and as soon as he got a job in the private sector, he planned on slowly depositing the money in a bank account to avoid suspicion. Since taking the money, he had noticed a change in his personality too. He had become braver, arrogant, and more cocky since spying for the Farahs, especially with women. He even started a workout routine at a local gym to bulk up. He felt that if he could steal top secret information from the U.S. government, he could certainly pick up girls. Using his new found confidence, he began to see Sarah, a thirty-five-year-old mother of one. She was a lot of fun, and she loved to spend time in the bedroom.

Kinsey got the phone call at 2:00 a.m. He rolled over, picked up the phone, and recognized the voice of Jim Thompson, the night commander for the information department at the Secret Service.

"Kinsey?" he asked. "This is Special Agent-in-Charge Thompson; we need you to come down to the office immediately. There has been a situation with the first son."

Kinsey sat straight up in his bed, "What do you mean? Is he okay?"

"Just get here. We need you working the computers. I will update you as soon as you arrive."

"On my way, sir," Kinsey responded as he hung up the phone.

He got out of bed and picked a pair of jeans and a blue button-down shirt out of his small bedroom closet. He thought to himself, *Could this really be happening?*

He left his apartment building and found a taxi despite the late hour; many taxis were already out picking up drunks from bars. When he arrived at the office, he paid the driver and went into the building where he met up with Thompson on the third floor. It was protocol to have a technology specialist on hand during a crisis such as this. Until a problem arrived, he was there just to wait until something went wrong; otherwise he would normally think of anything to keep himself occupied. He went on the computer and began to search the database to see what had happened to Charlie Seaborne. He realized that he didn't give Farah information about the drive home from the Rust Belt Brewery because the stop was not planned ahead of time; Charlie went there on a whim.

After getting caught up on the reports, he went to a bathroom stall. He took out his cell phone and wondered if he should use it to contact "Billy." He knew that the likelihood that the Farahs were involved was small, and he wondered if he should warn them. Thinking about more money in his pocket, he opened up the text messenger program and began to type to Billy.

"He is gone. No one knows where."

Kinsey had hoped that his message would be understood. He left the bathroom and went back to his desk to wait.

~ ~ ~

Youngstown, Ohio
Farah Hideout

Aahil and Taybah were sleeping in a bedroom that reminded them of something similar to what one would find in a third world country. The walls were bare with holes and peeling paint. The hardwood floors were worn, and the only thing in the room was a bed and a table that they used for a nightstand. Since Taybah had insisted on new sheets, Aahil had sent Maali to the local all-night department store, BucksMart, to pick a bed-in-a-bag set that contained sheets, pillowcases, and a comforter along with two new pillows.

His temporary phone buzzed on the table, and Aahil forced himself out of bed to retrieve it. He opened up his phone and read his new text message.

"He is gone. No one knows where."

Aahil was relieved that he had not thrown this phone away. He was planning on pitching it after the last payment but decided against it for a situation just like this.

Does this mean that the first son is missing? he asked himself. He wrote in his phone, "Keep me updated."

He walked over to his pants and shirt that were hanging on the closet door knob, got dressed, and before he left he looked at his sleeping wife and admired her for a minute. She was beautiful and brilliant, and he loved her with everything he was made of. But now he had to concentrate.

He went down the hall to Maali's room and opened the door. His bed consisted of a single mattress lying on the floor. He had no sheets and only a blanket was over him. His stained, caseless pillow disgusted Aahil. He kicked the mattress and demanded, "Get up. We have a problem."

Maali took a second to wake up and sat up and faced Aahil. "What's wrong?" he asked while rubbing his eyes.

"Kinsey has just informed me that the first son in missing. We need to get everyone, and we must be ready to move."

Maali got out of bed then went to put on his pants, "I will get them up now."

Aahil went back to his own room to wake Taybah.

CHAPTER 7

Washington DC
Exotica Gentlemen's Club

He turned around from the ATM and went to the bar tender to change his twenty-dollar bills into singles. The cute bartender smiled back at the man and gave him his change along with a new Budweiser.

"What would it take to get you up there," he gestured to the main stage.

The bartender had long blond hair and was wearing a short pair of shorts and a pink bikini top. She had a flat stomach with a belly button ring that was about an inch long and was silver with a fake diamond at the tip. She found that this outfit gave her the most tips.

"I don't think so. I just serve drinks," she refused as kindly as she could manage.

"What about a private show then? You can take a break, can't you?" he pleaded. "I'll pay you well."

"Maybe later," she said with a wink. She had no real intention, but if the man had hope, he'd tip her well for his drinks.

"I'll be back," he said feeling a little disappointed.

The man was about five foot seven and weighted around one hundred seventy-five pounds. He was in good shape, but no amount of exercise could keep the beer pounds off. He was a black man, with short hair, and a goatee that gave him a distinguished look. He had been drinking for about four hours with no end in sight. He would give his hard-earned singles out to the dancers, maybe buy a lap dance, and then head to the next bar.

As he took an empty seat at the main stage in the middle of the bar, he felt his phone vibrate. He pulled the phone out of his front right pocket and looked at the number. It was the office calling. "Shit," he said allowed, drawing the attention of the guy next to him. "Sorry," he said. The man was clearly upset about having the dance disrupted.

"Hello," he said.

"Agent Berry, this is Jim Thompson at headquarters. We have a situation that needs your immediate attention." Thompson heard the music in the background and a girl say, "If you are going to sit here, you have to pay!"

"Damn it, Berry. Are you at a strip club again?!" Thompson asked

"It is my night off," he said.

"Throw your beer away and order water. I will send someone to pick you up. You need to sober up. This is urgent, and it involves the first family. Everyone is being called in. What club are you at?"

"Exotica. How serious is it?" He left his beer at the stage and headed back to the bar.

"Serious. The driver will explain the situation when he takes you back to your house to shower and get changed. Then you are going to Youngstown. Sleep in the air to help sober up. I need you to have a clear head on this."

The bartender rolled her eyes when she saw him come back and said, "You are persistent, aren't you?"

"Work just called. I need to get sober and quick." He placed a ten dollar bill on the bar. "I need you to keep bringing me water."

She happily took the money and went and filled the first glass of tap water. She set it in front of him and said, "What do you do that makes it so important for you to leave here at this time at night?"

"I'm a cop, and I have to go chase some bad guys. I lead an investigative unit for the federal government."

Impressed she smiled and said, "Maybe this will sober you up." She lifted her top to reveal her small breasts and just as quickly pulled her top back down. "Did that help?"

"That was the best view all night," he said while taking a gulp of water.

He knew that the first lady was in Youngstown and had feared that something happened to her. He couldn't imagine it being Charlie because he was a low-risk target. The first lady would get more worldwide press attention.

Ten minutes and three glasses of water later, his phone vibrated again and he answered it. "Hello?"

"This is Agent Lopez. I am out front to take you home."

~ ~ ~

Mo Berry arrived at his house shortly after leaving the club. He drank a bottle of water that Lopez gave him on the drive as she explained the situation. Berry and Lopez went up to his fourth-floor apartment. It was small, but nicely furnished. He had two leather couches, a fifty-inch flat screen television, and an Xbox 360 in his living room. Lopez sat on the couch while Berry went to relieve himself of all the water he drank. After a quick shower, he left his bathroom and got dressed. His head was still spinning from the alcohol, but knowing that the first son was missing helped him think straight, plus he was anxious to get going.

Mo Berry worked for the Secret Service investigating potential threats to the first family. He was good at his job, when he was sober, and that is why Thompson had pushed for him.

Berry went to the University of Texas and majored in Criminal Justice. As soon as he graduated he applied for the Secret Service. He was highly qualified and was quickly accepted and sent to the federal law enforcement training center (FLETC) in Georgia. After his training in Georgia, he went to the James J. Rowley Training Center just outside Washington DC, where he specialized in protections intelligence investigations. The job was tough and for the first few years, Berry, like most new agents, spent a lot of time overseas. After proving himself capable, he moved back to Washington and concentrated on investigating threats against the first family. The vast majority of threats were not real, but all had to be taken seriously.

The Secret Service first started to protect President Grover Cleveland with part-time protection. The service offered full-time protection to presidents after the assassination of William McKinley in 1901. In 2002, the agency left the Department of the Treasury to join the newly formed Department of Homeland Security. The Service protected the first and second families, the president and vice president-elect, and visiting heads of state. The president may also issue an executive order to have other individuals assigned protection at his discretion. In addition, former presidents received protection up to ten years after leaving office.

Berry had Lopez stop at a McDonald's to eat some greasy food in the hopes of soaking up the alcohol. At the airport, he went to the bathroom one more time. When he boarded the plane, he was relieved to see that the private jet had a restroom in the back; he took his seat and was asleep before the plane began to taxi to the runway.

~ ~ ~

The White House
The Situation Room

The Emergency Response Team was gathered with the president at the long brown table in the Situation Room. Barbara Harper was in charge of the case, even though Secretary Matthew Jones was in the room. Jones was the Secretary of Homeland Security, which over saw the operations of the Secret Service. While he had outranked Harper, he let her lead the investigation. He would take over if he felt she was not capable, but at this point it would ruin the spirit of the Emergency Response Team.

"We are still trying to track the first son and Lindsey," Harper announced. "No sign of them yet. We have patrols looking for the green-and-white truck that struck our Suburban, but we have had no luck up to this point."

"It doesn't take luck, it takes diligence!" the president yelled.

"Yes, sir. The Secret Service is sending our best investigator to the scene, Special Agent Mo Berry." *If he stays sober,* she thought. "He will land at the Youngstown-Warren Regional Airport soon. As soon as he hits the ground, he will start the investigation."

CIA Director Host spoke up, "I have Bruce Maul that has just arrived in Youngstown. May I suggest an idea? Maul and Berry should team up and join forces to track them down. It is both a CIA and Secret Service mission. Let them come together and try to find them."

Jones spoke for Harper, "I like the idea, but I am afraid the CIA will try to control the situation and hold our man back. I would rather have Berry free to do the way he knows best."

Host responded, "I assure you that the CIA will only offer its assistance and resources to help track Jamin, ahhh, Charlie." The president did not like his family referred to by their code names. "We are all on the same team. The Patriot Act and the Department of Homeland Security were created to have all departments working together. Let's use that spirit to collaborate. If you feel we are in the way, just say so, and you can work on your own."

The president responded before Jones had the opportunity, "I like the idea. Have them work together. This is about finding my son, nothing else. I don't want any department trying to be the hero here; we all have the same mission. Harper, you will lead it up with Host. Jones, if you see that the plan is not working, let me know right away and we will fix it. Let's get moving. Harper, call Maul and have him pick up . . . what's his name?"

"Berry."

"Yeah, Berry, and they are to go right to the scene." Moving on to politics, Seaborne said, "What are we going to tell the press about Ann and Charlie both cancelling their events?"

"We can tell the press that they both came down with the flu," Wilder said. "Charlie flew back with his mother to recuperate in the White House rather than his dorm room."

"What about Lindsey?" the president asked.

"She was a concerned girlfriend and wanted to be there for Charlie."

"What about Lindsey's parents?" Austin asked.

"It depends how long Lindsey is gone. We should tell them the truth sooner or later, however."

"Fine," Seaborne said. "Get busy."

~ ~ ~

Youngstown-Warren Regional Airport
Victory Aviation

Bruce Maul pulled up to the curb of Victory Aviation as the plane taxied in. Maul was in his issued black Dodge Charger that he parked at the curb of the terminal. The airport was small with only three doors leading into the main terminal. The restaurant was only open when flights departed and on Wednesday nights for wing specials. The flights were mainly chartered flights to Atlantic City and a weekly flight to Orlando, Florida. The FBO was one of the best in Ohio, with great service and nice accommodations, despite the size of the airport. Maul went into the lobby of Victory Aviation and waited for Berry's plane to park.

Maul played football in the PAC 10 Conference for the Oregon Ducks. He was a middle linebacker and started his senior year. His stats were not good enough to get real attention from the NFL, so he looked into the CIA. The CIA was thrilled to have him because he was athletic, smart, and had great instincts. Being an operative also took a forceful personality, intelligence, toughness of mind, courage, and a great love of country; all of which Maul possessed. After playing four years of college football, boot camp was easy for him.

After his training, Maul started to drink and almost got kicked out of the CIA. To keep his job they made it mandatory for him to attend Alcoholics Anonymous at least three times a week. AA had helped him, and he was working on the twelve steps to recovery.

The worst case of his drinking came when he was at a little bar in Germany. He was there for undercover training when he and his unit went out for a drink. After shots of whiskey and too many pints of thick German stout, his sergeant found him on the ground in the alley behind the bar with his urine on his pants. He was also bleeding from his mouth and nose after a fight he could not remember. At first he fought with the idea of going to AA, but after a month he realized his life would have been ruined without it. He was thinking about becoming a sponsor to a new member of AA, but his road trips prohibited him from establishing a relationship that it took to be a great sponsor.

The CIA was restructured in 2004 when the Intelligence Reform and Terrorism Prevention Act was created by the director of National Intelligence that oversaw the intelligence community. The intelligence community was blamed for not sharing information about the terrorist activity before September 11. Even after the bill, they still had interoffice rivalry and did not like to hand over information. The CIA's primary goal was to collect, evaluate, and disseminate foreign intelligence to help prevent attacks. Since the Farahs were foreigners and were a part of a terrorist cell, it fell under the CIA's jurisdiction.

Maul wasn't sure how he felt about working with the Secret Service on a mission. He would do what he was told, but in the end he felt that the CIA was superior. He had never met Mo Berry and knew nothing about him; often that made a mission much harder.

The white plane pulled in where it was met by the line crew. After chalking the wheels, the door opened and a medium-sized black man descended the stairs. He was rubbing his eyes like he just woke up and was carrying a large cup of coffee in a Styrofoam cup. The man walked into the lobby and Maul approached him. Since it was in the middle of the night they were the only two in the lobby, the customer service representatives had already gone home for the night.

"Berry? I am Bruce Maul." He looked at his eyes and noticed that they were bloodshot. Maul wondered if Berry was drunk but assumed that an agent working to find the president's son would not be drinking.

The two men shook hands and Berry said, "Nice to meet you. I have orders to get to the scene first thing."

"Let's go then. I am parked out front."

"Are there any restaurants open around here? I need a breakfast burrito or something."

Maul put the Charger in gear and the headed south toward Fifth Avenue and Wood Street. He ignored Berry's question and said, "I am going to be honest with you, I don't like this set up. I like to work by myself, and I don't trust anybody, especially outside the CIA. Just stay out of my way, and I will stay out of yours."

Berry responded while rubbing his temples, "Listen, the president of the United States said we need to work together and share intelligence and that is exactly what we will do. Do you have any aspirin?"

"In the glove compartment. If it deals with the terrorists group I will take the lead. If it deals protection, you take the lead. Deal?"

Berry was searching the glove compartment for the aspirin and said, "Sounds good to me."

CHAPTER 8

Youngstown, Ohio
McGuffy Road

Steve Hines had been a cop for the Youngstown Police Department for the last ten years. Hines had enjoyed his job more than most cops did; he had a passion for fighting crime. Even when he was off duty, all he talked about with his friends were police stories and anecdotes. When he heard that he was on a top secret mission, all he could think about was telling this story over a campfire and beer.

He was featured in the news a few years back for fighting himself out of a situation, where he was surrounded by gang members. He pulled over a car in one of the roughest sections of the city for what he thought was a routine traffic stop. When he ran the plates, the computer notified him that the person had an arrest warrant on him. Hines had left his vehicle with the intention of arresting the man. The man did not resist until he noticed that his fellow gang members had come out of the homes to support him. They surrounded Hines's car and threatened violence if the arrest took place. Hines called for backed up and warned the onlookers to stay back. The man under arrest wanted to show off in front of the other members and began to fight. Fearing for his life, Hines then took out his night stick, hit the man over the head, threw him on the ground and put his knee against his back. He then put his back to the vehicle and moved his hand gun left to right. As he swung left the right side of the mob moved forward and the left moved back and vice versa.

When backup arrived the crowd refused to dissipate, so the officers released the K9s. As the dogs attacked the crowd, the crowd began to run into their homes, and Hines was able to complete the arrest. The black community was upset over police brutality, but the news media portrayed him as a hero for arresting a man suspected of selling drugs to school children. Hines had framed all of the newspaper articles and burned the local news broadcasts onto DVDs. He was eventually cleared of any charges of wrong doing.

Hines turned his cruiser down McGuffy Road, named after William McGuffy, the creator of the McGuffy Reader. About halfway down he noticed a green-and-white Ford F-150 with what appeared to be a smashed hood. The truck was parked in front of a small one story gray house. He parked his vehicle on the street and walked up the driveway to inspect the truck. He noticed that there was a bullet hole in the tailgate.

He walked back to his cruiser and used his cell phone, as ordered to keep the press in the dark, and dialed his commander, Jeff McCracken.

"Hello, this is McCracken."

"Commander, this is Officer Hines. I am on McGuffy Road, and I have spotted an old model green-and-white Ford F-150. As I approached the vehicle I noticed that it had a bullet hole in the tailgate, and the front end is smashed."

"Good work, stay on guard, but try to stay unnoticed. I am sending more units there now."

McCracken hung up the phone and dialed Jennifer Martinez to give her the news. McCracken also called the YPD SWAT Unit. Martinez called all available Secret Service units to the house, including Mo Berry. All agents responded quickly and surrounded the house. McCracken assumed command of the raid because it was led by YPD.

A battering ram was used to knock in the front door, and the SWAT members quickly followed in the home. As they cleared the rooms they progressed into the house quickly coming upon the master bedroom door. They busted the door down and swarmed in. The man in the bed began to yell, and the woman screamed in fear. The officers grabbed them both out of the bed, threw them on the floor, and put them in handcuffs. The man wore nothing but his boxer shorts and the woman was wearing a revealing night gown, and it was obvious she was trying to cover up the best she could with her hands cuffed behind her back.

"What the hell is going on here?" Scott Morgan demanded.

McCracken walked into the room, followed by Berry, Maul, and Martinez.

Berry answered the question, "I am Mo Berry from the U.S. Secret Service. I expect you to cooperate in my investigation." He was grateful that the aspirin was kicking in.

"Secret Service? Why would the Secret Service beat down my door in the middle of the night and pull my wife and me out of bed half-naked?"

Martinez felt bad for the woman and fetched a towel from the bathroom wrapping it around her shoulders.

"Is that your Ford F-150 in the driveway?" Berry asked ignoring Morgan's questions.

"Yes."

"What happened to the front end?"

"Why is my house being raided over a simple hit-and-run?"

"It was a little more than that I am afraid."

"Okay, fine. I was drunk when I came home from the bar. My wife and I got into a fight earlier today so I got stupid and drank too much beer then drove home. I ran a red light when I collided with a car. It must have been some gangster's car too because they started to fire at me. I almost didn't get out of there alive. Look, I know I messed up, but it was just an honest mistake."

"Sir, the vehicle you hit belongs to the Secret Service. It was following a car being driven by the first son. The 'gangsters' that fired at you were special agents."

The woman spoke for the first time, "You and your drinking! I swear I am going to kill you!"

"I am so sorry," Morgan said as tears rolled down his cheeks. He knew that this would result in jail time.

Berry turned to McCracken and said, "Looks like this is more your case than mine. I'm out."

He left the room, and Martinez caught up. "What the hell are you doing? We are not done here."

"This guy is no terrorist. He is a drunk with a pissed-off wife. I am here to track down the first son, not to handle the paperwork of a hit-and-run."

Martinez could not argue with him because he was right. She would assign the case to someone else. Maul and Berry left the house and got into the car.

"So what do you think?" Maul asked.

"I think the first son is on his way to have some fun. We get to chase him while he is on a vacation, and our job is to figure out where he is going. Do you still think the Farah cell is still here?"

"Yeah, I do. I'm to drive back to Secret Service headquarters. I'm sure there is an office we can use. I will call some of my sources."

When they got back to headquarters, the sun was beginning to come up. They found a conference room where they could set up their laptops and stretch out. Maul was focused on finding the cell, and Berry had to find out where Charlie and Lindsey were going.

As Maul was doing a search, he received a phone call from a CIA investigator stationed in DC. Liam Hughes had worked for the CIA for fifteen years and liked to work with Maul because he got results.

"Maul, this is Liam. I've got a hit on the Farah cell. I have been scanning the surveillance cameras in the Youngstown area, and we have a positive ID on Maali. He went to a local BucksMart to buy bedding of all things. You were right, they are in Youngstown. The parking lot cameras have him in a gray Honda Odyssey. Also, the YPD received a call from a neighbor about loud noises, and when the officers knocked on the door, a Middle Eastern man answered the door. He apologized for the noise and said it was his cousin coming in late. You want to know what kind of car was in the driveway? You guessed it, a gray Honda Odyssey."

"Send the address to my phone now, I am moving out," Maul said.

Maul looked at Berry and said, "I think we have a hit on the cell. We are moving out now. I will call McCracken and have the SWAT team meet us there."

Both men jumped up and went to the Charger parked out front and headed to the house.

~ ~ ~

Youngstown, Ohio
Farahs' Hideout

Aahil got another message from Kinsey saying that they think the first son has abandoned his protect. Aahil, Maali, and Taybah had left soon after. They grabbed AK-47s, Glock 45s, and ammunition and started to head south. They had no idea where Charlie and his girlfriend were heading, but they knew south would be a good bet. They headed south in case their instincts turned out true.

Just as the Farahs and Maali were fifty minutes out of town, the YPD SWAT unit arrived at the suspected Farah cell hideout. Normally the CIA would have their own men or the FBI would invade the house, but both were unprepared to conduct the raid. They had yet to have units in the area. McCracken's unit was ready to move in again; therefore the president gave the order to let the YPD lead the raid.

They rammed the door and swarmed the house using a snake formation. The formation was a single file line that minimized men in the open. The lead man had the most dangerous job, and it was the hardest in the sense that all decisions were a matter of life or death, including the possibility of killing a hostage. Before advancing into each room, the team used flash bang grenades to disorient the terrorists. Each member wore Kevlar vests and helmets and carried MP5 semiautomatic weapons with a SIG Sauer P220 as a handgun. They did not bother with silencers since they wanted to shock their targets.

In the living room of the house, the unit found four men, all of Middle Eastern descent. They did not resist arrest and were quickly immobilized with plastic handcuffs around their wrists and ankles. After the search of the house was complete, all four men were separated for questioning so that they could not collaborate their stories. Maul and Berry decided to interrogate the man who was giving orders since he seemed like the one in charge. They kept him in the living room and made him sit on a wooden dining room chair.

Maul said to the other officers in the room, "Guys, I need the room for a top secret interrogation with the suspect. Please shut the door on the way out." After everyone left, Maul and Berry continued the questioning. "What is your name?" Maul demanded.

"Jari Shad."

"Jari, I am Agent Maul from the CIA, and this is Special Agent Berry from the Secret Service." Maul nodded toward Berry and said, "We have some questions for you, and we expect you to cooperate. Do you understand?"

"I will not tell you a thing. We did not resist arrest and went under your control peacefully. I know my Fifth Amendment rights." Jari understood that the Fifth Amendment gave Americans the right not to self-incriminate and was one of the most important rights given to Americans.

"I don't think you understand," Maul said forcefully. "We came here for answers, and we plan on getting them. I will do whatever it takes to get them." Maul stepped back and retrieved a black gym back that he had carried in with him. He unzipped it and pulled out a rope. He then walked over to Jari and wrapped the rope around his chest. He pulled the rope tight causing Jari to gasp. Maul then tied a rope around his already bound legs.

"This can be easy. Just answer a few questions," Maul said.

Berry was fidgeting in the corner, obviously concerned about what Maul would do. He knew Harper would not be happy if she found out he was involved in torturing suspects.

Maul took both men by surprise when he punched the man in the gut. While Jari tried to catch his breath, Maul went back to his bag and pulled out what looked like a scalpel and a red bandanna.

"I am authorized by the president of the United States to do whatever I deem necessary to find the answers I want. Will you cooperate?"

"Fuck you."

"Okay, have it your way. This is for the screaming."

Maul went behind Jari and tied the bandanna around his mouth. Maul moved in front of him, took his scalpel, and cut the skin above his left eye. The man tried to scream but his cries were muffled by the gag.

"See, Berry, if you cut right above the eye you can say that he fell during the raid. Perfect cover up." Maul struck him again in the stomach and looked at him in the eye and said, "I am just getting started. You can end this. The next cut is your right eye, and then I go for the thigh. Your call."

Jari shook his head yes and Maul asked, "Does that mean you are going to talk?" Again Jari shook yes.

Maul went behind the man and untied the gag and asked, "Where is Aahil?"

"I don't know! I swear. Aahil, Maali and Taybah left not too long ago. They took some weapons and drove away in one of the vans. Aahil does not tell us anything, we are just here to do as we are told. Maali, however, mumbled something about heading south to chase down something."

"What are they after?"

"Not sure. They were in a hurry, and like I said, I am just a grunt."

"What are you doing in Youngstown?"

Jari paused for a moment and said, "It doesn't matter now."

"Fuck you, it doesn't!" Maul pressed the scalpel against Jari's leg hard enough to draw blood. He made a small incision about three inches long down his thigh.

"We were here for the first son," Jari yelled in pain. "We were supposed capture him when he was at Poland High School. Half the group would cause a diversion while Aahil snatched him and drove away. We were going to hold him for ransom along with the release of some prisoners in Guantanamo Bay."

In Guantanamo Bay the U.S. government kept many suspected terrorists. It had been controversial in the states but little had been done to shut it down because it was hard for any politician to look the American people in the eye and tell them they were bringing terrorist onto the U.S. mainland.

"Where were they going to take him?"

"Don't know that either. Aahil didn't trust us with the entire story because he was trying to prevent leaks. We were going to meet up with him after the demands were met."

"You trusted him to pay you?" Maul asked. "He was likely to take off and leave you hanging while he was out playing with your money."

"You do not understand Aahil. He would never do that. He was devoted not only to the mission, but also to his people."

Maul walked over to his bag and pulled out a bottle of aspirin. "Here, take these it will make you feel better." Jari had blood running down his face and was bleeding from his leg.

"What now?" Jari asked.

"Well, you are not done yet. Not even close. I am just a field agent, and we have the true professionals that will ask you more questions. Plus, they like to get a little more creative with the interrogation. Then you will probably be shipped off to join your buddies at Guantanamo."

Maul left the room with Berry following close behind. The four terrorists would wait at the house until the CIA agents arrived, and then ship them to Guantanamo Bay.

"What the hell do you have in the bag?" Berry asked.

"Don't worry about it."

"Well, next time you torture someone at least let me know," Berry said as Maul put his bag in the trunk then climbed into the driver's seat.

"It works better; just to go with it. Forget all of that, we need to focus. Where would Charlie go? We know that he is on his own, looking to spend some time alone with his girlfriend, but we have serious problems. I think Aahil knows they are on the run or else we would have caught them here. They must have a source on the inside. I am going back to the office, and we will call the president to see if he has any ideas on where Charlie will go."

CHAPTER 9

Parkersburg, West Virginia
Interstate I-77

P arkersburg was a small, poor town in northern West Virginia, and it was the city where Dan Seaborne called home. As the raid began on the Farah hideout in Ohio, Charlie and Lindsey pulled into his uncle's driveway.

"Are you sure this is a good idea?" Lindsey asked.

"They won't look here. Not at first anyway. Besides, we will not get far on a couple of hundred dollars. We will go in, give him a hug, ask for money, and split."

"You said you haven't seen him since your dad was elected. Why would he just give you money?"

"My dad hates him. With a passion. My uncle knows this will piss off my dad, and that will make him want to help us out even more."

Dan Seaborne and his brother William did not get along since they were kids. William worked hard to get good grades in school and was generally a responsible person. Dan was lucky to get a diploma and was reckless. As a teenager he would sneak out of the house to drink, do drugs, and meet up with girls. William was the one home trying to calm down his father and make him feel a little better about Dan's indiscretions.

Once Dan graduated from high school, he rented a small dirty apartment building on the south side of town and worked a minimum-wage job. When he couldn't afford his bills, he would run home and beg his parents for money, something that William always loathed.

When their father was sick, it was William who worked hard as a student at Youngstown State and worked nights to help pay the medical bills that were piling up. Dan still had the nerve to ask his parents for money, and for that, William never forgave him. When their dad died, William had to leave Youngstown. After graduation, William went to Boston to study law at Harvard. Dan still worked small jobs, lived poor, and was very irresponsible. William knew that Dan would never amount to anything, and William felt that eventually he would have the last laugh when he turned in his Harvard degree to receive a job at a law firm, making a large salary.

When he talked about his brother, he referred to him simply as the "hippie" because of his long hair, beard, liberal tendencies, and carefree view of life. In his final year of law school, William could not believe Dan's luck after he won $100 million in the Ohio lottery. *How is this fair?* he would ask himself. *I am working my ass off, and he wins the lottery!*

To William's surprise, Dan paid down all of his mother's debts and even bought her a new house in a nicer part of town. He also paid her living expenses for the rest of her life. Dan then decided that he wanted to get out of Youngstown, so he moved south to the state of West Virginia.

He bought several acres of land in the small town of Parkersburg. No one understood why he did not move to a warm or more exotic spot, but the randomness was a part of who Dan was. He built himself a small house outside of the city and created a liberal activists group. His goal was to clean up the environment, get rid of guns, end all wars, and push for socialized medicine.

When William began his political career as a conservative Republican in the great state of Ohio, he never mentioned to anyone that he had a brother. Dan never was an issue during William's time in the Ohio Senate and the U.S. Senate. The media had a field day, however, once he became a presidential candidate. They exposed Dan's group and started rumors that he smoked pot regularly, which William denied. William knew better and during the course of the campaign he warned Dan to stay out of the way.

When William won, he hoped that his brother did not get caught with marijuana, especially by a federal agency. That would have been political suicide to either have the attorney general press charges or to let it go. Either way, he would have caught heat from all sides. Thus far, the president had been lucky that his brother had not been caught.

As Charlie and Lindsey pulled up the long driveway, Uncle Dan was on the back deck with a blunt between his lips. When Dan heard the car, he quickly tried to hide the evidence. He did not know anyone who drove a black Ford Taurus and was curious to see who it was.

The car parked and he saw his only nephew get out of the car, followed by a beautiful young girl out of the passenger side. She was wearing a light colored pair of jeans and a fitting pink long sleeve shirt. Both stretched their legs as they approached the back deck.

"My god, my favorite nephew in the flesh." Dan had white hair and a matching thick and long beard. His shirt was tie dyed, which matched his hippie description perfectly. Dan noticed Charlie's beard and chuckled to himself, knowing his father would hate it.

Charlie noticed Dan's bloodshot eyes and responded, "That's because I am your only nephew. How are you, Uncle Dan?"

"Just fine. I take it since you're here you must be in trouble. The last time I saw you was when your dad's political advisor . . . what's his name?"

"Brad Wilder."

"That's it. Brad. He forced your dad to invite me to the inauguration, so it didn't look bad when his only brother didn't show up. Even made me wear a tux. Who is the young lady?" He took her hands in his and gave it a gentle kiss.

"This is Lindsey. She is my girlfriend from school."

"The pleasure is all mine," Dan said.

"Nice to meet you, sir. I have heard a lot about you," Lindsey said politely.

"Stop with that sir crap, this isn't the White House. What can I help you all with?"

"Well, you see," Charlie stuttered, a little embarrassed that he escaped his protection, "we got away from our protection. We figured we could go south and get some alone time. The problem is that we could only get $300 a piece from the ATM, and I hate to ask, but can I borrow some money? I promise to repay you as soon as we get back."

Dan found his blunt and lit it and took a puff. Lindsey was so surprised Charlie's uncle was smoking weed in front of them; her mouth almost hit the ground.

"Well, I guess so. But under one condition," Dan said.

"Yeah, what's that?" Charlie asked.

"When this thing is all over, you guys have to come down here and spend a week with me here in West Virginia. We can spend some time out on the land; show you how to reconnect with nature. What do you say?"

Charlie looked at Lindsey, who shrugged her shoulders and nodded her head.

"Sure. That sounds great," Charlie said.

Dan went through the back door to grab the cash and Lindsey said, "I can't believe that he is smoking weed right here in front of us!"

"That's Uncle Dan. He is a great guy, though."

"This property is beautiful, just look at the hills. It just might be fun to come down here for a little while."

"Yeah, and smoke some weed too," Charlie said with a smile.

"Shut up," she said as she punched him in the arm.

Dan opened the screen door and walked on the deck, holding two paper bags. He handed them both to Charlie.

"There you go. I put a little extra in there because I feel guilty that I haven't been around in your life too much. I always felt bad about that. The second bag is for you two to have a little extra fun."

Charlie looked in the first bag in saw a large stack of bills. "Wow, this is too much Uncle Dan!"

"No, it's not, kid. Remember I am not hurting for cash. There is ten thousand dollars in there. And you don't have to pay me back. I am actually enjoying the opportunity to help you guys get away."

"Why do you have so much cash on you?" Charlie asked.

"You never know when the banking system is going to collapse. I have a couple hundred thousand dollars here just in case something happens."

Charlie didn't know what to say and looked into the second bag and noticed a plastic baggie with two blunts in them.

"You know I can't take this Uncle Dan. What if I get caught?"

"Just take it and have some fun. If you really don't want it, just throw it out the window on the highway." Dan nodded toward the driveway and said, "Where did you pick that up? I didn't think that you drove stuff like that."

"Ahhhhh, well, we had to borrow it from a local dealership."

Dan let out a little laugh, shook his head and said, "See that garage over there? Drive over there real quick."

Charlie got in the car and drove to the garage, while Dan and Lindsey walked the short distance to the garage.

To break the awkward silence Dan asked, "What are you majoring in?"

"History. I am looking into graduate school now. I want to be a history professor."

"That's great. Just make sure you enjoy your life. You only got one to live. Don't get caught up in all this corporate greed stuff. Do what you love."

"I will, thanks for the advice," she said politely.

The garage looked more like big barn than a garage, but this is where he kept his collection of the most environment-friendly vehicles on the road. He had cars from the Prius to the Smart Car.

Dan took out a set of keys from his pocket and opened a locked cabinet on the wall. He pulled a set of car keys out and threw them to Charlie.

"This is for the blue Prius over there. It will save you on gas money and will help you go unnoticed. You better get out of here before the cops show up. We both know they will be here soon."

Charlie walked over to his uncle and gave him a hug. "Thank you Uncle Dan. I will never forget this. You are too kind."

"Just don't forget about our agreement. Now get out of here."

Charlie got behind the wheel and when they pulled out of the garage, Dan shut the main door and drove the Taurus back toward the edge of the property. The wooded area around his house was thick, perfect for temporarily hiding things. After he was sure no one could see the car from the house, he made his way back to the deck to roll another joint.

~ ~ ~

Washington DC
Oval Office

The president, first lady, vice president, Chief of Staff Austin, Director Harper, Secretary Jones, and Director Host were in the Oval Office sitting on the furniture surrounding the middle coffee table.

The first lady had made it in safely during the middle of the night and was not happy that she was kept in the dark. She got little sleep and was now ready to get her son back.

"Maul and Berry were able to track down the Farah cell using BucksMart surveillance cameras," Host said. "The three leaders, Aahil, Taybah, and Maali, were not there. After the onsite interrogations, we know that there is a leak inside one of our agencies. They know that Charlie is missing, but claim they do not know where he is going. Aahil is now on the road to track him under the assumption that he will go south."

"Do we believe him?" the president asked.

"Yes," Host replied. "Maul feels that they are telling the truth, but they will be further interrogated. What we believe is that they will use their source to track Charlie's movements and get to them before we do. We found both Charlie and Lindsey's cell phones in a trash can at a gas station near the

Interstate. They stole a car from a small car dealership in North Jackson, Bush's Quality Auto, and they are using it to escape from our detection. They also withdrew the maximum of $300 at a local ATM, which won't get them far."

"How did they get into the building?" the first lady asked.

"Ma'am, they broke a window near the back door and simply grabbed the keys and left," Host answered.

"The dealership didn't lock up the keys?"

"It is a small dealership in a small crime-free town. The keys were in a lock box, but it was not secured."

Harper spoke up, "We have not told the press yet, not that it will do any good with Charlie's change in appearance."

"What do you mean, change in appearance?" asked the president.

"He has grown out his beard, sweetheart, I almost didn't recognize him," responded the first lady.

Harper continued, "Normally it would be good for him to be recognized, but I don't think we will get lucky. To be sure we will scan the Internet for any sightings of him."

"What are you scouring the Internet for?" Ann asked.

"It is inevitable that someone will post something about him, which will lead us to his location. I need to ask you, is there any place where you think they would run or seek help?"

"If they are heading south, my brother's house would be on the way, but they haven't seen each other in years," the president said. "I'm not so sure if they would stop there or not."

Jones added to the conversation for the first time, "It is still just an assumption that they are headed south. They could be anywhere. They could still be in Ohio for all we know."

The president gave Jones a thanks-for-nothing look and told Harper, "Send some cops to my brother's house. Keep me updated."

~ ~ ~

Parkersburg Police Department
Parkersburg, West Virginia

Police Chief Owen Hunter was sitting in his office scanning reports when his assistant interrupted him.

"Sir, you have a call I think you should take. It is from Barbara Harper, the director of the Secret Service."

Immediately Hunter thought that Dan Seaborne was up to something since he got a phone call from the federal government. He had been trying to leave the guy alone. He knew that he smoked a lot of marijuana, but he didn't deal it, he kept it hidden, and he gave a lot of money back to the community. Plus the chief was too old to handle the press frenzy that an arrest on the president's brother would bring. Hunter was sixty-two years old and wanted to serve another two years to max his pension. He truly enjoyed protecting the community and working with good people of the city. He was also afraid that if he quit, he would sit at home and slowly die while no one noticed. His childless marriage was over a long time ago; now he went home to an empty house every day. He did save up enough money to be able to buy a large piece of property when he retired, and he was already looking into some just out of town.

"What line?" he asked.

"Line two."

He took off his reading glasses and set them on top of a pile of paperwork and picked up the phone. "This is Hunter," he said in his West Virginian accent.

"Chief Hunter, this is Barbara Harper from the United States Secret Service, and I am calling on a direct order of the president."

"Well, I will do what I can, ma'am." Hunter looked at a picture hanging on the wall. It was him with the president when he was campaigning in the area. He loved that picture and pointed it out to everyone that came in the office.

"What I am about to tell you is confidential. You may not tell anyone that is not absolutely necessary, and they must sign off on keeping quiet. Do you understand, sir?"

"I do."

"Great. Charlie Seaborne and his girlfriend Lindsey have gone missing. They are in no immediate danger, but for protection purposes, we need to find him now." She explained the story, but left out the part of the terrorists trying to track them down. "The president has asked that you personally go to Dan Seaborne's residence to see if they have been there. Can you do that for us?"

"I will leave right away."

She gave the chief her private cell phone number and hung up.

Hunter radioed his best detective, Lacy Frederick. Lacy was thirty-three years old, about five foot six with dark blond hair. She was a smart detective, and she used her pretty looks to help get the answers that she was looking for. Lacy met the chief at his cruiser then they left for the short drive to Dan Seaborne's house. On the drive the chief explained the situation, and he knew that he could trust her to keep it to herself.

They pulled into the driveway and parked near the garage. They did not see anyone, so Hunter beeped the horn twice to draw attention. A few seconds later, seaborne came through the small entrance door of the garage, leaving it open behind him.

"Good morning, chief, Lacy. What can I do for you?"

"Mr. Seaborne we need to talk about your nephew, Charlie. Do you have a minute?" asked the chief.

"Come on up to the deck. Do you want anything? I have beer, water, and soda."

"We are fine, thanks," said Hunter.

They made their way to the deck and sat at a patio table. On the table was a Bose radio playing Jimmy Buffet's *School Boy Heart*. Dan reached over and shut off the radio. The officers noticed the distinct smell of marijuana on him but ignored it.

"Late last night, Charlie and his girlfriend came up missing," Hunter said. "He is not in danger, but obviously they want to find them pretty quick before something happens."

"How did they get away?" Dan asked.

"Their agent's vehicle was involved in an accident, and Charlie took advantage of the situation by driving off."

"That life has got to be tough. They are always followed and have no privacy. I remember when I was his age, I was all over town chasing women and getting into trouble. Not poor Charlie, though, he will never be able to have his twenties. Something he will always regret. Sorry, but I still don't understand why you are here?"

"The president asked us to come here to see if they came here as a refuge. You are not too far from Youngstown, and this would be a perfect place to come."

Dan laughed out loud. "You can't be serious. I have not seen my nephew since William was inaugurated. Damn shame too. I love that boy. He has a lot of spirit; I just hope his dad's career choice doesn't ruin that for him. Hell, he went to YSU for college when he could have gone anywhere in the country, just to get back to his roots. Pretty cool if you ask me. But no, he wouldn't come here, especially with a girl. Just look at me." Dan tugged at his tie-dyed shirt.

Lacy spoke for the first time. "If they came here, we need to know. He could put this country at risk if he is held hostage. I know that life is difficult, but it is necessary."

"They were not here, and I don't expect them to come here. But if they do, I will give you a call. If you want you can look around."

"Do you mind if we looked in your garage?" Lacy asked.

"Let's go take a walk."

Dan led them into in the door that revealed his car collection. The collection had a total of fifteen cars.

"Wow, this is a nice collection," Lacy said.

"I like to collect environment-friendly cars. Most are hybrids. My favorite car is the Chevy Volt. Just look at it." The car was red with a black and gray interior. "When it is running on electric power it can get about ninety-three miles per gallon, plus it has a smooth ride."

"You don't seem like a person that would have a truck," said hunter, pointing at a shining black pickup.

"It does look bad, I know, but it is also a hybrid. My favorite hobby is to go kayaking and camping and unfortunately I need a big truck to haul the boat and the trailer."

Lacy and Hunter performed a fast search of the house, turning up nothing more than his lava lamps, bead curtains on the doors, Woodstock posters, and tie-dyed mushroom candles. Hunter was okay with the Haight–Ashbury picture, the area in San Francisco known as Hippie Mecca, but he wanted to rip the anti-Nixon sign off the wall. He was the local campaign organizer for Nixon in the 1972 election. Hunter felt that Nixon was treated unfairly and would argue to his death with anyone who felt otherwise.

"Well, that is all we need," Hunter said. "Please give me a call right away if you hear from them. Here is my card with my cell number. Thanks for the help."

"My pleasure, chief." He looked at Lacy and said, "Say, ahhh, Ms. Frederick, if you ever want to go kayaking, I would be happy to take you out."

"I don't think so. You are a little too old for me," she responded with a fake courteous smile.

"Age is just a number," Dan responded.

"Thanks anyway."

Frederick and Hunter got into the cruiser and headed back to the station. On the drive, Hunter used his cell phone to call Harper back.

Harper picked up after the first ring. "Harper."

"Ms. Harper, this is Owen Hunter. I am leaving Dan Seaborne's house now, and I don't believe that they were here. I took a look around the garage and house but nothing looked out of place or suspicious. If they are going south, they passed Parkersburg up."

"Okay, thanks. I will let the president know. I am sending some Secret Service guys down there anyway. Is there an office they can use at your station?"

"Yes, ma'am, I have a large conference room where they can set up."

"Thanks, chief. We will be in touch."

CHAPTER 10

West Virginia
I-77

Allen Kinsey was still at the office monitoring the situation closely. He was reading the new information that was coming in over the system about Jamin. He read that Harper requested that the Parkersburg Police stop at Dan Seaborne's house. The stop did not have success, but Harper had decided to send agents any way.

Kinsey took out his phone and texted Aahil. "Search at uncle's house in W.V. came up empty. No new information. Agents will be there in two hours."

Aahil saw the message and turned around the van. He had passed Parkersburg about thirty minutes earlier and wanted to back track to catch up with the president's brother. He told Maali to get out his phone and perform a search for Dan Seaborne's house.

Maali took out his prepaid phone and began to search. He found an organization that Dan Seaborne founded called the Democrats of West Virginia Standing for Liberal Principles. They supported candidates that stood for appealing the Second Amendment, the expansion of environment-friendly vehicles, and universal health care. Even Maali could understand why the conservative Republican president would not talk to his brother. Dan was supporting and giving money in direct support of William's opponents. The organization had yet to put a single candidate in office, but they did throw around a lot of money in support for their causes. The website said that the meetings were held monthly in the founder's garage. The eighteen-member group meets and has dinner at 6:00 p.m. every third Tuesday of the month. This month's agenda was posted, and it included starting a television ad to spread the word about hybrid vehicles. Maali put the address in the GPS app on his phone, and it mapped the way to Dan Seaborne's house.

Thirty minutes later they drove passed the house to avoid looking suspicious. They found a little area on the north side of the road, where they could park their van. Using the GPS as a guide, Aahil, Taybah, and Maali, made their way through the wooded area to the house. From the wood's edge they could hear the Doors' "Light My Fire" blaring from the deck. The man did not have a shirt on and was reading Al Gore's *An Inconvenient Truth*. He had a cigarette in his mouth as he highlighted and made notes in the margins of the book.

The three began the approach on the house when they noticed a black Taurus with Ohio dealer plates parked amongst the trees. They made it to the side of the house about forty feet from where the man sat reading his book.

"Taybah, go around the other side of the house and walk up the driveway as if you came from the street," Aahil ordered. "Act like you injured yourself on a walk, limp for good measure, and ask if you can use the phone to call a ride. Maali and I will go around and surprise him. Go."

As Taybah went to the side of the house, Aahil and Maali armed themselves with their pistols and waited for Taybah.

Taybah started to limp and called out, "Sir? Sir?"

The man did not hear her over the radio, so she spoke up louder, "Sir!"

Startled, Seaborne turned down the radio, sat his book on the table, and said, "Are you all right?"

"I think I pulled a muscle," she said with a limp. "Can I use your phone to call my boyfriend? I can't walk home."

Rushing to her side, he said, "Of course. Let me help you to the deck."

When he turned around, he was startled by two men that were right behind him. After he felt a gun poke him in his stomach, Seaborne asked, "What the hell is going on here?"

Aahil responded in a cool and calm deep accented voice, "Have a seat on the patio. We need to talk."

Maali and Aahil led him on the deck and forcibly sat him down in one of the chairs. The Bose radio began playing Bill Withers's classic "Ain't No Sunshine."

"Where is your nephew?" Aahil asked.

"I have no idea. I haven't seen him in years. Who are you?"

Aahil smacked Seaborne across the head with his pistol, leaving a large gash. "Only I ask the questions. Where is he?"

"I don't know!" Seaborne yelled.

Maali yelled back, "We saw the car with Ohio plates by the forest. Now tell me, why there is a car with Mahoning County plates hiding in the trees in West Virginia. Sure looks like you are hiding them."

"I have no idea what you are talking about."

Aahil pointed the weapon at Seaborne's left knee and fired. Dan screamed in pain as blood flowed to the deck. "I do not have time for this. I am getting impatient."

"Why are you doing this?"

"Still playing dumb, huh?" Aahil fired again, this time in the left foot. "You want me to stop? Tell me what I want to know."

"How do you expect me to give up information on my nephew?"

"Have it your way." Aahil raised the tip of the weapon and pointed it at his right shoulder.

Wanting to spare himself from more pain, Seaborne yelled, "He was here. A few hours ago. He wanted some money, I gave him a couple thousand dollars, and he was off. No idea where. I swear!"

"I don't believe you."

Seaborne saw black spots in his vision as the third bullet entered his body, this time in the right shoulder.

"Next, I will shot you in your right knee, then right foot, then left shoulder . . . you get the idea." Aahil got close to the man's ear and said softly and slowly, "Where did they go?"

"South. Down south. I think he said Florida. He didn't even know yet. They just wanted money; they were going to figure the rest out on the road."

Aahil looked at the bleeding man in front of him. He had blood running down his bare chest from the bullet hole in his shoulder. The bottom of his left pant leg was soaked in a dark color red from the knee down.

"You are pathetic, you know that? I would never betray my family," Aahil said.

As the series of "I knows" played in the background, Aahil raised his firearm and pulled the trigger twice, hitting the president's brother in the forehead. The man's chin hit his chest, and Aahil looked at Taybah and Maali, and said, "Let's go."

"Where to?" Taybah asked defiantly. "You don't know, do you? You just killed the president's brother; do you know what that means? Now we have every federal agency looking for us! What were you thinking?"

"Shut up! I do not take orders from a woman. I just put him out of his misery, like an injured race horse. We will head to Florida. We will figure out our destination on the way."

After a search of the house, the group returned to the van. "I agree, you did not have to kill him," Maali said. "We should have just left him there. We just made more trouble for ourselves."

"He would have called the police as soon as we left. This way when they find the body, we will be long gone."

~ ~ ~

Elkin, North Carolina
BucksMart

Charlie and Lindsey saw a sign from the highway for BucksMart in Elkin, North Carolina. The store was located on CC Camp Road, right off I-77. The couple needed an excuse to stretch their legs, plus they needed clothes and other essentials.

They pulled into the parking lot as they were listening to a Blink-182 CD. They wanted to buy enough clothes for the week, including underwear, bathing suits, toiletries, and snacks for the drive.

"Let's separate so we can move quicker," Charlie suggested. "Just the basics. It will be hot in Florida so get warm-weather clothes."

"I might need some help picking out a bikini though," Lindsey said with a coy smile.

"Sounds good to me!" Charlie kissed her on the check, and they agreed to meet up in thirty minutes.

The first stop Charlie made was in the electronics section. He searched for a prepaid cell phone, and he chose the most expensive one on the market. He wanted to make sure that he had a phone in case of an emergency and wanted Internet capabilities to search for hotels, restaurants, and maps.

Both had their own carts, and they met in the bathing suit department of the store. Lindsey had six swimsuits to choose from, and they went to the fitting rooms to try them on. Charlie enjoyed watching Lindsey model them, and the couple was finally able to choose two. The first was an all-black triangle bikini top with matching bottoms. The second was a pink-and-white striped string bikini.

As Lindsey put her bikinis into the cart, Charlie noticed a black, sheer, v-neck piece of lingerie. He picked it up and said, "Wow, look at this!"

"Put that back in there, that's for later tonight."

"This is going to be fun. I can't wait to get to a hotel. I am thinking of stopping in Savannah first."

"I have never been there. It sounds like a great time. I always wanted to see the historic city. They also have a fun party area by the river front we can go to."

"I figured tonight we can have some fun and tomorrow we can check out the sights. Then we will pick a spot in Florida to hang out in. Somewhere on the beach."

They transferred the clothes into one cart and went to the toiletries section of the store. After getting the things they needed, they went to a cashier and placed their items on the conveyor belt.

The cashier was fifty-three-year-old Daisy Flores. She worked at BucksMart for many years and enjoyed having the constant employment for the first time in her life. She dropped out of high school after becoming pregnant with her first of five children, with three different men. Most of her life was spent on the welfare system, and she was okay with that, she was after all a simple woman. One of the perks of her job was being able to look at the covers of all the magazines. She enjoyed looking at the pictures of the celebrities as she rang customers out.

She looked up from her register and could have sworn that she had seen this man before her. He did have a beard but those eyes looked very familiar. She looked at him closely and thought to herself, *It couldn't be the first son. What would he be doing here?*

The man paid in cash, and the couple walked out of the store.

In her spare time Daisy loved to post and follow people on Twitter. When she got off in a few hours, the first thing she would do is post how she thought the first son was in Elkin, North Carolina. Of course, no one would believe her, but she would stir up some conversation, making for some entertainment for the evening.

~ ~ ~

Parkersburg, West Virginia

As Charlie and Lindsey were paying the cashier at BucksMart, two Secret Service agents pulled into Dan Seaborne's driveway. Stuart Brands and Colin Levitt parked the car next to the modest blue house.

"If I was as rich as this guy, I would have a large beach house. Not some small house in the middle of nowhere," said Brands as they got out of the car and walked toward the house.

Levitt thought about it and said, "Me, I would travel the world. Start with Australia then make my way back."

"Australia, huh? The first thing I would do is a Mediterranean cruise."

As the men turned the corner, they saw a body covered in blood. Instinctively, both men reached for their sidearm and ran to the porch. It was obvious that the man was dead, so the two men stormed the house. Using military technique, they swept the house for the killer. After they were certain no one was in the house, Brands took out his cell phone and called Harper. Harper made a spot for herself in the Situation Room so she could stay close to the president.

"Harper."

"Ma'am, this is Agent Brands. Are you alone?"

"Yes, what is it?"

"We arrived at Dan Seaborne's house five minutes ago. As we approached the house we noticed a bloody body on the porch. We swept the house, no one is here. The body is the president's brother."

Harper took a deep breath. "What is the cause of death?"

"Not a good one. He has five bullet wounds. One to the left knee, left foot, right shoulder, and two to the forehead. It's not pretty."

"Shit. Okay. Do not touch a thing, and keep those local cops out of the way. This needs to be kept quiet to protect Jamin."

She hung up the phone and called the chief of staff.

"Hello?"

"Don, this is Barbara. We need to assemble the team now."

Chapter 11

The White House Residence
Living Room

The living room was on the second floor of the residency. Ann loved living in the White House because it was very formal and was always beautifully decorated. The Seabornes worked hard for all their successes. Both were Harvard-educated lawyers and had accomplished much during their careers in Ohio. After graduation from Harvard, they moved to Columbus, Ohio, and got jobs at the same large law firm. Ann always had a taste for expensive things, and in order to afford them, she worked eighty-hour weeks for many years, until she gave birth to Charlie. William still worked long hours, however, and eventually made partner at his firm.

He became an active member in the local Republican headquarters, and he aspired to test the waters in politics. Ann hated the idea at first, thinking that the part-time job in the Ohio Senate would mean less income, but she soon warmed up to the idea after she realized how talented William was.

Growing up poor himself, he connected to the voters when he spoke. He preached the American dream, hardworking values, patriotism, gun rights, large military, and a free capitalistic democracy. He lost votes when it came to the religious right, however. Seeing his dad die a hard death made him turn his back to God and rethink his stance on religion. *"What kind of God would do that?"* he asked himself. He was also more liberal on issues such as gay marriage, but enough voters in his district still supported him because of his speaking skills.

He won his seat in the Ohio Senate, and he rose as a leading figure in Ohio politics quickly. Just four years after his election, he ran for the U.S. Senate and won in a landslide. On Capitol Hill he took a leading role in economy and brought much-needed jobs and industries to Ohio.

When he had decided to run for president, he didn't think it was possible because of his moderate views. The Republican pool, however, was full; and while the other candidates beat each other up on the campaign trail, he slowly gained popularity. Even he and his staff were amazed that they had won the nomination. He asked Aaron Sewell to become his running mate because of his military experience. Although he took heat for being liberal on some issues from the right, he gained votes from the left, and Sewell's military experience proved to be a deciding factor in the general election.

Ann had a much different life than William. She grew up with a lot of money and was set for the rest of her life through a trust her father had set up. She would only date someone that she knew could keep up with that lifestyle. William always thought it was strange that Ann did not like Lindsey because of her background, since he had a life much like her, but now he had bigger things to worry about.

The living room was painted in a light brown and had tan leather couches. Some former presidents used the room as a bedroom, including John Kennedy and Lyndon Johnson. There were only two televisions in the residency—one in the living room and the other in the bedroom that Charlie used when he was in town. William and Ann did not have much time to watch it during the day, and at night they both read before falling asleep, so there was not much of a need. The president had never spent daylight hours in the living room, but today he needed to comfort his wife.

"Do you think Charlie is all right?" Ann asked her husband.

"I know he is. He is just looking for some fun. We have all of our resources and our best people trying to find him."

"I am just worried sick, thinking about the terrorists getting to him first."

"We have better technology and connections than they do. It will be fine. Just give it some time. He is probably at the beach right now."

"If he gets that girl pregnant, I swear . . ."

"Charlie is smarter than that."

There was a knock on the door and the familiar face of the first family's butler came through the door.

"Mr. President, I am sorry to interrupt but the Emergency Response Team is meeting in the Oval Office. Mr. Austin said he needs you there immediately."

The president jumped to his feet and turned to the first lady, "You should come too."

The couple walked down the historic hall to the private elevator. The elevator had a natural wood finish with an elevator attendant dressed in a black suit and a bow tie. They were quiet on the way down to the first floor, both nervous about the news.

The walk from the colonnade was normally a relaxing one. It ran beside the rose garden, but today the president and the first lady were at a fast walk, almost a run, and did not notice the perfectly trimmed hedges and flowers that lined the walkway.

A Marine stationed by the glass door saluted them as he opened the door, and the first couple was greeted by the Emergency Response Team. The president sat in his reserved chair in the sitting area of the office, directly in front of the fire place, while the first lady took an open seat on the couch.

"Sir, I am afraid I have some bad news," Austin said. "We just received word from our agents sent to Dan's house, and I am sorry to be the one to tell you this, but your brother has been murdered."

The chief of staff let the president gather his thoughts and waited for him to respond. The president leaned over in his chair and placed his hands on his temples and began to rub with his fingers.

"How did he die?" he asked.

Harper answered the question, "He was shot in the head, twice. He also had bullet wounds to his left knee and foot, and one in the right shoulder."

The first lady had tears in her eyes, but was relieved that the news did not involve Charlie. "Who would do something like this?" she asked.

Host spoke up on behalf of the CIA, and he knew the president would not be happy with the answer. "We cannot be certain at this point, but I believe it was the Farah cell. They are trying to track Charlie, they had the same thoughts we had about him stopping in to see his uncle, and they killed him in the process."

"Was Charlie there? Could they have taken my Charlie and killed Dan in the process?" the first lady asked in a nervous tone.

"We cannot be sure, ma'am," Host replied. "We will know soon though. This group has demands so they will not holdout long before they seek a ransom. It is my opinion that Charlie was not there or there would have been a sign of a struggle."

Wilder spoke up, "We need to keep this quite. The agents are keeping the area secure and will not allow anyone in or out, including PPD. The press cannot get wind of this."

Ann raised her voice and said to Wilder, "Is that all you care about? The press? Polling numbers? Do you have a heart?" She had tears running down her checks.

"I understand that you are mad, but it is my job. Plus, if anyone catches wind that the first son is missing, then other terrorist groups might come out of the wood work and try to take advantage of the situation. We need to be very careful." Wilder paused before he said, "Right now, politically, Charlie is a presidential liability."

Sewell responded, "He's right. This will keep Charlie safe. As far as the polling numbers are concerned, people will not think highly of the president if he can't keep his brother or son safe. Terrorists will wonder if he can really protect our country, which could potentially open us up to further attacks."

The president took a deep breath, let it out slowly, and asked, "What is the next step?"

Host fielded the question, "Maul and Berry are working on it and are following the leads the best they can. I have ordered them not to stop in Parkersburg, but rather continue south, our agents on the ground can handle the scene. I believe that they are heading toward Florida."

"Okay. Keep me updated. I will be in the residency if anyone needs me."

Everyone stood and headed for the doors, except for Austin and Wilder. As chief of staff, Austin got whatever time he wanted with the president. Don Austin had a great ability to organize and run large organizations efficiently and effectively. He had met the president when they both served on the Senate's finance committee. At that time, William Seaborne was the chairman and Austin was a rising star. Seaborne used Austin's knack of organization to set up hearings and organize questioning. The finance committee was charged with bills dealing with taxes, tariffs, Social Security, and the Children's Health Insurance Program or CHIP. Austin was a black Republican senator from Montana and jumped at the opportunity to become chief of staff of the White House. He knew that it would make him a major player in Washington politics, an opportunity that he would not even have in the Senate. He also knew that once his service ended he would make millions on the lecture circuit and book deals. Although they were not friends, they both had a lot of respect for each other, and Seaborne knew to listen when Austin spoke.

"We need a minute of your time, Mr. President," Austin said.

The president looked disappointed and sat back down. "What is it, Don?"

"We need you to be down here, sir, working for the American people. They need to know that you are still protecting them. If the press catches wind that you are hiding out in the residency, they will put it all over the news. I know it is a difficult time, but you need to make appearances."

"What do you suggest?"

"I was thinking about some photo ops," Wilder said. "Walk past the press room to say hello, take a few questions, and talk about the potential bailouts to the airline industry. I can have the CEOs of the major airlines here tomorrow because they need the money and fast. I also suggest you make an appearance on the State Floor, meet some visitors, shake hands, and give some history of the rooms. This will all make for some good distractions. The nightly news programs may even lead with it."

"Don?" the president asked, shifting the focus toward Austin.

"I agree. I would have the airlines here tomorrow. Americans are becoming worried about the potential failure of our airline industry. They are seeing major losses across the board. They are also upset with the increase of fees passengers face when flying. It can be an informal meeting, you do not need to stay long, we will have our people talking to them, just come and go as you please. Leave the rest to us."

"Honestly, I cannot think about anything else but getting my son back. I do not know how I will be able to take questions and contribute to the bailout meetings."

"You need to trust me. Trust your staff. We will take care of you, but you need to do these little things to keep the press off of you."

"Fine. My wife will accompany me to the State Floor; we will leave to go there now. I will then go to the press corps offices. Brad set up the meetings for tomorrow."

The president stood and headed toward the state floor.

~ ~ ~

The West Wing
The Office of the Deputy Chief of Staff

Dan Wilder had been involved in politics his entire life. He watched the news and read the newspaper every day in middle school. When he became a high school student he started a Young Republicans Club and as president of the organization he worked hard to campaign for their local congressman. He continued his political ambitions through college and law school. After graduation, he worked in the U.S. Senate as a top aide to Don Austin. Austin knew that he had great political skill, so when Austin was named chief of staff of the White House, he brought along Wilder as his right-hand man.

Most people, including the president, did not like Wilder because he was a conceited and arrogant man, but everyone put up with him because he was the best at what he did.

Wilder picked up the phone and dialed the number for Gideon Kosar, the CEO of Freedom Air, the largest airline in the country.

Kosar's secretary answered the phone and quickly transferred Wilder's call to her boss.

"Hi, Brad, how are you?"

"Good. Look Gideon, can you come to DC tomorrow? I finally got the president to sit down for the bailout meetings. We need the other major CEOs to be here with you to work on the bailout plan. All the president asks is that the White House needs to look good in front of the media. Now is our chance. Do you think you can pull it off?"

"I will make the calls right now. I am certain everyone will be there."

"I also want to up my fee."

"Are you serious? I already offered you a multimillion dollar consultant contract when this is all over!"

"Yes, but I have been pretty aggressive with the timeframe. I am trying to put money in your pocket now, and I am taking a big risk by moving up the date. Plus, it will be a year or so until everyone forgets about the bailout before I can come aboard. A lot can happen in that time."

"I understand the risks are high, but you will be rewarded. What kind of extra fee are we talking about?"

"An extra two million in salary spread out over the next two years. For you, I will get the process started tomorrow and have the president talk to the press to get the national conversation started."

"All right, I will agree to your terms. You better not disappoint me, though."

Wilder hung up the phone, and he sat back in his chair. He thought about all the money he would make from Freedom Air, and that put a big smile on his face. Now all he had to do is get the president to sign on and now.

~ ~ ~

The White House
The State Floor

The White House was the only executive house in the world that allowed visitors, and almost two million people toured it each year. The State Floor was the most recognizable area of the White House and was home to the Red, Blue, and Green rooms as well as the State Dining Room and East Room.

There was nothing more that William Seaborne enjoyed than shaking hands with everyday Americans. It made him appreciate his position and reminded him of whom he worked for. He would do it more often, but Barbara Harper and the Secret Service tried to keep his direct contact down to a minimum; it was where he was most vulnerable. George H. W. Bush enjoyed going to the fence line on the White House grounds to meet visitors, but the Secret Service put a stop to it because of concerns for his life.

The president and the first lady emerged from the private dining room and walked in the State Room to surprise the tourists visiting the White House. The West Wing had already sent up their private photographer and alerted a couple of members of the press to help record the event.

The president walked to the first person he saw and shook his hand firmly. The man was wearing a pair of khaki shorts, sneakers, and a polo shirt. "Mr. President, it is so nice to meet you."

"You too, sir. Thank you for stopping in today. Are you enjoying DC so far?"

"Yes, yes, sir," the man stumbled over his words. "My wife and I come every four years, all the way from Arkansas."

"That is great. There is a lot of great history here."

"Mr. President, I hate to ask, but can you sign my ticket?"

"It would be my honor. You can even take your picture with Mrs. Seaborne and I if you would like."

The man passed his camera to an aide accompanying the president, and the man and his wife posed proudly with the president and the first lady.

The president and his wife then made their way to the Blue Room, shaking hands along the way. The guard that was posted in the room quickly greeted the president. "Mr. President, is there anything I can do for you?"

"You don't mind if I give a little talk do you?" the president asked.

"Of course not, sir."

The president and the first lady went behind the rope barricade and began to shake hands, sign autographs, and take pictures; all while being recorded by the press.

"You know those windows over there are really doors." The president said as he motioned to the windows across the room. "They open to the South Portico. The top panes rise like a normal window but the wall below opens inward. Really kind of neat."

"I did not know that," a woman tourist said, impressed by the new found knowledge she would soon share with her friends.

By this time a group had begun to gather around the president.

The president continued his tour. "This is one of many oval-shaped rooms that George Washington loved. It would become a symbol of democracy; and the president would stand in the middle of the room, and everyone could be at an equal distance from him without being forced in a corner. The chandelier in the middle of the room is of French design, and the couches are made of a silk material with a gold eagle medallion sewn into them."

The president greeted guests for the next hour and the event gained breaking news status on the major network's website. After making their way back into the private dining room, the president kissed his wife, and she headed back to residency while he made his way to the press briefing room.

When he walked through the door he was quickly surrounded by the press as everyone had questions for the president as he took the podium.

"Quiet, quiet. I am here to discuss meetings that we have planned for tomorrow with our airline industries. As you know our airlines have been struggling to stay afloat. Passengers are also becoming upset about all the new fees that they must pay, including for bags. As a fiscal conservative, it is hard for me to allow the government to give money to companies who cannot afford to pay their bills. The question becomes, why should we reward incompetence? Well, the reason is simple, millions of people are employed by these industries, and our country's economy depends on our transportation systems."

The president stopped to take a sip of water and continued.

"This money will have conditions. First, they must repay all the money, with interest. Second, they must relieve some of the burdens on passengers, most notably the extra fees the airlines have been charging. Our country cannot afford our transportation systems being shut down.

"With that said, the CEOs of the major airline industries, including Freedom Air, will be here tomorrow. I have also invited the leadership of both parties of Congress to be here as well. I feel this is a necessary step in dealing with this major issue."

"Mr. President, what happens if an airline, like Freedom, goes bankrupt, will the taxpayers get their money back?"

Annoyed at the questions, the president said, "No, they will not, but that is just the risk we need to take. Thank you."

The president left the room as questions were being thrown at him. He retreated to the Oval Office where Brad Wilder, Don Austin, and Aaron Sewell were waiting for him.

"Great job, Mr. President," Wilder said. "We are all over the news, and the press will be distracted for a while, so they can have debates on their news programs. I called Kosar at Freedom, and he and his colleagues will be here in the morning."

"What about congressional leadership?" the president asked.

"They will be here as well," said Austin.

"Great, now we wait. I am going to the residency now. Let me know if you hear anything new about Charlie."

CHAPTER 12

Secret Service Headquarters
Washington DC

Kinsey was at his work station scanning the system to make sure there were no issues, at least that was his front anyway. He was really looking for any hits for new information on Jamin. It was relatively easy for him; he knew the team that was searching the Internet looking for new hits. It was similar to the programs that they used to track threats to the president and protectees; it looked for key words and red flagged a hit and an agent who would start an investigation. Kinsey could log into their computers to see what the other agents were working on.

In his search Kinsey found a memo that was written to Director Harper. The memo said,

There was a posting on Twitter of a possible sighting of Jamin in Elkin, North Carolina at a BucksMart immediately off of I-95. The Twitter said she saw him while checking him out and that he looked different because he had a beard. She also tweeted that she was probably wrong, but it would be "cool" to have seen him there.

Kinsey immediately took out his cell phone and hid it under the desk of his cubicle. He scrolled through his contacts until he found Aahil's alias, Billy. He texted, "Sighting in Elkin, North Carolina. Looks like he is still heading south."

After his text, he got out of his chair and walked down the hall to Jim Thompson's office. Everyone in the building was tired after the long night.

"Hey, boss. Do you mind if I go across the street to grab a fresh cup of coffee and some lunch? The coffee here is terrible, and I am just dragging."

"Sure. Bring me back a large cup, would ya?" Thompson asked.

"Sure thing."

Kinsey took the elevator to the ground floor and walked across the street to a small restaurant. It was a local place used mainly by Secret Service agents. Kinsey had prearranged to meet Sarah there. When she spotted him she was waiting at the table and she gave Kinsey a big smile.

"Hey, beautiful. Thanks for coming down. It has been a very long day, and I needed a break," he said.

"You look like shit. When was the last time you slept?" she asked.

"Been up all night. Thompson called me in while I was sleeping."

"What happened?"

"Can't say. You will find out soon enough."

A middle-aged waitress stopped at their table and asked, "Are you guys ready to order?"

"I will have the strip steak, medium, with mashed potatoes," said Sarah.

"I will have the same."

Sarah loved going out with Kinsey because he had money, and he did not hesitate spending it on her.

When the waitress left, Sarah continued the conversation. "So is it top secret or something?"

"Yes, and I still cannot tell you."

She placed her hand on his leg and asked, "You sure?"

"I'm sorry, but I would lose my job."

The food was delivered and they both ate while enjoying small talk, both happy to spend time together. When they were finished, Kinsey paid the bill, and they left the restaurant as they prepared to go their separate ways.

"Why don't you go to my apartment and stay there for a few days. I won't be there to bother you, and you can use the big screen TV and watch whatever you want."

"Thanks, but I will be fine at my place. Give me a call when you get off." She gave Kinsey a kiss, and she got in her car.

After he was back at the office, Kinsey gave Thompson his coffee, in part to suck up and draw attention off him. He needed to be left alone for the rest of the day.

~ ~ ~

Elkin, North Carolina
Home of Daisy Flores

Berry and Maul had been driving all day chasing a ghost. They were on a hunt without clues, and it was becoming frustrating. Harper had called to tell Berry about the Flores tweet, so he and Maul headed to her house for questioning.

They pulled into her driveway and walked to the door. It was a small pale blue ranch house in a rundown part of town. Since the Secret Service got the lead, Berry was in charge of the questioning.

They knocked on the door, and Daisy answered wearing an old pair of blue pajamas and slippers. It was obvious by her appearance that she did not get many visitors.

"What the hell do you want?" she asked.

"Ma'am, we are from the federal government. I am Special Agent Berry, and this is Agent Maul." Both men flashed their identification. "We need to ask you a couple of questions about your Twitter account."

"What for? Wait a minute; it was him, wasn't it? I knew it was Charlie Seaborne!"

"Not exactly. Can we come in?"

"I guess," she said as if it was a big burden.

The two men followed her through the door. They looked around the room and noticed that the lady loved the color blue. Her carpet and walls were both blue, although slightly different shades. The house was messy, but not dirty. There were used dishes scattered on the tables, and things were sloppy, but it looked like the floors were vacuumed, and the place was not too dusty. The men sat on the blue couch, and Daisy sat across from them on a blue reclining chair.

"So if it wasn't him, why are you here?" she asked.

"It is routine for us to look into any postings about the first family. Sometimes people try to impersonate them, which can cause problems," Barry lied. "We have an impersonator in this area, and we just want to check out the situation. When we saw your post, we decided to follow up. Can you tell us what they purchased?" Berry knew the woman was not too smart, and she would buy the line.

"A lot of clothes, warm weather stuff—bathing suits, shorts, that type of thing. It was like they were buying a whole new wardrobe. Let me see." She put her hand to her head as if it hurt when she thought. "Oh yeah, they also bought a prepaid phone with extra minutes."

"Did they mention where they were going?"

"No, just paid in cash and left. I never seen someone pay with that much cash before." Her grammar was not the best.

"What did the two look like?"

"The boy had eyes just like Charlie Seaborne, but with a beard. The girl was pretty with brown hair, about shoulder length."

That's them, Berry thought.

"Okay. Thank for your time, ma'am. I would ask on behalf of your government and the president of the United States that you please do not tell anyone about our conversation."

"I pinky swear." The woman held out her hand with her right pinky extended.

Holding in his laugh, Berry said, "That won't be necessary. Just your word will be fine."

Daisy was secretly disappointed that she could not tell her Twitter followers the crazy news.

They left the woman's house of blues and were relieved that the Charger was still in the driveway. Maul climbed behind the driver's seat, and Berry made himself comfortable in the passenger seat.

"That's them," Berry said. "They got all the clothes they need and a phone with minutes, probably data too. We just need to see where they are headed. Hey, I am a little hungry, what do you say we hit that bar and grill we saw before we get back on the highway?"

Ten minutes later the agents pulled into the parking lot of Tarheel Bar and Grill. It had a sports theme with flat screen televisions surrounding the entire restaurant, making it perfect for watching a game on the weekend. They were shown to their table and a brunette waitress wearing a North Carolina Tarheels jersey asked them what they wanted to drink.

"I'll take a soda," Maul said.

"I'll take a one and one," Berry said.

"A what?" the waitress asked.

"Give me a beer and a shot of whiskey," Berry clarified.

"I will be right back," the waitress said and went to the bar.

"Really? A beer and a shot?" Maul asked.

"It helps me think better. Besides, you are driving anyway."

"That could ruin your career, you know. The only thing that saved mine was going to AA. It changed my life."

"Unlike you, I can function while drinking. It helps me think outside the box."

The drinks arrived and Berry downed the shot and asked for another. They both ordered a burger from the menu.

"So what's next?" Maul asked.

"I say that we drive south until we get tired. My money is on Florida. Where else do college kids go? I went to Daytona Beach when I was in school, let's head that way. Those girls there were beautiful too. It is amazing how they act when their daddy's are out of sight. If I had a daughter, she would be homeschooled and sent to a nunnery." Changing the subject, he said, "When we get tired we will find a nice hotel with a bar and relax until morning."

"Daytona sounds like the best area."

Their food came and they took big bites of their burgers and Berry ordered another round of drinks.

"So what is your story with drinking?" Berry asked.

"It almost ruined me. I was like you, drinking every night, thinking I was invincible. Before I knew it I was making major mistakes. One time I was overseas tracking a target, and I wrecked the vehicle allowing him to get away. Luckily I could walk away before the police got there, and I wasn't arrested for a DUI. That would have looked great on CNN. The last night I drank, I pissed myself and got the shit knocked out of me by a guy I don't remember. My boss found me in an alley behind the bar. He gave me an ultimatum, go to AA or get kicked out the CIA. I chose the CIA. It was tough at first, I wanted to punch anyone I saw drinking a beer and take it from them to chug it. I was lucky to have a great sponsor that helped me through. Now I can watch you drink all night, and it doesn't bother me."

"Wow. That is rough. I won't get that bad, though."

The bill came and Berry excused himself to the restroom. A few minutes later Maul looked toward the bar and saw Berry on the other side ordering another shot. Maul shook his head, sighed and went to the bar. Maul could not believe how Berry was not even staggering a little.

Once they were in the car, Maul turned on the ignition and then headed toward I-95 south.

"We will drive two or three more hours then stop at a hotel, whether or not it has a bar," Maul said. "We will hit the road early. I hope you are not too hung over."

Less than five minutes later, Berry was snoring loudly and Maul set the cruise control at eight-five with Tom Petty's "Into the Great Wide Open" blaring from the speakers.

~ ~ ~

I-95
Georgia

Aahil, Maali, and Taybah were on I-95 heading south when Aahil asked, "Where are we?" Maali had been driving for the last few hours.

"Somewhere in the southern part of Georgia; we should be in Florida soon."

"Good, we are making decent time. Assuming he did not stop anywhere Charlie Seaborne should be in Florida by now. We will stop soon, somewhere near Coco Beach where we will wait until we hear from Kinsey. I did a search on my phone and most college students go to Daytona Beach, Pensacola, Panama City, and South Beach. Coco Beach will be a good stop, we can still get to where we need to in Florida, and if they don't make it this far, we can head back up north rather quickly."

Aahil did not always hate America. As a child he grew up here after emigrating from the Middle East. His hatred started when he was in middle school. As he was walking home from class to his parent's corner market; he experienced the worse day of his life. The family was well liked and respected in the community, and their store was popular in the area.

On that day, Aahil noticed a group of white males yelling at Aahil's father through the front door. The men were covered in tattoos, but the leader of the group had the most pronounced tattoos of all. His head was shaved bald and on the crown was a Nazi Swastika. In large thick letters, he had the word DEATH tattooed across the front of his neck. His arms had so many tattoos, they were impossible to distinguish. Aahil's father stood his ground and refused to let them in, yelling that they needed to pay for the damages to his store on their last visit.

The tattooed man pulled out a pistol and pointed it at Aahil's father, demanding to be let in. As the argument got more heated, Aahil's mother began to scream so loudly that it still gave Aahil nightmares.

Without warning the man shot Aahil's father twice in the chest then turned the weapon on to his mother, who was shot once in the heart. The man stepped over their bodies, went into the store, took a bag of chips and a soda, and walked down the street with his gang as if nothing happened.

At first Aahil was too stunned to move, but something forced him to run to his parent's side. He noticed that his mother was still breathing. She pulled him close to her and said, "We love you. Make us proud my son."

Those would be the last words the woman would ever speak. By the time the police and paramedics arrived both of Aahil's parents were dead. Being just a teenager, Aahil was taken into custody of New York's Children Protection Service.

Since Aahil and his parents had left his family behind in Saudia Arabia, he had no one to look after him and was placed into foster care. Many white families did not want him because of his ethnicity and his Muslim faith, so Aahil spent the next five years bouncing around foster families. One abusive foster father called Aahil the devil, Aahil spent three weeks in a hospital after the worst beating.

Police found the tattooed man who killed Aahil's parents a year later in Los Angeles after his involvement with another murder. California had jurisdiction and sentenced him to life in prison. The man died in a prison fight soon after, and was never tried for Aahil's parents' murders, an injustice that Aahil would never forgive.

At eighteen, Aahil left child services and quickly joined a radical Islamic Mosque. That is where he met Taybah and Maali. He fell in love with Taybah at first sight. She was just as brutal and radical as he was, and he soon asked her to marry him, knowing he would never find a woman like that again. It was Taybah's idea to start a Mosque. They rented a small building in New York City and began to recruit members; the result was named the Farah Cell by the CIA.

The Farahs had been waiting for this moment for years. They would make headlines and save their Muslim brothers in Guantanamo Bay, most of whom they had never met. With their monetary demands, the three would go back to the Saudi Arabia, where they would live out their days rich and living a happy life.

Charlie's disappearance had changed the cell's plans dramatically and Aahil was determined to track down Charlie to make his dreams come true. He did not care if the first son was injured in the abduction, just as long as his demands were met. If Charlie had cooperated, he would consider letting him go. He was sure Charlie would not go too far south; a long drive would ruin precious time alone with his girlfriend. Therefore, Coco Beach would allow the cell the ability to head south a few hours or north a few hours as needed.

CHAPTER 13

Savannah, Georgia
The River Inn

After trying to other hotels, Charlie and Lindsey were able to find one that had a vacancy. The River Inn was a historic and luxurious hotel. The building was known for its beautiful architecture and its prime location on the popular River Street. It was an expensive hotel, but with the money from Dan Seaborne, cost was not a concern.

After checking in, they went to the fifth floor to a room that faced north, allowing views of the Savannah River. Their room had hardwood floors with its own private balcony and an old canopy bed. It was early evening, and the sun was beginning to set, so after washing up, they decided to hit a small clothing store on River Street for club clothes. Lindsey was looking for something better than what she had from BucksMart.

They found a small shop, Alison's Formal Wear, close to their hotel and began to browse. Lindsey fell in love with the store as soon as she looked around. There were many cocktail dresses, and she knew it would be a difficult decision trying to decide which one to buy. She did not hesitate trying them all on, however.

She started with a strapless purple dress that was tight at the top and flared at the knees.

"It looks good, but a little tight up top," Charlie said.

"I thought you would like it tight."

"It doesn't leave much to the imagination, though. Why don't you try this one on?"

He handed her a black spaghetti-strapped dress that was ruffled in the midsection and flowed to the ankles. She tried it on, came out of the fitting room, and said, "I don't like it because it is uncomfortable."

Starting to already get frustrated, Charlie said, "I'll go over to the men's section and pick something out for myself. I'll see you in a little while."

Charlie walked to the other side of the store and began to pick out clothes. He chose a nice pair of kakis, a dark green button-down shirt, and a new pair of brown leather dress shoes. He carried his new items to meet Lindsey who had also picked up her outfit for the evening, including shoes.

"What did you pick out?" Charlie asked.

"You will need to wait until later!" Lindsey responded.

"The anticipation is going to kill me!"

Charlie paid the seven hundred-fifty-dollar bill, and they walked back to the River Inn. Once they got back to the luxurious room, Lindsey took a shower while Charlie pressed his clothes and got caught up on the news. He was relieved that none of the news covered his disappearance, which meant his father, was keeping it quiet. He felt guilty about not letting his parents know where he was and he contemplated on giving them a call in the morning before they headed south. He knew that they would track his call, but who cared, he would be out of town by the time they could respond. Lindsey came out of the bathroom wearing nothing but a towel around her body and another on covering her head.

"You're up. It won't take me too long to get ready. Just some make-up and my hair then I will be ready to go."

"Can I get a peak?" Charlie asked ambitiously. He was hopping she would open up her towel and reveal what was underneath.

"Not now, get in the shower," Lindsey responded with a sexy grin.

Charlie took a quick shower and still had time to spare as he waited for Lindsey to finish getting ready. He read the free newspaper he found in the lobby and was anxious to get the night started.

Lindsey emerged from the bathroom causing Charlie's heart to almost stop. She was wearing a white strapless dress that hugged her body showing off her perfect curves. The dress was plain and simple ending just above her knees, showing off her tan muscular legs, but in a tasteful fashion. She also wore a pair of silver heeled sandals giving it an elegant look.

"Wow. You took my breath away, sweetheart. You are truly beautiful."

Lindsey blushed and said, "Thank you. You don't look so bad yourself."

"I am taking you to the Exchange Seafood Tavern. It is in a historic building and is supposed to have great seafood."

"I'm in. Let's go, I'm hungry."

It was already dark when they left the hotel lobby as they began the short walk to the restaurant. The Exchange Seafood Tavern played a vital role in Savannah during the late 1800s and early 1900s. The building was headquarters to Savannah's Cotton Exchange, which became a leader in setting cotton prices around the world. Today, it served as a popular restaurant and bar that many people who visited River Street enjoyed.

The beautiful building stood out when driving down Bay Street. From River Street, they hung a wooden sign announcing the restaurant. Charlie and Lindsey went through the entrance and were greeted by a hostess. A few minutes later the two were shown to their table.

A waiter in his midtwenties came to the table and asked them for their drink orders. They ordered the expensive bottle of Merlot the waiter suggested.

"I can't wait to have a good time tonight," said Lindsey. "Now that we are done traveling for the day, we can finally relax for a while."

"I figured we will start drinking here then move on to the next spot. We can just walk slowly up the street, and if we find something we like we will stop in."

"Sounds good. Anything look good on the menu?"

"The Baked Stuffed Flounder sounds delicious. It is stuffed with crab meat."

The waiter brought their wine and asked for their order. Charlie and Lindsey both ordered the stuffed flounder, with a shrimp cocktail for an appetizer.

Van Morrison's "Someone Like You" was playing in the background. They both stopped for a minute to listen to the opening of the song.

Charlie looked into Lindsey's eyes and said, "I love you. Every time I hear this song I think about how I want to spend the rest of my life with you."

Lindsey's eyes teared up at Charlie's sincerity and responded, "I love you too. But your mom, she will never agree with us getting married. I don't come from an American political family like she wants. I am not a Bush or a Kennedy," she said mockingly. "Maybe one of the Bush twins is still single."

"She will come around. I promise. Just give her time. What is she going to do anyway? Forbid us? I don't think so."

The waiter slid the shrimp cocktail in between them as quickly as he could without interrupting the couple.

"Maybe she is right, you know. You are going to be a big shot lawyer, probably a politician like your dad. You need someone to compliment you, not a nerdy history professor." Lindsey smiled at her small joke.

Charlie thought for a moment, clearly irritated he said, "Then what are we doing? I am hanging my law school plans on your grad school acceptance. I want to be with you. If I didn't want this I would be ready to go to Harvard, but I will stay back for you. I will go anywhere to be with you—Ohio State, Cincinnati, wherever."

"I always feel uncomfortable around your mom. When I visit the White House it is like I don't belong. My parents are simple people. Your parents live a life of luxury and have dinners with royalty from all over the world. My parents go to the Golden Dawn for a nice night out." She took a deep breath to calm down. "I want to make this work. I love you, I just don't see how."

"I don't care about the White House or State Dinners or any of that." Charlie paused to take a bite of the shrimp and a sip of his wine. "You are the most beautiful women I have ever seen. You have a great sense of humor, you're intelligent"—he paused—"and those sexy brown eyes that drive me nuts."

They sat in silence for a few minutes while they finished their appetizer. When their food was delivered they ordered more wine and began to eat.

"This is fantastic!" Lindsey said after the first bite.

Ignoring the comment, Charlie said, "Let's do it."

"Do what, Charlie?"

"Let's get engaged. We can find a ring later, when we make it official. I will tell my parents, you tell yours, but that's it. Keep it out of the press for now. I love you so much, and I will do anything to be with you. I think you are going to be a great wife no matter what we decide to do, even if you are just a nerdy history professor," he said with a small smile.

Lindsey thought as she took another bite of her fish. "You're serious, aren't you?"

Lindsey was a beautiful woman with a calm demeanor, caring personality, and a good sense of humor, which made everyone enjoy being around her.

"Of course I am. What can be more romantic? We are eluding the Secret Service and every other agency that is looking for us. It is the only private time we will ever have together for a long time, especially if my dad gets reelected in a couple of years." Noticing that Lindsey was not buying any of it, Charlie sighed and said, "Look, I love you. I will do anything, anything, to be with you. I want to marry you."

"Yes, you idiot, of course I will marry you!"

Charlie was so excited that he wanted to jump over the table and give his new fiancée a hug, but he knew better and was somewhat disappointed that he could not. The two finished their meal, having a casual conversation about their friends in Youngstown. When the bill came, Charlie paid in cash and left a generous tip for the waiter.

Lindsey and Charlie headed down River Street, looking for a small bar to have a few more drinks. Lindsey was already a little tipsy after drinking more than her fair share of the two bottles of wine, and Charlie was ready to have a great time.

They walked hand in hand down the street and saw a bar called Funk. The bar was perfect for traveling college students. Its interior was decorated in loud colors, and they offered generous drinks. They sat at the bar, and Lindsey ordered a martini while Charlie ordered a rum and soda. They took sips of their drinks, and were surprised by the stiff pour.

"I think you will make a great first daughter-in-law," Charlie said.

"Thanks. Tell me how you really feel about being the first son. And not some answer you give to a journalist writing a story."

"It is not so bad," Charlie said, trying to avoid the subject.

"Be honest with me Charlie. We need to be honest about everything in our lives, no secrets. I know it is hard for you, but I hope you will share with me your feelings."

"It sucks, okay? Not just the obvious parts like protection twenty-four seven, but the part that no one sees. Everything I do is in the paper, from my grades to my friends. When I am around my parents or in their home, the White House, I can never relax because they are always surrounded by very important people, including heads of states." Charlie took a long sip of his drink before he continued. "The worst part is the attacks on my dad. It seems like he has a million enemies, and everyone wants the world to know it. Just look at all the Sunday morning shows. They attack his policies and his personal life. Hell, if my mom wears the wrong color dress that doesn't just match her skin tone, it is an article in every fashion magazine in the country." Charlie motioned to the bartender for another drink. "I try to not pay attention or to let it bother me, but it is unavoidable."

Charlie's drink was delivered and he took another big drink. He was noticeably bothered by the topic.

"I couldn't imagine, Charlie," Lindsey said trying to comfort Charlie. "A friend in high school called my father a no-brains factory worker, and it got me very angry. And he was just the school bully, not a national journalist. Do your parents know how you feel?"

"What good would that do? When my dad told me he was going to run, he tried to tell me how my life would change. He told me to ignore the criticisms and the attacks on his character, but how could he seriously expect me to do that? During the campaign I wouldn't see him very often, but I was at his side when I could. I would go on stage, wave to the crowd, and even shake hands. I was at his side when the reporters would ask him embarrassing questions about his past; questions about his sex life, drinking habit, drug use. It never seemed to bother him, all the while it tore me up inside and my parents never really understood that. He was running a national campaign, what was I going to do? Complain about my feelings and have him distracted? No, I sucked it up and kept it to myself."

Lindsey had listened closely to him, wanting badly to take away his pain. "I am here for you. We can talk about these things together; it will be good for you to get it off of your chest. I am in this for the long run. We will work through this, Charlie."

She reached over and hugged him. Beginning to feel like he was losing some of his masculinity, Charlie changed the subject.

"Did I tell you how good you look in that dress?"

Blushing, Lindsey said, "Maybe once or twice."

They both had a few more drinks, and it was almost one in the morning before they decided to head back to the hotel. They walked hand in hand next to the Savannah River not saying a word, but just appreciating each other's company and enjoying the alcohol flowing through their systems. They agreed to wake up early in the morning to visit some of the sites in Savannah before heading to Florida.

~ ~ ~

Charlie and Lindsey slept in longer than they had planned; it was almost nine before they began to stir. They both had a little headache from the night before, which was the reason for the slow start. They showered, got dressed, and went to explore the town.

After paying the hotel bill, they got into the Prius, and Charlie asked, "This is your trip. Where do you want to go?"

"Well, I wish we had more time," Lindsey said while looking at a Savannah map. "There are three things I want to see here. Forsyth Park, the Cathedral of St. John, and some of the major Civil War sites are on the top of my list."

"Sounds good, but I need some breakfast and coffee first."

They went to a small restaurant to eat breakfast and then headed toward Forsyth Park. Charlie was happy to have the small car to navigate the crowded streets of the historical town. Forsyth Park was on Gaston Street and was known for its large fountain in the center. The fountain was built in 1858 and had French influence. The park also featured a memorial dedicated to the fallen soldiers of the Confederate States of America during the Civil War. Lindsey was excited to give Charlie a history lesson as they explored the area.

Their next stop was the Cathedral of St. John. The church could make a nonbeliever become faithful; it was so beautiful. The stained glass depicted biblical figures, and at the front of the large and high sanctuary was the main altar made of Italian marble. Above the organ was the Great Rose Window with each of the ten pedals playing different musical instruments.

Inside the cathedral, Charlie said, "I don't think I have ever seen anything so breathtaking in my life."

After the cathedral, the couple used a guided map and drove to Civil War sites, including a prison camp used by William Sherman.

Charlie pulled out his cell phone and used it to perform an Internet search for places to visit in Florida. They wanted to go somewhere small on the Atlantic Ocean so they could minimize the risk of being recognized. A little town called Vero Beach was one of the results.

"What about Vero Beach? It is a small beach town with some hotels on the water, and it is right off of I-95. What do you say?"

"Vero Beach it is."

CHAPTER 14

Washington DC
The White House Residency

The president skipped his morning workout, instead opting for breakfast in bed. Don Austin made sure the butler did not make the normal early wake-up call to allow the president to get some extra sleep. While Charlie and Lindsey were sleeping off their hangover, the president had a busy day in front of him. Even though he would not be in the room for the entire meeting, the airline bailouts would take up a considerable amount of his day.

The meetings with the airline CEOs were to commence at nine o'clock, later than most meetings, but some of the executives needed the extra hour to make the short notice trip to DC. The president wanted to be present at the start of the meeting and then he would spend the rest of the day between the Oval Office and the residency. Ann Seaborne would spend the day in the Yellow Oval Room, available if needed for any official business. Kate Jenner, her chief of staff, would be able to handle the day's business in her absence.

The president demanded that Harper meet him in the Oval Office before going to the Roosevelt Room for the bailout meetings. He arrived at eight forty-five and didn't hesitate before he began asking questions.

"What is the news, Barbara?" he demanded.

"Good morning, Mr. President. So far, nothing. Apparently Charlie is very good at keeping himself hidden. Maul and Berry have been tracking him for some time now and have turned up absolutely nothing. They are on the road now heading to Florida where they will continue their investigation. Charlie will make a mistake sometime soon."

"Why Florida?"

"That is where most college students go to have a good time."

"Fine, what about the Farah cell? Any word on them?"

"Not that I am aware of. We will keep looking."

"Okay, thank you."

Harper left the office and Wilder was next on the agenda.

"Good morning, Mr. President. All the CEOs and congressional leaders are in the Roosevelt room helping themselves to refreshments while they wait for you. I have a good feeling about today, sir. I know it is just a hunch, but I think we will make significant progress."

"Great, I will be there in two minutes. Get everyone seated."

Wilder left the room while the president sat in his large chair behind the *Resolute* desk and looked at the garden just beyond the window. He thought about Charlie and how great of a son he was. He did not complain much, always got good grades and was never in trouble. Seaborne remembered how proud of him he was when Charlie had told him he would attend Youngstown State. It took a strong person to give up an Ivy League school for a small university in Northeast Ohio. Charlie insisted that he wanted to know Youngstown, so he could connect with his family roots and follow in his father's footsteps. When William complained, Charlie was quick to point out how successful his father was. William could not argue with the reasoning and figured it would be good for him to go to school in a hardworking area like Youngstown. Charlie would still make it to an Ivy League school; he would just take a four year detour.

The president got up from his chair, left the Oval Office and walked into the waiting crowd of CEOs and members of Congress. Wilder could have sworn that the president had tears in his eyes. Everyone in the room stood for the president, who took his reserved chair at the head of the table.

"Good morning, everyone. It is nice to see you all could make it. Our goal today, ladies and gentlemen, is to come to an agreement that is best for this country, not to line anyone's pockets. Although I have reservations, I feel that a bailout is important to our country's economic stability. If we can agree to give the taxpayers money to you, the airlines, it better be a good deal for the people that elected me, or I will not sign on." The president looked around the room, making sure that he had everyone's attention. When he did, he continued, "The airlines must repay the principal in full, with interest. In addition, the extra fees that you are charging need to cease. The taxpayers will not be happy if their airline charges them two dollars for a blanket after they gave it billions of dollars."

Gideon Kosar was sitting to the president's right and was the self-assumed leader of the airlines. He said, "Mr. President, I want to thank you for meeting with us to discuss helping us out. I promise that you will be happy with the outcome of today's meeting. I believe that after leaving here we will have a good deal that works for the American people."

The president and Kosar were not close friends, but they were political allies. Kosar gave money and supported Seaborne during the presidential election. Kosar felt like he was owed the bailout money in exchange for long supporting the president.

"Thank you, Mr. Kosar. Now, I have other meetings that I must attend to, but I leave you in good hands. Mr. Wilder is more than capable of negotiating on behalf of the White House. I will be stepping in as my schedule permits in order to check your progress."

The president returned to the Oval Office to attend to his usual schedule, including a delayed Presidential Daily Brief. At noon, the president met with Vice President Sewell for their weekly lunch. The lunch was a tradition that had started during the Carter administration. The two sat for lunch in the private dining room connected to the Oval Office. Today they talked over a turkey club with a side of potato chips.

"Good afternoon, Mr. President."

"Aaron, how are you? Any word on Maul and his search for Charlie?"

"I talked to him this morning. He and the Secret Service Agent Mo Berry were just hitting the road heading south. I honestly can't believe that Charlie has escaped our sights for this long; it must be the new beard. He will make a mistake that will lead us to him sooner or later."

"Then what, Aaron? We wait until the Farahs catch him? We need to step it up here. What about military technology?"

Sewell was easily frustrated when he talked to the president about the military. He felt like these were topics that should be common sense, especially to a president. He did not know how he would serve another term with the man.

"Charlie is not using credit cards, cell phones, nor does he have his car that we would be able to track," Sewell said. "At this point the military will not be much use to us. We will send Maul and Berry to continue their investigation and wait until something turns up."

"Honestly, Aaron, I don't know how you can expect me to just sit here and accept that answer. This is my son we are talking about. Do you know what can happen to him if he falls in the arms of the terrorists? He could be tortured and have the video spread all over the Internet for the world to see. And they can keep him for ransom. I honestly feel that I would not be able to make a clear decision at that point. My son or my country is an impossible question."

Sewell thought the president was being too timid about the situation. "Mr. President, you took an oath to protect and serve this country." He emphasized the word *protect*. "You must do what is best for the country. If you were to give in to terrorist demands you would be setting a terrible precedent for the future of this country. We cannot allow that to happen."

"Let's hope we never get there," the president responded.

~ ~ ~

After lunch the president moved to his private West Wing office that sat in between the Oval Office and the private dining room. He evaluated the people that he had surrounding him, and he knew that he had made one main mistake; not hiring anyone he truly trusted to be a critical player and a close advisor in his administration. When he was elected he opted for Don Austin because of his experience, Brad Wilder because Austin had trusted him, and Aaron Sewell because he needed the bump in the general election. He had offered advisor jobs to his people that worked for him in the Senate, but they all declined because it was an insult. Most of them took jobs with other Senators or left for the private sector.

The president picked up the phone and asked the operator to connect him immediately to Kate Jenner, the first lady's chief of staff. The first lady worked in the East Wing of the White House and had her own staff to assist her.

"Yes, Mr. President, what can I do for you?"

"Kate, can you sneak away for a minute? Don't make a big scene, but I need you to come down to my private office so we can talk."

"I am on my way, sir."

Jenner had worked with Seaborne when he was in the Senate. She was his deputy chief of staff and was also in charge of the office operations. He wanted to have her in his office, but Ann had asked for Jenner to work for her instead, citing that she was the only political aide she had gotten along with. William was disappointed, but agreed to have her work with the first lady. Now, Jenner was the only person he could trust, and he wanted to touch base with her.

When Jenner arrived at the office she knocked on the door and Seaborne asked her in. Jenner was five foot two and had long brown hair. She was a sweet person, but she was feisty when someone got in her way, a trait the president admired her for.

"Please, Kate, have a seat. How is everything?"

"Just fine, Mr. President."

"Kate, how is your deputy chief of staff?"

"He is wonderful. He will be running his own office somewhere soon I am sure."

"Great. I need him to start today."

Jenner thought she was getting fired and said, "What is the problem? I have done nothing wrong!"

"Calm down, Kate. It is nothing like that. I need you here with me, at least for a couple of days. I realized I made a mistake when I first took office by not bringing my staff with me. I was too tangled up in the politics of the place; I wanted to have the person with the best resume. What I should have done is brought in the people that I could trust. I am assigning you as my senior chief advisor. You report to me and no one else, including Austin. I want you in on every meeting that concerns Charlie, and I am depending on your honest feedback. I do not want anyone playing games with my son's life. Do you accept?"

"Of course, sir."

"There is one more thing, Kate. If the terrorists get a hold of Charlie, I need you to give me solid advice on how to handle the situation. My mind might be a little cloudy if we get to that point. Can I count on you?"

"Mr. President, I will not let you down," Kate said confidently.

"Great, I will go write up the change now. You can use this office until we find you a home here."

The president went back to the Oval Office feeling better that he had someone on his side. Jenner, however, was scared out of her mind that she now had to play hardball with some of the biggest players in Washington. This was not going to be an easy assignment. She knew she could work with Austin, but Wilder and Sewell were a different story. Wilder only cared about politics, and he did not let anyone stop him. If she messed with him too much, he could ruin her career in Washington politics. Sewell was a strong powerful man who had connections throughout the government. He could have the CIA or DIA, Defense Intelligence Agency; make her life hell by investigating her and her family's background including performing an intense investigation. She had to play this carefully, but she knew she was there to protect the president, the first lady, and the first son, and she would do whatever it took.

~ ~ ~

Jacksonville, Florida
I-95

Maul and Berry had arrived in Jacksonville as the president was finishing up his conversation with Jenner. The ride was uneventful, boring even, and they both needed to get out and stretch their legs. They stopped at a McDonald's to eat, and when they were finished Berry excused himself for the restroom. Instead, he walked past the restroom and used the exit and went to a local drugstore with a liquor department adjacent to the restaurant. He picked out two flasks and purchased a medium-quality whiskey to fill them with. He placed the flasks in his pocket and set the bottle next to the passenger side door, with hopes of sneaking it in when he entered the car.

"What the hell? Took you long enough," Maul said as Berry took his seat at the table.

"Must have been the food from last night, didn't sit well is all."

"I want to go further south. I say around Daytona."

"I heard they have some fun bars down there," Berry said.

"No bars, am I clear? We are trying to track down the president's son. We can't screw this up. We will get there, tap into our respective agencies' computers, and do some research. I am going to get a good workout too. I think the way you have been drinking, you can get rid of some those toxins in your body."

"I can still outrun your ass after a bottle of whiskey."

Maul laughed and said, "You are kidding me! I am a CIA operative. You are Secret Service. I have respect for you guys, but you don't have a chance."

"What about a wager? If I win we go out tonight, have some fun, and maybe pick up a few beers. If you win, we stay in the hotel and watch pay-per-view on the taxpayer's dime. What do you say?"

"Deal."

They stood up, threw away their trash and walked to the door. When Maul unlocked the Charger's doors, Berry opened the door, acted like he was stretching his legs, and slid the half-full bottle of whiskey in the backseat. Maul did not notice to the delight of Berry.

A few hours later, Maul and Berry pulled into a beachside hotel in Daytona Beach and used a government credit card to pay the bill. They both checked into the respective rooms and prepared for the battle between the CIA and Secret Service. They agreed to meet on the beach in one hour.

Maul was the first one to the beach and said to Berry, "You sure you want to lose to me? It is something that your ego will never let you live down."

"Ha-ha." Berry pointed to a sign and said, "To the sign, fifty push-ups, fifty sit-ups and back."

Maul put his hand in the sand and said, "On three. One. Two. Three."

The men exploded down the beach toward the "Lifeguard Zone" sign about one hundred yards away. Maul arrived at the sign a few steps ahead of Berry and both counted the push-ups and sit-ups aloud, drawing a lot of attention from the bathing-suit-clad spectators. Berry had the edge in the exercises and began the final leg of the competition, but it seemed like Maul was just getting warmed up, and he caught up to him taking the lead with about twenty-five yards left.

Berry, refusing to lose, tackled Maul, elbowed him in the jaw, and proceeded to finish the race. Maul just caught his ankle enough to force Berry into the sand. Maul then leapt on Berry using a Peterson Roll that he learned on his high school wrestling team.

The men fought for a few minutes until a lifeguard showed up to the scene on an ATV. It was obvious that the man wanted nothing to do with the fight, but he was duty bound to stop it. "Gentlemen, stop it. Please, stop it before I call the police!"

Maul and Berry had their faces covered in sand and looked at the man with the squeaky voice.

Maul started to speak, but he had to spit out the sand in his mouth first. "Uh, sorry. We are just in a race. Harmless fun. We will get out of your way."

"Yeah, sorry about that," Berry added.

The young lifeguard was too stunned to do anything but nod.

On the way back to the hotel Berry said, "Looks like a draw. I figure I go out tonight, you stay in and watch pay-per-view."

"I had you beat, you son of a bitch!"

"Hey, in the Secret Service, we play to win."

"You know what; I think I need a break. Let's get a few hours of work in, meet to discuss any progress, and then we will go our separate ways for the night."

"Sounds like a great idea," Berry said pleased.

CHAPTER 15

Vero Beach, Florida
Driftwood Resort

Charlie and Lindsey pulled into an old hotel on the Atlantic Ocean called the Driftwood Resort. The Driftwood was built in the 1930s and was listed in the National Registry of Historic Places. Many people visited Vero Beach just to stay at the hotel. The hotel was famous for its collection of bells, including one owned by Harriet Beecher Stow, the author of *Uncle Tom's Cabin*. Vero Beach was a perfect location for Charlie and Lindsey, a small quiet town that was not yet infested by the snow birds looking to get away from the northern snow. Besides the residents of the small town, most people in the town were tourists from Europe, looking for a small, warm, safe place for vacation.

Charlie and Lindsey managed to get an ocean front room on the second floor and paid for three nights in cash. On the last day, they planned on calling the president from Vero and then wait until the Secret Service picked them up.

For dinner they decided to stay at the Driftwood and eat at Waldo's, a beach front restaurant. Waldo's was as old as the hotel and featured dining on the deck directly on the beach of the Atlantic Ocean. The restaurant was a one of a kind with distinctive architecture and antiques.

They were seated on the deck, Charlie ordered the Waldo's Draft, a lager made just for the restaurant, and Lindsey ordered a glass of Merlot. Lindsey was dressed in casual clothes, a pink button-down shirt, tan Capri pants, and a pair of brown sandals. Charlie wore a blue polo shirt with tan cargo pants, and a brown pair of sandals.

When the waiter brought the drinks he asked what the two wanted for dinner. Lindsey answered, "I need something semihealthy. We have eaten nothing but junk for the last couple of days. I will take the Oriental Chicken Salad with the dressing on the side, please."

"Good choice," the waiter said, "and for you, sir?"

"Screw it; I am having fun on this trip. I will take the Baby Back Ribs."

The waiter left to put their orders in, and Charlie and Lindsey relaxed while staring at the ocean.

Charlie spoke first, "It is beautiful, isn't it? All we have is Lake Erie and Mosquito Lake. When we graduate from grad school, let's move down here. Vero seems like a nice town."

Lindsey thought about it and said, "Maybe for a vacation home, but this town is just too small for me. Plus, there are no universities around here where I could teach at." Lindsey could not help but to think about her parents. She knew they would be extremely worried. "How do you think my parents are doing? I hope they are not too worried about me. I haven't talked to them in a while."

"I am sure my parents have talked to them by now. They will be fine. This is for us now. Let just enjoy the view."

In the distance they could see a cruise ship lit up as it sailed across the horizon.

"I always wanted to go on a cruise, but I couldn't because it is too big of a security risk."

"I was on one when I was about fourteen. My parents saved for years, it was supposed to be the trip of a lifetime. Instead we spent the entire trip below deck because it rained the whole week. It was just our luck. My parents were so disappointed; they've never been on another vacation since."

After their dinner and a few drinks the couple asked the waiter where to go to hang out for a while.

"What kind of place are you looking for?" he asked. "A small town bar or a happening place?"

Charlie thought it would help to avoid detection by going to a small bar.

"My favorite bar in town is called the What-A-Tavern. Great prices and drinks. I will call you a cab, they are cheap around here. I have a friend there, her name is Red O'Malley. She and her husband will be there; let them know I sent you."

Twenty minutes later they arrived at the bar. They ordered their drinks and asked for O'Malley.

"She is over there at the end of the bar."

They introduced themselves and they began to have a conversation, which soon got around to her job.

"I coach girls' basketball at the high school where I teach," O'Malley said.

"That is awesome. How did your girls do last year?"

"We have been to the Elite Eight the last two seasons. Not bad for a small school. Where are you guys from?"

"Ummm . . . we are from Ohio, down here to visit my grandparents," Charlie said trying to sound convincing.

"You look familiar. Did you go to school down here?"

Lindsey spoke up and said, "Nope, first time here."

"Where have I seen you before?" O'Malley asked.

Charlie tried to turn the attention on the guy singing Frank Sinatra's "Luck Be a Lady" on karaoke. "This guy is horrible! He sounds more like a kid that got kicked out of his high school choir."

O'Malley gave Charlie a "be quiet" look and nodded her head toward the guy sitting next to her.

"You got a problem with the way my buddy sings?" the man asked. He was short but clearly did not back down from a fight. He had short man syndrome; he was small but wanted to gain respect from everybody and was willing to fight for it to make up for his lack of height.

"No, no. Just kidding around," Charlie said.

The man stood from his stool and asked, "Do you want to say that again?"

"Come on, Brian, why do you always try to start a fight? Let me buy you a beer," O'Malley said to the man. She motioned to the bartender indicating that she wanted to buy him a drink, so the bartender returned with a token for his next round. Satisfied, the man took his seat and continued drinking his beer.

"Thank you for saving me there. I've got to learn when to shut my mouth."

Three hours later Charlie and Lindsey were feeling no pain when the bartender called them a cab. They thanked O'Malley for the good time, secretly paid for her tab, and went back to the Driftwood.

When they arrived at their room, Charlie and Lindsey quickly got cleaned up. When Lindsey came out of the bathroom, she was barefoot and wore nothing but a T-shirt that barely covered her. Charlie was looking forward to having a good night.

~ ~ ~

They woke up the next morning with the sun on their faces. It was a great way to wake up while they ordered coffee and cereal for breakfast. They sat on the balcony in silence for a while just watching the waves. They decided to spend the day at Sebastian Inlet Sate Park. The park was one of the most popular in the state because of its long pier and great surfing conditions.

Lindsey and Charlie tried to take advantage of the sun while they had it, so they got dressed in their bathing suits and covers and went to the front desk. They were looking for a place to grab a book for the beach, so the front desk manager suggested the Vero Beach Book Center.

It was a large bookstore in Vero Beach known for its children's section and used-book section. Both Lindsey and Charlie were avid readers and immediately fell in love with the store. The main building contained the new-book section, and the second building was divided up with the children's section on the ground floor and the used-book section on the second floor. The ground floor was large, and the middle area was used for story time and other programs. The outer portion was for children's books and toys, including play areas. Charlie and Lindsey went to the second floor to the used-book section and began to browse the large selection of used paperback books.

After a few minutes, Charlie selected a comedy book entitled *Rugged Knuckles and Painful Chuckles* written by a local author, and Lindsey got an old Jennifer Wiener novel.

When they arrived at Sebastian Inlet State Park they headed straight toward the beach and laid out their towels. The waves were rough and they spent their day swimming and sunbathing. Charlie rented a surfboard and tried to surf, even got some pointers from a local kid who was skipping school.

The young skinny blonde kid said, "All right, here comes a wave, man. Lay flat and when the whitewater is two feet behind you start paddling toward shore. Then act like you are doing a push up and slowly get to your feet. Here comes one now, bro."

The wave hit and the boy seemed like a pro as he caught the wave and headed into shore. Charlie, however, was quickly thrown off his board and was struggling to get back on. The boy tried to encourage him to keep trying, but after about forty-five minutes Charlie was ready to read his book.

He joined Lindsey, where she was sunbathing, and put the board down, feeling somewhat defeated. As he was huffing and taking deep breaths Charlie said, "Well I think I got my workout for today. I also found out that I am not much of a surfer."

Lindsey chuckled and said, "Do you mind if I try?"

"Good luck, it is a lot harder than it looks."

Lindsey took the board, went into the water and began to paddle out into the water when she met up with the same boy that tried to help Charlie.

"Hey, your boyfriend had a tough time out here. I would be willing to give you some pointers."

"I would appreciate that, thanks," Lindsey replied.

The boy went through the same instructions that he gave Charlie, with one exception. "Be careful though, not many girls wear bikinis surfing. You don't want to give the beach a show, though I certainly would not mind."

Lindsey blushed and was beginning to rethink whether she wanted to continue. "I think I will try it. I will just stay under until I get myself fixed."

The boy shrugged his shoulders and said, "Okay, your call. Here comes one now. Remember, push up, knees, and then to your feet. Ready, go."

They both paddled in and Lindsey began the process but soon found herself in the ocean. Not to be denied she tried four more times before she had some success. While she was not ready for competition any time soon, she was able to ride waves long enough to have some fun.

On the last wave, she got to her feet and was able to ride the wave well, until she lost her balance and hit the water hard enough to take her top with the wave. She looked around to see if anyone saw, but luckily her instructor rode the wave to the shore and no one on the beach was paying attention to her so she was confident that she was unseen. Though undetected, she could not find her top and she desperately hoped that it did not float away. Franticly, she began to splash around in hopes of finding it, while trying to stay under the water shoulder deep. As she noticed the boy making his way back out to her, she stepped up her searching efforts. As she kicked, she felt it with her foot and she reached down grabbed it with her hand just as the boy made it to her.

She turned her back toward the open sea and said, "Look back at the beach; I am having that bikini malfunction you were talking about."

He turned and she quickly put the top back on, hoping that the boy was honest.

"I think I have had enough fun for today," she said. "Next time I come out I will make sure I have the proper attire. Thank you for all the help, you are a great teacher."

He smiled and said, "Come on, you got one more in you."

"Good try."

He had a mischievous smile on his face and said, "It was worth a shot, and the lessons were my pleasure, sis."

Lindsey paddled back to shore meet Charlie on the beach. "Did you see me out there?" she asked Charlie.

A little upset and embarrassed that she did better than him, he said, "Yeah, you did great. Your new boyfriend looked like he enjoyed himself out there."

"Are you jealous? He looks like he is still in high school, just relax. He was just teaching me a little. Besides, he didn't see me when my top came off."

Taken by surprise, Charlie said, "What! Your top came off! What makes you think that he, or anybody else for that matter, didn't see?"

"Because he was just as surprise as you and no one was looking at me. If someone would have noticed, they would have been ogling."

Getting more jealous by the minute, Charlie asked, "You told him?! Why would you tell him?"

"I had to make sure he wasn't looking at me. It's no big deal."

Charlie relaxed and said, "I wish I would have seen, anyhow."

He was a little irritated when Lindsey had better success at surfing than him. Determined to find something he was good at, he tried his hand at saltwater fishing from the pier while Lindsey stayed on the beach. He caught a few small fish then decided that his time would be better spent with Lindsey.

They took a long walk down the beach where they had another heart to heart talk. Lindsey felt that the little vacation was worth it, just for the talks that they had.

Out of nowhere Charlie opened up. "You know life wasn't so bad at first. It was fun when my dad was in the Ohio Senate. I always got to go to fun parties, meet interesting people, even got treated differently by my teachers. When he won a seat in the U.S. Senate it all changed. Dad was always in DC, he came home almost every weekend but he was out meeting with 'the good people of Ohio who put me here.' That was when Mom started putting the pressure on me. God forbid that a Senator's son earns a B in his math class or be seen at a professional wrestling match because it was not prestigious enough for her. I just wanted to have fun and be a kid."

Lindsey was not sure what to say and she was surprised by his frankness. "Charlie, I know that you had a tough life." She paused. "Just think of the positive experiences that you have had; all the trips you got to go on; the world leaders you got to meet. Don't just focus on the negative. It will bring you down. Just look at my life. I was born to a lower middle-class family that had to pinch pennies to survive. I lived in a rough neighborhood and went to a subpar school. It was a good summer break if we made the hour-drive to Lake Erie. But when it comes down to it, I wouldn't change a thing because it made me who I am today. My parents love me and they did what they could to help me be successful. Your parents did their best too."

"I guess I do sound like a spoiled brat," Charlie said. "I just wonder what life would be like having a normal childhood."

They both started to tap their hands to Kenny Chesney's "When the Sun Goes Down" on Lindsey's MP3 player.

Charlie continued, "I can't even have a normal conversation with anyone without thinking that they only want to be friends with me because of my dad. When I first started dating you that is all my mom warned me about. She was afraid you were trying to use me. I will never know a normal life like you have, or at least had before we get married." He playfully elbowed her in the ribs and smiled at her.

"I will do anything to be with you, Charlie. Even if that means I have to put up with all the crap that comes with being married to the first son," she said jokingly. "I remember one time I found my dad downstairs at the kitchen table at three o'clock in the morning. I was thirsty, and I was getting something to drink. He was just sitting there in the dark with his hands on his temples. I almost gave him a heart attack when he saw me. He said he couldn't sleep because he was worried about our bills. He said we had to cut back, and he was trying to do anything to keep the electricity and water on. He even told me to be prepared to lose the cars because they might be repossessed. He then talked about how he wished he was a better man that could take better care of his family. That is what I grew up with."

"I feel like an ass," responded Charlie. "At least we both had parents that loved us. It is like they always say; the grass is always greener on the other side. When we get married I promise to give you a good life, and I will be a devoted husband and father. My family will come first."

"You are going to be a great husband, I know it. When do you think we can get married?"

"It would be smart to wait until after grad school. And it would be easier to please my parents. Who knows, maybe we can push them for a closer date?"

After their walk they headed back to the Driftwood to get dressed for dinner. They choose Mulligan's, a small restaurant with a fun atmosphere on the beach. The bar area had a one-man band playing music, and they both enjoyed the setting. After a few drinks and full stomachs, Charlie and Lindsey walked back to the hotel for a much needed night of sleep after all day in the sun.

CHAPTER 16

Washington DC
The President's Private Office

While Charlie and Lindsey were having fun in Vero Beach, Kate Jenner was in the president's private West Wing office trying to get conformable. Even though the president let her use his office, she still felt out of place using it. Her job was to help the president keep track of Charlie and to make sure that he was in the right frame of mind when he made decisions, which meant that she had a lot of catching up to do.

Jenner's first task was to contact Matthew Jones, Secretary of Homeland Security; Barbara Harper, Director of the Secret Service; and Thomas Host, Director of the CIA. Jones, Harper's boss, wanted to play a bigger role in the search for Charlie since Harper had been unsuccessful.

Kate made her way down to the Situation Room where the three were waiting for her.

"Good morning," she said as she entered the room. She was trying to hide her nerves. She sat at the chair at the head of the table, usually reserved for the president, and Jones was quick to point out her mistake.

"Ms. Jenner, that chair is reserved for the president," he said.

Jenner stood and found an acceptable chair at the side of the table while continuing her introduction. "The president has asked me to report directly to him about Charlie's search. I am asking, through the Oval Office, for an update of the situation. In addition, I would like updates throughout the search until he is found."

The other three in the room were upset that Jenner was taking charge of the case and resented being ordered around by an outsider of the West Wing.

"As of now, we have no new information to pass on," Harper said. "Maul and Berry are in Daytona Beach and are stuck until new information is available. We have every available resource, with the cooperation of the CIA, trying to track them. We are trying to be as proactive as we can, but until Jamin makes a mistake, there is nothing we can do."

"Jamin?" asked Jenner.

Sighing loudly to demonstrate her frustration in dealing with an amateur, Harper said, "Jamin is the code name used by the Secret Service to track Charlie's movements."

Ignoring the tension in the room, Jenner asked, "What about the Farah cell?"

Host spoke for the first time, "I am sorry Ms. Jenner, but that information is classified."

Digging through her binder Jenner took out a sheet of paper and slid it to the middle of the table. "This is an executive order from the president, signed last night, stating that I have all clearance as it relates to Charlie's search, including all information on the Farah cell." She was relieved to have been on the winning side of the argument.

Without a choice, Host said, "They have also gone underground. Our men, including Maul, believe that the cell is tracking Charlie. They are very good at hiding their tracks, as well. What makes this case different is that any move now is unpredictable because they don't even know where they are going at this point. When we tracked them to the Youngstown area, we were able to follow points of interest and past behavior. For example, the first lady was in town, which would give them a good reason to go to that city. We were then able to track the Farahs using a store's surveillance camera system. In this case, they don't know what their next move is so it is next to impossible to try to predict where they are going, with the exception of Florida, assuming that is in fact where Charlie is going."

Jones added in his slow, deep voice, "This is extremely classified. I just want to remind you that this conversation cannot be conveyed to anyone, and I mean anyone, outside of this room with exception of the president. If the president wants the first lady to know, he can tell her."

Jenner snapped back, "I understand what classified means, I need no lecture. The president wants me on this team because he trusts me and believes that I am the best person for the job. I hope that you will feel the same." Feeling that she needed to make her status known she added, "I expect updates in real time."

With that she excused herself and went back to the president's private office. Since the president had asked her to help him make decisions, she decided to check into the airline bailout meetings, which were rumored to be almost finished. She left her office and headed to the Roosevelt Room, where the meetings were being held. No one was in the room, so she decided to go to Brad Wilder's office to see if she could catch up with him there.

When she approached his office, she noticed that the door was left slightly open and heard Wilder talking to another man. She figured that she would catch up with him later, but as she turned to walk back to her office, she was caught off guard by something that Wilder said to the unknown man.

"Listen, the president is distracted now, I know this is not the exact plan that we want, but if we push hard we can get this money now," Wilder said.

The other man then spoke up and said, "The dollar amount is low and we were hoping for more favorable interest rate. Now he wants no extra fees. I'm not sure I like the deal."

"This is the best you are going to get. And you can start to receive the money now. In a little while I will be working for you, and I will hit them up for more."

Jenner had heard all she needed. She decided that if she waited any longer someone would catch her snooping. She wanted to know who the man was, so she knocked on the door and stuck her head in.

"Hey, Brad, I was wondering . . ." She stopped in midsentence and said trying to put on her best Oscar performance, "Oh, I am sorry; I didn't know that you were in a meeting. Hi, I am Kate Jenner."

"Gideon Kosar, nice to meet you."

"Brad, we will catch up later, it is not important."

She turned and left the room and knew that she had some investigating to do. She wondered what Wilder was up to. She almost did not believe that Wilder would try to do that to the president or the American people because he was such a valuable person in the White House. She felt an obligation to investigate further because she would need more information before taking it to the president. An accusation this large needed solid evidence. The only problem was, how was she going to get it? No one would authorize a formal investigation. She decided that she would sneak into his office and search for anything she could find, but doing that in the most secure building in America was not going to be easy. She had to first find his daily schedule, which was available to her as a top advisor to the president.

She pulled the schedule up as soon as she returned to her office. He was scheduled to be off White House grounds in two hours to speak at a journalists conference. Beside the speech, the rest of his day was spent in the West Wing; so this would be her only opportunity, and she would have to risk it to help save the president from a possible scandal involving the White House.

~ ~ ~

Two hours later, Kate Jenner was trying to catch herself up on the issues that she was not privy to when she worked in the East Wing. One of the issues included the situation in Iran and the threat of nuclear weapons. She felt that if the situation got any worse, she would need to advise the president to take action, either through military force or through diplomatic channels.

Brad Wilder left his office just in time and stopped by Jenner's office on the way out.

"Not a bad office for your first day on the job," he said.

"Yeah, I know. Too bad it is temporary."

"I wanted to tell you that I am sorry that I didn't get back to you. I was preparing for this speech I need to give in a little while. When I get back, I promise we will sit and talk."

Trying to sound polite, Jenner said, "No problem. We can catch up when you get back."

She waited about fifteen minutes before she entered Wilder's office. Her heart was racing so fast she thought it would burst through her chest. She took a deep breath, walked down the hall and turned the corner. She could see his office, and it seemed much farther than the thirty feet it really was.

As she approached the door and went for the door knob she heard someone coming from behind her, which caused her to keep on walking. She rounded the next corner and went into a supply closet to grab a pack of pens in an attempt to disguise her real motive.

Pens in hand, she walked back down to his office and with all her senses on high alert, she opened the door and then quickly shut the door behind her in what she felt like took no more than a half a second. Wilder's office was not too big, but had a nice size desk and two doors: one from the outside hall, from where she just entered, and the other leading to his secretary's office.

She could hear his secretary talking through the side door and knew that she needed to be quiet. Not having much time, she began to sift through his stuff on his desk finding nothing there to hint at what she was looking for.

She noticed a black leather briefcase under his desk. She figured that if he was in fact keeping something like this hidden, he would want to keep the evidence somewhere else besides the White House, and the best place for that would be his briefcase, which he could take home every night. She reached down and pulled out the briefcase and opened it. She noticed many files and began scanning the tabs.

She noticed one that had "Airlines" written on it so she pulled it out. Inside the folder was an agreement between Wilder and Kosar worth millions of dollars. The only reason she could figure why they would sign such an incriminating agreement was too keep one another honest. If one went public, the other would have the incriminating evidence too. She took out her phone and took several pictures of the document, included the briefcase that it was in. She was certain that she had found the evidence that she would need to take to the president.

Now she would need to leave Wilder's office, but it would be more difficult because from the inside of the room she was blind to who was in the hall. She eased the door open, hoping that no one was there. Her luck had run out though as Don Austin walked by as she emerged from the room.

"Hi, Ms. Jenner. I thought Brad was out giving a speech at a conference this afternoon."

"He is."

"Then what are you doing in his office? This is not a good thing, Ms. Jenner. A person's privacy is highly regarded around here."

Acting like a school girl getting caught by the principal, Jenner said the first thing that came to her mind, "I was leaving a note on his desk. I wanted to get caught up on the airline bailouts, so I can report to the president."

"He has a secretary for that. There is also voicemail or email for that matter. I still do not see why you would need to enter his area."

Giggling like she just made a minor mistake she said, "I guess I didn't even think about that. I really didn't see why it was a big deal. In the East Wing we . . ."

She was cut off by the unimpressed chief of staff, "This is not the East Wing. We deal with a wide variety of national security issues that need to be protected. We do not go into other people's offices around here. Do we need to set up a meeting to have a discussion of West Wing protocol?"

"That will not be necessary, sir."

"All right, then. Have a nice day."

Jenner was relieved that she did not get into more trouble than just a lecture. Little did she know that Austin went directly to the president's office to complain about Jenner's whereabouts.

~ ~ ~

Three hours later, Jenner was exhausted and was in need of a good nap, but she had her prearranged meeting with the president. She waited in the reception area outside of the Oval Office. She had her presentation to him memorized and was anxious to get started.

"You can go in now," the young secretary said.

Jenner nodded her head in response and headed into the office. The president was sitting on one of the couches in the center of the room and motioned for her to join him. The president had a coffee mug in his hand and by the bags under his eyes it looked like he needed it.

"How is it going, Kate? Are you up to speed on everything?"

"Not quite, Mr. President. I still have a lot of material to cover."

"It will come." Trying to get to his next meeting, the president did not want to waste time with small talk, so he decided to get right to the point. "I talked to Don Austin. He was very upset about you being in Wilder's office. I must say that I am too. There is information around here that must be protected and everyone must understand that."

"I do, sir, but I have reason to believe that Wilder is not as honest as you think."

"Where is this coming from, Kate?"

"This afternoon, I went to Wilder's office to discuss the bailouts. As I went to knock on the door, I overheard him talking to someone. Wilder was saying that he will be out of here soon and that he should take the deal on the table to get the money now and that Wilder will be working for Freedom Air soon. Trying to protect you, sir, I knocked on the door to see who was in there. It was Gideon Kosar from Freedom Air. I think Kosar is paying off Wilder to get the bailout money."

"You are making very big accusations, Kate," the president said.

"I know. I snuck into his office to get evidence. I told Mr. Austin that I was in there to leave a note."

"Which he did not believe," Seaborne interrupted.

"I know it was a bad excuse, but it was the best I could come up with at the moment. Under his desk, I found a briefcase and inside was a folder labeled 'Airline.'"

The president interrupted again and said, "I am sure you know that in order to search someone's possessions, you need a search warrant. Anything you have found cannot be used against him."

"I understand." She took out her cell phone and pulled up the photo of Wilder's agreement with Kosar and passed it to the president. The president put down his mug and took the phone from Jenner.

"I took a picture of this and put the file back. This makes it clear that he has a multimillion dollar contract with Kosar, and he is using the White House to his advantage." Jenner stopped for a moment before continuing. The president was still analyzing the photo when she said, "You asked me to protect you and that is what I did here. I do not want to see you get hurt. America does not need a scandal."

She couldn't tell if the president was upset at the fact that she stole the evidence or that Wilder was working behind the scenes. It seemed like an eternity before she found out her answer.

"Kate, what you did is highly illegal, but I know that you were acting in my best interest. I cannot use this against him, but I also cannot let him get away with it." Seaborne stood and walked to the fireplace and paced in front of it for a few minutes.

"Who else have you told about this?" the president asked.

"No one."

"Good. Call Kosar and tell him that I want to see him. Keep it under the radar, though. Get him here as soon as you can. Maybe I can use the leverage of this office to get him to talk. Make sure that no one sees him here. Call Harper. She will help you send an undisclosed vehicle to pick him up."

"Yes, sir."

"Also, let Don Austin know that Kosar is coming. Tell him it is about the airline bailouts and that my schedule will need to be cleared while he is here."

Jenner nodded to the president and walked out of the Oval Office heading back to her temporary one. She wondered why she had dreamed about one day working in the West Wing since her first day had turned out to be such a disaster.

When she got back to her office she shut the door and called a White House operator to put her in touch with Kosar. She was amazed by how fast she was able to accomplish that goal.

"Mr. Kosar? This is Kate Jenner calling on behalf of the president."

"I met you today in Brad's office."

"That is correct. Good memory. The president wants to have a private meeting with you. We will send an unmarked car to pick you up. He will consider it a favor."

"What is this about?" Kosar asked.

"I was instructed not to discuss it."

"Well, I guess I don't have a choice anyway."

"Great. This trip is to be confidential; it would be appreciated if you did not tell anyone where you are headed. Now, can you tell me where you are located?"

After writing down his location, Jenner called Harper to set up the pickup. Her next call was to Austin.

After two rings the chief of staff picked up the phone.

"Mr. Austin, this is Kate Jenner. The president has asked me to notify you that Gideon Kosar is on his way back to the While House to discuss the progress of the bailout meetings. He asked that you clear his schedule while he meets with him."

Austin was clearly upset about Jenner giving him orders, even on the behalf of the president. "I don't understand, Kate. Wilder will be back soon, and he will be able to brief the president. What is it that you are not telling me?"

"I am not at liberty to say."

"Ms. Jenner, I am not playing games here. I am the president's chief of staff, and I demand to know what the hell is going on over there!"

"I wish I could. Can I tell the president that you have taken care of his schedule?" Jenner asked.

"You can, indeed. But you and I need to have a conversation real soon about how things work around here."

Kate agreed and hung up the phone.

Shortly after, she met Kosar at the West Wings main entrance. Kosar was ushered through without signing the visitor log in the lobby and followed Jenner through the West Wing to the Oval Office. Jenner asked the president's personal secretary to alert the president of their presence and they were immediately ushered in and the door was closed behind them.

"Gideon, how are you?" the president asked.

"Just fine, sir. Can you tell me what I am doing here?"

CHAPTER 17

Vero Beach, Florida
Later That Night

As the president was getting ready to meet with Kosar, Charlie and Lindsey were walking down Ocean Drive toward the Driftwood. Both were exhausted from the sun and Lindsey was looking for a good night's sleep. Charlie secretly wanted to stop back at Waldo's to have another beer, but felt that Lindsey would not be up to it. As they strolled hand in hand, they looked at the stars and dreamed of what the future held. They both knew that despite the consequences, the vacation was much needed and well worth it.

"I had a great time, it is too bad our little vacation is going to end soon," said Lindsey.

"Once we graduate from grad school and start working we will have plenty of time go on great vacations."

"Yeah, but this one is different. It has the thrill of running away, no one knows we are here, and we have nothing to worry about, like work."

~ ~ ~

About fifty feet ahead, parallel parked in front of the Driftwood was an old, dark colored van. Inside sat Aahil, Taybah, and Maali, who had been waiting for the last fifteen minutes. They finally spotted Charlie and Lindsey. Aahil was the first one to notice them and was quick to point them out.

130

"There they are," Aahil said slowly in his thick accent. It was as if he was in a zone because he was in such deep concentration.

The three pulled down their black ski masks over their faces and took out their pistols. Taybah and Maali were waiting for Aahil to signal when to move on their targets. Aahil had parked the van on Ocean Drive so that it was strategically placed in front of the Driftwood. The parallel parking spot was in a location where they could easily jump out, grab Charlie and Lindsey and leave the area quickly.

When the couple was five feet away from the van, Aahil commanded, "Get ready."

Just when he was ready to give the order, Aahil noticed from the corner of his eye a black Dodge Charger screaming down the street.

~ ~ ~

Maul and Berry were driving wildly, trying to catch the couple before anything could happen to them.

"There they are!" Berry yelled.

Since there was no oncoming traffic, Maul went left of center and prepared to jump out of the car and apprehend the first son.

Maul said to Berry, "We got to make this quick."

"No shit," Berry quipped.

~ ~ ~

Aahil's instincts told him that the car was a federal agent's because of its model, color, and high speed so he yelled to his team, "Go!"

The three terrorists jumped out of the van with their weapons drawn as they approached their target.

"Stop! Stop!" Aahil yelled to the stunned college students.

~ ~ ~

In the Charger, Maul yelled, "Shit, look!"

Maul slammed on the breaks, leaving a long line of tire tracks. Berry left the vehicle before the car came to a stop and took out his pistol without saying so much as "police!" He fired his weapon, hitting one of the masked men in the upper arm. The other two terrorists quickly took a position behind their targets using them as shields.

Maul was now out of the car alongside Berry with his pistol pointed at the two terrorists. The people in the area, who were used to living in a small, low-crime city, began to flee the area, many women screaming as they ran.

Aahil knew that one of the witnesses would most certainly call the police, so he needed to act fast before they arrived.

"You do not want me to kill the first son, do you?" Aahil asked. "How would you explain that to the president?" Trying to reassure the agents, he continued, "We just want to keep him until we get our demands met. Then, we will let them go unharmed."

Maul responded, "That's not going to happen. Just let them go, and I will think about not killing you."

"Do you think I am dumb? I have the upper hand here. I am going to walk to my van, and we will drive away. If you try to stop us, I will shoot them, starting with the girl."

At first, Charlie and Lindsey were too surprised and scared that they hardly moved; but with the idea that she might be shot, Lindsey let out a small cry.

"Let her go, I am the one that you want," Charlie pleaded. "She will not get you anything."

Aahil twisted Charlie's arm behind his back and shoved the pistol further into the side of his head and said, "Shut up!"

Charlie had no choice but to listen.

Aahil then heard a faint sound of sirens in the distance. He began to slowly moving toward the van while the other terrorist followed close behind.

"Don't do anything stupid!" Aahil yelled.

"Shit, what the hell are we going do?" Berry asked Maul.

Maul said nothing in return, which Berry took as a sign of defeat. He also knew that the terrorists had the advantage and that there was nothing that he could really do but watch as the terrorists moved toward the van. Aahil, who was still holding Charlie, stayed outside the van while the other terrorist loaded Lindsey into the vehicle. Once Lindsey was secured, Aahil moved Charlie into the van and restrained them.

Keeping a close eye on the two agents, Aahil climbed between the seats and took his place behind the wheel.

"What about Maali?" a female voice asked from the back.

"He is on his own now. We cannot risk trying to save him."

Aahil shifted into drive and drove north on Ocean Drive.

Taybah thought about Maali bleeding on the side walk and wondered what would have happened if she was shot. Would he leave her on the side of the road like he had left Maali? Would Aahil really sacrifice her to complete the mission? It was one thing for Aahil to say that he would do anything to complete a mission, including letting her die, but was it really possible that the man that she had grown to love would really leave her there for the federal agents?

"Aahil?" Taybah asked.

"What is it?" Aahil responded slightly annoyed that she was trying to ask a question now. He was trying to keep an eye on the agents and was also trying to navigate their way out of town.

As he turned left on to Route 60, Taybah asked, "Would you have left me there?"

"What do you mean?" Aahil asked, making no attempt to hold back his agitation.

"You left Maali back there and who knows what the U.S. government is going to do to him. If that were me, what would you do?"

Aahil looked in the mirror at Charlie, who stared right back at him. Aahil was almost embarrassed that she would be asking this question in front of another man, let alone the hostage that they just captured.

"We will talk about this later!" he said firmly.

"Would you have left me behind so that those men would do God knows what to me?" she demanded.

In a dark, deep, slow voice Aahil responded simply, "Yes."

Although she had expected it, the news hurt Taybah. She knew she was doing this mission to serve a bigger purpose, but this was the man she loved. She prayed that this would end quickly, so she could begin thinking about a possible change of lifestyle.

~ ~ ~

Berry yelled to Maul, "Let's get him," referring to the wounded terrorist.

Holding their firearms in front of them, the men approached the wounded man. He was holding his shoulder and was in obvious pain. Once Maali noticed that he was being approached he reached for his weapon and pointed it at no one in particular.

"Stop or I will shoot!" Maali yelled.

"Don't be stupid, put down your weapon before I shoot you again," Berry said.

Berry also wanted to leave the area before the local police showed up; he didn't want to fight over who had jurisdiction over the case. The Vero Beach

Police Department would have claimed that this case was theirs because shots were fired within the city limits. Berry and Maul from the Secret Service and the CIA, respectively, would not allow that to happen, and ultimately they knew that they would win the argument. But why go through the hassle if they could have avoided it. They needed to get Maali talking, the sooner he talked the faster he would lead them to Charlie.

Berry aimed his pistol on Maali's right arm and fired, skinning his left hand, and the gun dropped to the sidewalk. Maul took advantage of the moment and in what seemed like a flash, quickly apprehended the terrorist.

Not worried about the pain he caused Maali; Maul roughly flipped him on his stomach, placed his knee in the small of his back and handcuffed him. He then forced him to his feet and walked him to the car where Berry was ready with the back door open. Maul shoved him in the vehicle, smacking Maali on the head as he was forced into the car. Berry chose to sit in the backseat with him with the hopes of getting him to start talking.

Maul retrieved his cell phone from his pocket and hit the speed dial to CIA headquarters.

"Operations," the voice over the phone answered without emotion.

"This is Agent Maul; I need to have a satellite track a high priority target. This has precedent over any other case at the order of the president."

"Hold on," the male operator said, seemingly not realizing the urgency.

Maul peeled out as he started down the street. He needed to make a u-turn to head in the same direction as the Farahs. Just as he completed the turn the first VBPD police vehicle arrived at the scene. Maul knew that it was only a matter of time before one of the pedestrians ratted him out.

He turned on to Route 60 and made his way quickly toward I-95.

"Maul? This is Liam." Liam Hughes was working on another case when he heard Maul's call come in, but dropped everything to take the call.

"Liam, I am glad that you are on duty tonight. Your help in Youngstown was priceless. I am in Vero Beach, Florida, and I am heading toward I-95. I need you to track a black 1980s Chevy van. They have Charlie Seaborne."

After a short silence, Liam said, "Shit. I am on it. The problem is there are not too many satellites over Vero Beach. I will make this urgent and get everyone here on it."

Maul noticed a VBPD cruiser with its lights on passing him in the other direction. Suddenly in his rearview mirror he saw the car take a quick u-turn to head his way.

"We got company," Maul said to no one in particular. "Liam, I am going to need a nice quiet place to hang out for a couple of hours. Any ideas around here?"

Maul heard Liam talking in the background but could not make out what was being said. A few seconds later Liam came back on the phone.

"Maul, keep heading west on 60 and once you hit Sixty-sixth Avenue, turn north. That is a very rural area and I am betting there are some old farmhouses there."

"Thanks, Liam. Keep this line open in case I need to talk to you. Call me when you have something." Maul hung up the phone and turned his full attention to the police chasing after him. Maul was sure that his super charged Charger could out run a small town police cruiser, but he was outnumbered and he had a long drive on Route 60 before he got to Sixty-sixth Avenue, most of it in thick traffic.

Maul hit the gas and felt his powerful engine kick in. He began to dodge traffic as he drove over the Barber Bridge. He made a sharp left turn as the windy road made its way through the beautiful business district. In some areas he needed to slow down because of the thick traffic. Before he knew it, he had three police vehicles following him, two VBPD and one Indian River County Sheriff's.

He swerved his way in and out of traffic until he finally hit a straight stretch of road. He was able to get the car going well over one hundred miles per hour and quickly out ran the cruisers following him. Going these speeds, he was surprised that he did not catch up with the Farahs.

Berry took this opportunity to start the interrogation of Maali. He began the questioning by plunging his finger in his bullet wound. Maali screamed in pain, which only made Berry stick his finger in his a wound even further.

"This is going to be a long process if you don't start talking to us," Maul said candidly. "Just tell us where they are going, and I will take it easy on you."

Maali spit on Berry's face and said, "You will get nothing from me. I am trained to resist your interrogations. Whatever you do to me will not work."

Although organizations around the world, including the CIA, KGB, and even al Qaeda, train their agents on how to resist torture, most experts claim that no training can prepare someone for torture. It is a person's character that allows them to deal with torture, and Berry was determined to see how far Maali would go before he broke down.

Berry responded by hitting the terrorist over the head with his pistol. Maali let out a small cry but quickly turned his pain into a laugh.

"Ha-ha. You think you can really break me? I am too determined to carry out my mission."

Berry let out a laugh of his own, "We will see about that. We have a lot of interesting things lined up for you."

"Your words do not scare me."

Maul's phone began to ring in his pocket.

"This is Maul."

"It's Liam. We found your van. We could not track the van, but we are checking the traffic cameras now. I'll call you when I get something."

Maul hung up and repeated the news to Berry.

Berry decided that it was time to call Barbara Harper to tell her the updated status. They had been sitting around waiting for so long that it was a small relief to finally have something to report.

"Hi, Maul, I hope you have good news."

"Not really. We found Jamin and Lindsey, but not before the Farahs."

"Damn it," was Harper's only response.

"I shot and hit one of the terrorists in the arm as we first approached them." Berry told the rest of the story, including that he had taken Maali into custody.

"I got to tell you, Berry, I am beyond disappointed. How could you have the president's son taken into their custody right in front of you?"

"I understand, but I assure you that there was nothing else we could have done. If I would have approached them, I think he would have injured Charlie. Maul just got a hold of his contact at the CIA, and they are trying to locate the van now."

"All right. What is next?"

"We are going to try to find an abandoned house where we will try to get some information from the prisoner."

Harper quickly spoke up, "Nothing that even resembles torture, you hear me? You know very well how much trouble the Bush administration received and Seaborne does not need any bad press right now. Plus, I do not want to sit through hours of depositions."

George W. Bush and his administration received much criticism during his presidency for the torturing of known terrorists. The Bush administration maintained that the methods worked and caused key terrorists to tell all. The critics claimed that torture does not work and that the methods just cause the terrorists to say what the examiner wants to hear and that other methods were more effective.

"Yes, ma'am," was Berry's only response.

"Berry, I want you to hear me loud and clear. No torture."

"I assure you, Director Harper."

"Good. Talk to me soon."

Harper hung up the phone and called Vice President Sewell, CIA Director Host, and Homeland Security Secretary Jones. She told them to meet in the Situation Room immediately; she could not stall from telling the president any longer than needed.

When Berry hung up the phone, he reached down and grabbed the flask that he had hid earlier in the day. He unscrewed the lid and took a big gulp.

Maali was looking at him strangely in which Berry responded, "Do you want some too?" Before Maali could respond, Berry poured a stream of liquor on the terrorist's gunshot wound.

"Ahhhhh!" Maali screamed.

Ignoring the man, Maul took another long gulp and replaced the lid.

"Jesus Christ, Berry. You got to stop," Maul said. When Berry did not respond, Maul continued, "We are going to find an abandoned house up here off a little ways. I will drop you two off, and I will head to that hardware store I just passed to get some tools that we need."

"I saw a liquor store back there too," Berry said. "Do you mind stopping and picking me up a bottle on your way back?"

"You have issues," Maul responded.

Berry finished the flask and began to wonder what Maul had in mind to get Maali to talk. Going to the hardware store was not a good sign of what was to come. Was he just trying to scare the hostage, or was he really planning to get tools to torture him? If he did plan on torturing the man, how would he keep it from Harper? She was very clear with her instructions. One thing he knew, regardless of his orders, he would do whatever it took to get the first son back.

CHAPTER 18

Washington DC
Allen Kinsey's Apartment

Since his newfound wealth, Kinsey had experienced a profoundly different lifestyle. He was paying off his student loans; he had no need to worry about his rent or car payment, and he was able to buy whatever video or entertainment system he wanted knowing that the government did not track those types of purchases. He also found that it was easier to pick up women when he had the money to take them out and show them a good time.

Since his last meeting with Sarah he had started seeing a new girl, Maria Thome. Maria was a decent-looking petite brunette that he had met in a bar just a few days earlier, but now their short relationship was beginning to pick up.

They began to kiss on his bed and then she took off her shirt.

"This is moving so fast," Maria said.

"Shhhhh," Kinsey said he continued to kiss her, now removing his shirt.

He knew that he had a good thing going with Sarah, but this was the first time in his life that he had so much opportunity, which he felt he could not pass up. To him, it was worth the risk of losing her.

He took a second to look around his room. While he felt guilty for taking terrorists's money, he felt that if the government had paid him more, he would not have financial troubles to begin with. His education and experience were fantastic, how could the federal government seriously think that he would be satisfied making his salary? Wouldn't they just expect people to do what he was doing? It had to be common, right? In his room he had a brand new flat screen high definition television and a new Xbox with all the games he could every want. Of course he felt guilty, but his guilt was short-lived.

As things were heating up in the bedroom, Kinsey heard the front door open. He jumped like the time when his mom caught him with a girl in his bedroom during high school. Trying to put his shirt back on he looked up and saw Sarah standing at the door. There was no denying what he was doing and there was no sense of even trying.

"What the hell are you doing!" yelled Sarah. Her face was red with anger.

"I'm sorry, I'm so sorry," were the only words that Kinsey could muster.

"You bastard! I thought we had something special here. I am such a fool. I should have realized that you are nothing more than a lying jerk."

Maria soon got in on the conversation, "Is this your girlfriend? You are a jerk." She put on her shirt and left the apartment without saying another word.

Kinsey thought it would be smart not to try to go after her, so he just let her go.

"I am so sorry. I guess I wasn't thinking clearly," he said.

"You are damn right you were not thinking clearly! How could you betray me like that?"

"I got stupid," Kinsey responded.

Sarah smacked him across the head, "That is all you can say?"

"I deserved that. Look, is there any way I can make it up to you?"

Ignoring the question Sarah said, "Is it because she is prettier than me?"

"No, nothing like that. I just got arrogant."

"We are over!" Sarah said as she walked to the front door.

As she reached for the door knob, the front door flew open and smacked her in the face, breaking her nose. She was then pushed to the ground as FBI agents wearing black uniforms stormed the apartment.

"FBI! Get on the ground!" one of the agents yelled.

Despite her broken nose, two agents restrained Sarah and quickly put her wrists in handcuffs which stained the carpet red. The others stormed a terrified Kinsey.

"What do you want?! I didn't do anything!" Kinsey said.

"Put your hands in the air!" the agent yelled back.

Kinsey quickly did as he was told and placed his hands in the air. While Agent Mark Bailey, the lead agent, had his weapon pointed at him, two others slowly approached Kinsey, took hold of his arms, and pulled them behind his back to restrain him.

"What is this all about?" Kinsey asked, despite knowing the answer.

Ignoring Kinsey, Bailey said to his team, "Take them to the car."

The agents swiftly carried Kinsey and the battered Sarah to a black Tahoe waiting for them outside a side door of Kinsey's apartment building. The windows were tinted so Kinsey and Sarah could not track where they were headed. Two agents sat in the front seat and the others followed in an identical vehicle. They were headed to an undisclosed location just south of Washington DC. The building was plain and had a large attached garage. The building was where the FBI brought fugitives that were a threat to national security.

As they pulled onto the street, the blood from Sarah's nose was now rolling down the front of her neck. The pain began to kick in as the adrenaline was slowing in her system.

"I need to go to the hospital, you bastards broke my nose," Sarah said.

"We have questions for you first and then we will take you to our best doctor to fix you up. Just relax," Bailey said.

"Just relax? I have blood rolling down my face, and I can't even stop it because my hands are tied behind my back."

"Ma'am, we are close to our destination, you are just going to have to wait."

Ten minutes later the van pulled into the garage, and the vehicle parked next to a large steel door. The garage was dark, with only limited lighting coming from two single bare light bulbs that hung from the ceiling. The large door opened from the inside and Kinsey and Sarah were ushered in.

The hall was narrow and just as dark as the garage. It had doors along both sides of the corridor that looked more like doors you would find in a prison. They forced Kinsey aggressively toward the third door on the right, Sarah was taken to the forth.

The rooms were bare and had concrete floors; no bed, no chair, no windows, and more importantly, no toilet.

Kinsey looked up as the agent shut the door as it made a loud, piercing sound that caused to shiver. It was as if he was in the world's worst prison.

This was the first time that Kinsey realized he made a terrible mistake taking the bribe. Now he was in a cold cell only God knows where, with the first girl he truly cared about in the room next door. How could he do this to her? They were a happy couple who enjoyed each other's company and they always had fun together. It seemed that when they were together, nothing else mattered.

He remembered one time they went to the movies to see a new comedy with his favorite actor Adam Sandler. They left early because they talked through half of it before they were kicked out. That was just it with her, even during a movie he was dying to see, he still enjoyed the conversation with her better.

Just like many things in life, a person doesn't know what they have until they lose it. What had he been thinking? He had a great relationship with a great person, and he screwed it up all because he got a big head. When he told Sarah that he got too arrogant, he was not lying. With money came confidence and confidence brought women. One thing he always dreamed of was having money and a great woman. He never thought that the money would drive off the woman.

He needed to find a way to get her out of here soon. He knew he would never get out, but she had nothing to do with this, and he would tell them whatever they wanted to hear to protect her.

~ ~ ~

Washington DC
The White House

Matthew Jones had been working in the White House since he decided to take a more active role in the Charlie Seaborne case. When he was asked by the president to become his Secretary of Homeland Security he was excited at the prospect of helping keep the nation safe. Unfortunately, he quickly learned that he would not have as much influence over the country's security as he thought. Even though the departments had merged, many of them felt that they were better off by themselves, especially the Secret Service. The Secret Service was controlled by the Department of the Treasury until the creation of Homeland Security. Its agents felt that they did just fine on their own and did not need anyone else to run them and that included Director Barbara Harper. While Jones thought that she was extremely good at her job, he felt that they should listen to him more. Adding to his lack of influence, he was not the president's first or even second choice to become secretary. The first choice decided to withdraw his nomination to take a private job at a security firm, and the second choice had his nomination denied by the Senate. The rejections gave the impression that Jones was just a fill in for the job and thus no one trusted his judgment.

Jones felt that this would be a great opportunity to prove his worth and his authority. He also felt that being stationed in the Situation Room with

Harper would put him closer to the action. When Harper called him with urgent news, he was ready to prove his value.

"Good evening, gentlemen," Harper started. "I just received a call from Mo Berry in the field. Thomas, I am sure that you will be hearing from Maul soon, he has been in contact with your office. Berry and Maul located Jamin and Lindsey in a town called Vero Beach, Florida. After finding their location, they headed south and spotted them walking on a sidewalk toward their hotel. Before they were able to make contact, the Farahs intercepted."

As Harper spoke, she could almost feel the air leaving the room as everyone took in a deep breath.

Harper continued, "Berry and Maul got into a confrontation with the Farahs, but only after the terrorists had positioned themselves behind Jamin and Lindsey. At the onset, Berry fired a shot and hit one of the terrorists in the arm. Unable to hold the upper hand, our agents watched as the Farahs were able to take the first son and Lindsey hostage. The Farahs drove away in a van that the CIA is currently tracking. Berry and Maul apprehended the wounded terrorist and are currently trying to find a quiet place to question him."

Jones was the first to respond, "Call the president and get him down here immediately." Directed to Harper, he added, "I can't believe that you didn't tell him earlier."

Defending herself to her boss, Harper said, "Sir, I asked that everyone come here first to devise a plan before we go to the president."

It was no secret that Harper and Jones did not always see eye to eye. She felt her department was capable of handling the job on their own. Jones on the other hand was loyal to the president, and his decisions reflected that. He felt that as commander in chief, it was the president's responsibly to gain insight from him because ultimately Seaborne would get the blame.

Because of these two conflicting ideologies, it seemed like they were in a constant state of disagreement. As secretary of Homeland Security, Jones had the final say.

"What kind of plan, Barbara?" Jones asked.

"As the president's advisors on this issue, we need a clear course of action that we can bring to the president and feel confident about. This is an emotional issue for him, as we can all understand; therefore, I believe that when we approach the president we need to be clear. We will serve the president better if we have an agreement."

"I understand, but at this point it seems clear what we need to do. First, we need to see where that vehicle goes. Once we know what kind of hideout the terrorists are using, we can begin to draft a plan to get Jamin back. In the meantime, have the FBI and the Secret Service assemble teams and head to Florida where they will remain on standby. It seems pretty clear to me, Director."

Host spoke up, "Mr. Secretary, I believe that the CIA can be very useful. It was one of our agents that helped to track down Jamin in the first place. I would like a CIA team there as well."

Jones thought for a moment and finally said, "Fine, but your men will only be there for surveillance and backup."

"Except for Maul, of course," Host added. Jones did not respond, so Host added, "He has been on this case since the beginning."

"Agreed. Director Harper, get the president please."

It was everything Harper could do to contain herself. She was wondering why he was now trying to be so involved. Was he trying to impress the president, or was he trying to make everyone aware of his power? Harper suspected it was a little of both.

Harper turned around and asked an assistant to call the president's personal secretary with an urgent message that his presence was needed immediately in the Situation Room.

CHAPTER 19

Gideon Kosar had been to the White House on many occasions but all for positive reasons. He had attended formal state dinners in the East Dining Room and had watched the Super Bowl with the president's family in the White House theater. But never before had he been ordered to see the president on his way out of town and by a staffer that he had just met.

He knew why he was summoned: the bailouts. He was unsure, however, how they found out. Did Brad Wilder turn him in and expose the deal? It had to be Wilder, Kosar was certain. How could Wilder be so stupid when he had much more to lose than Kosar did? Kosar knew that he would lose his job, get bad press, and maybe do a short stint in a minimum-security jail. But when he got out, he would have millions in the bank and could live a life of luxury, traveling around the world. Wilder would likely serve more time and did not have a large nest egg to fall back on.

As he rode in the back of his limousine toward the White House, Kosar needed a strategy to get himself out of this situation. He felt that he had two options. The first was to flat out lie. He would deny the charges until he turned blue in the face, then lie some more. This would at least give him time to contact counsel and begin the process of a plea bargain.

His second option was to admit that he was wrong with the hope that his honesty would save him. Sometimes being honest helps smooth over the victim. He and the president were friendly, and he could gamble that the president would not want him to take the fall.

He looked out the window and watched the history pass him by. Washington DC was the symbol of America, our version of Rome or Athens. Rome may have thousands of years on Washington, but now Washington was the epicenter of freedom. Everyone throughout the civilized world could recognize the Washington Monument, Capitol building, and the White House and could associate them with freedom.

The first time Kosar was at the White House he was being honored as one of America's great entrepreneurs. Now he was being called back because he got greedy. He did not work because of the money; he had enough for his children and grandchildren to not have the need to work. What he cared about was making more money than his friends and then being able to brag about it. Now his greed had him summoned to the White House to be reprimanded personally by the president.

He felt like a child. He was greedy and tried to pull a fast one. It was all fun and games until it was time to face reality, and he would have given anything to go back in time.

His driver pulled up to the gates where his vehicle was met by a uniformed guard who asked for identification. Two more uniformed guards approached the limousine—one with a mirror to check underneath the car and another with a canine to search for illegal items. Once they were cleared, they headed toward the front entrance of the West Wing.

As he entered the doors of the lobby, Jenner nodded her head hello, and Kosar placed his briefcase on the X-ray machine, then he preceded through the metal detector.

"Mr. Kosar, thank you for coming."

"Good evening."

"I will walk you to the Oval Office, and the president will see you as soon as he can."

The walk to the Oval Office was short, and Kosar was asked to have a seat in the reception area. Jenner knocked twice on the door and entered the office without waiting to be invited in. It was clear that the president was waiting around just to see him. A few seconds later, Jenner invited Kosar into the room.

"Good evening, Mr. President," Kosar said.

"You have already met Ms. Jenner. She is my new senior advisor and will be joining us for the meeting."

"That sounds fine, sir."

The president led them to the couches in the center of the room; Jenner and Kosar took their seats on opposing couches while the president sat in his normal chair in front of the fireplace.

"Gideon, I am just going to be blunt. What the hell is going on with you and Wilder?" the president demanded.

Kosar needed to make his decision. He decided that it would be best to admit his involvement with Wilder.

Kosar sat tall in the couch and said, "Mr. President, we go back a long way. I consider you both a personal friend and a political ally."

"We are not that close, Gideon," the president interrupted. "Tell me what the hell is going on."

"Sir, I hope that what I am about to tell you will in no way affect the bailouts. They are too important to the country's economy. To be honest, on my way back to the White House, I was thinking about denying my role with Wilder. However, after thoughtful consideration, I believe that it is best for the country that I admit my wrongdoing in hopes of keeping it out of the press. Mr. Wilder and I did have an agreement on the bailouts. The plan was that Wilder would help Freedom Air, as well as the other airlines, obtain the most from the bailouts. In return, I promised him a job making a multimillion dollar salary. He would start once the bailouts were out of the press, and we could sweep it under the rug."

"Son of a bitch," was the first thing that came to Seaborne's mind. "I cannot believe that two men I trusted and respected would do that to our country."

Just as the president was about to continue, a Secret Service agent opened the door and said, "I am sorry to interrupt, Mr. President, but you are needed in the Situation Room immediately."

The president jumped to his feet and practically ran for the door, ignoring Jenner and Kosar. The halls were cleared by lead agents, where they had to move people with force as they led him to the elevator that would take him to the basement. The president's heart was beating so fast that by the time he arrived at the elevator, he had to close his eyes and take deep breaths in an attempt to not have a heart attack.

The Secret Service agent saw the sweat on his brow and asked, "Are you all right, sir?"

The president ignored the questions for a minute to concentrate on his breathing before he responded, "I'm fine."

When he heard the ding of the elevator indicating that he had arrived at his destination, the president opened his eyes and walked toward the Situation Room. An agent was waiting for him and opened the door as he arrived. The president was the only person in the world that was allowed in there without a hand scan.

As he walked into the room, everyone stood and in unison said, "Good evening, Mr. President."

"Good evening. Please have a seat."

Seated around the table were Thomas Host, Aaron Sewell, Barbara Harper, and Matthew Jones.

Jones decided to speak first, "Mr. President, I am sorry I have some bad news. This evening we got word that Charlie and Lindsey were in a small town called Vero Beach in Florida. We promptly sent Berry and Maul to retrieve them. As they spotted them, the Farahs were hiding in a van nearby and were able to take them hostage."

The president had lost all color in his face, and everyone in the room could hear him breathing. A military aide poured Seaborne a glass of water and set it on the corner of the table. Seaborne barely noticed him.

Jones continued, "Maul and Berry felt they did not have a choice but to let the Farahs take Charlie and Lindsey. They believed that if they would have advanced toward the terrorists, they would have taken more drastic measures against Charlie and Lindsey."

"Including shooting them?" the president asked in a dry tone.

"Yes, sir. We do have a lead though. Berry was able to shoot one of the terrorists, and they now have him in custody for questioning."

"Make sure they do whatever they can to get him to talk," the president ordered.

"Sir, are you suggesting that he be tortured?" Harper asked, alarmed.

"Not torture but enhanced interrogation," the president responded.

"With due respect, sir, everyone in this room knows that means the same thing."

"Barbara, this is my son we are talking about. My flesh and blood. As a father, I will do everything in my power to get him back."

"Sir, you are not just a father, you are more than that. You are the president of the United States and you cannot go beyond the boundaries of the Constitution, even if it is your son. The powers of commander in chief do not give you that right."

Seaborne turned to Thomas Host and said, "Thomas, what is your definition of enhanced questioning?"

Host sat up in his chair and said, "Enhanced questioning is not torture, and I am a proponent of it. We will use methods that break down a person mentally rather than physically."

"Like water boarding," Harper said.

"Yes, Ms. Harper, like water boarding."

"Mr. President, research shows that these methods do not work. Most of the information that is obtained from torture is misleading. The person would want the pain to stop, so they will say anything."

"That is not true. I have read many reports on information obtained during enhanced questioning, and I am convinced that it works," Host replied.

"Are you admitting that the CIA uses torture?"

"No. Enhanced interrogation."

Harper's tone was getting louder. "It is torture. I cannot believe that the director of the CIA just admitted to using torture! Do we not set an example for the rest of the world? If we do this, we are no better than a dictator of a third world country. Anyone that participates in it should be held accountable."

The president had heard enough. Finally he said, "All right, quiet. I want to remind everyone in this room that whatever is said here is top secret. If this ever leaks, that person will be subject to the full penalty of the law."

Everyone knew that the comment was for Harper, just in case she decided she wanted to make some trouble in the future.

"Enhanced interrogation, even torture, is used from time to time to keep America safe. I do not even know about a lot of it because I do not want to know. The men that run the interrogations are under order from their superior officers and should not be held accountable. How can they serve this country well if they think their country is going to turn on them? That will not happen on my watch."

The president took a deep breath before he continued. "And to answer your question, Director Harper, this is not only a father of a kidnapped child speaking but also your commander in chief. Charlie's abduction does indeed threaten national security. He can be used as a political bargaining chip, and we need to get him back."

The president then turned his attention to Host and said, "Tell Maul to use whatever means necessary to get that terrorist to talk."

"Mr. President, I am sorry, but I cannot give that order to my people in the field," Harper said. "Mo Berry will not receive that order."

"You are right, Ms. Harper. He will not hear it from you, he will get that order from Host. And I am warning you, do not get in my way."

The secure door to Seaborne's left opened, and everyone around the table focused their attention on the man in his full marine uniform. Colonel Vernon Lee had a serious look on his face, even more so than a typical marine would have on any given day.

"Mr. President, we have a serious situation brewing in Iran that needs your immediate attention," Lee said. "The secretary of defense is standing by for your call."

The president's evening had started out with Kosar in his office about a bailout scandal. Then his meeting with Kosar was interrupted when the word reached him that Charlie had been taken hostage by a rogue terrorist. Now he was being informed that there was a serious situation brewing in volatile Iran.

This is when he realized that George Washington could not be more correct when he told John Adams that he would not wish the burden of the presidency on anyone.

CHAPTER 20

Dasht-e Kevir Desert, Iran

It was hardly a secret that the Iranians have been attempting to gain access to nuclear technology for many decades. They figured that building a facility in a remote desert would allow them to do research without attracting too much attention. The large building blended in with the sand, almost as if it was a chameleon and was known as the Environmental Research Lab.

The Iranians were not naive in the fact that the building would go without notice. They realized that Americans had satellites and unmanned drones that would document the construction. What they were trying to hide was the reason it was built. They disguised it as a research facility studying the arid desert; what they wanted to keep secret were the subfloors.

The subfloors took a long time to build, almost four years. There were no main roads to the building, so they needed to sneak the construction materials in with supply trucks over rough terrain. The trucks carried pieces of equipment into the facility, along with the equipment necessary to begin a nuclear program.

The piece-by-piece plan worked and ran for almost three years before the Americans caught on. The Americans could not claim that their vast and expensive equipment won the fight. They received a tip from a disgruntled employee regarding the legit function of the building. The dissenter was born in Iran and was educated in the United States. He became irate when he was passed over to become the lead scientist on a project at the Environmental

Research Lab. The project was designed to study the particles in the air to determine their effect on the environment. Although their work was just a cover, the scientists were making progress in their studies, and the scientists took their work seriously.

One day the scientist recognized equipment that was not used in the authorized studies of the facility, and after performing an independent quarry, he inferred what the equipment was really for. He intended to keep it a secret until he was passed over for the promotion. Disgruntled, he made contact with a local U.S. embassy and gave them his secrets in exchange for protection.

Vice President Aaron Sewell was approached by the Secretary of State Debra Sharp about the dissenter, and Sewell promptly took it from her desk. Working only with the Secretary of Defense Adam Royal, CIA Director Thomas Host, and a few select staff from both departments, they were able to develop a plan of action to take down the facility that the president would eventually approve.

This was the type of situation Sewell lived for—fighting a covert operation in a hostile area. His adrenaline had never been higher.

Royal did not hesitate on choosing the lead man for the mission. Thaddeus Klug was a commander in the navy, and he did not exist on paper. He led the Zeta Force, or Z Force, a highly classified special forces group. The president of the United States and the secretary of defense were not told about their existence until the time was necessary. That information was held with the secretary of the navy and the director of the CIA until they felt a mission was important enough to break their silence. Some presidents were not aware they existed until late in their term of office like Bill Clinton, when he sent them into Bosnia. George W. Bush learned about the Z Force on September 11, 2001, which was early in his first term.

Zeta Force was made up of thirty highly skilled soldiers. One secretary of the navy once called them "the elite, of the elite, of the elite." When they were not performing missions, Z Force participated in intense training. To keep active and contribute to key missions for the United States, the Z Force often worked with the CIA.

Members of the Z Force have no families and are handpicked. If one of them dies in action, no one at home will miss them. Thaddeus Klug's parents died when he was young and shortly after he joined the navy. As he completed boot camp, he realized that he had incredible skills as a soldier. The navy recruited him for the Navy SEALs, and before he could ever get a serious girlfriend, he was asked to join the Z Force. He did not regret his decision to join Zeta, but he did wonder what it would be like to be able to drink a beer while grilling burgers in his backyard surrounded by friends. That is a feeling that he would never have. The perks in Z Force were good though. After missions, the taxpayers would send them to exotic places around the world, where they would indulge in relaxation, booze, and women.

Klug and twenty of the thirty Z Force soldiers were prepared to launch an attack on the Environmental Research Lab. They also had five scientists from the Nuclear Emergency Search Team (NEST), headed by Pete Hill. While NEST was trained just to handle weapons, this type of an attack required the skills of the Z Force.

Hill and Klug met for the first time at an army base in Iraq. The army allowed them to make use of their conference rooms under the guise of a NEST operation.

Hill was waiting by himself in the room when Klug entered the room. Hill looked at the well-built man in plain camouflage and stood to shake his hand.

"Pete Hill," he said, introducing himself. He tried to play off the pain in his hand from the firm handshake.

"Commander Klug. Have a seat." Both men sat at the old conference table. The room had no artwork on the wall, and the tan paint was peeling. The army had more important concerns than a nondecorated room.

"Tell me what you saw," Klug continued.

"We were in the desert last night and went close to the research facility. Using our Geiger counter, we were able to trace radioactive material, more so than there should be in a desert. I can say that with the dissenter and my numbers, they do have nuclear operations taking place beneath the building."

"Were you detected?"

"No. They showed no signs of knowing we were there. Our vehicles got us close, and we traveled on foot another five miles, not easy to do in the sand."

Klug shook his head and said, "You need to come with us. My guys can get us in, but you need to tell us what we are looking for. You and four others will go with us."

"I don't know about that. We are trained to defend ourselves, not to infiltrate a building."

"We will take the lead. Your mission is to follow us in and point us in the right direction. Once we confirm the nukes, we will blow the building to hell and get out of there. Since the Japanese nuclear meltdown, I am sure the Iranians made the material stable enough to handle an explosion. The experiments on the top floors make the risk of explosion that much greater, I would be very surprised if they did not take every option to protect it."

"And if they didn't?"

"We will have a team on standby that will be ready to secure the building if needed. We will then use NEST to safely remove the material from the building. It should be rather easy, assuming that they do not have enough time to organize a counterattack."

"I did not know that the army could run such an intense operation," Hill said.

"You'd be surprised with what we can do," Klug said, satisfied that Hill bought his cover.

Hill scratched his head and said, "I don't understand how you expect to know your way around the facility."

"The deserter drew us a map from memory. That will give us a good guide. What doors we cannot open we will blast open. I am not too worried about that."

Still clearly confused, Hill said, "What do you need us for? It seems like you have it all under control."

Now Klug was starting to get annoyed. In an agitated tone, he answered, "Your job is to use the Geiger counter to detect the radiation. When we penetrate the subfloors, your men will help us identify the equipment and you will photograph them for analysis. NEST will then prepare to remove all material related to nuclear technology."

"What happens if the Iranians respond?"

"We fight our way out, just like we fought our way in."

Taking a deep, nervous breath, Hill asked, "When do we leave?"

"As soon as the sun goes down, we will deploy. Have your men get their gear together and try to relax a little so they are fresh. Just follow us and you will be fine."

Hill stood and walked to the door, "I'll see you tonight?"

"Yeah," Klug said without enthusiasm.

Klug locked the door behind Hill and walked toward the secure phone. He dialed Secretary of Defense Adam Royal.

A female voice answered, "Adam Royal's office."

"Hi Marie, this is Commander Thaddeus Klug, and I am calling for the secretary."

"One moment, commander."

A few seconds later, the secretary of defense (SECDEF) answered. "Klug, how did it go with Hill?"

The secretary of the navy told the SECDEF about the Zeta Force six months into his confirmation at the advice of Thomas Host. Host thought it was a good idea to tell Royal about Zeta Force from the beginning of his term because of what the Z Force could do against the war on terror.

"Honestly, sir, I am a little worried about Hill. I thought he was a little more trained for a mission like this. I think that he is petrified about going into battle."

"These guys might not be elite, but they will be able to lay down some firepower. Your team will go in first. They will be fine backing you up."

"Are you sure that my team can't handle identifying the nuclear material on our own?"

"Stick with the mission, commander!" Royal barked.

"Yes, sir. We will move out at sundown, assuming that the president will give us the green light."

"I will let the president know soon," Royal said. "I believe that the president will give us the go. You will leave the base at 2100 local time, about noon in Washington DC. I will call you before go time."

The line went dead, and Klug went to the barracks housing Zeta Force. The group was participating in physical training—men in great shape on their third set of one hundred reps of push-ups—this room was any woman's dream.

When he walked in the room, he yelled, "Attention!"

The men quickly got to their feet and stood at attention as Klug addressed the unit.

"Men, we are going into action after sundown. Make sure that you get a decent meal in you and try to relax a little. We will commence here in one hour to go over the mission details." Klug took a minute to look around the room. He looked every man in the eye and said, "Gentlemen, this one is coming straight from the top, and it is a sensitive issue. The mission must be executed flawlessly. If not, we could unleash World War III with Iran and the rest of the Arab world. We will be going into a fully sovereign country, and it will be looked upon as an act of war. We will let the politicians work out the diplomatic stuff—our job is to kick ass and move on. You've got to have your heads straight. Move out."

The men looked around at each other and realized the negative effects the mission could have. The elite force focused to shut all distractions out.

~ ~ ~

The White House
The Situation Room

"Mr. President, we have a serious situation brewing in Iran that needs your immediate attention. The secretary of defense is standing by for your call," Colonel Vernon Lee said.

The president thought for a moment and said, "Let me have the room."

The vice president and CIA director waited for the others to exit the room, leaving only Seaborne, Lee, Host, and Sewell in the room.

"Mr. President, I know what this call is about, and I think we should stay for this," Sewell said.

"Very well. Colonel, put the SECDEF on the phone."

Royal's face was displayed on the big screen mounted on the wall. Royal was in his sixties with salt-and-pepper hair and had an exhausted look on his face. He was wearing a blue tie, but the top button of his shirt was undone, and the tie hung loosely around his neck, which was out of character for the usually sharply dressed man.

"Royal, you look like hell, what is going on?" the president asked after seeing the bags under Royal's eyes.

"Sir, we have a major situation brewing in Iran. We have a mission that will need your final approval."

"Should I get the rest of my national security team in here? Certainly the SECSTATE would want to be in this decision, especially if it deals with a sensitive area like Iran."

The president was referring to the Secretary of State Debra Sharp, who would have been irate if she found out they were planning this behind her back.

"She can be called in shortly, if you like, but for now this conversation needs to be confidential between only us in the room," Royal said. "Colonel Lee received this information just a moment ago, and I think it is time I share it with you."

The president was unsure of what to think. With all that was occurring in that last couple of hours, he wouldn't be surprised if it turned out that Iran was behind the kidnapping of his son. He still had not told his wife that Charlie was being held hostage. His ears began to ring as a massive headache was developing.

"Let's hear it, Adam."

"Sir, the military has a top-secret military force."

"We have a lot of those, what is the big deal?" the president interrupted.

"Not like this, sir. This group is so well hidden that not even I was aware of them until shortly after I took this job. The only people that know this information are the secretary of the navy and the CIA director. It is customary that no one else is told, including the president, until there is a need to."

"How can a special forces group be kept from me? I am the commander in chief! I have access to all of our nation's secrets. Who says I can't be trusted with this information? How can I effectively protect this country if I do not know what weapons I have at my disposal?" The president blew up. He was now yelling.

Royal continued, "The secretary of the navy and the CIA director have the responsibility to keep them hidden until they feel that the president needs them. All presidents just need to trust the system. It has never failed us."

"This is unbelievable! I should have all your asses for this!" That was the first time that anyone in the room had seen the president so out of control.

"I know that this is upsetting to you, Mr. President, but right now we need to concentrate on the mission," Royal said, trying to talk some sense in to the president.

"Tell me already!"

"We have good evidence that the Iranians are far along in their nuclear program," Royal said. "The vice president and I are recommending that we go in and take the facilities out."

"You can't be serious. Do you know what kind of diplomatic ramifications this will have? How can we do this without Sharp being involved? We have diplomatic procedures to follow, including UN sanctions."

The vice president took over the conversation and said, "No, sir, she cannot be involved. Not yet anyway. I agree with you that this will look bad for us, but I also believe that it is necessary. The Iranians will more than likely try to keep this quiet, just like we are."

Royal explained Klug's mission to which the president asked, "Why the hell would they keep it quiet?"

"They do not want the world to know about this facility. If the UN finds out about Iran's nuclear programs, they most certainly face tough repercussions. If we penetrate the facilities, destroy the technology, and get out without making too much commotion, I think we can agree to keep this a secret. In return, we will promise to not slam them as much when making public statements about them. We lead the world in condemning Iran. If we leave them alone, that will mean a lot less pressure for them. We can even offer aid to build some schools."

"Can you get this done?"

The vice president looked at Seaborne in the eyes and said, "Yes. I will go over myself to negotiate. I will fly into Iraq and sneak out for a few hours. It will not be that difficult."

"What about Congress? The Wars Powers Resolution requires me to let them know of any military action within the first forty-eight hours."

"They will have no knowledge, even the intelligence committees of both chambers of Congress do not know of Z Force, and we must protect their identity," Sewell said. "Unless we come across the worst-case scenario, they will never know. If a member of the Z Force is killed, no one will miss them. If a member of the Nuclear Emergency Search Team is a casualty, we will make it look like an accident. We are very good at this, sir."

"Why not bomb them?"

"The entire world would know. That is exactly what we are trying to avoid. At least with sending in our men, it will appear as if it was an internal explosion. Maybe an experiment gone bad. Remember, the world does not know what is on the lower floors."

It was getting late in Washington, and the president was starting to feel the fatigue. "Okay, you have the green light to prep for the mission. I need an hour or two to chew on it before I give the final go. But we will tell Secretary Sharp, and I will leave that up to you, Royal. Tell her you are letting her know as a courtesy. The operation is going forward."

"Yes, Mr. President, I will call her right away," Royal said.

As the president stood, everyone in the room stood as a sign of respect for the president. He was on his way back to the Oval Office to meet with Kate Jenner to let her in on the brewing situation in Iran. He needed an outsider to give her point of view, especially the political ramifications if Congress finds out. He had; after all, asked her to keep his mind straight; it seemed that he did not really understand a word in the Situation Room because all he was concerned about was Charlie. Kate Jenner was about to be told what seemed to be the nation's most held secret, and Seaborne hoped she was ready for it.

CHAPTER 21

Vero Beach, Florida
Route 60 / I-95 Interchange

On the western edge of Vero Beach there was an outlet mall that included restaurants and hotels, all of which had heavy tree coverage, and Aahil thought that this would be the perfect place to switch cars. The trees and darkness would provide them enough coverage to hide from satellites, steal a car, and continue west on Route 60. With the amount of traffic going in and out of the area, providing a decent distraction, it would buy him some time.

He pulled into the parking lot of a fast food restaurant and parked under a large oak tree next to an older blue Ford Escape. He retrieved his slim jim to unlock the car door and slid the long metal strip device between the window and the weather stripping of the door. He jiggled the slim jim around until he caught the control arm of the locking mechanism with the slim jim's notched edge and unlocked the door. He opened the door, and the alarm sounded, but Aahil quickly found the fuse box and pulled the fuse for the alarm system.

"Hey! That's my car, asshole!" a man yelled from behind him.

Aahil turned and saw an angry Hispanic man in a brisk walk toward the car with three kids and a woman in tow. He made it to about ten feet away from the car before he repeated himself.

"That's my car! What the hell are you doing?"

In his thick accented slow drawl voice Aahil said, "Yeah, I'm busted. How about I do you a little favor—I will get back in my car and I will leave yours alone. No harm done."

Aahil tossed the pulled fuse to the man, who was obviously not happy about the compromise.

"I'm calling the cops. Stay right there, buddy."

"That would be a big mistake."

Trying to get out of the situation as fast as possible, Aahil lifted up his shirt revealing a pistol. The other man instinctively took a step back.

"Now I am going to get back into my vehicle and drive away. If you try to stop me, great harm will come to you and your family," Aahil said blatantly.

"Okay, okay. Just calm down," the man said as he backed away toward his family. When he reached them, he said something in Spanish, and they walked back toward the restaurant.

Lindsey tried to take advantage of the situation and began to knock her head against the tinted window of the van in an attempt to draw attention. Taybah hit Lindsey in the side of the head with the butt of her pistol.

"Be quiet before I hit you again!" Taybah promised.

Aahil got in the front seat of the van, started it up, and backed out of the parking space. As the van peeled out, Aahil said, "What did you do?"

"She was banging her head against the window," Taybah answered. "What else was I supposed to do to stop her?"

Aahil reached Route 60 and made an illegal left-hand turn heading west.

"See what happens when you don't follow directions?" Aahil asked Lindsey. "Now you will have a headache the rest of the night."

Charlie looked at Lindsey and lifted his eyebrows, gesturing "Are you okay?" Lindsey nodded slowly.

"Now what are we going to do?" Taybah asked Aahil. "I am sure that man called the cops by now. We need another vehicle because every cop in the state will be looking for us, not to mention every federal agency now knows what direction we are headed."

"Give me a minute, I need a minute to think," Aahil responded.

They continued west for about ten minutes until Aahil saw a sign for Blue Cypress Lake. Aahil thought that he had as good a chance as any to steal a car here. Plus, there was no place else around that he could see where he could steal another car. Western Indian River County, just like much of Central Florida, was nothing but citrus farms, cattle ranches, and swamps. Route 60 could be a lonely place if a person had car trouble.

As the van approached the County Road 512, Aahil decreased his speed and turned on his right-turn signal. He headed north on 512 until he reached a small parking lot on the left. The lot was mostly vacant with exception to a few old pickup trucks with airboat or kayak trailers attached.

Blue Cypress was the largest lake in the area, and it was a great attraction to both air boaters and kayakers alike. Fishermen loved coming here for the largemouth bass and many other fish that made the lake their home. Bird-watching groups also enjoyed searching for bald eagles and ospreys that made nests in the trees.

Aahil found a parking spot in the corner of the lot and began to look for the best vehicle to take. He needed something that was large enough for four people, and an SUV would have been the perfect vehicle, but there were none available. The best available was an old extended cab pickup truck that was parked underneath a large Cyprus tree near the water. After noticing that the truck's doors were unlocked, Aahil walked around the rear of the truck and removed the trailer from the hitch.

As Aahil walked under the tree, he stopped in his tracks to stare at a large alligator waiting to catch its next meal. Besides what he learned about in school, this was the first time that Aahil had seen an alligator in his life. He was unsure of what he should do. He thought about running, but what he remembered is that the animal could run fast. He could shoot it, but how many shots could he get off before the animal attacked him?

Aahil was relieved when the animal instead turned around and slid into the water, looking for a better meal. Aahil continued around under the tree, being very alert of what could be crawling around him. Alligators, snakes, spiders—this area of the world seemed to have it all. He reached for the door handle of the passenger door when he felt something land on his head. His first reaction was to reach up and swipe it off, but as he did, the animal slid down to his face. Aahil heard himself scream as his field of vision was blocked.

"What the hell?" he called out.

He reached up and smacked the animal from his face, causing it to hit the ground. The animal was a green frog with red spots on its body. Its feet were large with red ball-like toes. In the background he could hear Taybah laughing hysterically.

"What's the matter? A little frog got you scared?" She was laughing so hard she was hard to understand.

"Shut up! Who can live in a place like this? It is full of alligators, snakes, and . . . and frogs! It could be poisonous for all I know!"

"Calm down, Aahil. I am just having some fun. Hey, maybe we can use the frog to torture the hostages!"

"Why are you joking right now? We are in a very serious situation and you want to make jokes? All of the United States might be looking for us right now and you want to have fun. Grab our supplies from the van and start loading the truck."

Taybah chuckled to herself as she got out of the van and opened the rear door to begin transferring the supplies. She could see that even Charlie and Lindsey got a little laugh out of the ordeal.

After all of the supplies were placed in the bed of the truck, Charlie and Lindsey were moved to the rear of the truck. Aahil was worried about how close the two would be to him, so he tied ropes around their already handcuffed hands and attached them to the inside door handle. Assured that his two hostages could not break free to cause any disruptions or problems, Aahil hot-wired the truck and began driving back toward Route 60. Now he was ready to begin the next stage of his makeshift plan.

~ ~ ~

Near Lake Whales, Florida

Central Florida was home mainly to wooded areas, and Aahil noticed many signs indicating camping areas along the way. He pulled off of Route 60 onto a small dirt road. He found this road while researching the area and thought that it would be a perfect area to set up camp. It was secluded and had many areas that he could hide.

Four miles down the road, Taybah pointed out a small trail, barely wide enough for their truck. As they drove, the tree branches rubbed against the side of the vehicle and made a maddening screech. Aahil found a small clearing on the side of the road that he pulled into. He stopped the car and got out to retrieve Charlie while Taybah kept an eye on Lindsey in the tuck.

Aahil and Charlie walked to the back of the truck, and Aahil opened the tailgate. He pulled out the tent's bag and wrapped the straps around Charlie's shoulders.

"Hold out your arms," Aahil commanded Charlie.

Charlie did as he was told, and Aahil placed a large box in his arms. Aahil grabbed all he could carry and began to head into the woods with Charlie close behind. They walked into the wooded area for about five minutes until they found an opening large enough to set up a tent. Two trips later, Aahil and Charlie had successfully carried all the equipment to the site and had the tent set up.

Taybah took Lindsey out of the truck and held Charlie and Lindsey at gunpoint while Aahil covered the truck with brush, trying his best to conceal it from any aircraft that may pass overhead in search of the first son. If a passerby noticed the vehicle, he would assume that it was just a hunter or a camper in the woods.

Charlie led the group to the site while Aahil brought up the rear just in case Charlie or Lindsey wanted to try to pull a stunt. It was hard to navigate in the dark, especially with what could be lurking in the Florida night, but the group pressed on while Aahil and Taybah tried to light the area as best they could.

Charlie and Lindsey sat on the ground while Aahil built a fire. He had purchased fake logs at a country store that the manufacturer claimed was made out of natural materials that would burn for four hours. He lit two of the logs, making just enough heat to cook a small meal.

Aahil prepared bland white rice over the fire and served it onto four paper plates. He walked over to Charlie and Lindsey and took off both of their gags.

"This is all the food you will eat for a while," Aahil said. "I suggest you eat up. Here is a bottle of water for you to split."

"I really need to pee," Lindsey said. "I have not gone to the bathroom in a while."

"You American girls have dirty mouths. Women in our homeland would never speak like that."

"Women can't even show their beauty to the world either," Lindsey quipped, referring to long robe-like dresses and veils worn by many women in the Middle East. "In some cultures, their eyes and hands are the only part of the body that is shown. If they are exposed to someone other than their blood or their husbands, they could be beaten."

"Do not lecture me on my own culture! At least our women have some respect!" Aahil responded.

"They cannot even drive cars in some places! You call that a respectful society?"

"That is not the norm, and you know that. I treat my wife differently, and most Muslims do the same."

"That's right. You would just rather kill Americans."

"Americans are infidels that threaten the world. Are you hungry or not?" Aahil asked.

"Are you going to let me pee or not?" Lindsey responded.

"I will take you," Taybah stepped in. "Let's go."

"Fine, then we will all go," Aahil said.

While the women searched for a good spot, Taybah said, "You should not test him like this. It will only make him angrier."

"Why are you trying to be nice to me? You took me hostage, remember?"

Taybah shrugged her shoulders and said, "Just some friendly advice. Take it or not, I do not care."

When they returned to the campsite, Charlie asked Lindsey, "What the hell are you doing? Do you want to get us killed?"

"I am not going to sit here and take any more of this. I am going to make him as miserable as possible. You should too."

Charlie thought for a moment. "I am not so sure. Just be careful."

Aahil placed their now cold rice and one bottle of water in front of them.

"You will need to eat with your hands. Do not forget to drink up," Aahil said.

Taking the advice from Lindsey, Charlie decided to be defiant for the first time. He said, "You know this is just going to end badly for you, right? My father is the commander in chief of the United States. He will find us and kill you."

"Why would I let you and your grubby girlfriend live, huh? I have the resources and the connections to get away and hide for a very long time. You are dispensable."

Aahil rose to his feet, pulled the pistol out of his belt, and walked over to Charlie. If it was daylight, everyone would have noticed that Charlie was as pale as a ghost. Aahil raised the gun and pointed it at Charlie's forehead.

"I could end this right now." He paused to let it sink in for a minute before he continued. "No no, I would rather watch you suffer."

Aahil grabbed Charlie's gag and rubbed it in the dirt before putting it back in Charlie's mouth.

"Now you will starve and be left to your thoughts because I am done listening," Aahil said.

Lindsey spoke out and said, "Leave him alone! At least let him drink some water."

"Shut up before I gag you too. Look on the bright side, at least you have the entire bottle of water to yourself now. Hurry up and eat."

Lindsey looked to Taybah for help, but she looked off in the distance, trying to ignore the situation. Lindsey decided that it was probably a good idea to shut up, eat her rice, and drink her water.

Charlie was trying to distract himself from the dirt in his mouth. He did not think that this situation could get any worse. He knew he made a mistake trying to speak up. He was just trying to follow Lindsey's lead; now he was sitting here with a dirty rag stuffed in his mouth. It was not the hunger that bothered him; it was the dehydration that was getting to him. His mouth became parched, and that was all he could focus on. He wondered how he could survive the night. He looked at Lindsey who was doing her best trying to shove rice in her mouth while being restrained. Charlie began to feel a little bitter because he felt that what Lindsey said was far worse than what he said. He was comforted, however, that at least Lindsey was able to eat and drink. He placed a lot of hope in all of the federal government agencies in search of him.

He also prayed to God for the first time in many years. When he went to church, it was always for the press. He and his family did not enjoy being there, but it looked good politically. He prayed mostly for Lindsey wishing that she would be saved. He loved her with all of his heart and could not bear having something happen to her.

From this point on, he would play it smart. No more disrespectful comments or outbursts and he would only do what he was told. Charlie considered himself a smart and charming person and would use that against his captors.

CHAPTER 22

The West Wing
The Oval Office

"That is my favorite painting in the Oval Office. I've always loved all the beautiful American flags meshing together. It is a great symbol of our country," Gideon Kosar said. He was referring to the painting "Avenue in the Rain" by Childe Hassam. President Seaborne had the painting hung next to the french doors that lead out to the rose garden.

"It is beautiful," Kate Jenner agreed. Trying to continue the uncomfortable small talk, she added, "But I like the picture of Theodore Roosevelt over there," as she pointed to the far wall.

"I wondered about that painting," Kosar said. "TR was a pretty progressive president for a Republican to hang his portrait on the wall. He was known as the trustbuster, his administration created many new regulations making it harder on businesses, he sided with the labor unions in the mining strike of 1902, and he reformed big banks."

"Despite these liberal ideas, he also believed in the idea of responsibility of the individual, family values, and patriotism. He was also a great sportsman."

"Yes, he was a dedicated outdoorsman. He enjoyed hunting and the peace that came with the open wilderness. Roosevelt also served our country courageously with the Rough Riders in Cuba before he became president, the secretary of the navy, and the governor of New York."

Jenner shook her head and said, "That's just it. The president obviously is not a promoter of all of TR's politics. Nevertheless, he admires what he was able to accomplish in his lifetime and how he used his time as president to get things done, something that does not happen anymore because of the gridlock of Washington politics. The president has a high regard for his accomplishments. He was able to make our food healthier as a result of the Pure Food and Drug Act, every American enjoys the federal parks that were a result of his conservation ideas, and he helped to get the Panama Canal built."

"You seem to have a lot of information about the man. Did you know that the Republicans never wanted him to be president?" Kosar asked.

Jenner responded, "No, I did not."

"It is true. He was governor of New York at the time, and the Republicans wanted him out. They convinced William McKinley to add him on the presidential ticket in 1900 as the vice presidential candidate. Back then, the office of the vice president was inconsequential, like John Nance Garner said, 'the vice presidency is not worth a bucket of warm spit.' The Republicans assumed that his popularity would eventually die out. When McKinley was shot in 1901, good ol' TR became president. He won in a landslide in 1904 and eventually had had his face carved on Mount Rushmore. Not too bad for a man who was never meant to hold the office."

"That is interesting. Of course his friend William Taft and Roosevelt did not get along once Taft became president, which helped TR decide to run as the Bull Moose candidate in 1912, only for both of them to lose to Woodrow Wilson."

Kosar was enjoying this nerdy conversation that most people would run away from. He added, "He would have won a third term in 1908 too, but he respected the tradition set by George Washington to only run for two terms. TR said that was one of the biggest mistakes that he ever made. Who else do you admire, Kate?"

"Ben Franklin and Thomas Jefferson are my other two favorites. Franklin because he was a well-rounded man—he was an inventor, philosopher, postmaster general, and an entrepreneur. He created the bifocal glasses, a more efficient woodstove, and the lightning rod, which he gave to the world for free. His political thoughts and ideas were considered before the Revolutionary War when he came up with the Albany Plan of Union, which would have joined the colonies for protection. His ideas were also put to good use during the debates for the Declaration of Independence. His printing business was also very successful. It was rumored that as he was crossing the Atlantic Ocean to and from Europe and North America, he would swim next to the ship. He even discovered new species while swimming. The idea of the Gulf Stream was his too"

"He was also quite the ladies man!" Kosar said with a smile.

"That is all you think about?" Jenner kidded back.

"The man makes me look like a bum compared to all of his successes. Why is Thomas Jefferson on the list?" Kosar inquired.

Almost astonished by the question, Jenner said, "He was so important to our new nation. He was the first one to stand up for our country during the Barbary State conflict . . ."

"The what?" Kosar interrupted.

"The Barbary States were in North Africa and demanded tribute from American ships that passed into the Mediterranean Sea. That is where he said that the U.S. would only negotiate through the mouth of a cannon and where the 'to the shores of Tripoli' phrase came from in the Marines' Hymn. The event resulted in the world's respect for the United States and extreme popularity for Jefferson. He also bought the Louisiana territory, more than doubling the size of our country, when many argued that it was unconstitutional for us to buy land because it was not specifically stated in the Constitution. This is now known as implied powers. He also commissioned the Lewis and Clark expedition in search of a waterway to the Pacific Ocean and to explore a widely unknown area."

"Well, you sure did convince me. I think I now have three new favorite historical figures," Kosar flirted.

"I can go on if you like, Mr. Kosar."

"Call me Gideon, and I think that is all the history I can learn in one night."

He reached in his pocket and pulled out a business card and handed it to Jenner.

"I could use some more history lessons in the future. Why don't you call me sometime?"

Jenner said bluntly, "Not with the trouble you are in, sir. I am surprised I am standing in the same room with you."

"I can make you very happy, you know, and I am not a jerk like you think. Spend some time with me and you will see that I am a good and caring man."

Jenner reached out and took the card. "Maybe I will."

Before Kosar could respond, the main door to the Oval Office opened, and the president walked in. Jenner and Kosar stood and said in unison, "Mr. President."

The president ignored them and walked behind the desk and sat in his armor-plated chair. For a minute he looked around the room as if he was taking it all in for the first time.

"You know, I am tired. Real tired. Most of what I deal with the public will never know. That is why I get so pissed when I come across stupid stuff that I should not need to deal with. Take you for instance," he gestured toward Kosar, "you are a smart and successful person. You have made enough money to pass down to several generations. You have it all. Probably ten houses in the most desirable areas of the country, you have vacationed in areas most people could not even dream of visiting. So it always surprises me when someone like you would try to pull a stunt like this against the country that gave you the opportunity to have that lifestyle. Furthermore, you have a good acquaintance in the president of the United States. This has been the most stressful day of my life, and because of your actions, I am slightly distracted today."

"I am sorry, Mr. President, I made a mistake," Kosar said.

"No, you are not sorry. Do you know what I hate? When someone says an action was a mistake when that person knew that action was wrong in the first place. A mistake is accidently bumping into somebody on the street. It is not a mistake to knowingly try and persuade a senior advisor to the president to make more money for your company."

"Sir, I need time to explain this to you, and you will see that this deal would have benefitted this country more so than it did me or Brad Wilder," Kosar said. He felt like he was being lectured by his parents after getting caught taking something from the liquor cabinet.

"I am simply not buying it," the president said candidly. "I like you, Gideon, but you got greedy. Frankly, I am not sure what I am going to do about this. For now, I had my staff set you up in a hotel down the street, on your dime, of course, and we will meet as soon as we can. I will have an agent posted outside your door to keep an eye on you. I have about a million meetings tomorrow which means you will be on call so be ready to meet with me at my pleasure."

"Yes, sir."

"Gideon, do not mess with me on this or I promise I will bring you down."

"I understand, sir," Kosar said.

"My assistant is waiting for you."

"Have a good evening," Kosar said trying to smooth over the president.

Kosar left the office, and an assistant walked in the room as he left.

"Mr. President, Mrs. Seaborne called and was asking for you. She wants to know when you will be heading to the residence," the assistant said.

"Tell her it will be a long night and that she should go ahead and get some sleep."

The assistant left the room and made the call to the first lady, leaving the president alone with Jenner. He got up from behind the desk, walked to the couches, and asked Jenner to have a seat across from him.

"Kate, I am tired. There are some major events going on as we speak, and I need to run something by you. This is of the highest confidentially. Not even Don Austin knows what I am going to tell you."

"Thank you for trusting me."

"I gave the go-ahead to begin preparations for an attack on Iran. Royal is waiting for the final order."

"Iran?" Jenner questioned. Her reaction was both surprised and terrified.

"Iran's built a facility where they are actively advancing their nuclear weapon capabilities. A disgruntled former employee escaped to the U.S. embassy, claiming that the building used by the Iranians for an environmental research lab was in truth a nuclear facility. Members of the Nuclear Emergency Search Team confirmed this claim by getting positive Geiger readings."

Seaborne paused to let the news settle in. Jenner just sat there for a minute, trying to comprehend the news.

"Now is where it gets complicated," the president said.

"I can't believe that it gets more complicated," Jenner replied.

"We have a highly secretive special forces team called the Zeta Force. I was just told about it this evening, that is how undisclosed the team is. The Z Force is made up of a total of thirty men, twenty of which will be used for the attack. At about twelve noon, local time tomorrow, we will send the Z Force, with five members of NEST, to infiltrate, take pictures, and destroy the facility."

Jenner looked like she was staring off into space and said, "The diplomatic repercussions could be horrendous. Their first strike could be on the Israelis, our closest allies. They could also incite many sleeper cells here in the United States to carry out terrorist attacks on our homeland. OPEC could respond by raising the price of oil. It could shatter our relations with Egypt and Syria. Sir, this could put us in a very bad situation."

The president was happy to hear candid advice from Jenner, and that was exactly what he expected from her when he made her a senior advisor.

"Yes, I know it could go wrong, but I feel that it would be worse if we sat around and did nothing. Could you imagine Iran with a nuclear weapon? Israel would never be safe, and they would most certainly sell it to the highest bidder." The president thought for a moment before continuing, "I still feel that it is best to go in and blow up the facilities."

"Sir, do not let Charlie's situation cloud your decision making."

"Kate, I have not even updated you on Charlie yet."

"What is going on?" Kate asked.

"I will get to that in a moment. First, we need to discuss Iran."

Seaborne chose to discuss Iran first so Jenner's judgment on Iran would not be distracted. He was sure about what needed to be done to save Charlie; Iran is where he needed the advice first.

He continued, "I am sending the vice president to Iraq, and soon after the attack, we will slip him into Iran so he can negotiate a settlement. We believe that they do not want the world to know how close they are, and keeping that fact a secret will also help them save face. In addition, we will be less critical to them in the UN, and we will also send some aid to help construct schools."

"What did Secretary Sharp say about the plan?" Jenner asked.

"She does not know yet. Adam Royal will tell her soon. I assume she is going to be upset when she finds out."

"She will be irate. I can see the wisdom behind the mission. We certainly do not want the Iranians with a nuclear weapon. I am just concerned about the repercussions. Are you sure that the Iranians will keep this quiet?"

"No, I cannot be 100 percent certain, but it will benefit them more for us to keep this quiet," the president said. "We will get a slap on the wrist for not telling the world community about the facility, but they would have to admit that they have nuclear capabilities. Sewell is good with negotiations, and I believe that he can get this done."

"As your senior advisor, Mr. President, I agree with your decision. Something needs to be done about the facility, and the United Nations will take too long to investigate and make a decision on how to handle it."

"Thank you for your advice, Kate. It gives me comfort that you agree. Now we need to talk about Charlie. He was taken captive not too long ago."

"Oh my god. Mr. President, I am stunned. How did it happen?" Jenner asked.

"They were in Vero Beach, Florida, when they were tracked."

"Tracked how?"

"You know what, I forgot to ask." The president could have kicked himself for not asking before. He continued, "They were walking down the street after dinner, and as our agents spotted them, they were overtaken by the Farah cell. We wounded one and took him into custody, but two got away with Charlie and Lindsey."

"Where did they go? There had to have been satellites available?" Jenner asked.

"Unfortunately, there were none in the area, but both the Secret Service and the CIA are trying to analyze traffic cameras. We have also launched helicopters in the area and put out an APB. At this moment, I have no idea what to expect. They have to give their demands soon, but until then, we will just need to continue the search."

The president picked up the phone that was sitting in the middle of a small coffee table at the head of the couch.

When his assistant picked up, he said, "Where is Don Austin?"

"Sir, he is at a function for the Republican caucus."

"Tell him I need him here now."

"Yes, sir."

The president hung up the phone and turned his attention back to Jenner.

"Does Mrs. Seaborne know yet?" Jenner asked.

"No, she does not know yet. I do not have the heart to tell her."

"Sir, you must tell her. I have worked with her for a long time, and trust me, the first lady does not like things to be kept from her."

"I know. I will tell her first thing in the morning."

CHAPTER 23

Vero Beach, Florida

Bruce Maul and Mo Berry were headed west on Sixty-sixth Avenue in search of an abandoned house. This area of Vero Beach was widely used for citrus farming. Citrus was a large and prosperous business in Indian River County for many years but had recently been struggling. The downtrend was largely due to a disease called canker that renders citrus plants useless and the freezes the area had experienced over the last few years. The county was also hit especially hard by the recession, and it was not uncommon to see an unemployment rate of 12 percent in the area.

The circumstances made it easy for Maul and Berry to find an abandoned home. Maul turned west on a small road two miles later and began their search. The dirt road was dark and bumpy, but they found a house that was perfect for their mission.

The house had peeling lime-green paint and rotting plywood on the windows. An unattached garage sat next to it in the same decrepit condition.

"What is it about Florida that makes people paint their houses with crazy colors like this one? I have seen more pink or lime-green houses than I ever thought I would see. You would not see those in the north," Berry said.

"Is that all you are thinking about right now?" Maul asked in an annoyed tone.

"It is just an observation, that's all. I am surprised that I haven't seen any orange houses yet."

172

Maul shook his head, trying to ignore Berry as he pulled into the driveway.

The house sat about forty yards off the dirt road, and Maul turned on his parking lights in place of his headlights as they approached the house.

"Let's just hope this house is as abandoned as it looks," Maul said. "We really don't want to get caught torturing a Middle Eastern man by a poor old couple."

"Yeah, my uncle lived like this. He had an old boarded up house just like this, but don't worry, he was so deaf that we could torture this punk right next to him, and he wouldn't know we were there."

"Let's hope that there is no one home."

"My uncle was a crazy old bastard. Boy, he could drink too," Berry went on.

These comments made Maul pause for a minute and almost respond before he decided it was not worth his breath.

"I remember one time we showed up on Christmas Eve," Berry continued. "It was dark and snowy, but my pops wanted to go see him, said it would be a nice thing to do on Christmas. All I wanted to do was go home and open my presents, but I didn't want to piss him off after he had been drinking all day."

Maul now knew where Berry got his drinking habit from; his dad, his uncle, who knows how many other family members were alcoholics.

"Anyway, Dad didn't turn off his headlights, and my uncle must have looked out the window just as we pulled in. I never saw a drunken old guy move so fast because by the time we got to the top of the driveway, there was the drunk, mean, old man waiting for us with a shotgun in his hands. Since he was deaf, it wasn't as if we could just roll down the window and yell. We had a hard choice to make—either open the car door and risk getting shot or backing out and have him take a few shots at our car.

"Well, my pops, being the brave man that he was, handed over the rum bottle, told me to take a swig. I was twelve and had my first taste of liquor. Rum is still my favorite, by the way. Come to think of it, I haven't stopped drinking since."

"Could hardly tell," Maul said sarcastically as he brought the car to a stop at the top of the driveway. He thought it was best to hear out Berry's story.

"After the drink, my dad said, 'Go say hi to your uncle.' My hands were shaking as I opened the door, and that old man took a shot at me, took the mirror right off the door, just missing me. Seeing that my uncle was distracted with me, Pops opened his door and ran toward my uncle. The shotgun was moving toward Pops, but he collided with Uncle first, knocking the gun up. Uncle got a shot off, and I was hit with two pellets from the round in my left arm. I held my arm as I remained standing while my pops and uncle were on the ground. My uncle started to laugh as he realized who it was. My arm was hurting as I made my way toward them.

"They took me inside to examine my wound and declared that it was nothing but a scratch, put on a few Band-Aids, and in return for my silence, I got to spend my Christmas Eve sharing drinks with my uncle and pops while they told me stories. Needless to say, I was too hung over the next morning to really enjoy Christmas, but it is a night I will never forget."

Berry looked at the house and said, "But I am sure we are not going to have that problem here."

Ignoring Berry, Maul got out of the car and said, "Wait here."

Maul pulled out his sidearm and approached the back of the house. The sidewalk that led to the back door was cracked, and Maul was careful not to trip. Instead of a step, the owner placed two cinder blocks at the foot of the door.

Maul decided it was best to peer into a window first before entering the door and carried one of the blocks to the nearest window. The block gave him just enough height to see into the house through a broken piece of plywood.

The kitchen was old, looking as if it was straight from the 1950s. White cabinets sat on a black linoleum floor and brown countertops ran the length of the wall. The cabinets gave way to an authentic 1950s refrigerator that even Maul could respect. It was a two-door freezer on the bottom unit that had large chrome handles. Families in the 1950s often made the refrigerator the focal point of the kitchen, and Maul thought how neat it would be to have this unit in his man cave.

The floor was littered with paper and dusty boxes that gave the impression of them sitting in the same spot for years. Maul felt that it was probably likely that the owners were long gone, so he decided to enter the old house.

He jiggled the doorknob only to find that it was locked. He took a step back and kicked the door, but it barely budged—1950s craftsmanship was clearly better than houses that are thrown together today, Maul thought. Four more kicks and the door gave way, allowing Maul to step foot in the house.

Using his flashlight, Maul walked around to inspect the house as the floorboards creaked beneath him. The single-story dwelling was empty, but there was furniture throughout that was tipped over or ripped up. Overall, the house was in bad shape, and it was clear that no one had lived here in a long time. His best guess was that an older couple lived here for years together until they both died. After their deaths, the kids decided that they did not want the house and kept the valuables. There were no valuables and the walls were devoid of pictures, just the shadows of old frames on the wall, so Maul assumed that the kids went through it before leaving it to Florida's rodents.

Maul thought that the best place to put the terrorist was in the kitchen because of the dark linoleum floor, which would make cleanup the easiest. The counter space would also come in handy for all his tools. He moved the boxes, cleared the floors and set up an old dining room chair in the middle of the floor.

"It is about time," Berry yelled as Maul was walking toward the car. "The CIA does everything slow."

"That is because we want to get it right," Maul said.

Maul opened the trunk to retrieve rope, two battery-powered lanterns, two head flashlights, and a small black bag. He shut the trunk and then opened Maali's door.

Maul put one headlamp on and tossed the other to Berry.

"Get out," Maul said to Maali.

Maali slowly rose from the back of the car, and Maul took the back of his wrists. Berry went around the back of the car to help Maul with materials, then Berry led the way into the house.

Maul and Berry forced Maali to sit in the chair that Maul positioned in the middle of the room. Berry set up the lanterns on the countertops while Maul worked on the rope. Maali's wrists were still bound as Maul began to tie the rope around Maali's body. Maul tied his ankles together and then tied the same rope around the legs of the chair.

He checked the rope to make sure that it would hold as the terrorist fought for his life.

"You are pretty good at that, you had some practice with your girlfriend?" Berry said.

"No, she ties me up," Maul said proudly. "What, you have never been tied up before by a woman?"

"I don't think I have ever trusted a woman enough to tie me up. Half the girls I date would have left me spread eagle on the bed while they rob my place."

"You haven't lived yet. Besides, everyone at the CIA learns how to bind someone because we do the work of the people while the Secret Service looks pretty running next to the president's limo."

"This Secret Service agent can kick your ass though."

"You will have your chance later. For now, keep an eye on him, I will get us some tools."

Berry opened his mouth to say something about his uneasiness toward torture, but before he could get it out, Maul said, "This is something that I have been trained in, trust me, let me handle this one."

"Fine, but I get to lead the questioning."

Maul thought for a moment and said, "Deal. I will be back soon, then the fun will begin."

When Maul left, Berry looked around the room and thought out loud, "I wonder if there is any booze around here."

"You know that stuff is bad for you. It will shorten your life," Maali said.

Berry did not respond as he looked around the room. He noticed a short, old broom handle in the dining room and picked it up. He raised it like a baseball bat, then hit Maali in his wounded arm.

Maali cried out in pain.

"All-Conference on my baseball team in high school," Berry said proudly.

Before Maali had a chance to respond, Berry hit him again.

"Not another word, do you understand?"

"You are going to need to do better than that. I think your friend was right, the Secret Service is not as good as the CIA."

The comment earned Maali another hit in the arm. Berry ignored his cry as he looked through the cabinets when he noticed the cabinet above the refrigerator.

"This is where old men hide their booze," Berry said aloud.

He reached above the refrigerator and opened the cabinet door where he found two bottles of whiskey hiding in the corner.

"Jackpot."

Berry retrieved the full bottles and opened the first bottle, taking a long gulp. Feeling relaxed Berry walked to the bag that Maul had given him. This was the same bag that Maul had used on the terrorist in Youngstown. He opened it up and laid the contents on the counter.

"This guy does know what he is doing," Berry said to Maali. "Do you see what he has over here?" Berry asked while pointing to the items on the counter.

Berry went through each item, allowing Maali to get a good look at each one. Berry's goal was to begin the psychological torture on the hostage. The first item that Berry inventoried was a taser. Next, Berry picked up a large and a small pair of pliers, which he assumed would be used to pull out fingernails. Lastly, he saw six vials of medicine and a pack of twenty syringes. Three of the bottles were marked with plain red labels, and the other three had plain blue labels.

Berry held up one red and one blue label and said, "I am assuming that one of these is a truth serum. I can only guess what the other one is for, and I have a feeling that it is not going to be good."

Maali responded by saying, "Truth serum is only a myth. It is like drinking alcohol. It may make you slip and say something, but there is certainly no guarantee that the subject is not lying."

Maali was right, but Berry did not want to downplay the drug in front of the man he was about to torture. Truth serums do make a person speak more freely, but they only have the same affect of a person drinking all night. Berry knew that just because they tell you more does not mean that they are telling you the truth.

"We will find out tonight, I am sure," Berry said.

Berry's phone began to vibrate in his right pocket; he pulled it out and identified the caller as Barbara Harper.

"Hello?" Berry asked into the phone.

"Berry, this is Harper. I am calling you so you can reassure me that there will be absolutely no torture involved tonight."

"Yes, ma'am, I can assure you that there will be no torture."

"Thank you. I am also sending down Rich Maxwell and Ray Turner to help with the search for Jamin."

"Those guys are the worst! Maxwell is old and got tore up in the accident, and Turner just complains the whole time. They may be good at protecting, but they are not made to investigate. They will just slow me down."

"Maxwell is a good agent, and Turner has learned a lot from him. They feel that since Jamin was their charge, they should be involved in the case."

"Then they should not have lost them in the first place!" Berry shot back.

"It was a fluke. That drunk driver could have hit anyone in their situation. I think that you will be surprised by what they are capable of."

"I just hope that Maxwell keeps his mouth shut. We all know how much he can talk."

"He will be fine. They are leaving Youngstown sometime early in the morning, and they will fly directly to Vero Beach where there will be a car waiting for them, then they will meet you at the house."

"Can't wait, ma'am," Berry said sarcastically.

Harper hung up, and Berry was disappointed that he now had Maxwell and Turner to deal with. Turner was not too bad. He was personable and had some good jokes, but he tried to copy Maxwell too much. Maxwell, on the other hand, was a great agent and had good instinct but not as an investigator. As long as Berry could keep him quiet, he would be fine.

Chapter 24

Near Lake Whales, Florida

"Do you have a blanket I can use? I am freezing over here," Lindsey said.

She was still wearing her clothes that she wore to dinner. It was a tight-fitting tank top with a small pair of shorts and sandals. Aahil retrieved an old blanket and threw it to her. It smelled like old urine, and Lindsey almost threw up.

"This is awful," Lindsey complained.

"Your American arrogance never surprises me. You are at a point of desperation and you will not use it because it has a little odor. You can freeze or keep the blanket. It is up to you."

Lindsey chose to be warm, so she kept the blanket. She glanced at a sleeping Charlie and was grateful that he wore a pair of jeans.

Aahil and Taybah took turns with two-hour shifts watching the couple. Taybah emerged from the tent to relieve Aahil, and he kissed her on the check before he took his turn to sleep.

~ ~ ~

Two Hundred Yards from the
Farah Campsite

"Did you see that deer?" Otis asked excitedly in his southern accent.

"Yeah, we could have made a lot of jerky out of that," Kevin responded.

"Jerky? I would have made steaks and sausage. Too bad you have a horrible shot and missed it by a mile. Shoot, all you did was scare everything away."

"I missed it? You shot too," Kevin said as he tripped over a branch and landed on his face.

Otis took the opportunity to laugh hysterically at his buddy.

"I see you can't drink just like you can't shoot," Otis said.

"Hey, screw you. It's dark out here."

"I can't wait until your party tomorrow night. It is going to be a train wreck! With all the girls and beer there, we will be in all our glory."

"Just don't run all the girls off like you did last time."

"It's not my fault they can't take a joke."

"You stripped and danced on the picnic table. I wanted to leave too, but unfortunately it was at my house."

After twenty feet, Otis stopped. "Do you smell that smoke?" he asked.

"Sounds like you're the drunk one. There ain't no one out here for miles but our dumb asses."

"Shut up. Seriously, I smell smoke over there."

The pair changed directions and headed toward the smoke smell.

"I hope the forest ain't on fire," Kevin said.

"Only one way to find out, let's go check it out."

As they approached the campsite, they saw three people sitting at a fire who all appeared to be staring at the flames.

"Do you want to go say hello?" Otis asked.

Kevin thought for a minute and said, "I don't think so. We will scare the shit out of them this late."

"They look like nice people, I'm going over."

"How do they look like nice people when you can only see the back of their heads?"

"You need to have more trust in people, Kevin."

When Otis was about ten feet away from the makeshift campsite, he yelled, "Hello? How is everyone doing over there?"

Taybah was startled and responded by firing her weapon, which hit Kevin in the chest. Charlie woke up from his deep sleep, Lindsey fell out of her chair, and Aahil almost ripped the tent open trying to get out.

"What the hell did you do that for?" Otis cried out as he went to assist his friend.

Kevin was bleeding from his chest and was instinctively clutching the wound. Otis kneeled next to him and did his best to add more pressure to the injury.

"Kevin, Kevin, Kevin, can you hear me?" Otis asked in panic.

Otis saw Aahil approaching him on his right, and he twisted around to face him. To protect himself, Otis pointed his shotgun at the man's head.

"Don't come any closer or I will fire!" Otis yelled.

From the corner of his eye, he saw that Taybah was pointing her gun at him while standing in front of two other people. There was a girl lying on the ground, and she looked like her hands were bound. The boy looked as if he was struggling to get his hands free. Otis knew that these were not simply people hanging out by a campfire but much more than that. He began to think about how he could get himself out of the situation. He thought it was best to lower his weapon and lay it on the ground.

"Let me take my friend to the hospital. Please, he has a family at home," Otis pleaded.

"You are not going anywhere. What the hell are you doing out here?" Aahil asked.

"Kevin and I were doing some late-night hunting. Please, let me get him to the hospital."

Lindsey jumped as she heard another shot fire.

When she looked up she saw smoke at the end of Taybah's pistol. Her first thought was to look toward the man pleading for his friend's life, but all she saw was the bottom of his boots.

Otis was killed with a bullet wound to the head. Lindsey heard the signs of a struggling life as Kevin began to breathe heavily. Lindsey hoped that the Farahs would put him out of his misery, but Kevin would not be so lucky.

Aahil looked down at the slowly breathing man and turned and walked back toward camp.

Disgusted, Lindsey broke her pact to keep quiet and said, "At least kill him. Don't let him suffer like that."

Aahil ignored the girl and walked to his wife.

"Good shooting, looks like the time at the shooting range has paid off," Aahil said.

"I learned from the best," Taybah responded proudly.

180

"Help the man out!" Lindsey yelled.

Aahil offered the gun to Lindsey and said, "Go ahead, put him out of his misery."

"Screw you!" Lindsey yelled.

"Americans cannot even kill to put a man out of his misery, that is what makes you weak. Do not worry, he will not last long. In the meantime, I am done listening to you speak."

Aahil put Lindsey's gag back on her mouth and was satisfied that she could no longer talk. He felt like she spoke too much like a typical American woman.

"What do we do now?" Taybah asked.

"We will keep with our plan. I am going back to sleep."

Taybah looked at Lindsey, who was still on the ground. Lindsey was able to kick the chair off of her and was covered in dirt. Taybah worked her way over to Lindsey's chair, set it upright, and then helped Lindsey to her feet and back into her chair.

"I know you do not understand what we are doing, but there is an extreme injustice taking place by your country," Taybah said. "To imprison our people in Guantanamo Bay without a trial is wrong."

Taybah looked at the gag on Lindsey's mouth and said, "If you could talk right now, you would tell me that the prisoners are not American citizens and they do not deserve American rights. Maybe you are correct, but they deserve some kind of military tribunal at the very least. The best scenario would be a trial before the international community. You and Charlie will help us get some of our people out. You do what we say and you will be fine and you can continue to live your plush life with your rich and noble boyfriend. If not, you will be like those men over there, and we will be long gone when they find your bodies."

Taybah brushed some of the dirt off of Lindsey like a mother would do to a child.

Lindsey thought that deep down Taybah could be a good person. She took care of Lindsey when she needed it, and she had a gentle hand as she brushed the dirt to the ground. Lindsey wondered how she could be so brainwashed to follow these evil men.

Lindsey was not a very religious person, but she did believe in God. Since she believed in God, she also believed in good and evil, and these guys were truly evil people. She had a hard time believing how a small group of people could ruin a beautiful religion. Islam has been practiced for centuries and had brought much good in the world. It was a disgrace that radicals could destroy the beauty with their view of infidels. The truth was many Americans were afraid of Muslims. After September 11, many Americans stopped shopping at Muslim businesses and harassed many of their people. Lindsey wished that everyone could gain a better understanding of what Islam really stood for.

Lindsey wished that she could tell Taybah what radicals like her were doing to the great faith. How they were pushing Americans to hate both radical and good Muslims and that they were needlessly fueling the war on terror.

~ ~ ~

Two hours later, Aahil unzipped the cheap tent to relieve Taybah. The sun was coming up, and he was surprised by how much energy the two-hour nap gave him. Charlie and Lindsey were both sleeping uncomfortably in their chairs.

"How long before we need to move out of here?" Taybah asked.

"We will leave this evening," Aahil answered.

"We still have some cover of night, but do you really want to wait until the middle of the day? More people are liable to walk up on us like those stupid hunters."

"Relax, it will be fine. We worked through the situation fine last time," Aahil said, referring to the two dead hunters.

Charlie began to moan, so Aahil walked over to him and took off his gag. Hearing the commotion, Lindsey also began to stir.

"My neck is killing me!" Charlie said. "This chair is the worst, and I need to go to the bathroom."

Aahil helped Charlie up and led him to the woods to relieve himself while Taybah did the same for Lindsey. Both Charlie and Lindsey had mosquito bites all over their bodies from being unprotected during the night, and they were growing miserable.

When they got to the campsite, Charlie asked, "Can I have some water?"

Taybah retrieved a bottled water for both of them, and Charlie and Lindsey drank them quickly, eager for more. Taybah ignored their request and instead prepared rice for breakfast. Charlie and Lindsey did not have gags, but they learned from last night that they should not talk. Instead, they just sat and watched Taybah prepare their meal.

When everyone was through eating, Aahil left the site in search for another vehicle that he could steal. He was sure that by now the authorities had the information on his stolen truck, and he knew if he got another vehicle it would buy him some time.

When they left the woods of Lake Whales, they had one more stop to make. St. Augustine was where he would call in his demands and would prepare for an exchange of money for the first son. He would kill Charlie if he needed to, that was not the problem; his goal, however, was to get the release of the prisoners of Guantanamo Bay and make some money in the process.

He would keep the shares of those on his team that had died and any that were captured. That would mean that Aahil and Taybah would have a good life in the Middle East. A nice car, a nice house, maids, butlers, and cooks—he would finally have a life that he dreamed of.

He was driving down a small residential street in what seemed like the middle of nowhere. All the houses looked the same, and at the early hour, the town was asleep, which made his task easier.

He noticed a small salvage yard ahead and decided that it would be less noticeable to steal from a place that was full of old cars. The only problem was finding a car that was in good enough condition to take them to St. Augustine.

Aahil used a pair of bolt cutters from his trunk and severed the lock securing the gate. He decided that he wanted a small sedan to help them blend in. He spotted a small red Taurus with black primer dots covering it. The late 1990s vehicle started up easier than he thought as he hot-wired it. Aahil figured that he could steal another car if this one broke down during their travels.

He shut the gate and drove back to the campsite. He assumed that it would take a while for the salvage company to figure out which car was stolen out of the many that were in the yard and that the place would not throw a big fuss over an old vehicle.

When he returned to the campsite, Taybah was sitting around the fire pit.

"Where the hell are they at? What did you do?" Aahil asked Taybah.

"Calm down, they are in the tent trying to get some sleep. I think they are going to have permanent neck damage from sleeping in those old camping chairs."

"Who cares about their necks? This isn't the White House!"

Aahil walked to the tent to see if they were still there. To his delight, both were asleep on the tent floor, and Charlie had his arm around Lindsey's back. Aahil figured that there really was not any harm in letting them sleep together for a little while. He decided that he would join his wife as they waited for their trip to St. Augustine to carry out the plan.

CHAPTER 25

Vero Beach, Florida

While the Farahs were dealing with the illegal hunters, Maul was driving from the local department store with hardware that he felt would be sufficient to make Maali talk. He decided that he was tired of working with Mo Berry, whom he felt was nothing more than a drunk amateur. He normally would have taken care of the situation himself, but with a direct order from the president, Maul felt that his boss Thomas Host would be better able to address the situation.

Host was still in his office, same as everyone working on the Charlie Seaborne case, and he was eating a greasy burger and fries while reading files. His desk was a mess, and no one—not even his personal assistant—was allowed to touch it. He claimed to know where everything on the desk was, and it was a better system than using filing cabinets. Most worried, however, that his system would leave their country at risk with sensitive material being left out for any custodian to see or even lose something easily.

"This is Host," he answered on the first ring.

"Sir, this is Maul. I would like to speak to you about Mo Berry. I know that you do not have time to play a middle-school principal, but I would like to request that I take this case on my own."

"Why is that, Bruce?"

"Frankly, sir, he is the biggest drunk I have ever met."

"Maul, are you aware that the president himself has ordered Berry to work on this case? He feels strongly about this. I am not sure if I can persuade him otherwise."

"Berry is going to put Jamin in danger, and I feel that it is our duty to let the president know that there are better people out there to work this case."

"Hold on a minute." Host rummaged through his files to find Berry's file, and in the process he knocked the ketchup-covered french fries on his lap. "Damn it!" he yelled at no one in particular. Maul knew that it was best just to ignore him.

"Here it is. I had the same thoughts as you. I had my team pull his file. Several years ago, a group of senators went to Iraq when our forces were still a major player over there. Berry was sent on a protection detail with the group and was assigned to one particular senator. The trip was highly publicized but what was not in the news were the events that took place one early morning. Two senators left their hotel early to go into the countryside to see the real Iraq without the press, and Berry's principal was one of them. As they were driving on an isolated road, they were attacked by four armed men.

"A Secret Service agent in the lead car was shot and damn near drove off the road. Berry was in the passenger seat in the second car and singlehandedly killed all four assailants without anyone else being hurt. It is customary for agents involved in a shooting to undergo a blood test and his came back positive for alcohol. I am not condoning his drinking, but his file is full of commendations for his field work. The man is a hero with connections, and it seems that he controls his alcoholism. Give him a break on this one."

"Who was the senator?" Maul asked.

"Don Austin, the president's chief of staff."

"You are telling me that the chief of staff is signing off on a man that is drunk half the time to help protect the president's son?"

"No, I am saying that Mr. Austin believes that Berry can control his drinking and will stop before he gets too drunk. Austin said that there is no one else in the world that he would rather have protect him, including you, Maul."

"If he gets sloppy, I am taking this directly to the president."

Maul hung up the phone and was very disappointed in both Host and Austin. He wondered how they could let Berry work while drinking. When he told Host that he would call the president, he meant it. He was sure that the president would take his call if he tried. For now he would keep a close eye on Berry and look for any signs of stumbling and slurring. Maul smiled while he thought that it would be fun to tie Berry up and try some of his tricks on him.

Maul pulled into the driveway, parked in front of the garage, and went into the back door. He was pleased to see that Maali was still alive and that Berry was not passed out on the floor. Maali's shirt was off, and he had some large bruises on his upper body. He also noticed that the contents of his black bag were organized on the countertop. He motioned for Berry to go into the other room, out of earshot of the terrorist.

"I see you got a head start. You could have screwed everything up. I'm sure that you were taught that there are steps involved in interrogating a suspect. Oh wait, I forgot that the pretty boys of the Secret Service do not know how to properly question someone."

"If by that you mean torture, you are right, we are not taught that. Besides, I was having a little fun in there. I took everything out nice and slow so he could see it and explained what everything was, trying to get him nervous of what is to come."

"And the bruises?" Maul asked.

"Those were just for fun."

"I see."

"Just as a reminder, as per our earlier conversation, I am in charge of the questions. You are in charge of the pain," Berry said.

"I remember clearly. Let's get started."

The two went into the kitchen, with Berry trying to prepare for what was about to come. He knew that Maul was just crazy enough to do anything to get Maali to talk. He hoped that he did not need to call Barbara Harper with the news that he was involved in the torture that killed the suspect. There was a lot that she would turn her head to but not torture. Berry would need to tread very carefully, especially with Rich Maxwell and Ray Turner expected to show up soon.

Maul went to the countertop and opened the bag of syringes and stuck the needle into the bottle with the blue label. He filled the cylinder and approached Maali.

"Hold him still," Maul said calmly to Berry.

Berry took his arm and held it until he was sure the man could not move.

"Your vein is hard to find. Looks like I am going to go on a search," Maul said.

He tapped him on the inside of his elbow and roughly stuck the needle in his arm and just as fast pulled it back out.

"Nope, that wasn't it. Looks like I need to try it again."

"Ahhhhh," Maali cried out.

On the third attempt, Maul was successful in finding the vein, so he administered the liquid.

"That will do it. What you have now running directly in your veins is a type of truth serum. You will feel funny shortly. We don't have time to fool around here. Berry, come give me a hand."

The pair retrieved some of the items from the car and brought them back into the house in two trips. Berry was surprised by the number of torture materials available at a twenty-four-hour department store in small-town America.

"Why did you buy a cooler of ice? Is that for my drinks?" Berry joked.

"I see you already took off his shirt, thank you for that. Now grab some ice."

They each carried two ten-pound bags of ice, and Maul placed the first one around Maali's lap, then stacked the other on top. From one of the mystery bags, Maul used a rope and tied it like an "X" across his chest to hold the ice in place.

Then Maul said softly, almost in a whisper, "The ice will lower his body temperature pretty quickly, and it will make him real uncomfortable. You will see him squirm soon, and then he will call out in pain. It won't take long."

"I hope it doesn't take long because Harper is sending two more agents down here. They were Jamin's personal agents, and they want to be involved. We need to get him talking . . . fast."

"You weren't able to stop her from sending them down?"

"I tried, but she is a stubborn woman."

"Fine. When will they be here?" Maul asked.

"Early morning."

"Shit, you're right. I'll do what I can."

Maul started for his bag of tricks when Berry stopped him saying, "Hey, what are in those two vials?"

"Don't worry about it."

"Just tell me."

"Trust me, you don't want to know. You will be able to deny it later," Maul responded.

"Okay," Berry said, disappointed that he was not able to find out more.

After about thirty minutes, Maali was beginning to get dizzy and was feeling the effects of the ice. He felt like he was bare-chested on an Alaskan glacier. Maul went to him and untied the rope, then placed the ice back into the cooler across the room. Maali's chest was red, and he was noticeably uncomfortable.

Maul took his open hand and slapped Maali's chest, causing Maali to scream in pain. Maul proceeded to hit him ten more times without taking a break. The cold intensified the pain with every strike, and Maul wished it was enough to get the man to talk.

"It is all you, Berry," Maul said.

Berry took over. "Where are they taking Charlie Seaborne? That is all we want to know. You tell us that and the government just wasted a lot of money on those things in the bags over there."

"And I go to prison where no one will ever hear from me again. No, thank you."

"Maybe we could work out a deal to have you go into witness protection. You tell the U.S. government everything you know about terrorist activities and you get a rather good life right here in the states."

"I could never live here among infidels."

"The way I see it, you will be held by the U.S government either way. You might as well tell us what we want to know which will get you off rather easy. Or you can hold your tongue, not tell us, and feel an incredible amount of pain, ultimately ending up in a dark cell, never to see light again. Your call."

Maul interrupted, "Did you say hold your tongue? That is a great idea."

Maul took hold of the large pair of pliers, and before Maali could react, he forced the pliers into Maali's mouth, clamping on his tongue. He pulled his tongue out farther than it was intended for, and Maali's muffled moans could be heard.

When Maul finally released, Maali's tongue was bleeding, and Maul was satisfied with the pain he caused.

"Now do you want to tell us?" Berry asked.

Maali did not respond and instead spat blood onto his chest.

"Okay, fine," Maul said as he bent back Maali's left pinky finger and snapped it.

As the man screamed in pain, Maul snapped his ring and then middle finger almost simultaneously. Berry was impressed by how fast Maul moved; it seemed as though Maul broke the terrorist's fingers before he could even blink his eye. It was clear that this was not Maul's first time using advanced interrogation techniques.

"Start answering some questions before I begin using some more of my special potions over there," Maul said. "I also plan on pulling out your fingernails and sticking some cotton swabs up your nose before the night is over." He paused before saying, "You know what? I am going to use the cotton swabs now. I can't believe they sell the long-stem type at the store."

He walked to the tied man and stuffed the stick up his nose far enough to hurt and to be real uncomfortable but without doing much damage. The act was similar to a patient having his sinus cavity examined by a doctor but without the numbing agents.

"Ahhhhhh!" the terrorist said as tears came to his eyes.

"I got a whole pack of those, so we can explore more of that later. I think we are ready for some more ice."

Maul and Berry stacked and tied the ice like they did before. Maul went to the garage and came back in ten minutes later to find Maali beginning to shift in his chair. He brought in a pair of sawhorses used to stabilize wood while cutting and an old piece of plywood. He set the sawhorses so that one was higher than the other, then he secured the plywood on top of it.

"Do you know what this is for?" Maul asked Maali. "It is a little technique we call water boarding. It is designed to simulate drowning, and even some of the toughest men will say anything after experiencing it. I can actually set it up pretty easily right here. I will just cover your head with that towel, pour some water on your head, and you will feel as if you are dying. Pretty easy. You have one last chance to answer my partner's questions before we start the procedure. No? Okay."

Maul untied the ice from Maali's chest, set it in the cooler, and then began to release him from the chair. With his hands and ankles bound, they walked him to the makeshift water-boarding device where together they picked him up and laid him on the board. It took everything Berry had to hold the man down while Maul placed a rag over his head and picked up a five-gallon bucket of water he bought from the store.

As the first couple of drops landed, Maali said, "I will talk, I will talk!!" in slurred speech because of his tongue injuries.

"Now you are finally making the right decision," Maul said.

"Where are the Farahs going to take the first son?" Berry asked, almost yelling.

"I do not know the exact location, but I know the city," Maali pleaded.

"I don't believe you. How could you be this involved and not know where they are going?"

"It is true. Aahil never told us much. I will tell you the city as long as you promise to keep that evil man away from me."

The rag was removed from the terrorist's face as Berry and Maali looked over at Maul who was filling a syringe using the red vial.

"I am going to honest with you," Maul said. "This one is going to hurt. It will burn as I inject it into your body."

Maul walked toward Maali with the filled syringe, causing Maali to blurt out, "St. Augustine! They are taking him to St. Augustine, I swear. He never told us the exact location in the event one of us got captured. All I know is that they were planning on arriving there after the sun goes down tonight. Once the hostages were secure, they would wait for the demands to be met."

"Why would he carry out his plans now, after he knows that you are being tortured for this information?" Berry asked.

"There is not much time left to change plans, and he hates to deviate. Plus, I have no idea where they are going, so I could not tell you exactly what you want to know anyway. I believe he will carry out these plans. It is your best shot anyway."

"Liar!" Maul said as he stuck the needle in Maali's arm. Maali screamed in pain as the burning liquid entered his arm.

"I promise I am telling the truth! I do not want to be water boarded! Please believe me!"

"Let's go in the other room for a minute," Berry said to Maul.

They secured the terrorist back in the chair, and the federal agents went into the old living room.

"He is telling the truth, did you see how afraid he is of you?" Berry asked.

"I agree. I have been tracking Aahil for a while, and he always kept things close to the cuff."

"Once Maxwell and Turner get here, we will head to St. Augustine." Maul gave Berry a dirty look but Berry continued, "We will be in separate cars, it is a favor for Harper."

"Fine, but if I lose them, I am not waiting for them to catch up."

"They will be here soon. In the meantime, I will be in here trying to get some sleep."

CHAPTER 26

The White House
The Oval Office

The president finished filling in his chief of staff on everything he knew about Charlie, Iran, and the bailouts. When Seaborne was finished, it was clear that Don Austin was disappointed that he was left out of the loop for so long. The two were sitting on the couches in the middle of the room, and both men were secretly beginning to hate them because it seemed like this was where they sat when they were working on the toughest problems they faced during their day.

"Sir, I am your chief of staff, and in order to serve you, I need to be in the know on everything."

"I am telling you now, Don."

"Mr. President, I am sorry, but if you do not value my opinions, I cannot continue in this capacity."

"Come on, Don, we are not in the fifth grade. It was just a matter of convenience. You were at the fund-raiser, and I had Kate Jenner with me. Plus, I needed to make sure that you were not involved with Wilder and Kosar."

"How could you even say that?" Austin asked, obviously hurt.

"You are the one that brought Wilder on board in my administration." Austin opened his mouth to say something, but the president cut him off and said, "I made a mistake, and I want you to continue as my chief of staff."

"Only under one condition, sir," Austin said directly.

"What's that?"

"I need the assurance that I am not going to be left out of meetings, I must always be in the loop, and I must be in charge of your schedule, who you meet with and why you are meeting with them, just like a chief of staff is supposed to do. This is not negotiable."

"I can agree to that. Also, Kate Jenner will be taking a more active role in this administration."

"I will need some time to sit down with her to explain how things work down here."

The president nodded his head and picked up the phone on the table positioned next to the couches.

"Yes, Mr. President?" an assistant on the other line asked.

"Is Kate Jenner still in the building?"

"One second, sir." The assistant checked the Secret Service's digital log of persons in the building and said, "Yes, she is still here, sir."

"Send her in, please."

"Right away, sir."

Jenner was in her temporary office, the president's private office, when she received word that the president wanted to speak to her. Although Jenner's office was connected to the Oval Office, she thought it was inappropriate to use the door connecting the offices; instead she walked around to the official entrance of the Oval Office.

After knocking, she let herself in and was greeted by the president and Don Austin.

"Kate, Don is caught up, so now you two are going to discuss Iran and the bailout fiasco. I want you both in bed in a half hour, and that is an order. Sleep on the couches in your offices, if you have to. Hell, use one of the bedrooms upstairs, but I need you both fresh tomorrow. We will meet here at seven thirty, and Don, please set my wake-up call for six forty-five. Good night."

"Good night, Mr. President," Austin and Jenner said in unison.

Austin turned to Jenner and said, "Let's meet in my office to start a road map for tomorrow. We need to cancel most of the president's day without anyone picking up on something being wrong."

~ ~ ~

The White House
The Residency

William Seaborne walked into his bedroom at three o'clock in the morning. He was up all night working on the search for Charlie, nuclear weapons in Iran, and the Kosar-Wilder bailout scandal. He wanted to work through the night, but he knew that he was in dire need of sleep in order to be fresh for the next day.

Austin was not very happy about being kept in the dark, but that was to be expected. He understood about the Zeta Force, but he was adamant that he should have been made aware of the bailout scandal. After a long conversation, they agreed that they would not make a decision on Wilder or Kosar until they had the opportunity to talk to them both in the morning. Austin wanted to go the legal route and have the attorney general involved, but the president felt that they needed more time to see if they could dance around it.

Thus far, Seaborne was happy with the work Jenner had done. She had been clearheaded, honest, she openly disagreed with the president, and had made right decisions. Wilder would be gone one way or the other, and the president was prepared to move Jenner into his position.

He opened the door to his bedroom quietly, trying not to wake the first lady. He was proud of her for being strong, at least publicly, throughout the ordeal. She still managed to make all of her public appearances. Thankfully there were no speeches planned because the president was sure she would not be able to speak clearly.

He made his way to the bathroom to clean up for the night before he joined his wife in bed. When he opened the bathroom door, the lamp on his wife's side of the bed was on, and she was sitting up waiting for him.

"It's late, don't you think?" Ann asked.

"Yes, it is, but as you know, I have a lot on my plate right now."

"What is going on down there?" she asked as she rubbed her eyes.

"Well, of course we are still searching for Charlie, and there are two issues that need my direct attention."

"What the hell could be more important than finding our son, William? Your priority is your family."

"I know very well what my priority is, but I also must see to the country's business. I am the president of the United States, and the American people demand that I deal with the country's problems, or I will need to give up all of this and let Aaron Sewell take over."

Ignoring her husband's explanation, Ann said, "Since you tried to sneak in here, I can assume that you have not found Charlie, but I hope at least that you have some news."

The president looked out the bedroom window to the dark city beyond it. In the distance he could see the Washington Monument's lights flashing.

"Ann, there has been a development."

"What the hell do you mean there has been a development?"

"We found Charlie's location. Charlie called the White House, asked for me, but hung up while the Secret Service tried to trace the unknown number."

"Why would they do that?"

"If Charlie would have used his cell phone, the number would have matched with the database, and it would have been patched right through. Charlie threw away his cell phone and must have bought one from a store on the way to Florida."

"Where at in Florida was he hiding?"

"A small city called Vero Beach. The service did not have an absolute hit, but then ten minutes later, the same number called Lindsey's parents. The call was only connected for five minutes, but Lindsey's parents verified that it was in fact Lindsey that called."

"So why didn't you just go get them, for god's sake?"

"We sent our people down as soon as we tracked the call."

"Then what the hell is the problem," Ann said, becoming more and more irritated.

"The agents spotted them walking down the street but before making contact . . ." the president paused and took a deep breath. This was going to be the hardest sentence he ever spoke.

"What?" Ann asked eagerly.

"A small group of terrorists took them as hostages."

Ann stood and threw her pillow at the most powerful man on the planet. "Hostages? What kind of morons let the first son become a hostage?"

"The kind of agents that didn't want them to kill the first son." After a pause, the president continued, "The bright side to all of this, if there is one, is that we shot and took captive one of the terrorists. He is being questioned as we speak."

194

"I hope they are making him scream!"

"I assure you that they will do everything they can to get him to talk."

"You also assured me that nothing would happen to Charlie and how did that work out?"

"We need to remain calm."

"Remain calm?" she yelled.

"Yes, remain calm so we can make the right decisions to save Charlie. If we are not calm, we may make a mistake."

"If something happens to him, I will never forgive you!"

"What is that supposed to mean?"

"It means that if your being president hurt my son, I will never let you forget."

William was becoming upset and was raising his voice. "I care about Charlie just as much as you and don't you for one minute sit there and believe that I don't. Do not forget how much you pushed me into running. Hell, you practically signed the papers to file for the candidacy yourself."

"Get out of here. Go find someplace else to sleep until you find Charlie."

"Do you really think that this is helping to bring home Charlie? We need to be rational right now."

"Out!"

The president turned toward the door and before he opened it, he said, "You will regret this. When you think back at this tragedy, you will always remember how you acted and that I was the one with the clear head."

Ann knew her husband was right, but instead of admitting she was wrong, she turned her back on him and walked to the window. William nodded his head and opened the door leading to the West Sitting Hall.

He looked at the agent on duty and said, "I need to see a butler now, please."

"Is everything all right, Mr. President?"

"Yes, I will just need different sleeping arrangements," Seaborne said, embarrassed.

The agent did as he was told, and in a matter of moments, the butler showed up.

"How can I help you, sir?" the short butler asked.

"I will need another place to sleep tonight. Is the Queen's Bedroom available? I have never had the opportunity to sleep there."

"Of course, sir, just follow me."

"I know where it is, thank you. Just make sure people know where to find me."

"No problem. Good night, sir."

The butler thought how awkward the president must feel at this moment. He was kicked out of his room by his wife, but he could not simply retreat to the couch like every other man. Seaborne instead had to ask for a place to stay by the midnight butler.

The president entered the Queen's Bedroom and could not help but feel at least a little bit excited despite the fight with his wife that forced him to sleep here. This room had been a favorite room for many people, including the Queen of England and Barbara Bush during her son's presidency.

William pulled back the right side of the covers and tried to fall asleep, but no matter how tired he was, he could not relax long enough to sleep. Instead, he just laid there and stared at the ceiling with nothing more than his thoughts.

He drifted back to when Charlie was a little boy growing up in a wealthy and powerful family. It was vastly different than what William himself had experienced growing up. Charlie always managed to put up with the pressures with a smile. William knew that most children grew up wishing that they were the son of someone like him, a president of a country; but then like they say, be careful of what you wish for as you might just get it.

William had many regrets when it came to Charlie. Since he worked so often, Charlie was often in bed by the time he got home. Charlie was a three-sport athlete in football, basketball, and baseball, and although not a star in any of them, he was a solid player in each, and William missed most of his games. That was probably his biggest regret—not being there for the big hit, or the three pointers, or the homeruns. It was especially hard when he had to hear the highlights from one of the other fathers.

He also regretted not standing up to his wife in regards to Lindsey. Charlie obviously loved her, and he wanted so desperately for his parents's approval. William understood that Ann wanted him to find someone that would help him be more successful, but love was a strange thing. William would let Charlie marry a bum off the street if he loved her enough. Ann was different—it always had to be the perfect girl on paper, not what was perfect to the heart.

Now Charlie was presumably somewhere in Florida under the control of terrorists. He left because he needed to get away from the pressures of being the first son and to spend quality time with the love of his life.

William started to tear up when he thought about his brother Dan. His brother was not the best person in the world and certainly had his issues, but it was not all bad. He remembered playing catch in the backyard and watching the Cleveland Browns play on Sunday. He was too busy trying to be president to spend more time with his brother trying to work things out when their relationship went south. Now his brother was gone, and he had lost the opportunity to at least have a cordial conversation with him.

The weight of the office of presidency was becoming more than what William could bear, and he thought of how it was not too late to bow out of the race.

In the master bedroom, Ann also could not sleep. She looked at the Washington Monument and thought about all the first ladies before her. How did they do it? She heard the stories about Mary Todd Lincoln going insane after her son Willie died during her stay in the White House. While mostly rumors, Ann really could not blame her; if something were to happen to Charlie, she too might go insane.

Ann knew that she was being unfair for not allowing William to stay in their room, but what could she do now? Beg him to come back? He was a big boy, and he should be able to handle his own problems. Besides, he was the president of the United States, and that was expected of him.

She instead thought about her son and if she had been fair to him for all these years. Sure, Charlie was under more pressure than most people his age; however, that would be forgiven when he grew up and realized the privileged life he had. He had met world leaders, traveled across the world, had the opportunities to go to the best schools, and he could get a job anywhere just because of his name. He would have nothing to worry about.

Ann still could not believe that he chose Youngstown State over an Ivy League school. She tried to explain to him what he was giving up but to no avail; he just would not listen. Of course, that is where he met Lindsey. Lindsey was smart, pretty, active, and nice enough, but a college professor? How much money could she really make? And what a boring job to boot. Maybe Charlie would see the light when he went off to law school and met other future attorneys.

CHAPTER 27

Washington DC
Brad Wilder's Apartment

Brad Wilder's alarm clock went off at two minutes past six in the morning. He felt that the extra two minutes would make him feel like he was able to get extra sleep, and he recognized that the notion was ridiculous but whatever gave him a boost in the morning was worth it.

Wilder always enjoyed nice things, and he spent most of his budget acquiring items that were too expensive for his government salary. He did not care because he knew after his stint in the White House he would be able to find a high-paying job anywhere, allowing him to pay off all of his debt.

He lived in a modest apartment in Old Town Alexandria. Old Town Alexandria was his favorite neighborhood in the Washington DC area. It was historic, and the bars and restaurants were full of classy women that he was often able to bring home due to his expensive style and high-profile job in the West Wing. Gadsby's Tavern was his most beloved place to have a nice dinner, and it was conveniently only a few blocks from his apartment.

This particular morning, Wilder woke up alone and headed for a shower and a shave. He got dressed in his expensive suit and went into the kitchen to prepare an egg-white omelet with feta cheese, spinach, tomatoes, and hot peppers.

After his heart-healthy breakfast, he left for the Metro to take him into the city. The Metro gave him time to read the newspaper and catch up on the day's current events. He stopped and got a small cup of black coffee from a small street vendor and drank it as he entered the West Wing.

He said hello to his assistant as he passed her and went into the office, shutting the door behind him. His desk had a pile of messages, and he went through them determining who would get a callback and who was not important enough to receive a call from the deputy chief of staff and senior advisor to the president.

~ ~ ~

That night, Don Austin slept on the couch in his office and did not bother to change his wrinkled pants, shirt, and tie when he was told Wilder had entered the building. He only got two hours of sleep, which was more than what he thought he would get, so he was grateful. He rubbed his eyes and gargled mouthwash. Two minutes later, he knocked on Wilder's door and entered before Wilder could respond. Austin wanted to catch him off guard, giving him a chance to question Wilder alone.

"How are you, Brad?" Austin asked.

"I'm okay, Don, but you look like hell. Long night?"

"You can say that. I was grateful for the two hours of sleep on my couch that I did get."

"Why didn't you call me? I could have been here to help you out," Wilder said, trying to act sympathetic.

"Most of it you do not have clearance for, and to be honest, much of my stress is because of you."

Wilder's heart started to beat fast in his chest. He felt like he was in a scene of Edgar Allan Poe's "The Tell-Tale Heart," and he knew he had to play it cool. Trying not to let his voice quiver, he said, "Me? What are you talking about?"

"I know about the bailout scheme that you and Gideon Kosar had, and I have to say that I am very disappointed. My first hire as chief of staff was you. It was the first major decision that I ran by the president, and it took convincing that he shouldn't hire one of his own. I went to bat for you because I believed that you would have done a good job."

Wilder's father told his son when he was a kid that if he was ever in trouble to never admit fault no matter what. It would be harder for someone to find guilt if you consistently lied and that, eventually, the accuser just might believe you even as the evidence piled up. He used this strategy often when he was in high school with teachers and principals, and the advice managed to get him out of a lot of trouble. He knew that the chief of staff would not be so gullible.

"Don, I do not know what you are talking about," Wilder said.

Austin yelled back so loud that Wilder's assistant jumped, "Kosar already told us everything last night when he had a private meeting with the president."

Wilder knew that this was a good time to stop talking before Austin was subpoenaed to testify before a grand jury about this very conversation.

"I am taking my Fifth Amendment rights to not self-incriminate myself, and I will defer to my attorney for any further questioning."

"Did you really think you would get away with this, you bastard? That was incredibly stupid to trust someone like Kosar. He sang like a canary to the president, did you really think that he would keep his mouth shut?"

"I am sorry, but I have no idea what you are talking about, and again, I am taking my Fifth Amendment rights to not self-incriminate myself, and I will defer to my attorney for any further questioning."

"I want to walk you right over to the Department of Justice and have the attorney general and the FBI take a run at you, but the president does not want to do that just yet. So instead I am going to allow you to sit in an office with an intern and let you read a magazine until we can figure out what the hell kind of mess you got us into. If you try to convince him to allow you to make a call or leave the office, I will have you arrested."

Austin escorted Wilder to the second floor and put Wilder in a young intern's small and cluttered office. The young black male was intimidated by Wilder's presence, and he attempted to force himself to get some work done while trying to ignore one of his bosses sitting in the corner as punishment.

"Can I turn on the TV?" Wilder asked, referring to a small television set hung on a wall in the corner.

"Ahhhh, sure."

Wilder turned on SportsCenter and prepared for a long day.

~ ~ ~

South of Washington DC
FBI Detainment Center

Allen Kinsey was sitting in the FBI detainment center that housed terrorists who posed an immediate threat to the security of the United Sates. It was a nondescript building that a passerby would assume was just another abandoned building in the area. The building was titled to Franklin's Consultants, and the company paid its property taxes every year; therefore, the building was left alone.

The building had twelve cells, four interrogation rooms, and a control center. Kinsey and Sarah made up two of the three prisoners in the detainment center. The third was Chip Zinn, a British tourist, who was held after one of his phone conversations was flagged for making threats to blow up the Capitol building's Visitor Center. Zinn claimed that he was joking around with a buddy, but both the British and American governments had been trying to keep close tabs on him for two years, and neither believed his story.

Kinsey sat in a pitch-black windowless room, unaware of the sun coming up outside. He did not sleep through the night, and he had to break down and urinate in the far corner of the room.

In the room next to him, Sarah was finally being treated by a doctor for her broken nose. She had sat there all night in moderate pain, and like Kinsey, she did not sleep well. After her nose was examined, Sarah was administered a pain pill and a modest breakfast before she was again left to nothing but her thoughts.

Kinsey's mind began to drift off to his family in Wisconsin. His grandma was approaching ninety-four years old. When Kinsey was growing up, Grandma Gladys lived three houses down from Kinsey, and he was a regular visitor, mainly because she made the best fudge in town. To the annoyance of many of the moms in town, Kinsey and his friends would stop in every day in the summer for a piece of fudge as an afternoon treat. Kinsey was a decent basketball player in high school, and his grandma was always in the stands cheering him on. She was also there for every big moment of his life—from proms, breakups, and the loss of close family members. He was grateful that she was such a large part of his life, which made him sad when he accepted the Secret Service job in the nation's capital. He almost did not take the job, but she told him that he would be crazy to pass up a great opportunity to work in Washington DC while helping keep America safe. Since he had been in DC, he called her every week to touch base, and he flew home for every major holiday to see her. Now he imagined her coming to visit him in a federal prison with him wearing an orange uniform standing behind thick glass.

Kinsey jumped when he heard the large clank of the door unlock and squeal open. Two large men entered without saying a word then led Kinsey to one of the interrogation rooms. Kinsey sat in one of the chairs that was bolted to the floor and waited for the interrogator to walk in.

Mark Bailey entered the room, sat across from Kinsey, and opened a file folder.

"I am Special Agent Bailey of the FBI. Do you know why you are here, Mr. Kinsey?"

"You are the man that arrested me at my house, aren't you?"

"That's right."

"How is Sarah?" Kinsey asked concerned.

"Sarah is fine, Mr. Kinsey. She suffered a broken nose but otherwise is doing okay."

"I want you to let her go now. This has nothing to do with her."

"So you do know why you are here. I am glad that we got that out of the way. Now are you going to start telling me your story, Mr. Kinsey?"

"I am not going to tell you anything until two things happen. First, you let Sarah go and, second, I have a lawyer in the room to represent me."

"You are going to jail, Mr. Kinsey. How long you go away for is up to you. If you help us now, the government will promise it will give a plea deal that may provide you with a chance of getting out of jail before you die. If not, the government will make sure that you will be in prison until you die."

When Kinsey did not respond, Bailey closed his file folder and walked out of the room. Two minutes later, he came back pushing a media cart that held a small television and DVD player and plugged them both into the wall.

"I thought that you might want to see this, Mr. Kinsey," Bailey said.

Kinsey thought it was strange that Bailey referred to him as "Mr. Kinsey" so often. Bailey hit play, and the video showed Sarah sitting in the corner of her cell, still with dried blood on her chin and a doctor standing over her. Then Sarah screamed in pain as the doctor attempted to reset her nose. The sound of Sarah screaming made Kinsey's hands sweat, and tears built up in his eyes. Bailey knew that he had him.

"Let her go. This is not about her," Kinsey pleaded.

"You know the deal, Allen. Talk and she goes free. You can start by telling us how you are communicating with the Farahs."

"Let her go!"

The DVD was on continuous play mode, and the doctor was setting her nose again on the replay. It was perfect timing as the screaming forced Kinsey to yell, "They contact me on my cell phone!"

"We have your cell phone, what is the number they are using?"

"Let her go."

"Just as soon as you tell us something of substance, Mr. Kinsey."

"That wasn't the deal."

"What is the number?" Bailey demanded.

"The name is listed under 'Billy' in my contacts."

"Thank you, Mr. Kinsey."

The agents listening to the conversation in the control room began to relay the information to the appropriate agents. Those agents began to track the calls made from Kinsey's phone, specifically calls to Billy, then they tried to track the location of the phone using its GPS.

"Now are you going to let her go?" Kinsey asked.

"Soon enough, Mr. Kinsey," Bailey responded.

"You told me you would let her go!"

"The process of her release is already under way. We have agents listening to this conversation, and they are getting the paperwork done as we speak. Right now we need to focus on the Farahs. Where are they headed, Mr. Kinsey?"

"I do not know where they are headed. I was not involved in the planning."

"What exactly were you involved in, Mr. Kinsey?"

"I think I need a lawyer now."

"Your lover is not gone yet. I would plan your next move very carefully."

"You can't do that!" Kinsey yelled.

"Mr. Kinsey, clearly you can see that I have the upper hand here."

"Why the hell do you keep on addressing me as Mr. Kinsey?"

"That is your name, is it not, Mr. Kinsey?"

Kinsey responded, "But it is just weird!"

"What are we going to focus on here, Mr. Kinsey? How I address you or how you are going to help us stop the terrorists and help your girlfriend leave here faster. Your choice, Mr. Kinsey."

Bailey made sure to emphasize his name this time, now knowing how much it bothered him.

"I have a buddy that is a lawyer, I can call him and have him here in minutes," Kinsey said in desperation.

Bailey took an aggravated sigh and said, "Look, you have the right to call an attorney. However, it would be more beneficial for you to talk to us now. Our main focus right now is saving the first son's life, the life, I might add, that you put in danger by working with these scumbags. If you help us now and make an attempt to help save his life, it could go a long way. If you choose, Mr. Kinsey, to instead lawyer up, I assure you that the federal government will not hold back when prosecuting you. Your name will be on every news program in the country. You will look like a traitor to your country, and it will be the ones you care about most that will be watching all of it. If you help us now, we might be able to help you, Mr. Kinsey."

Allen wanted to say "I will do anything as long as you stop saying my name." Instead, he asked, "You cannot guarantee this deal but you are expecting me to just agree?"

"It is your choice to take the risk. I just want to save Charlie Seaborne's life," Bailey said matter-of-factly.

Allen considered his options. He did not want to have his name scattered all over the media outlets and have his family embarrassed. He was mostly concerned about his grandmother; how would she explain this to her bible study group? It would devastate her. He could not imagine what she would go through if she knew that his actions could put the president's son in harm's way. He went to Washington to protect the first family, but all he did was put them in danger.

"I don't know much, Agent Bailey, but I will tell you what I know in good faith."

"Very good," the FBI agent said.

"All I was paid to do was help keep an eye on Charlie's movements. I did not do a lot until the last couple of days when I was asked for his schedule. Once he left and went to Florida, I gave them updates as they came across the system. They never told me where they were going to take them or what their demands were."

Bailey sounded both disappointed and skeptical and said, "Why should I believe you?"

"I have my life on the line," Kinsey shot back quickly.

"Very well. I will pass along to the prosecutor that you helped us, assuming that what you have told us is true. In the meantime, get comfortable because it will be a while before you will go anywhere."

"What about Sarah?"

"She will be let go." Bailey paused for a moment and said, "But I think it will be a while before you see her again, Mr. Kinsey."

CHAPTER 28

Undisclosed Army Base in Iraq

"Attention!" a voice rang out in the room.

The Zeta Force members stopped what they were doing and stood at attention as Commander Thaddeus Klug entered the room. The members of the Nuclear Emergency Search Team were out of place, so to fit in the best they could, they stood at attention with the other men in the room; albeit not with the precision the Z Force had. Pete Hill looked the most awkward as he stood with his hands crossed around his chest.

Klug took a commanding stride to the front of the room, a walk that made everyone in the room know who was in charge. Klug loved the feeling that everyone had to wait on him. He had studied the leadership of George Washington during the war for independence. Washington was able to get men to die for the cause even though it seemed like everything was working against them. They were fighting the most powerful nation in the world, had little funding, limited food and supplies, dealt with devastating losses and the takeover of cities like Philadelphia, along with smallpox and the horrible conditions of Valley Forge. Despite these downfalls, Washington kept his armies together and was able to win the war.

Klug tried to display the strength, calmness, and confidence that Washington had displayed during the war for independence. He stood behind the podium, grasped both sides firmly, and looked around the room. The men were standing next to their chairs at full attention, so Klug stood for a minute taking the power in. A projector screen next to him displayed an aerial photograph of the Iranian nuclear research facility.

Klug took a big breath then said, "Gentlemen, we are ready to go to war. The consequences will be profound if we are not successful in completing our mission in a timely manner. We cannot allow the Iranians enough time to launch a counterattack. If they do, it will force our president to make the decision to respond, and we could find ourselves in an all out war. You all are experts in your respected fields. You all are in fantastic shape. Most importantly, you all have a deep love for your country. There are no men that I would rather go to war with. I am confident that we will use precision to execute our mission and will emerge victorious."

Klug used the presentation remote control in his hand to move to the next slide. The screen changed to a close-up satellite view of the facility.

"This is where we will land," Klug said as he pointed to an area north of the building. "We will be transported in a top-secret helicopter that your wife cannot even know about."

The comment was meant for Hill's Nuclear Emergency Search Team because they were not used to traveling in a top-secret aircraft and performing sensitive missions. Klug knew that the members of the Z Force would always keep their mouths shut because the release of top-secret information could get someone killed.

The Black Hawks for this mission, were of the same model used to kill Osama bin Laden, made famous because one of them crashed and had to be blown up. The remaining tail caused a small diplomatic problem for the United States when rumors surfaced that the Pakistanis would sell the tail to the Chinese. Eventually Pakistan gave back the remaining tail, but it was anyone's guess what technology they were able to steal from it.

The helicopter was oddly shaped similar to the iconic B-2 stealth bomber and had covers over its tail rotors. The aircraft also had a complicated system of exhaust ducts in its tail to give it further stealth capabilities. Its ability to fly close to the ground also gave it greater cover. Although it was made to fly in stealth mode, helicopters consisted of too many moving parts to be truly stealth. The aircraft made it perfect for this mission because the Iranians would be unsuspecting. Combined with the quieter technology it would give Klug and his men the best chance for a surprise attack.

Klug continued, "After we land, Alpha Team will take down anyone that poses an immediate threat. Once the area is clear, Beta Team will advance to the front doors. Once we gain access to the facility, blowing up the doors if necessary, Charlie Team will advance with NEST team into the building.

Alpha Team will remain on the perimeter to fend off any counterattack that may be coming our way."

Pete Hill shifted in his seat, nervous about knowing that he was entering a building with men yielding a large amount of firepower and with the distinct possibility of being in the middle of a large fight. He was trained to use an M-16 rifle, but the training was only for protection. He would not tell anybody about how petrified he was to be on the brink of going into battle. He just hoped that he would not wet himself as the first bullets flew.

"Hill, do you understand?" Klug asked, drawing Hill's attention back toward the screen.

"Can you explain that one more time?" Hill asked with a small chuckle, embarrassed in front of the hardened soldiers.

"It's sir."

"I'm sorry?"

"When you address me, you will call me sir. I may not be your direct superior, but on this mission, you will be treated like any other solider," Klug said, unwavering.

Repeating the question, Hill asked, "Can you please explain that one more time, sir? I just want to make sure I did not miss any details, sir."

Hill's voice was quivering as he spoke to the commander.

"NEST will move with Charlie Team into the building. You are not allowed to fire unless you are in direct danger. Beta Team will lead the way into the building until we get to here."

Klug pointed to an area on a computer-generated map. The map was created using the information the deserter had given the Americans. Klug pointed to a door in the middle of the compound. The door was protected by two armed guards and required a key card to open.

"We will take out the guards and then put explosives on the door to take it down. The strength of the door will determine how many times we will need to blow it. My guess is that we will not need more than two attempts. Beta Team will remain at the top of the stairs, and Charlie Team will take the lead into the basement.

"The basement is three stories below ground, which allows for the large equipment needed to research nuclear capabilities. This is where we will go blind because our informant has never been to the lower level. NEST's job is to take pictures of the equipment that is stored in the lower level and confirm with your Geiger readers and your knowledge of nuclear technologies. The pictures will automatically be uploaded into the CIA and Department of

Defense servers. While you are taking pictures, the upper level will be rigged to blow, then we will get the hell out of there."

"What about the scientists working?" Hill asked.

"They will be given the opportunity to leave, and if they refuse, they will go down with the building."

The image of Iranian scientists dying in the lab did not sit right with Hill, but he knew better than to share his feeling with Klug.

Klug continued, "If for whatever reason there is a massive amount of nuclear material, we will have a team standing by that is ready to secure the building. The facility will be secured until the NEST team can safely remove all nuclear material, which may take some time. Assuming that everything goes as planned, the explosives will be set, and we will work our way out of the building, load in our helicopters, and leave in a hurry. I believe that we will be able to get in and out of the building relatively quick. Any questions?"

"Sir," a well-built Z Force sergeant said, "Will we have any air coverage if we get attacked by the Iranian air force?"

"Sergeant, we will have F-22 Raptors if needed, but it will take them time to get in to position, which means we will hunker down until help arrives."

F-22 Raptor fighter jets were considered by many to be an elite fighting machine because of their speed and agility and their air-to-air and air-to-ground capabilities.

Klug continued, "We have to be quick, gentleman. If we get engaged in an air-to-air fight with the Iranian air force, all hell is going to break loose. The world will be at war. Iran will probably go after Israel, and we will more than likely face a war that could involve the entire Middle East. It is on our shoulders men. Move out."

As the men were filing out of the briefing room, Klug called Hill over.

"Sir?" Hill asked.

"I just wanted to let you know that you and your men will be fine. Just stay next to us and follow the battle plan. I need you to take those pictures to not only confirm Iran's nuclear activities but also to show how advanced their technology is."

Klug put his hand on Hill's shoulder, surprising even himself with the act of caring.

"Listen, I know you and your men are nervous about being in a war zone and, believe me, we are too. The only difference between me and you is that I can suppress those feelings and get into a frame of mind that allows me to focus on getting the job done, allowing me to forget about the rest. You need to be strong for your men. When the bullets start to fly, they will not be looking at me, they will be looking for your reaction. If they see an ounce of nervousness in you, they will break down, which will put every one of us at risk. Stay strong, at least on the outside, for the rest of us. I know you can do this."

Hill responded with a wavering voice, "I am not so sure, commander. I am not made for this."

"You went through training. You know how to fire your weapon and you understand how to protect yourself when you are under fire. All of those skills will come back, and you will surprise yourself on how well you do."

"Thank you for the confidence, but I must tell you, I am not so sure."

"You will be, because you have to be."

Klug started walking out of the room, and when he got to the door, he said, "Your country needs you. Now, is your chance to step up and be the hero the nation needs you to be."

Klug walked outside leaving Hill in the empty room. Hill sat in one of the chairs and placed his head in his hands. He was not sure how he was going to be able to pull himself together to fight. He longed for a cushy job at a nuclear power plant, maybe somewhere in California. He would make enough money to have a large house with a big television and a pool. But instead, he chose a job where he worked in one of the most dangerous places in the world. He remembered why he did it though—to look out for the country that he loved. Now was his biggest opportunity to step up and defend it.

When Hill walked out of the room, he was determined to fight for his country, even if it resulted in his death.

~ ~ ~

The Situation Room
The White House

The president sat at the head of the table as he considered the pros and cons of the attack. In the room were Vice President Aaron Sewell, Chief of Staff Don Austin, Advisor Kate Jenner, Secretary of Defense Adam Royal, Secretary of State Debra Sharp, and Colonel Vernon Lee, and CIA Director Thomas Host.

Sharp opened the conversation. "Mr. President, there are other options that we can pursue. It is not too late to call off the attack. We need to give them time to allow us to search the facility through diplomatic means. None of us want to start a third world war."

Royal responded, "That would take away that element of surprise, Debbie. By the time they let us search the facilities, the nuclear equipment will be long gone. Now is the time."

"I am sorry Adam, but I respectively disagree. This is the reason why we have the UN—"

"The UN is a joke!" Royal interrupted.

"Let me finish! No reasonable person can dismiss the benefits of an organization based on diplomacy. A system that was set up to allow the world to work out its disagreements without going to war is worth pursuing. We need to see this through using the right means."

"Just like the United States tried before taking out Saddam Hussein? I cannot count how many UN resolutions that were issued that Hussein just dismissed. It took a brave president in George W. Bush to say enough is enough and go in and take him down. You also cannot deny that the world is safer because Hussein is dead."

Sharp rubbed her temples with her index fingers. "But at what costs, Adam? Too many Americans died in that fight."

Sharp was in her late sixties and still dyed her hair blonde, its original color before it began to turn gray. She had two grown children and three grandchildren that she hardly saw. Her husband had begged her not to join the Seaborne administration in exchange for a happy retirement. They did not need the money since he was a successful investment banker, but she felt a need to serve. She promised her husband that she would only serve one term without being sincere, but now was the first time she seriously thought about leaving the post. She had served many roles in the State Department beginning with an internship out of college. She served as the ambassador to Brazil and Australia before she served as deputy secretary of state. When Seaborne was elected, she was on the short list amid concerns that she was too liberal for the job. It was no secret that Seaborne and Sharp did not agree on every issue, but Seaborne enjoyed having someone in the job that would argue her side privately while supporting him publicly.

Seaborne spoke up saying, "Iraq is not up for discussion right now. We need to focus on Iran. I agree with you, Debbie, that going into Iran is not something that we take lightly. However, given the situation that we are in, I agree with Adam that we must attack now. Since both sides want to keep this issue quiet, I believe that it will work out in the end. The world will be safer by controlling nuclear weapons, and this will send a clear signal to Iran that the U.S. will not sit back and let them build them. The vice president will leave soon for the Middle East so he can be in position to begin negotiations with Iran." Seaborne looked at Lee and said, "You have the green light to take over the facility."

"Yes, sir," Lee said. He picked up the phone receiver directly in front of him on the table and said, "We have a green light." Lee hung up the phone and announced, "Klug and his men are getting on the helicopter right now. They should be there shortly."

"Royal, stay here and keep me updated," Seaborne said.

"Yes, sir," Royal responded excited to go to war.

"Don and Kate, come with me. We will work on our other problems."

CHAPTER 29

The Residency
The White House

"I just got off the phone with Mrs. Skeffington," Ann said as William walked through the door, referring to Lindsey's parents. "I still believe that their daughter put Charlie up to this. Do you think that our son would ever get an idea to do something like this on his own?" Before her husband could answer, she said, "Absolutely not! Don't you know some king somewhere with an unwedded daughter?"

"Are you suggesting that I use my influence as the leader of the free world to arrange a marriage for my son? A son who, may I remind you, is in love with another woman?" William asked.

The couple was in the West Sitting Hall where Ann was reading a magazine.

"Don't be silly. Not arrange a marriage but to give our son an idea of what is out there."

"Charlie knows what is best for him, he is a smart boy."

"Why do you insist on supporting their relationship?"

"Why do you always try your hardest to bring it down?"

"I want Charlie to be successful in life. I do not want him to ever worry about money or paying for his children's college education. I want him to take vacations of luxury and own houses all across the country. I want him to be able to become president of the United States if he so desires."

William sighed and looked at the floor, shaking his head.

"Do you have a problem with Charlie being so successful?" Ann asked.

"You don't get it. Of course I want all those things for Charlie, but I feel that he needs to be able to make his own decisions. Plus, after I leave the White House, I will make $200,000 a speech and sit on multiple boards of directors making even more than that. Charlie will be fine when he gets his inheritance."

"I cannot believe that you do not want Charlie to make a life of his own!" Ann was beginning to get irritated.

"I was not raised a rich man nor am I of royal blood. I was born in Youngstown, Ohio, just like Lindsey, and I did fine. I still became the president of the United States! You need to let Charlie decide for himself or we will lose him forever." William took a deep breath to calm down. "None of this is important right now. What did Mrs. Skeffington have to say?"

"She is naturally worried about Lindsey. At first she was a little worried, but she assumed, like we did, that the kids were on a vacation. Then Lindsey called and confirmed which made her more at ease. Now that the number that Lindsey called her from is not working, she is getting worried again. Imagine the first lady taking calls from a poor woman from Youngstown."

"Did you give her an update?"

"No, I did not."

"She needs to know what is going on."

"You can't be serious. That woman will tell the world, and as I recall, it was you and your people that said this needed to be kept quiet."

With a raised voice, William said, "Just because she does not have a fancy college degree or live in the White House does not mean that Mrs. Skeffington is dumb. When we explain to her the significance of keeping quiet, I know she will do what is right."

"There is no we in this. You are the one that is going to make that phone call, not me!"

The president picked up a phone receiver and said, "Operator, I want you to connect me to Mrs. Skeffington immediately, please."

The first couple stared each other down while the operator connected the call. In what seemed like eternity, the operator said, "Mr. President, Mrs. Skeffington is on the line."

"How are you today, Mrs. Skeffington?"

"Mr. President, I am not doing too well as you can imagine. I am just worried sick about Lindsey and Charlie."

"How many times did I tell you to call me William?"

"I will call you Mr. President for as long as you call me Mrs. Skeffington."

"Fair enough. I wish that I was calling under better circumstances."

"I figured you weren't calling to invite us to a state dinner."

The president explained the kidnapping and the current situation.

"How close are you on getting them back?" she asked.

"We have a lead that we are pursuing, and I am confident that it will direct us to Lindsey and Charlie. Mrs. Skeffington, I need you to make sure that you do not share this information with anyone else besides your husband."

William looked at his wife, and he saw that she was listening intently to the conversation.

"I'll do what you say is best, but why is that necessary?" Lindsey's mom asked.

"We do not want the press to know that Charlie and Lindsey are missing because it may put more pressure on the terrorists who may in turn cause harm to the kids."

"I promise that we will keep our mouths shut. I wouldn't do anything to put those kids in danger."

"I do have another question for you."

"What is that, Mr. President?"

"What did Lindsey say when she called?"

"Just like I told your people, she said that she was safe and that she was just having a good time. She didn't want me to worry."

"Well, it was a good thing that she did call because it gave us her location. We would still be looking for them while they were in the terrorist's hands."

The president thanked her for her time and hung up the phone.

William turned to Ann and said, "She promised to keep the situation quiet, and I believe she will."

"I am glad that you are hopeful."

"I need to get back to the Oval Office."

"How was the Queen's Bedroom last night?" Ann asked, trying to get under William's skin.

"Not too bad. I know why everyone likes it so much." He said, attempting to make it seem like it did not bother him. He added, "You know I am not a bad man. I work hard for you and our family. I have spent my life serving our country. Do you realize that we are fighting over our son's girlfriend? They are young and who knows what is going to happen. They are liable to break up soon anyway. We need to stop this fight."

"No, you need to find Charlie."

William walked out of the room, frustrated that his wife refused to be rational. He understood why some presidents had separate rooms from their wives; he just never thought that it would happen to them.

~ ~ ~

Iranian Airspace

The helicopters were flying low to the ground as they crossed into Iranian airspace. One could feel the tension in the aircrafts as they moved toward the facility. Every man was well aware of the consequences of a failed mission.

Commander Klug was flying with Alpha Team and was prepared to help clear the area as they landed. Unlike the other members of Alpha Team, Klug decided that he would not wait in the landing zone, but instead he would accompany NEST into the lower floors, if nothing else but to provide moral support. The second and third helicopters held Beta Team and Charlie Team, respectively, with all three helicopters flying in tight formation.

Klug was looking out of the side window when he heard a crackled voice in his headphone system. "Sir, we have a problem."

"Shit," Klug whispered to himself before responding into the headset, "What is it, captain?"

"Beta helicopter is reporting that they have a malfunction. They may need to turn back."

"What kind of malfunction? This is not the time to be of little details."

The captain spoke into his headset to the captain of the second helicopter before saying, "They are reporting a hydraulic leak. It is bad enough that they needed to break radio silence. This early in the flight they may want to head back."

"These aircrafts are supposed to be war ready! Especially on a sensitive mission like this!"

"I understand, sir, but what should we do?"

"How bad is the leak?" Klug asked.

"Any leak is bad, but we will not be able to tell how severe it is until we hit the ground." The pilot waited a moment before he said, "Sir, you need to make the decision. Should they go back?"

Since they were on strict radio silence orders, meaning they could not call back to headquarters, it was up to Klug to give the orders in the field. He knew that the risk was too big to allow the helicopter to continue on the mission. For the safety of the men on board and to avoid the risk of another helicopter ending up in the hands of the enemy, he had to send it back to base. It meant the Beta Team would not be there to help clear the building. He could abort the mission, but the president was depending on the Z Force to carry it out, and if Iran did pick them up, he did not want to risk word of an attack leaking to the Iranians, putting them in even more danger. He also considered if Charlie Team had enough explosives to finish out the mission, but he concluded that all the men had training in explosives and they carried enough to improvise.

The captain interrupted Klug's thoughts, "Sir, what are your orders?"

"Send the helicopter back to base. We will continue the mission with two teams."

"Are you sure, sir? This could jeopardize the mission."

"I understand the risks, captain. You have my orders."

The captain alerted the other pilots of the orders, and the second helicopter fell out of formation, heading back to the base. The men sitting next to him in the cramped confines had a look of surprise on their faces as they watched the aircraft head back toward base. Klug switched his headset on so that everyone on board could hear him.

Trying to raise his voice above the rotors, Klug said, "Listen up! Beta Team had a malfunction, so we will be down one team, which means that we will need to make some changes. Alpha Team will clear out the landing zone just like before, but this time we will need some help getting into the building. Garfield, Brimley, Star, and Tindall, come with me. The rest will stay on the outside perimeter. We are going to be severely shorthanded and will need to do most of the mission on the fly, so make sure you pay attention to my orders."

Tindall spoke up, "We have your back sir, but it won't be easy."

After asking the captain to relay the message to Charlie Team, Klug looked out his window at the desert below.

~ ~ ~

The White House
The Treaty Room

After leaving his wife in the West Sitting Hall, the president needed a minute alone. He sat behind his desk and stared blankly at a file in front of him. He had to be honest with himself, he was confused. He felt anger toward his wife for the things that she had said and done to him. He was also sympathetic because of the stress she was under.

He was under a tremendous amount of stress too, however. He had all the pressures of running the country while worrying about his son, the Iranian crisis, and the bailout scandal. He also felt terrible about his brother. Even though they did not get alone very well, he still loved him.

William had one lingering question, how could he and his wife ever recover from this? She was a good woman at heart, he knew. He could not figure out when she began to change from the woman he loved to the woman who would not allow him to sleep in her bed during the worst event in both of their lives.

Maybe it was when he became a star in Ohio politics? She loved being the guest of honor at major functions throughout the state. He knew deep down, however, that it was the White House that had changed her. She no longer had her friends around her every day to keep her grounded, and the new Ann was a result.

He still had time to back out of the next election. There would be no shortages on candidates; Aaron Sewell was certainly an option. There were at least five senators that also would make good runs, not to mention all the governors of the large states.

The phone on his desk rang, and the president picked it up on the first ring. It was Kate Jenner on the other line.

"Mr. President, I am sorry to interrupt you, but there are several pressing issues that we need to touch base on."

"What are they, Kate?"

"First, you need to have that meeting with Kosar. He is getting antsy, and it is becoming more difficult trying to convince him to stay in his hotel room."

"Tell him that it is in his best interest to stay there."

"I tried that, sir. I think we need to meet with him as soon as possible."

"Very well, tell him to make his way back to the White House. I will meet with him as my time allows. In the meantime, have Don talk with him."

Jenner continued, "We do not have any more information on Charlie's kidnapping. The FBI is still interrogating Kinsey, but the agents do not believe that he will be of any more help."

"Isn't that the man who gave us the contact?"

"Yes, but he does not know any more than meeting with the terrorists when they contacted him. We did receive some information from Berry and Maul. The terrorist said that they are taking Charlie and Lindsey to St. Augustine. Maul and Berry will go there now, and we will also send two extra teams of Secret Service agents."

"Do we want them to be tied up like that?"

"No other choice. They will have an agency plane available to move them where they need to go." Someone whispered to Jenner in the background. "I am sorry, Mr. President, give me one minute, please."

Kate covered the phone as the spoke. When she came back on, she said, "Mr. President, one of the helicopters is heading back toward base."

"What the hell is going on, Kate!"

"Not too sure because they are on radio silence."

"Then how the hell do we know they are on their way back, Kate. I want answers now!"

"We know that they are on their way back because they crossed into Iraqi airspace, and our radars just picked them up."

"Only one has shown up, correct?"

"Affirmative, sir, only one helicopter has been spotted, and as of now we do not know where the other two are. Excuse me, sir." Jenner put the president on hold, and when she came back on, she said, "Secretary Royal is requesting your presence in the Situation Room to discuss the matter further."

"Tell them I am on the way, but Kate . . ." The president paused for a moment.

"Yes, sir?"

"As soon as I am through with Royal, I need to have a . . . private and personal conversation with you."

"Is everything all right, sir?"

"We will talk in a few minutes," the president said, then hung up the phone.

As William left this office, he wished that there just might be a little chance for his family to go back to the pre-White House days. His life was much simpler then, and even though he did not live in luxury like he does now, it seemed like his family was happier, and he would not change that for the world.

CHAPTER 30

The White House
The Situation Room

"Mr. President, we should be close to starting the attack on the Iranian facility. At that time, we will end radio silence," Adam Royal said.

"Why is that, Adam?" Seaborne asked.

"Once the first shots are fired, someone at the base will alert the Iranian military. Therefore it will not put our men in harm's way by lifting radio silence. On our way back to base, we will enter radio silence again so they will have a hard time tracking us."

"What the hell is going on with that helicopter, colonel?"

Colonel Vernon Lee responded, "Sir, they are just about to land. We will receive a full report once they hit the ground. Right now our best assumption is some type of leak, either oil or hydraulic. I will give you an update as soon as I know."

"When does the transmission start?" Seaborne asked.

"Any moment now, Mr. President," Royal said.

~ ~ ~

Environmental Research Lab
Dasht-e Kevir Desert, Iran

The guards of the Environmental Research Lab felt like they had the worst job in Iran. They loved the idea of guarding a top-secret facility, but at the same time, all they did was stare at sand. They were paid well, although they did not know what exactly they were guarding. It was almost like guarding Fort Knox in Kentucky—there was prestige and mystery about guarding it and that helped keep a person alert while on patrol. A squad of soldiers was spread around the perimeter of the base and were armed with high-power rifles.

They did not hear the two helicopters as they approached the facility, until the aircrafts were about two hundred yards away, that's when one of the guards spotted it and radioed the others. The guards retreated to their battle stations and prepared for whatever was coming. When the helicopters were just one hundred yards out, the guards began to fire at the Americans as they went into their descent.

"We are under fire!" the captain told Klug.

"Fire at will," Klug ordered.

The helicopter's machine guns exploded on the facility below, aiming specifically for the guard towers that stood along the wall. The second helicopter began to fire its 70mm rockets. Even Klug was impressed by the firepower the two helicopters were able to unload.

~ ~ ~

One of the guards immediately called in the attack to his superior officer in Tehran. He said in Persian, "We are under attack. I say again, we are under attack!"

Nassir from central command responded, "Who is attacking?"

"I cannot be for certain. Both helicopters are plain in color with no insignia. I can only assume that they are American because of the technology of the helicopter. I have never seen anything like it."

"The Americans, huh? Why would they risk an attack on us?"

"What should we do?"

"Defend yourselves until you hear otherwise."

~ ~ ~

Iranian Central Command

Nassir called the Iranian president's office direct. After only one ring, an aide picked up, and Nassir demanded to speak to the president directly.

"What is it? This better be good!" Iranian president Saeed Jafari said.

"We are under attack at the Environmental Research Lab!"

"That is impossible, we would have seen them coming."

"I think it is the Americans with their stealth helicopters."

"Why would they attack there?"

"We both know why they would attack there, sir. They must know about our research."

"Tell our men to defend the facility at all costs."

The Iranian president hung up the phone and demanded to speak to President Seaborne.

~ ~ ~

Environmental Research Lab

The Charlie Team helicopter went to the rear of the facility and fired its rockets toward the guards' strongholds. It also used its machine guns in an attempt to mow down soldiers that were seeking safety.

Pete Hill was near the door of the aircraft, tapping his foot nervously as he saw the destruction outside. He positioned himself so he could look west where saw a man dissected by the machine gun's fire. Hill quickly jerked away and tried to remain calm for his men. He took a deep breath as the aircraft jerked left.

The captain's voice came over the headset. "Get ready men!"

The helicopter made its way to the front of the small building, and Hill watched as Alpha Team's helicopter made its descent to the ground. Charlie Team stayed in the air, continuing to fire upon the enemy below. The helicopter shook as it launched its rockets and its machine guns roared, and finally the amount of guards trying to advance began to lessen.

Alpha Team's helicopter hit the ground and the Z Force members jumped out of both sides of the helicopter, taking out whatever targets that posed a threat. As the captain of the ship lifted the helicopter back into the air, the counterattack came from the main entrance to the building. Klug and his men found cover behind concrete columns, and they began systematically taking out the guards that were defending the entrance.

Klug radioed to Charlie Team and ordered them to land. Alpha's aircraft was now in the air to provide support while Charlie Team began its descent. Hill took a deep breath and said a little prayer as he felt the falling sensation in his stomach.

~ ~ ~

The Situation Room
The White House

"We have just ended radio silence. The attack has commenced," Colonel Lee said.

The president shook his head and stayed glued to the television screens on the wall that showed a live-feed signal that came from both helicopters. The president saw the first helicopter ascend as explosions erupted all around them.

As he watched the second helicopter land, Secretary of State Debra Sharp said, "Mr. President, the Iranian president is on the phone demanding to speak to you."

"Patch him through." Seaborne picked up the phone and said, "Mr. President, this is William Seaborne."

Seaborne heard a thick Persian accent on the other line. He looked to his translator for the interpretation. "Mr. President, this is a courtesy call, and I hope that you will be truthful with me. Right now my country is under attack, and I want to know if it is you."

Seaborne responded, "Yes, the Americans are on a mission to take over a nuclear facility that you are illegally keeping below the building."

"You have no proof! You are attacking a sovereign nation. We will have no choice but to respond."

"That would not be a good idea. We need to negotiate."

"You do not attack then ask to negotiate," the Iranian president said.

"I do not want to see a war just as much as you do not want to see a war. This could turn out to be a world war before we know it. However, I feel that we can prevent that."

"How can that possibly be? My people will not stand for being attacked and have their government do nothing about it."

Seaborne answered directly, "Mr. President, if the world finds out about this, we will both look bad. The United States attacked a sovereign nation. But I believe that Iran harvesting nuclear weapons would be an even bigger deal. If the world finds out that you have these weapons, there will be hell to pay. We will go into your facility, destroy it, and leave."

"That is unacceptable."

"We will also promise to be less negative toward your country in front of the United Nations and to the press, which will relieve you of some pressure."

"We will see about that," the Iranian president said as he hung up the phone.

"I thought that went well," Seaborne said sarcastically.

"I think they will call back. They will have no choice once we take down the building," Royal said.

"I hope so or we just started World War III."

~ ~ ~

Iranian Presidential Palace

The Iranian president slammed the phone onto the base and cussed.

He yelled at no one in particular, "How could we not see them coming? Get our missiles ready. Our first target is Jerusalem."

The general nodded his head to an assistant, and the assistant ran out of the room to give the order.

"Mr. President, I understand you are upset, and I also think it is a good idea to get our arms ready to attack," the general said. "However, I must warn you that if you do this, the United States and the world will put all of their resources into destroying us. They have been waiting a long time for this opportunity. I am recommending that we negotiate a deal with the Americans. It would be good for us if they got off of our backs for a little while. If the UN finds out how close we are to the weapons, they will go after your head." He paused and gestured to the room, "All of our heads! We need to hear what they have to say."

"You may be right, but right now I want some American blood! Have the guards fight to the death."

The general called central command and relayed the message.

~ ~ ~

Environmental Research Lab

Hill felt the jolt of the helicopter as it hit the ground. When the door opened, he followed the team out and into the battle. Charlie Team ran for cover next to Alpha Team who was still laying down rounds of bullets to the guards protecting the main entrance. After Charlie Team evacuated, the stealth Black Hawk took off and went dark again. To avoid being sitting ducks, the helicopters flew back into the desert using their stealth capabilities. They would return when the men on the ground were ready to evacuate.

Klug ordered his men to throw grenades through the open door so Charlie Team could make its way into the facility. As the shells exploded, Klug began advancing, and the Iranians quickly shut the heavy metal door. This is where Klug needed Beta Team and the explosive experts that accompanied them. Klug and two of his team members rigged the door with what he had and walked away to ignite it.

"Blow it!" Klug ordered.

A few seconds later, the door exploded, and three guards emerged firing their weapons, even though they were all slightly burned from the explosion. Klug's men quickly took them out, and Klug gave the order to advance into the building.

Hill grabbed his gear, advancing into the facility with his fellow NEST member Derrick Miller running beside him.

Klug placed covering fire into the building, and Charlie Team followed behind soon after. Hill and his men were followed by Tindall who took up the rear. The smoke in the air forced Hill to blink his eyes rapidly as he entered the building. He heard a gun fire, and he hit the floor as a reflex. Tindall was next to him and picked up Hill by his collar and shoved him down a small hallway.

Hill looked back and saw Miller lying on the ground with the left side of his head missing. Hill thought seeing his friend dead would make him freeze in fear, but instead it made him want to take revenge for his death. Hill narrowed his eyes and focused on seeking revenge against those who killed Miller.

Klug led the team down the hallway, and even as they went farther into the building, they could still hear the fight outside. The offices were vacated by scared scientists who sought refuge in a large break room in the back of the facility. Klug ordered two of his men to keep watch while the rest of the team searched for the door leading to the nuclear research lab.

Klug was the first to spot the nondescript and well-protected door. Using intuition and the description of the dissenter, he knew right away that it was the door he was looking for. Klug used the explosive material that he carried and rigged it to the door. When Tindall finished the opposite side of the door, they prepared for the explosion.

After a loud bang, the door came ajar, much to the relief of Klug. Hill jumped at the sound and took another deep breath.

An Iranian soldier jumped up from behind a wall and fired, hitting Garfield in the upper arm. Klug and Tindall fired back killing the Iranian.

"What the hell are you waiting for? Get down there and take those pictures!" Klug said to Hill.

Tindall led the charge as Hill took a deep breath and moved down the stairs with the rest of the NEST men.

~ ~ ~

The Situation Room
The White House

"What happened to the video feed?" the president asked Colonel Lee.

"The Black Hawks left the area, the feed will return as soon as the Z Force completes their mission. In the meantime, we will need to listen to the radio transmissions."

"Man down! They have shot Miller from NEST," an announcement came over the radio.

"Damn it! Make sure to get him out of there," the president ordered to Lee.

"They will make sure to get the body out, sir," Lee responded. "We like to make sure that there is no man left behind."

"We found the door and are ready to take it down," Klug said over the radio. "We are heading down to the nuclear facility now. Stand by for updates."

"Well, this is it," the president said. "If we don't find anything now, we will have hell to pay. Keep your fingers crossed."

"At this point, sir, we need more than luck," Sharp said, immediately regretted her comment.

~ ~ ~

Environmental Research Lab

Tindall moved down the stairs, cautious of what lay behind the closed doors, his M16 leading the way.

Hill pulled his Geiger reader out of his backpack and turned it on. There was definitely nuclear material down there.

When Tindall and three other Z Force members hit the bottom of the stairwell three stories below the ground, they turned a corner and saw one large room with scientists holding their hands above their heads.

Hill recognized a small reactor immediately as he entered the room. "That is definitely nuclear, but it is not as much as I thought."

"If you want to live, I suggest that you get out of here now!" Tindall said to the scientists.

The Iranian scientists held their hands in the air as they left in single file formation up the stairs. All except one man, who quietly moved into a small lab in the rear of the facility.

Tindall radioed to Klug, "The scientists are making their way upstairs now. Hill said that he can confirm that the material is here. He will take the pictures, then we will head out."

"Copy that. We will clear the top floor and set the explosives."

"Hurry up and take those pictures," Tindall said to Hill.

Hill nodded to his men, and they took pictures of the equipment in the room. Hill made his way toward the back when a dark-skinned Iranian came out of a small lab. He was holding two large vials in his hands.

In broken English, the man said, "Stop! You do not want me to drop these vials!"

~ ~ ~

The Situation Room
The White House

"Commander, we have a problem." Tindall radioed to Klug.

The president stood up. "What the hell is going on?"

"What is wrong?" Klug asked.

"There is a man saying the he has vials of . . ." the radio broadcast broke up.

"Fix it now!" the president ordered.

"It is not on our side, it is on theirs," Royal said calmly.

"Say again," Klug commanded. After a long minute, Klug said, "Tindall, say again!"

"Sir, we have all just been exposed to smallpox!"

~ ~ ~

Environmental Research Lab

The man holding the vials threw both of them into the middle of the room, allowing the highly toxic virus into the room.

"What the hell did you do that for?" Hill yelled.

The man just responded by laughing hysterically.

Hill did not think for a minute as he lifted his M16 and shot the man twice in the chest.

"Sir," Hill called to Tindall.

"What is it?"

"I don't think we can go back. We cannot expose smallpox to the world."

"What the hell are you suggesting? That we all die here? I'm getting the fuck out of here right now."

Hill lifted his weapon and pointed it at Tindall.

"I will not hesitate to shoot you."

Tindall turned and looked at him. "What the fuck are you doing? You think you carry a big gun so now you can use it? I will kill you faster than you can even think about pulling the trigger."

"If we leave, we will cause great harm to everyone we come in contact with. We must stay here and go down with the building."

"You are one crazy son of bitch. Do you really expect the rest of us to stay here and die?"

"You joined the military to save lives. You risk your life every day to save the lives of innocent Americans. Now you need to give up your own life so that this disease can never leave this room."

"What if it is not smallpox and that guy was just messing with us?"

"He died to let that vial drop and paid for it with his life. Why else would he do that?"

One of the other NEST members came out of the backroom holding a stack of reports. "Pete, all of these papers hold scientific research on smallpox."

Hill looked at Tindall and said, "Do you think that they staged this just in case the Americans attacked a top-secret facility in the middle of the desert?" Answering his own question, Hill said, "I don't think so either."

~ ~ ~

The Situation Room
The White House

"Commander, those of us in the lower level have been exposed to smallpox. We need to go down with the building," Tindall said with surprising calm.

"What the hell are you talking about? Get your asses up here now!"

"If we leave, we will expose everyone we come into contact with. Just go."

Royal looked over to the president. Seaborne had his head in his hands.

"Mr. President, it is the right choice. We cannot allow them to leave the building and risk spreading the virus. Humans have not been exposed to smallpox in many years. We cannot risk it."

"I know," Seaborne said. "It does not make it any easier though. I will never understand why good men will need to die in the face of evil."

"They are true American heroes."

"I know, but because of the secrecy behind the mission, there will never be a statue or memorial honoring their deaths. Get me the president of Iran."

~ ~ ~

Environmental Research Lab

Klug knew deep-down inside that Tindall was right. He rounded up the rest of his men after they set the explosives and prepared to take off. All Iranian civilians and military personal left in and around the building were told to get as far away from the building as they could.

The pilots of the helicopters made their way toward the building and spotted the red-signal flare indicating that the mission was over. The aircrafts landed and were quickly filled and took off with lighter loads than what they landed with. Miller's body was thrown into the Black Hawk, and it stood as a harsh reminder of the cruelty of war.

As the helicopters were about two hundred yards away from the facility, the walls exploded and the building collapsed into one big mound on top of the nuclear and smallpox labs below.

The men in the helicopters all stared blindly as they made their way home.

CHAPTER 31

The White House
Don Austin's Office

Don Austin had a surprisingly large office in the West Wing. While Z Force was carrying out their mission on the Environmental Research Lab, the chief of staff was sitting at the large mahogany conference table that sat in the far corner of his office. Across from him was Gideon Kosar, who did not appear nervous. Kosar just wanted to get the meeting over so he could go back to his office and begin his normal routines. He had a large lifestyle. He ate heavy meals, exercised whenever he could, worked hard, and played even harder. He was scheduled to run in a local adventure race on the upcoming weekend. The race was three-and-a-half miles long with twelve obstacle courses that included climbing a net wall, crawling through tunnels, and running through quicksand.

Austin started the meeting, "Why the hell did you do it, Gideon?"

"I am not so sure I did something so wrong. I was doing what I could to get this deal passed as fast as I could. The deal would have been better for both the taxpayers and my company. The American people are getting reduced fees, including no baggage fees, and the airlines will get the extra money they needed to expand, allowing for a larger profit. In addition, the loans will be paid back with interest. How is that a bad deal?'

Austin could not believe what he was hearing. "Is that your explanation? No jury will ever buy that excuse. You realize that the president is the only thing keeping your case from being prosecuted."

"I don't understand why I am here or what you and the president are looking for. You know I did it. I admitted to it. I gave you Brad Wilder. What else do you expect from me?"

"How did you get Wilder involved?"

"Brad and I have known each other for a while. We worked on a couple of campaigns together, we even worked together in the private sector for a while. He came to me and said that he would be able to speed up the process, plus fight for Freedom Air to get a larger share of the money. In return, I would hire him to be my government liaison once the dust settled."

"How much money was he promised?" Austin asked curious to see how much his former assistant would make.

"Millions in salary and millions more in bonuses and incentives," Kosar said without blinking an eye.

"You still do not see anything wrong with this?"

"I see it as a win-win."

Austin had heard enough. He walked across the room to his desk and began to shuffle through some papers. He was more upset about Wilder betraying him than he was about Kosar making the deal. Austin had fought to bring Wilder in the Seaborne administration, and he had convinced the president that Wilder was the best man for the job.

"I want you to tell me one thing," Austin said. "Tell me why the hell should the president let you go instead of dragging your name through a publicized trial and sending you to jail for a very long time."

Kosar did not need to think of his answer. He quickly responded, "It will destroy this county like Watergate. I would even wager that it will hurt the country more so than Watergate because the public trust of the government is already low. The public needs to deal with politicians fighting the debt ceiling, shutting the government down, and a prolonged war in the Middle East. It will take years to regain that trust. This is not the time for us to move in the wrong direction with so much on the line."

Austin did not respond because he knew Kosar was right. It would take too long for the country to recover, and no one wanted to see that happen, and he also believed that the president would have the same thought.

The president opened Austin's door and walked in without being invited. He had more pressing concerns than hurting the chief of staff's feelings. Kate Jenner walked in behind him as they both just left the Situation Room. Kosar stood while the president sat at the end of the table, Jenner to his right.

Without acknowledging anyone, Seaborne said, "Here is what we are going to do. You are going to fly back to your headquarters and announce your resignation in the morning. You will say that you want to spend more time with your family. You will stay out of the airline industry for the rest of your life. It is my belief that the county does not need this controversy now. I do guarantee you, however, that if this ever leaks, all of us will go down in the future. Who else knows about this?"

"Just us in this room know about the agreement. As the CEO of Freedom Air, I had the ability to hire whom I chose at whatever salary I wished."

"Can I trust that this will not go any further?"

"Absolutely. I have set up a very nice nest egg for me and my family, and it would give me nothing but pleasure to spend my time traveling the world and doing charity work."

"If Wilder talks, we are all done. I just want to be very clear on this point."

"I will not talk, and I have a funny feeling that Wilder will also keep his mouth shut."

"Okay. There is an assistant waiting in the hall to walk you out. I hope you will hold up your end of the deal."

"You have no worries, Mr. President." Kosar was anxious to leave, but as he was halfway out the door, he stopped and said, "You know, with all of this free time, I can organize some fund-raisers for you."

The president responded in annoyance, "I don't think so. I never want to see you again."

Kosar turned and left the room.

"What do you guys think?" Seaborne asked.

"To be honest, I do not feel too comfortable making this deal, but I understand, and I can live with it," Austin said.

"What about you, Kate?"

"Mr. President, I think that he got off too easy, but like Mr. Austin, I can live with it."

"Mr. President, can I talk to Wilder?" Austin asked. "I want to handle this one on my own."

"Yes. He gets the same deal. Now, I want us to all have lunch together. Don, can you get us menus?"

~ ~ ~

FBI Detention Center
Washington DC

Allen Kinsey fell asleep in the interrogation room while the agents were discussing what to do with him next. Sarah was released and sent to the hospital to have her nose examined after the FBI concluded that she did not have a role in helping Kinsey.

Mark Bailey slammed the door shut as he entered the room, waking up Kinsey. He wiped the drool from his lips and rubbed his eyes. He was not fully awake when Bailey started to grill him again.

"Kinsey, we have released Sarah. Right now she is at the hospital getting her nose checked out. By the way, she was swearing your name. I have a funny feeling that she is never going to visit you in prison." Bailey chuckled and said, "Kinsey, in fact, I don't think many people are going to come visit you. You are going to be a lonely man."

"What happens to me next?" Kinsey asked.

"From here, we will take you to our processing unit where we will set up a hearing before a judge. Do you have a lawyer?"

"Not a good one."

"I don't think it is going to make much difference, Mr. Kinsey, you will be denied bail. When a man conspires with terrorists, bail is never granted, at least from my experience. You will be given an attorney, but he will probably hate you too. After your hearing, you will be moved to a federal prison until your trial."

"What if I make a plea agreement? Do you think I can get out before I die?"

"Not my department. I will pass on that you were helpful here, which will help your cause, but I imagine you will be gone a very long time."

"I don't want a trial. I cannot put my family through that."

"Mr. Kinsey, I can't blame you for that, but I can guarantee that this case will be all over the papers. There is going to be no hiding from it."

"When can I lie down in a bed?"

"We will move you out soon, Kinsey, sit tight."

~ ~ ~

Undisclosed Army Base, Iraq

The stealth Black Hawk helicopters landed, and the men disembarked and headed toward the hanger for a debriefing. There was a somber mood as each man was well aware of their comrades they lost on the mission. Thaddeus Klug was the saddest of them all. Good men like Tindall had died in the service of their country. Peter Hill had died a hero, something that Klug would never have guessed. It was his idea, after all, to stay in the building and die to help prevent the exposure of smallpox. All of the men would be tested to ensure that they were not infected, although the odds were low because they were upstairs when the virus was released.

Klug's men were sitting in their briefing room chairs when Klug walked in. All of them stood as they noticed his presence. He told them to be seated and did not hesitate to begin the briefing.

"We lost a lot of brave men out there today, including the entire NEST team. Let's have a moment of silence in their honor." A few moments later, Klug continued, "You should be proud of yourselves and the way that each of you fought. You were brave, and we were able to destroy the weapons inside the facility. Our men did not die in vain, they died as heroes defending our country."

A young corporal with bad acne entered a side door and said, "Sir, I am sorry to interrupt, but there is an important message I need to give you."

"This better be important, corporal!" Klug barked.

"Sir, the president wants to have a word with you and your team. He is standing by."

Aggravated by the young corporal, Klug said, "What are you waiting for? This is the president we are talking about!"

In a wavering voice, the corporal responded, "If everyone could please follow me into the next room, we have a teleconference ready to go."

The tired soldiers slowly rose from their seats. Klug did not like this disrespect and yelled, "The commander in chief is waiting for you, and I suggest you get a move on!"

The men picked up their pace as they exited the room and crowded in front of a large flat-screen television that displayed the famous White House emblem. Klug positioned himself in front of his men and waited for the president to appear. Ten seconds later, the president's frowning face appeared on the screen. He was sitting behind his desk in the Oval Office.

"I wish I was calling under better circumstances," the president said. "We lost some good people out there, all of which died with honor. I am truly proud to call them Americans. They all died knowing the risks, but they put their country first and they will forever be heroes. I want to thank all of you for your contributions to this mission. Each and every one of you put your lives on the line to protect not only our country but the world from the Iranians. If they would have been able to go through with their nuclear and biological ambitions, this could be a very unsafe world. It is undoubtedly possible that they could have attacked Israel, and we would have come together to protect them. What each of you did tonight was save us from that fight." The president took a deep breath, and the Z Force could see the president tearing up as he continued, "I wish I could tell the world about what you did today. You deserve that much. Unfortunately, because of security issues, we cannot do that. To me, that is what makes you true American heroes. When I go to bed every night, I think about all of the men and women that have died for us, and I cannot be grateful enough. I want to personally thank you for what you have done for our country. As a small gesture, I am sending you the best steaks money can buy, out of my pocket, for what you did tonight. While I know this is but a small token, please understand that what you did potentially saved millions of lives. Commander Klug, good job tonight."

"Thank you, sir, it was our pleasure to serve our country."

"Thank you, commander. It is no secret what you found tonight. We now can confirm that the Iranians were in the process of developing nuclear material for what we believe would have been used as weapons. We also can confirm that the Iranians were producing smallpox. Some believe that smallpox could have been more dangerous than nuclear weapons. Vice President Sewell is on his way to Iraq as we speak. He will then fly to Iran to negotiate a peace agreement that I believe both sides will be willing to accept. Do you men have anything to say to me?"

The soldiers looked at each other, unsure if they should say anything; this was, after all, the president of the United States.

A man stood in the back row and said, "I just want to say how brave the NEST team was today. They were brave up to the end."

Another warrior stood and said, "I agree, and if I could add that it was a pleasure kicking some Iranian ass tonight!"

The president smiled for the first time and said, "Yes, it was gentlemen. Yes, it was. Did I mention before that you will eat those steaks in Aruba? Tomorrow morning you will hop on a plane and head to Aruba for some R & R. Enjoy yourselves."

"I think I speak for everyone in the room when I say thank you," Klug said.

"Have a good night, gentlemen," the president responded before signing off.

The screen went black, and Klug turned to his men and said, "We will all need to go back and shower and hit our beds. Looks like we have a little vacation tomorrow, and while we will think of those who gave the ultimate sacrifice, we need to relax for our own mental health."

The men of the Zeta Force knew that Klug was right. They retrieved their gear and headed toward the showers, all looking forward to a little time in the Caribbean waters with girls in bikinis.

CHAPTER 32

The Oval Office
The White House

The president ended the conference call with Klug and the Z Force as the technical staff cleared the office of the equipment needed to broadcast the teleconference. When they vacated the room, Kate Jenner and Seaborne were left alone, sitting on the office's couches.

"Mr. President, you said there was something that you wanted to talk to me about?" Kate asked.

"Yes, Kate, I am worried about Ann. She is handling this situation pretty badly. Last night she made me sleep in a different room"

"I had no idea it was that bad."

"It's pretty bad. With the way she has treated me lately, I can't imagine things ever going to where they were before. I don't think I could ever look at her the same way."

"It will be hard for a while, but you will get through it, you are both strong people."

"I wish I was that confident."

Kate tried to console him the best she could, but she had never been good at giving advice. "Mrs. Seaborne is going through a difficult time right now. Her only child is being held hostage, and she cannot reach out to anybody because it is held confidential. You can come down here and work while she is stuck up there by herself left to nothing but her thoughts. Give her some time and space. Come to think of it, it may not be a bad idea to call a friend or family member here so she can have someone to lean on. Maybe watch a movie in the theater or something."

The president agreed and said, "I think I might do that, thank you. I don't mean to bother you with my issues. I wanted to ask if you knew a good psychiatrist."

"Let me think. Yes, a friend of mine used Dr. Kryptoforski."

"Kryptoforski? His name doesn't sound too positive."

"She raved about him. I think you should give him a shot."

"All right, give his office a call. Tell him that the president is calling and he is needed at the White House. Remind him that even the first family is afforded patient-doctor privilege."

"I will make it very clear, sir. And by the way, it is not a bother to help you talk through these things." She let out a soft laugh and said, "This reminds me of how it was back in your senate office. More personal."

"I kinda of miss those days too. Do you remember Rodger Robbins?"

This time letting out a loud laugh, Kate said, "How could I ever forget Rodger? He was the nicest intern you could ever meet, but he did some stupid things."

"The first time he met the president, he was so nervous that when it was his turn to shake his hand, he didn't say a word."

Kate took over and said, "The president had to ask him if he was all right because Rodger just stood there with wide eyes and a terrified look on his face."

"The next day, the president's office called me to make sure that Roger was never at another event with him because he freaked him out." The president let out a loud laugh and said, "Explaining to Rodger why the president never wanted to see him was the most awkward conversation I have ever had with an intern." The president took a deep breath and asked, "Whatever happened to Rodger?"

"The word on the grapevine is that he is a big executive on Wall Street, probably making more money than the both of us."

"Your time will come, Kate. Just be patient. I get to have an office staff after I leave the presidency, as you know, and I am sure that there will be a place for you on my staff."

"Thank you, sir. I will make sure I keep that in mind."

"I wish that I never left that office. I could have been a senator for a long time, maybe even be like Senators Byrd or Thurmond. I could have stayed and served forever."

"Why didn't you?"

"Ann wanted this. It did sound good to me too, I must admit," Seaborne said.

"I thought you were a great senator and you are a terrific president. Just try to stay positive because you have another campaign to run," Kate said with a smile.

"I don't even want to think about another campaign now."

"Tell me you are going to run, Mr. President."

"Kate, we both know I will. It is just not fun to think about right now."

Jenner stood and said, "I will call the doctor right now."

"Thank you, Kate."

Jenner turned and headed to the door when the president reached out and grabbed her forearm. "I appreciate your time and listening to me babble. I just want this to be over."

"It will be over soon, sir," Jenner said as she released her arm from Seaborne's grasp, and headed toward the door to call the doctor.

~ ~ ~

Vero Beach, Florida

Rich Maxwell and Ray Turner arrived at the abandoned house with two other agents. Rich had his arm in a sling from the accident, and Ray had a couple of scrapes on his face. Maul and Berry spent time cleaning up the house, including most of the blood. The blood left behind would not raise any suspicions of foul play when the house was used again.

"Hey Berry, nice to see you again," Rich said as he walked in the door.

"Guys, you remember Bruce Maul from Youngstown, I'm sure," Berry said.

"Of course, where is the prisoner?"

"He is on the floor in the living room trying to get some sleep. He has a couple of injuries."

"Come on, Berry. Don't tell me you hit him."

"He was shot in the shoulder at the scene. He also received a minor wound to his hand when I attempted to disarm him."

"Okay. Our orders are to take him back to the airport with us and put him on the plane to Washington. Ray and I have asked and have been granted permission to join you for the duration of the investigation."

Maul spoke up for the first time, "All you are going to do is slow us down. You are in a sling and you guys don't know anything about our investigation. You guys stay here."

"Sorry to rain on your parade, son, but this is not my first rodeo. I have been doing this a long time. Plus, it won't hurt having two extra people working together to figure this out."

"We are doing just fine on our own, thanks. And don't call me son. Besides, you couldn't protect him to begin with, what makes you capable to help track down the person that you lost?"

"That wasn't our fault."

"All I know is that your protectee is now in the hands of some dangerous people."

"Son, I am not afraid of you. The Secret Service has been authorized to run this investigation while the CIA has asked to assist us. My boss has overruled yours, so you better get used to the idea real fast."

Maul stepped forward and leaned down to the shorter man in order to look him in the eyes. "If you get in my way, I will leave you behind."

"I think this will work out just fine. Let's go check out this piece of scum."

Rich and Ray walked to the old living room only to find Maali lying on the ground with his hands tied behind his back, wearing nothing but his underwear. The bruises and blood showed signs of the intensive questioning from the night before. Rich walked over to him to make sure the man was still breathing when Maali opened his eyes.

Rich walked back into the kitchen and asked, "What the hell went on here last night?" Rich yelled. "You were given very clear orders."

"Listen, Agent Maxwell, this piece of scum gave us the lead on Charlie. Without our questioning, we would not know to head toward St. Augustine."

"We don't even know if he is telling the truth. He can't even give us the exact location of where they will be taking Charlie. For all we know, the Farahs could still be right here in Vero Beach."

"Right now I have no reason not to believe him. Plus, if he is lying to us, he knows that we can start the questioning over again. Come to think of it, if you want we can go ahead and water board him right here to see if his story changes."

Finally Ray spoke up, "That won't be necessary. Look, we need to drive our vehicles to the airport, get on our plane, and head toward St. Augustine. The two agents that are with me will stay on the plane while we drive around the city looking for clues."

"Nah, I am driving," Maul said. "You two go ahead and meet Berry and I there."

"Not going to happen," Ray said. "We need to fly so we can get there in good time. The Jacksonville branch will have a vehicle waiting for us when we get on the ground."

"Looks like I just lost my Charger for some piece of shit standard-issued vehicle," Maul said bitterly.

The agents made their way back to the Vero Beach Municipal Airport where they loaded on the government plane headed toward Jacksonville. The plane was an executive jet used by most federal government agencies. Maali was cleaned up to look like an average FBI prisoner so that his presence did not raise any concerns among the airport employees.

Once they were in the air, Rich started the small talk. "I went out to dinner the other night, and my wife insisted on eating at Kilika's Steakhouse. I told her that we could get a steak anywhere and did not need to spend the extra money."

"Maybe she just wanted to get out for a nice dinner," Ray said. "Who can blame her for that?"

"Honestly, we could have gone to that little place downtown and probably could have saved five or six dollars a person."

"That place is dirty! I can't believe you would ever go there. So what if it cost you a little more, you made your wife happy."

"I could have stayed at home, cooked a steak on my own grill, saving ten dollars a plate."

"Did you actually do the math?" Ray asked, not surprised by the man's gift of being frugal.

"Of course I did. I should not have mentioned that to my wife though. She was pretty pissed and said I ruined the dinner. So while I am waiting in line at Kilika's, we noticed one of her friend's and her husband. The next thing I know I am paying for everyone's meal! For a dinner that I could have cooked on my grill for fewer than ten dollars I ended up spending over one hundred, including drinks. But of course my wife doesn't stop there. Because she had a few drinks in her, she wanted to go to the shoe store and buy like her ninth pair of shoes! In case you are not counting, I spent almost two hundred dollars just for a night out."

"Ha-ha. It made your wife happy. Besides, with your side jobs over the years and your pension, you will be fine once you retire."

"Not if she keeps on spending money like this. I will end up living with my daughter and son-in-law. And don't even get me started on them. I loaned him two thousand dollars to help them put a down payment on a car, and the little bastard has not paid me one cent of it. I might go repossess the car."

"You can't do that. Your daughter and wife would never forgive you."

"You're right. I will just have him work the money off next time he is in town. I have some wood that needs stacked."

"Will you shut up?" Berry yelled from the back of the plane. "My head is killing me."

"Why you are so upset? I am just trying to have a conversation with my partner. You can just close your eyes and go to sleep. I think I even saw some ear plugs up here." Turning to Ray, Rich said, "My generation never did stuff like this, and I lived through the sixties."

"He is not wrong, it would be nice to get a little sleep around here," Ray said. "We have a long day of ahead of us."

"Well, I guess I will use this time to hit the head. I just hope I don't clog the toilet again. That was so embarrassing when I was assigned to the secretary of state years ago. We were on a mission to Asia, and I made the restroom unusable until we landed. I've had trouble using them ever since."

Berry turned to Maul and said, "I told you this guy could talk. Great guy, but he will tell you everything you want to know about him and then some."

When Rich was in the restroom, Maul called up to Ray and asked, "How do you do deal with that?"

"What, Rich? He's not so bad. It makes him feel better to talk through things. I just listen to him and tune him out when I am tired. When it comes down to it, he is a great agent that does his job more meticulously than anyone I have ever met."

"If he is so good, how did you guys lose Jamin?" Maul asked.

"We were blindsided by a drunk driver, there was nothing we could have done. Nor could we have prevented Jamin and Lindsey from taking off to go on a little vacation. There was nothing we could have done differently, and every committee that investigates this case will find that we are not guilty of any wrongdoing."

"Unfortunately, no matter how good you and your partner are, you will always be known as the guys that lost Jamin."

"I can take that with a clear conscience."

"I'm glad you could because I would never be able to get over that."

Rich emerged from the restroom and took his seat in front of the plane next to Ray completely unembarrassed about his bathroom trip. "When we get there, I suggest we spread out," he said. "I have been to St. Augustine before, and it really is not too big of a city. I suggest that we separate with our partners and begin searching the city."

"I think splitting up is a great idea," Maul said.

Berry chimed in, "You two can take the outskirts of town while Maul and I stay in the downtown area. Start at Anastasia State Park and work your way around town from there."

Maali spoke up for the first time in hours and said, "The original plan did not include St. Augustine, so they do not know the city well. Expect them to be in a public place and to only move in under the cover of darkness."

"Why should we believe you?" Berry asked.

"I don't want to spend the rest of my life in Guantanamo Bay. Maybe you guys will have some mercy on me."

"Mercy? You plotted to kidnap the first son," Rich said. "We are going to throw the book at you."

In a soft and defeated voice, Maali said, "They left me behind."

Rich opened his mouth to say something, but Maul cut him off and said, "What?"

"They left me to die right there in the streets. They didn't even try to save me. They don't deserve my silence any longer."

"What about your mission?"

"I completed my end of the deal. I provided support to Aahil when I could. Now it is time for me to protect myself. If you don't believe me, that's fine, but they are going to St. Augustine, and my best guess would be that they will be near the heart of the city to make an easy exchange."

"Being in the city will just mean that there will be more opportunity to get caught, why would they risk that?" Berry asked.

"Their demands will be simple," Maali explained. "Just an easy wire transfer. That means that Taybah will stay and watch the first son and his girlfriend. Be careful because she will kill them if she needs to. Aahil will also demand that certain prisoners in Guantanamo Bay be released, but I believe that he will be willing to negotiate this demand. Right now he is desperate, and he may very well just take the money and run."

"How much money?" Berry asked.

"Not sure now, since so many of our men were captured, including me."

"How does he expect to leave the country?" Rich asked. "He and his wife will be the two most wanted fugitives in the world."

"They will assume that since the boy's kidnapping has not yet shown up in the news, no one will recognize them in the streets. That means you will just have federal agents looking for him, not the entire country. He is very good at keeping hidden, and I suspect that you will have your hands full."

"Then what? He thinks he will just disappear forever?"

"He will try. Probably end up in a Middle Eastern country somewhere."

"Do you have any idea where he might be?" Berry asked.

"I don't know anything about St. Augustine, but if you give me a map, maybe I could make an educated guess."

CHAPTER 33

The White House
The Oval Office

D r. Kryptoforski left his office as soon as he received the call from Kate Jenner. He gave his patient load of the day to his partners. As soon as he entered the White House, he was ushered to Kate Jenner's office.

The assistant knocked on the door and announced, "Ms. Jenner, Dr. Kryptoforski is here."

"Great. Can you let the president's secretary know he is here and we will be in the Oval in just a few minutes?"

"Sure."

Dr. Kryptoforski entered the room, and Jenner was surprised by the man's appearance. He was tall and looked like he played tight end in college. His head was shaved bald, and he wore a Hawaiian shirt with long cargo shorts and a pair of white shoes. The feature that Kate could not help but notice was his calves. His calves were the largest calves she had ever seen. She almost thought about not taking him to the president, but she valued the opinion of her friend that recommended him, so she took a leap of faith.

"Hi, doctor, I am Kate Jenner. Thank you for coming here on such short notice."

The doctor's words were quickly spoken, "No problem. It is not every day that I am asked to come to the White House."

"I just want to make it clear again that your patient must receive the highest level of doctor-patient privilege. This could look really bad if it got out to the press."

"I would never. I am assuming that I am not here to see you."

"I will let the president talk to you about that."

They walked to the Oval Office, and without knocking, they let themselves in. The president was sitting behind his desk, working on a stack of files that were situated in front of him. He stood and invited them to sit on the couches.

"Dr. Kryptoforski, it is nice to meet you," the president said.

"I can't believe that I am here right now. This is one of those places that I thought I would never go."

"Well, unfortunately, you are here under these circumstances."

"Before we talk, I think we should be alone that way you can be more open with me," referring to Jenner.

"You are not here for me, you are here for my wife, Ann. Charlie was taken hostage by a rogue terrorist cell. My wife is alone upstairs, and since we are keeping it from the press, she cannot grieve like a normal mother."

"My god, I am sorry to hear that. May I ask why this is being kept from the press?"

"We believe that it would put Charlie in more danger."

"Well, this is a terrible thing for her to experience by herself. What behavior is she exhibiting that concerns you?"

"She has being yelling at me an awful lot, and I cannot have a normal conversation with her. She also did not allow me to sleep in our bedroom last night."

"It is a good thing that you called me. She is going through the worst experience of her life, and she desperately needs someone to talk to right now. Is she expecting me?"

"No, she has no idea you are here. I wasn't sure how to approach it."

"I think it would be better for you to introduce us. I will then ask you to leave, allowing her open up to me. I find that a spouse often will not be honest and upfront when their partner is in the room."

"Of course. Can I ask you to step in the reception room? I will be right with you."

While Dr. Kryptoforski was comfortably waiting outside the Oval Office, Seaborne said to Jenner, "Are you sure this guy is the best? He doesn't look like a normal psychologist. It doesn't help that he is wearing cargo shorts and a Hawaiian shirt."

"My friend did nothing but rave about the guy. You shouldn't judge a book by its cover, remember? You also need to consider the fact that he did not have the opportunity to change."

"You're right." He chuckled and joked, "Did you see that guy's calves?"

"Ha-ha. They are huge!"

The president walked to the door and said, "Here goes nothing. Ann just might divorce me over this."

"I am sure everything will be fine. Mrs. Seaborne is a sensible woman," Kate said, not even believing her own advice.

"I'm not so sure. Wish me luck."

~ ~ ~

The White House
Briefing Room

Lisa Campbell was the White House press secretary and had been so since William Seaborne took office. Campbell was a young and very attractive African American woman that was an up-and-coming star in Washington. She was known to be witty and never got frazzled under fire. The first time Don Austin met her, he knew that she was perfect for the job. She planned on staying on the job until after the election when she would decide her future. She could move on and earn large amounts of money as a public relations consultant, but she preferred instead to move up in the administration.

She was sitting in her office when a seventy-year-old, longtime veteran of the White House Press Corps knocked on her office door.

"What can I do for you, Howard?" Campbell asked.

"I have a story I want to run by you," Howard Pinkus responded. Pinkus had the White House beat since the Reagan administration. He used a cane to help stabilize his weight.

"You know I have a staff for that, Howard. Just leave it with my assistant and she will make sure that someone gets to it soon."

"I can't wait that long, Lisa. If you don't want to comment, that is your choice."

His urgency got Lisa's attention. She put down her pen and invited him in.

"What is it?" she asked.

"It is about Charlie Seaborne. There are some rumors that he is missing."

"Missing? I am not sure what you are talking about."

"The first lady and Charlie were supposed to have a public event in Youngstown before they both cancelled."

"They both came down with the flu. We covered this in the gaggle the other day."

A gaggle was an informal press conference where the press secretary provided information, such as the president's schedule, and the journalists gave heads up on topics that may come up at the formal press conference.

"Well, Charlie and his girlfriend have not been seen at any of their classes since. This is not so weird if they have the flu. The thing is, they have not been seen anywhere on campus. Not even by close friends. No one has heard from them either. With all the social media out there, that is very strange behavior for a kid his age. Any more if a kid so much as farts they post it as their status. I need some answers before I print this story. If you do not give me anything, my report will be all speculation."

"I know nothing about this, Howard."

Pinkus used his cane to help himself stand and said, "It is your call."

"Can you give me a day or two?"

"I'll give you two hours."

~ ~ ~

The White House
The Residency

Ann Seaborne was sitting in the Yellow Oval Room, flipping through old scrapbooks. When William entered the room, she asked, "Did you find Charlie yet?"

"Not yet."

"Then get out."

"Hold on a second, honey."

"The next time I see you, it better be to tell me you found my son."

"There is someone here to talk to you."

"A shrink?"

"Yes."

"Tell him to go away."

"It is important that you talk to someone."

"Charlotte will be here soon. I will be fine until then."

"Will you please give him some time? Just a half an hour. Then if you still don't want to talk to him, I will tell him to go."

"Fine."

William went to the door and asked Dr. Kryptoforski to come in. After one look at the doctor, Ann refused to see him. "This is a terrible time to play a joke on me."

"This is no joke, ma'am. I am Dr. Kryptoforski. I am a psychiatrist and trained at Boston College, where I graduated at the top of my class. Give me thirty minutes and I promise that I will have you convinced that I am the real deal."

William left the room, closing the door behind him. Ann looked at the doctor's attire and asked, "What are you wearing?"

Without a word, the doctor took out his notebook and began writing.

Ann could not take the silence and asked, "What are you writing down?"

"I am wondering why you are so concerned with what I am wearing."

"It is not often that a person comes to the White House wearing shorts, even visitors on tours. I would expect that a doctor coming to work here would dress up a little more formal."

"I do agree that my clothes are not what you are used too, but I hope you can understand that I was called here just this morning and I came right over."

"So what is it exactly that you expect me to tell you? That I am a grieving mother of a missing child and I am torn up inside?"

"That is a good start."

~ ~ ~

The White House
Press Secretary Lisa Campbell's Office

As soon as Howard shuffled out of the room, Lisa called Don Austin's office.

"Mr. Austin's office," the receptionist said.

"Hi, Jean, this is Lisa Campbell, can I please speak to Don?"

"I am so sorry, but Mr. Austin is not available. I will have him call you as soon as he can."

"Jean, I need to talk to him right now."

"Hold on."

After a few moments, Don Austin picked up, "What is it?"

"Don, Howard Pinkus was just in my office and he wants to run a story that I think we should talk about."

"What does that crazy old bastard want now?"

"He is ready to run with a story about how Charlie is missing. I assured him that Charlie is just sick with the flu, but he insisted that it was something more."

"What did you tell him?"

"The truth, that Charlie is fine. He gave us two hours to respond before he gives the story to his editor. He said he wants to give us the opportunity to respond." Lisa took a deep breath and said, "Sir, is there something I should know? I know this sounds silly, but Howard Pinkus has been around a long time, so when he runs with a story, I tend to get a little worried."

"Why don't you make your way to my office now? We need to talk."

"Don, don't tell me something is wrong with Charlie and I didn't know about it. I am the press secretary, and if I did not know pertinent information like this, I cannot do my job effectively."

"Spare me the lecture and get your ass down here right now."

On the short walk to the chief of staff's office, Lisa began to feel sick to her stomach. She was worried about Charlie and what could be going wrong. She was also upset that if there was something wrong with Charlie and she was not told, she could not do her job correctly. Her job was to deal with the press, which meant she needed to be kept up to date on everything that went on in the White House. She was always amazed by how the press seemed to find out about situations like these. She would not be surprised if the press had every room in the White House bugged.

When Lisa arrived at the chief of staff's office, the door was ajar waiting for her.

"Come on in, Lisa," Austin said. Lisa took a seat across from his desk. He continued, "Believe it or not but the crazy bastard is right. Charlie has been missing for some time now and is in grave danger."

"When did this happen?"

"The night before the first lady was supposed to give her speech. We told everyone that she was sick, and luckily most people bought the story."

"Okay, back up. I need you to start from the beginning."

Austin explained the story to Lisa, including Charlie and Lindsey being taken hostage in Vero Beach. He also filled her in on the current plan to try and track down Charlie in St. Augustine.

"Why wasn't I told?" was Lisa's first response.

"I needed you to tell a good lie. The first son's life was at risk, and I needed you to make it look like he was fine."

"You know that I could have played it off well."

"I needed your reaction to look authentic if you were asked a question in front of the entire country. Look, we can either sit here and argue about how I should have told you or we can use our time to figure out how to keep Pinkus quiet."

"Obviously we will need to offer an exclusive interview with the president. But that will not stop him from running the story eventually."

"What about telling him that Charlie went on a short vacation and we wanted to leave it out of the news. If he keeps it quiet, he can be the first to break it and even have an interview with Charlie."

"That is if his face has no bruises. The terrorists could have knocked him around already."

"Let's hope not. If he is a little knocked around, we can say that a rough wave hit him while swimming in the ocean. Maybe say that he hit a rock or something when the water took him under. If Charlie can't absolutely go, Pinkus can sit with the president for the interview."

"I have never had a reporter turn down an exclusive," Lisa said. "I think that will work."

"There is one more thing that may come up soon. The president's brother was murdered by the Farahs. He was killed in his home in Parkersburg, and for obvious reasons, we have kept that hidden too. As soon as Charlie is recovered, we will say that he had a heart attack, but it won't be long before Dan Seaborne's friends also start to get nervous and they begin to look around. We will need to break this story soon, so I need you to come up with a plan so we will be ready to go if it does come up."

"What happened to the body?"

"The Secret Service has it off site."

"How was he killed?" Lisa asked concerned. She did not know the man well, but Dan always made her laugh.

"Multiple gunshot wounds. They took their time."

"How is the president handling the news?"

Austin took a deep breath and said, "Not too good since he has been so focused on finding Charlie he has not had much time to let it sink in. His last couple of days have been rough."

"Is there anything else that you are not telling me?"

"Yes, but they are national security issues that you are not cleared for."

Lisa knew not to press him on national security issues that even Deputy Chief of Staff and second in command Brad Wilder was not privy to.

"Sometimes I hate my job because of the stress, but never in a million years would I want to be the president." Changing the subject, Lisa said, "I will give Pinkus a call to set up that deal. I will let you know as soon as I get off the phone with him."

CHAPTER 34

St. Augustine Airport
St. Augustine, Florida

Mo Berry, Bruce Maul, Rich Maxwell, and Ray Turner disembarked from the FBI's plane at the airport and agreed to split up. Berry and Maul chose the downtown areas, including the famous St. George Street and Flagler College. Maxwell and Turner went on the outskirts of town, which included the lighthouse, Anastasia State Park, and the beaches. They thought that Maali was on the right track about Aahil and Taybah going to a busy area. For the cell's own safety, they would probably be hidden in a different location with access to a faster get away.

Maul and Berry started near the historic St. George Street. The lively street was home to many restaurants, bars, and shops. The street was open only to pedestrian traffic and was a hot spot for tourists. Maul was able to find a parking spot nearby, and he and Berry walked the long stretch of the road.

"I never realized how pretty this town is," Berry said

"Okay, grandma, we are not here for the tour. We have a mission to complete," Maul said.

"Just saying, that's all. We need to look for spots where it would be easy to hide Charlie. A small secluded space, so far what I see of this street, I don't think we will find it here."

"That is if they are here already. What about a place like that?" Maul said while pointing the country's oldest wooden schoolhouse.

"I guess there could be some spots hidden in there, but I don't see how they would pull it off without somebody noticing. There would be at least a worker that would stumble upon them."

"Let's go find out."

Maul and Berry paid the admission and looked around the small courtyard for good hiding spots. They went into the old classroom, the small building that served as the kitchen, and the grounds.

"I don't see anything here that could be used as hiding spot because every area is too accessible to employees," Berry said. "The problem is that there are probably a hundred other areas just like this that would be more suitable than here. I just don't know how we are going to find him."

"Let me see that map."

They inspected the map looking for the most probable areas a person could easily be hidden. They made a short list and chose to continue at Flagler College.

~ ~ ~

Anastasia State Park
St. Augustine, Florida

Rich and Ray were walking around Anastasia State Park looking for anything out of the ordinary. They met with the park manager, Nick Rash, to look for clues.

"We are looking for two couples, we don't think they are here, but we need to be on the safe side," Rich said.

"They are not violent, are they?" the manager asked. Nick was a skinny man in his midforties and had worked in the state park system since graduating from high school.

"No. They are just wanted for questioning. If we thought they were dangerous, we would evacuate the park."

"I don't know if that makes me feel better or not. What do they look like?"

"One couple is Middle Eastern and the other is a young white couple."

"I will ask my guys at the guardhouse, and I can spare a man or two to search the park. The park is large with plenty of hiding spots if someone wanted to seclude themselves badly enough."

Rash pointed to a park map on the wall. "You guys should take these trails and the beach areas. I will send my guys off the beaten path. Is there a number I can contact you at in case we find something?"

The men exchanged numbers, and Rich and Ray began their search. They parked at the beach and combed the area. Besides a few scattered sunbathers, there were no signs of anyone else.

They proceeded to a trailhead where they hiked a few trails, finding nothing but trees and random animals. Rich got a good laugh at Ray when he jumped at the sight of a snake that was stretched across the trail.

"Wow! That thing is huge!" Ray said.

"We will just go around it."

"I'll go back the other way."

"The end of the trail is just right up here."

"I would rather walk back around than be attacked by that thing."

"Come on, it won't hurt you."

Rich stepped over the tail end of the snake, and it acted like it hardly noticed.

"Come on, you little girl, we have work to do."

Ray approached the reptile cautiously and slowly lifted his leg to get around it. The snake did not move as Ray ran away as fast as he could, unscathed by the harmless snake.

~ ~ ~

Flagler College
St. Augustine, Florida

"Why are we here again?" Berry asked.

"There could be many secluded areas here. This is an old building that may be a good spot to hide," Maul responded.

"This place is way too crowded. There are too many students and staff roaming around here." Berry noticed a group of girls walking past him, and he quickly changed his mind. "You know what? Since we are here, we may as well look around. We need to split up to cover more ground."

Before Maul could respond, Berry was chasing after the girls. Maul took the opportunity to walk around the campus in hopes of finding something. Before becoming a college, the campus was used as a luxurious hotel. The rich and famous would flock here and spend large sums of money to stay during the winter. The small campus today is arguably the most beautiful in the country. The Spanish architecture and light orange-tiled roof gave the building its character.

Forty-five minutes later, Maul was done taking his tour with the head of security that showed him around the areas closed off to the public. He was waiting in the courtyard for Berry to show up. Maul glanced up and saw him walking down the stairs arm-in-arm with two girls, and all were laughing at one of Berry's jokes.

"You got to be kidding me," Maul grumbled to himself.

"Hey Maul! I want to tell you that these girls showed me around campus, and everything seems fine!"

The girls wore tight tank tops and short shorts and giggled as Maul tried to explain where he was. Berry continued, "I made sure that I looked around the girl's dorm real well, and it was clear."

"I'm sure you did," Maul said like a disappointed father. "We need to leave."

Berry turned to the girls and gave them both a kiss on the check, "Give me a call sometime!"

"We will!" they responded in unison.

Maul and Berry walked toward their car parked on the street outside of the campus when Maul let his frustration out.

"Have you been drinking?" Maul asked, still portraying on the father figure.

"I had one shot. And one beer. But other than that, no."

"Listen to me! We cannot screw this up! The president has made it our responsibility to find his son. If you do anything stupid again, I will leave your ass behind. Do you understand?"

"I had to blow off some steam and have a little fun. Now I have a clear head, and I am ready to find Charlie."

"You make me sick! They are only in college!"

"You don't think I slept with them, do you?"

"You were drinking in their dorm room, what do you think?"

"Apparently we have some miscommunication going on here. I had a couple of quick drinks and searched the dorm. That was it."

"Just forget it. We have work to do."

"When I get a chance, I am going to tell my kids about this place. This has to be the most beautiful campus I have ever seen."

Maul stopped, looked at Berry in disbelief, and then asked, "You have kids. As in plural?"

"Yeah, I got so many kids I can field my own football team—all boys too."

Maul started to walk again, saying, "How often do you see them?"

"Not very often. The job keeps me on the road, and their mothers really don't like me being around that often. But twice a year I have a big party at my place, and we spend the weekend together."

"How can you continue to amaze me?" Maul asked.

"You are just scratching the surface," Berry said with a grin.

They reached the car, and Maul sat in the driver's seat. "How do you afford the child support?"

"My great-granddaddy left me some decent money."

"Is that the drunk you told me about?"

"That was my great-uncle," Berry said, annoyed that Maul could not follow along. "Anyway, each mom received a large lump sum of money and an account for college if the boys chose to go."

Maul merged into traffic and said, "Do you still have some money left over?"

"I got a little. With the inheritance and my pension, I will be fine."

"Unbelievable."

~ ~ ~

The White House
Lisa Campbell's Office

The old reporter and Lisa Campbell were sitting in her office. Lisa was doing her best trying to convince Howard Pinkus to hold out on reporting the story, but thus far Lisa had been unsuccessful in her endeavor.

"I am an old man, Lisa; this could be my last big story. This is like a manager retiring after winning the World Series. I want to end my career with something big and something that I will always be remembered for."

"Howard I know that this story is important to you, but the president is asking you to hold off."

"The president is not asking, you are."

"You know that I am speaking on his behalf. Listen, if you wait, I will give you an exclusive with the president."

"Everyone gets exclusives from time to time."

"Fine. Off the record, I will admit that Charlie is not on the Youngstown State campus. He and his girlfriend are currently on a little vacation. They needed some time alone."

"Then why not tell the press?" Howard asked as if he felt insulted that he was not told.

"Charlie hates the media. They needed some time away without being followed."

"Where did he go?"

"I can't tell you that. When Charlie gets back, I will give you an exclusive with him and Lindsey."

"Who?"

"His girlfriend, Howard. I might be able to get the president to make a surprise appearance during the taping."

"Go on," Howard said, finally listening.

"You can talk about his vacation and why they went away without telling anyone. Then you can talk about life as the first son and ask Lindsey about life as the girlfriend of the first son. Your story will get much attention."

"And no one knows about this little vacation?"

"No one."

"How could the first son go on vacation without anyone noticing him? I know Americans are ignorant when it comes to the first family but someone would have recognized him, I'm sure."

"That is a question that you can ask him in the interview. If that won't convince you, I have another big story that you can break." She was referring to the death of the president's brother, Dan Seaborne. She figured that someone will need to break it, and Howard needed something to push him over the edge.

"What is it?" Howard asked, very curious of what this new information could be.

"You are just going to have to trust me on this one. This will be headline news."

"With me getting the exclusive with Charlie and getting to break this mysterious headline, the other reporters are going to wonder why I am getting the special treatment."

"Leave that to me," Lisa said confidently. "Most of them have played the game long enough and understand how it works here. Like you said, they have all had exclusives in the past."

Howard thought for a moment then said, "I can agree to this. You better make this worth my while."

"I can promise you that."

"We will be in touch," Howard said as he returned to his office to call his editor and tell his editor to hold off for now.

Lisa's first call was to Don Austin. "Yeah, Lisa," he said into the phone.

"Pinkus is on board. I had to promise an exclusive with Charlie and Lindsey and have the president make a surprise appearance."

"Why do I get the feeling that is not all you offered him?"

"I also offered him the opportunity to break the Dan Seaborne story."

256

"What?"

"Relax. I didn't tell him what it was but promised that it was big. Like any reporter, he couldn't help but to take the deal."

"What are you going to tell the other reporters?"

"That is was a retirement gift. They may be upset, but that will only last so long because deep-down inside they know that they are just jealous and would make the same deal if given the chance."

Austin was pleased with Lisa's work. She was good at her job and was glad to have her on board. He had hopes that she would be willing to move up and become a senior advisor to the president when her current job became too stressful.

"Good job, Lisa," Austin said. "I hope you know how much I appreciate you being here. You do good work."

"Thanks, Don."

CHAPTER 35

The White House
The Oval Sitting Room

"I gotta tell you, doctor, I am glad you came," Ann said to Dr. Kryptoforski.

"I am glad that you opened up." Dr. Kryptoforski was just as surprised as anyone that Ann was willing to talk to him. She was keeping everything bottled up, but she felt much better off now that she talked through it. "Remember, next time you feel stressed, try to calm down and most importantly avoid taking it out on the people that you love."

There was a knock on the door, and a stunning woman in her midforties was at the door. She had long blonde hair and was wearing a long, black skirt with a white button-down blouse. Dr. Kryptoforski was interested the moment he laid eyes on her.

"Hello, Charlotte! I am so glad that you came," Ann said to her friend.

Charlotte had been a good friend from Ohio and had been around the Seabornes as they made their climb to the White House. She was one of the only friends that Ann still talked to from before they became famous. Behind her was a butler with a warm tea kettle and three cups.

"Dr. Kryptoforski, this is my longtime friend from Ohio, Charlotte," Ann said, introducing the two.

"Nice to meet you, doctor."

"Call me K. The pleasure is all mine," Dr. Kryptoforski said. He felt like he was coming on too strong, so he decided that it was a good time to leave the women alone. "Ladies, I have other business to attend to, so I better get going."

Charlotte was clearly disappointed and said, "So soon?"

"I would love it if you could join us for a cup of tea," Ann said, picking up on the vibe in the room between the doctor and her friend.

"I think I can make time for one," Dr. Kryptoforski said. He was a little apprehensive about joining the two for a social event.

"Great, okay!" Charlotte said. The three took a seat in the sitting area while Ann poured a cup of green tea for each. "Where did you go to school?" Charlotte asked.

"I went to Boston College. I played tight end during my undergrad, and I loved it so much I went back for my doctorate."

"You know my son's girlfriend is trying to get in to B.C. Is there anyone you could call?" Ann asked hoping this would be her opportunity to get Charlie to go to Harvard.

"I will be happy to see what I can do. I still have a lot of connections."

"I can tell you played football," Charlotte said, clearly flirting with Dr. Kryptoforski. "Wasn't it hard to get hit all the time?"

"It is not that bad. That is why we spend so much time in the weight room."

"Why did you choose Boston College?"

"I had other offers from Syracuse and Miami, but B.C. seemed like the right fit. I had a lot of respect for the coaching staff, and the players were good guys."

"You turned down Miami? You could have been in the sun every day."

"I am from Michigan, so the lack of sun and mountains of snow never bothered me." Dr. Kryptoforski was now openly flirting with Charlotte. As he took a sip of his tea, he felt uncomfortable socializing with his new patient and a woman that he was attracted to. He was waiting for his opportunity to leave the room as soon as it came up.

Ann placed her tea cup on the table and said, "When this thing is all over, why don't you come join us for dinner one night. We can double date and have dinner in the private dining room. After, I can give you a personal tour of the White House."

"I'm not so sure that is a good idea," Dr. Kryptoforski said.

"Is it because I am a patient?"

"That does have something to do with it, yes," he replied.

"Don't be silly, I will not take no for an answer."

"In that case, I have no choice," Dr. Kryptoforski said. He set his cup on the table and announced, "I am sorry, but I do need to get going. Let me know if you need anything else."

Dr. Kryptoforski left the room and was escorted by a Secret Service agent to the see president.

When he was out of earshot, Charlotte said, "He is cute!"

"You like those calves?"

"I think they are sexy. Good call on the dinner so I can see him again."

"The calves just scare me. He is a good doctor though."

"What is going on, Ann? You sounded so frantic on the phone."

Ann and Charlotte spent the next couple of hours discussing Charlie. Charlotte offered whatever comforting words she could, but it was hard keeping her mind off of the psychiatrist.

When Dr. Kryptoforski arrived in the West Wing, he was ushered right into the Oval Office. Seaborne sat behind his desk while Kate Jenner gave him updates of the day's business.

"Dr. Kryptoforski, how did it go?" Seaborne asked, hoping for a positive answer.

"Great. She seems to be in a much better mood now. Her friend Charlotte just showed up, so I let them talk for a while."

"Okay. Send the bill to Kate, and you will be paid soon."

"Thank you, Mr. President."

Dr. Kryptoforski left the room, and the president said, "He is good. Ann always swore she would never talk to a shrink—another wonderful decision on your part, Kate. Thanks again for being here."

~ ~ ~

The White House
Don Austin's Office

"You are a real jerk, you know that?" Austin said.

"You can't tell me that you are naive enough to think that I would be here forever," Brad Wilder responded.

Both men were standing in the middle of the room about three feet away from each other.

"But to go out like this? I put my reputation on the line for you. The first major decision I made for Seaborne was hiring you as my assistant and you go behind our backs and screw us. I should kick your ass for this."

"I would have given you a job, you know that."

"You know that this is my dream job, and I would never do anything to screw that up. Did you ever consider how I've always looked after you while you were sneaking around making your deal?"

"This isn't personal! I was trying to look after myself. You know that my skills are worth the money." Wilder took a deep breath and said, "I screwed up."

Austin closed his hand into a fist, swung, and connected on Wilder's temple. Wilder was knocked off balance but remained standing. Wilder stepped forward and responded with a quick uppercut to Austin's abdomen, which earned Wilder another shot to the temple. Wilder put Austin in a headlock and squeezed hard enough to cut off his air supply. Austin slapped at Wilder's leg, causing Wilder to release his grip.

Both men collapsed to the floor, breathing hard, trying to regain their composure. A full two minutes passed before Austin said, "You could have killed me!"

"Looks like I am definitely out of a job now," Wilder said.

"Get your stuff together and get out. Kosar agreed to resign from Freedom Air and to keep his mouth shut in return for his freedom." Austin stopped for a moment to take in more air. "You resign and stay away from the airline industry, do you understand?"

"I appreciate the president sweeping this under the rug, but I must say that I am surprised. I didn't think he had it in him." Wilder raised his hand to his temple and flinched when he pressed on the fast-forming bruise. "When you hit me, I saw stars."

"Trying to get to the gym more. Look, resign and go quietly. We will leave you alone and you will leave us alone. It is best for all of us."

"Since it is obvious that we will never see each other again, for what it's worth, I enjoyed working with you."

Austin looked Wilder in his eyes and said, "Have a nice life."

~ ~ ~

Washington DC
Secret Service Headquarters

Liam Hughes was working in the Secret Service office, on loan from the CIA for the duration of the search for Jamin. Working at the offices of the Secret Service allowed him greater access to their files.

Hughes was sitting at his desk, looking through security tapes from Ray's Hot Spot and Grill, the bar where Kinsey and Taybah exchanged money and information. The bar's owner was always cooperative with police because on his side of town, he never knew when he would need the favor returned.

This was the first opportunity Liam had to look through the tapes. One of his subordinates went through the tapes and created a file that contained only the nights that Kinsey and Taybah meet. He wanted to see the interaction with his own eyes so he could get a feel for Taybah. He believed that if he knew the personalities of the targets, he could use the knowledge to his advantage when trying to follow a suspect's movements.

He evaluated every scene, finding each one was the same. Kinsey went into the bar and met Taybah, she then passed him an envelope and stayed for only one drink, presumably to avoid raising suspicion.

He was eating a small bag of chips when someone looked out of place. He replayed the video of the couple's fifth meeting. He was sure that he saw that person in one of the earlier videos. He watched the first meeting again, and the same person was sitting in a small booth in the corner. He scanned every video of the drop-off and there was that same person, always sitting in different places in the bar, but it was clear what the purpose was. Being at every meeting was too much of a coincidence.

He zoomed in on the face to get a better look. He was sure he saw that person before. Yeah, that's right, he saw that person at the White House. He needed to notify the president. There was a terrorist working in the West Wing.

~ ~ ~

The White House
The Oval Office

Debra Sharp, Don Austin, Adam Royal, and Kate Jenner were standing around the president's desk as Seaborne discussed the attack on Iran's sovereign land with President Saeed Jafari of Iran.

"Yes, Mr. President, I am sorry for the attack, but can we focus on the future?" Seaborne asked. Thus far, the president had done nothing but apologize for his country's actions.

"How dare you attack us! You had no right!"

In an attempt to move on, Seaborne ignored the man and said, "Sir, Vice President Sewell is flying to Iraq as we speak. Officially he is there on a diplomatic mission, but he will sneak over to Iran to negotiate the final terms, and I assure you that you will be pleased."

"Nothing can take back what you did."

"I understand, sir, but again we need to move on and look to the future. We will not tell the UN or the world about your nuclear and biological programs. We will also send a couple of billion dollars to help you build some schools, including schools exclusively for girls. You just need to give us your word that you will discontinue your illegal weapons programs." The line was quiet. "This is a good deal. If you want, we can tell the world what you have been hiding and even the Middle Eastern world will turn against you."

"Fine, it is agreed."

"When the vice president gets there, you can discuss the terms of the weapons inspections."

"I will refuse weapons inspections."

"You have promised not to build weapons, now you need to let us in. This is a deal breaker."

"All right, but they need to be kept out of the public's eye."

"We will do our best. Thank you."

The president hung up and asked Sharp, "How do you think that went?"

"Fairly well. It will depend on how much access they give our inspectors. You will be criticized for giving them money. It will make it look like you support them."

"Lisa will be able to spin it for us. Thank you, everybody, that will be all."

The president was alone, relieved that the Iranian problem worked out. He was almost sure that it would blow up in his face like many top-secret missions of presidents before him. Like Jimmy Carter's attempt to free the American hostages at the U.S. embassy in Iran, but the helicopter crashed before it made it to the embassy. Sometimes a president needed to take risks such as when Barack Obama sent the Navy SEALs to kill Osama bin Laden. Obama believed that it was a fifty-fifty chance that bin Laden was actually in the compound. He believed in his intelligence and that our military personal could carry out the mission perfectly, however, and he gave the order to attack despite the odds. The mission was a success, and Obama was a hero. This would be Seaborne's defining moment in the White House, but his situation was different. The public would not know how courageous of a leader he was, and they would never know who the heroes of the Z Force were or how brave the members of the NEST team really were. This is what Seaborne thought made a good leader. Making decisions that were best for the country and not taking any credit for it. He would find Charlie and then focus on running for reelection because he knew he was the best man for the job and for the country. This was his purpose in life.

~ ~ ~

Bright Days Café
St. Augustine, Florida

Maul, Berry, Rich, and Ray sat around the table at the small café as the sun was going down. They each ordered sandwiches and coffees as they compared notes and brainstormed about what to do next.

"I don't know about you guys, but I am damned tired," Rich said, taking a big sip of black coffee.

"He walked some trails today, and I thought he was going to pass out on me. He was sweating, his face was all red, and he was huffing and puffing. It was quite a sight," Ray said, looking for a laugh.

"When you get to be my age, you will understand. It is not as easy as it used to be."

"You are supposed to be in the Secret Service and you are expected to be in great shape at all times," Maul said. "No wonder Charlie got lost on your watch."

"Why do you keep on bringing that up?" Rich asked in his defense. "We need to focus on finding Jamin."

"We can blame the terrorists taking Charlie on you then," Ray said, referring to the partners losing Charlie in Vero Beach.

"This will get us nowhere, gentlemen," Berry said, trying to calm everyone down. "We need to concentrate on the details here for a moment. Maul and I called the local police and sheriff's office, and they are on the lookout for people fitting the Farahs' descriptions."

"Was that wise? I thought we were supposed to do this quietly. Now who knows who is going to find out what we are doing," Rich said.

"Relax," Berry said. "They don't know why they are looking for them. We need all the help we can get right now, so if that means getting the help of the local police we need to do it. The respective organizations have my phone number and will call me it they find anything. Is there something we are missing?"

"We searched the city pretty hard. I sincerely don't know what else we can do. After we eat, we can drive around some more and see what we can find."

CHAPTER 36

St. Augustine, Florida
Castillo de San Marcos

"Enough about Canada already!" B-Mac said.

"Obviously you haven't been listening. Canada has a lot of great history. They started hockey, the greatest sport on earth. The band Guess Who is from Canada, and who doesn't like them?" Fleck asked. Fleck was five feet eight inches tall, had a runner's body, and a full beard from his Canadian ancestors that he was grateful for. He was an American history teacher, but a person would not know it by how much he talked about Canada. His parents moved to the states when he was a young boy, and he grew up in Michigan, all the while clinging to his Canadian roots.

"We live in the United States, and there is a reason for that. Just think about who protects Canada militarily. The U.S. does. Where do you earn your living? America." B-Mac was a calculus teacher and never backed down from a debate. He was an inch shorter than Fleck and had 100 percent Irish in his blood, red hair and all.

"Did you know that the Unites States lost a war to Canada?"

"What the hell are you talking about? We never lost a war with Canada."

"Sure we did. It was the War of 1812. A couple of decades before the war Jefferson said that all America needed to do to take over Canada was to march there. They tried it in 1812, and the British-Canadians responded by burning down the White House. The Treaty of Ghent ended the war, and all prewar lands were returned, which is why some historians call it the "strange war." Nothing was gained."

"I don't think that means that we lost the war. Using that logic, Canada lost too."

"But the U.S. was supposed to win big, but the Canadians held strong."

"Never mind all that. We are here at this great fort thousands of miles south of the Canadian board, so let's just enjoy this."

"How did you get us in here again?" Fleck asked.

"My buddy is a ranger here. He said everyone should be gone. He gave us this key to get into the front gate."

"I don't feel right about this, B-Mac. I say we just go back to George Street and have a stout," Fleck said nervously. He was not used to breaking the rules. He was the kind of person that hesitated to go above the speed limit.

"We can have some drinks later. We will just lock up when we leave." B-Mac was slightly annoyed that his Canadian friend was thinking about backing out. "Do it for Laura Secord."

Laura Secord was a legend from the War of 1812. The myth claims that after dragging her wounded husband home from the battlefield, Secord's house was overran by American soldiers. She hid and overheard them discussing a surprise attack near the Nigeria Peninsula. She walked about twenty miles and warned the British army, and at the battle the Americans were the side that was taken by surprise and lost.

"Why couldn't we do this during the day?" Fleck asked.

"There are ghosts in here."

"Don't tell me you believe in ghost stories now."

"I'm going in. You can stay here like a girl or you can come in and have a little scare."

B-Mac continued up the path to the old fort. Fleck decided that it was really not a big deal and joined him.

"I didn't think you would change your mind that easily," B-Mac said proudly.

"I figured Laura Secord would do it."

"Ha-ha. That's more like it. I will buy you some Irish whiskey tonight."

"I'll stick to my stouts."

When they got near the main entrance, both men slowed down and became vigilant of their surroundings. To their relief, the grounds looked empty like they were promised.

"You ready?" B-Mac asked.

"Sure."

B-Mac put a key in the lock that was securing the gate and opened it only wide enough for the two of them to slide through. B-Mac ran his hand along a sharp piece of the fence, leaving behind a two-inch laceration. "Ouch!"

"Who does that?" Fleck asked. "You were the kid that always got beat for crying for little injuries, weren't you? Man up."

"I'm not complaining. I'll be fine." B-Mac removed his outer shirt and tied it around his hand to stop the bleeding.

"Hurry up, eh," Fleck said.

The teachers walked across the drawbridge into the main courtyard, astonished by what they saw. The Castillo de San Marcos was a late seventeenth century fort built by the Spanish. For many years, it was the main fort between Spanish Florida and Colonial America. The fort boasted thick walls, and like many forts of its time, it was shaped like a star to see in all directions. Its history included surviving hurricanes, violent attacks and changes of ownership, but it still stood. Visitors could witness live demonstrations of firing cannons and view many of the rooms that supported the fort and the city around it.

B-Mac heard rumors of ghosts being present at the fort during the night. His ranger buddy claimed it was the scariest thing he had ever experienced. B-Mac called him on it, and now B-Mac was here to settle a bet. B-Mac said that he would be able to stay at the dark fort for two hours without being freaked out. The ranger said he would never experience a visit at night again, so Fleck came on the trip because of the promise of free beer afterward.

They approached another gate that B-Mac easily unlocked, and they entered the dark fort. Besides the security lamps lighting the outside, it was almost pitch black. B-Mac and Fleck grasped their flashlights tight in their hands as they walked slowly into fort. The pair waited until they arrived at the courtyard before they said a word.

"It is supposed to be over here," B-Mac said, pointing to his right.

"What are you talking about?"

"The gun deck-powered magazine room," B-Mac said as if Fleck were an idiot.

"You didn't say anything about going into a room."

"Shut up and listen to the story. They used this room to hold gun powder but it was too moist. Eventually the room was sealed off, and no one knew about it for years until it was found on a fluke accident. When they opened it back up, it was rumored that they found old bones and ashes inside. Because of the bones, some people believe that this room was used as a dungeon."

"You cannot honestly think that I am going into an old dungeon, B-Mac."

"This coming from the guy that doesn't believe in ghosts?"

"I don't need to believe in ghosts to get freaked out. Come on, man, you are not really going in there, are you?"

"We both are. I just want to go in look around a little bit and leave. We will spend the rest of our time in the courtyard."

"Exactly what ghost stories are out there?" Fleck asked, now seemingly interested.

"Some believe that old soldiers still walk in formation around the courtyard. Others claim that they have seen a woman searching for her husband. The stories are endless, really. If you go in the dungeon, it will be an experience of a lifetime. Don't chicken out."

"All right, all right. You lead the way."

~ ~ ~

Aahil got lucky. He followed the two into the fort, opening the gates as they went. He came to the conclusion that both men were idiots. One thought that Canada was the best place on earth and the other one believed in ghost stories. To him they were both infidels that needed to die. Aahil's luck got even better when the Irish one started to talk about a secluded dungeon within the fort. He planned on stowing his hostages in one of the storage rooms. An old dungeon would make his demands that much better.

Aahil could almost see the money now. When Charlie and Lindsey were secured, he would call and make his demands. He decided that he could no longer worry about the Guantanamo prisoners. His time was running out. He would demand fifty million dollars that would be wired to a Swiss account. For a fee of one million dollars, Aahil contracted a professional hacker who would then move the money through several accounts until the remaining forty-nine million ended up in Aahil's account. He would use the new money to start his own terrorist network in the Middle East with the goal of bringing down the Americans.

Aahil snuck back to his vehicle parked in the main parking lot of the fort. He didn't like the idea of leaving his car in the middle of a vacant, well-lit parking lot adjacent to a busy street, but he had no other choice.

"Remember what I told you," Aahil said to Charlie and Lindsey. "We need to walk quickly to the fort, trying to stay in the shadows. I will have my gun on me, don't try me."

The gagged couple had no other choice but to nod their heads yes. Aahil removed the gags in their mouths to not draw attention but left their hands bound in front of them. They slowly made their way to the entrance, dodging the lights as they advanced through the big lawn. They entered the two gates, then once they entered the foyer area, Aahil told Charlie and Lindsey to sit.

"Things have changed," Aahil whispered to Taybah. "Stay here and keep an eye on them. We are about to pick up two more hostages." Before Taybah could protest, Aahil was turning the corner.

~ ~ ~

"I'm out!" B-Mac yelled.

"What the hell, B-Mac? This was your idea," Fleck said. They began weaving their way through the maze of rooms to get back to the courtyard.

"I am not going to sleep for a week after that. I was fine until we turned out our flashlights. I swore something was rubbing my neck."

"It was probably a spider."

"You were freaking out too, don't deny it."

"I was crapping my pants, but this was your idea."

"When you get homesick, do you know what you can do to feel more at home?" B-Mac asked.

"I can't believe that I am going to subject myself to this. What is that?"

"Fill a refrigerator full of maple syrup and stick your head into it." B-Mac laughed but was not joined by his friend. "You get it? Because it is so damn cold in Canada, and the best thing from Canada is maple syrup."

"I get it just fine, but it was the stupidest joke that I've ever heard," Fleck responded, not amused. He then pulled out his phone and held it up, saying, "I have you flipping out on video. I can't wait to post this on your wall."

"You are not going to post anything on my wall. This stays between us!"

"Is that the new bro code?" Fleck asked, making fun of him. "Can't post anything embarrassing on a friend's wall? Does that mean that I am not invited to your next Tupperware party?"

"Hey man, I have a couple of girls in the works, this could ruin it."

"They will find out you are afraid of the dark sooner or later."

B-Mac pushed Fleck out of his way and went through the door leading to the courtyard. They jumped when they heard the deep, slow, monotone voice, "Where is this dungeon you speak of?"

Fleck jumped, hitting his head on the door frame, while B-Mac stood still in his tracks.

"Well, come on, guys, I heard you talking about this great dungeon. Don't you want to show me where it is?"

"Listen, I know that we broke in here, but we can explain," B-Mac said, stumbling his words. "We will leave, no harm done."

"You gentlemen won't be going anywhere for a while, I'm afraid."

"Screw you, call the cops but we are leaving," Fleck said. He took a step toward the exit, and Aahil revealed his pistol he concealed behind his back. Fleck and B-Mac took a deep breath and were too stunned for words.

"On second thought, stay right here. If you move, I will shoot you. We have already killed two today." Shouting over his shoulder, he yelled, "Taybah! Bring them here."

Charlie and Lindsey emerged from the darkness with Taybah following them. Charlie and Lindsey were tired and hungry, and they were struggling to stay focused. They walked slowly to the annoyance of their captors.

"Hurry up!" Aahil yelled. "I do not have time for this nonsense. We have the perfect spot for you."

Aahil pointed his gun at the frightened teachers and said, "Lead the way."

Fleck and B-Mac reluctantly headed back toward the dungeon. Fleck wasn't sure what B-Mac would be more afraid of, the man with the gun or the haunted room. Using their flashlight, they stopped in front of the door. "There it is," B-Mac said.

"What are you waiting for?" Aahil asked. "Go in."

"Nah man, I'm not going in there again," B-Mac said.

Aahil raised his gun between B-Mac's eyes at pointblank range. "Looks like I'm going back in," he said without hesitation. He opened the squeaky door and entered the room, with Fleck following close behind. "Give me your flashlights," Aahil ordered. Both men hesitated but knew it was in their best interest to hand them over.

"Good, now clean out your pockets." Aahil held a flashlight on them while they turned over their possessions. The two men emptied their pockets, which contained mostly their wallets, cell phones, and keys.

"Now lift up your shirts so I can see if you stashed anything in your waistbands." The two men did as they were told, and when Aahil was satisfied that the men were unarmed, he forced Charlie and Lindsey into the room.

"Charlie and Lindsey, it has been fun, but now I leave you. If my demands are not met by sun up, I will come back and kill you. If I am paid, you will be rescued once the tourists start showing up."

Aahil shut the door and used miscellaneous items lying around to barricade them in, including a shovel handle in the door handles. Taybah and Aahil walked out of the old fort to their car in the parking lot, headed to their next destination.

The four were sitting in the dark room, this time with no way out and no way to illuminate it. All four were scared out of their minds.

"Where the hell are we?" Charlie asked.

"The old haunted dungeon of the fort," B-Mac blurted.

"What the hell, B-Mac?" Fleck asked. "Why did you have to frighten them?"

"Sorry, sometimes I don't think before I speak."

"Great." Charlie said. "I can't wait until this whole thing is over."

"Who the hell are you guys?" B-Mac asked.

"I'm Charlie Seaborne, the president's son, and this is my girlfriend Lindsey."

"What the hell did you get us into," Fleck asked B-Mac. "You and your stupid midnight tour. When we get out of here, I am going to kick your ass."

"Did somebody just brush up against my arm?" B-Mac asked with a sense of urgency. When no one responded, he said, "Seriously, who the hell just brushed up against me? I am freaking out over here. Your dad better hurry and pay that dude off!"

"My father is the President of the United States, don't you dare make a threat!"

"There it is again! Where is the door at?" B-Mac felt his way to the door and pushed, using all of his might, but the door didn't budge.

CHAPTER 37

St. Augustine, Florida
Castillo de San Marcos

Aahil swore as his stolen junker's engine did not turn over. "I can't believe it! We need to get out of here! Taybah, grab the phone and tell me where we are at."

Taybah reached deep into the bag and searched for a phone while Aahil attempted to start the car. He popped the hood and started fooling around with some wires near the battery. She felt the phone with her fingers and pulled it out of the bag. She clicked the menu button, but the phone did not respond. Looking for the problem, she flipped it over, noticing that the battery compartment was empty. She found the battery in the bag and inserted it then turned the phone on.

Returning from the hood of the car, Aahil said, "No! Not that phone!"

"Sir, do you need some help?" a man asked from behind him.

Aahil spun around and saw two St. Augustine police officers standing behind him. For the first time in his life, Aahil was speechless. "Ahh, no, we are fine. I think the battery died on me."

"Do you want me to call someone for you?" the older police officer asked.

"No, that will not be necessary. My brother is on his way."

"Are you sure?"

"Yes, we are fine."

"You know that it is illegal to park here after dark."

"My apologies. We are not from around here."

"I should be giving you a ticket."

"I understand!" Aahil said, not doing a very good job concealing his annoyance.

The cop was not pleased with Aahil's disrespectful comment. "I will be back in ten minutes, and this car better be out of here or I will tow it out!"

"Yes, sir." Aahil watched as the police officers walked back toward the main street. He turned to Taybah, who was searching area maps on the phone she found.

"Taybah, what are you doing?"

"I am just using the phone like you told me to."

"That is the phone that I used to contact Kinsey!"

~ ~ ~

Washington DC
Secret Service Headquarters

Jim Thompson was talking to Liam Hughes when a notification menu appeared on Liam's computer. They were going through the tapes from Ray's Hot Spot one last time to confirm what they saw before taking it to the president.

"This is something big, sir. The Farahs just turned on their phone," Liam said.

"Where are they?" Thompson asked.

"Give me a minute." Liam typed commands into the computer eager for results. As they came across the screen, he read them to Thompson, "They are in Florida, North Florida. Sir, they are right where we thought they were, St. Augustine."

"Get Berry on the phone now!"

Liam dialed Berry, and without a salutation, Liam said, "They are there. In St. Augustine."

"Where the hell at?" Berry asked.

"Hold on, it's coming. They are at the Castillo de San Marcos. It is on."

"I know where it is at," Berry interrupted him. "We are on our way." Berry hung up the phone, then the federal officers ran to their vehicle without paying the bill.

"Sir, when are we going to tell the president about the infiltrator?" Liam asked Thompson.

"I'll call Harper now."

~ ~ ~

St. Augustine, Florida
Castillo de San Marcos

"We got to go!" Aahil said.
"Where?" Taybah asked.
"To the fort."
"Why are we going to go there? We will be trapped. We need to go and disappear. Start a family. I am over this mission."
"That is not what we are here for. We need to finish our operation."
Aahil took Taybah by the arm and led her to the path of the old fort. The police officers were now three hundred yards away, they noticed the couple sprinting toward the landmark and knew that something was amiss, so they began to chase after them.
"Stop!" the older man yelled. "This is the police!"
Without skipping a beat, Aahil and Taybah continued up the hill running toward the open gates. "When we get to the gates, keep on going and find something to lock us in the area where we put the hostages," Aahil huffed. "I will lock the gates behind us."
Taybah did as she was told when they reached the gates and Aahil closed and locked the first gate behind him. This gave the out-of-shape patrol officers time to make up ground.
"I said stop!" the older cop repeated, not yet realizing the magnitude of the situation they were in. Aahil disappeared across the drawbridge when the cops spun around to see a standard-issued Secret Service vehicle bounce up the footpath that led to the main entrance of the fort. The cops saw sparks underneath the vehicle as it made its way toward them.
The younger cop aimed his pistol at the car before his partner could stop him; he took a shot that reflected off of the roof of the car.
"Hold your fire! You can't shoot just yet."
The local cops held their ground with their weapons when the car came to a screeching halt. Maul emerged from behind the wheel of the car, and Berry opened the passenger door. Ray and Rich were hesitant to get out at first because they were unsure of what the cops would do. The local cops were nervous and were ready to make a move.
"We are Secret Service agents!" Berry yelled. "I am reaching for my badge."

274

On edge the cops placed their fingers on the triggers of their pistols. Berry slowly reached for his badge in his front pocket and held it in view of the cops. "I am Agent Mo Berry, this is Agent Maul. We are with two fellow agents that are too afraid to get out the car right now. Just relax and put your weapons down."

"Bring your badge here," the older cop commanded.

"Okay. Here it is." Berry walked slowly to give the man his badge.

"Thank you. What is going on here?"

"Those two you are chasing are terrorists, and they are holding the first son hostage," Berry said. "We need you to stay out here to watch the perimeter. And get help fast!"

Maul was trying to open the gate, and after a short time with no success, he shot the lock with his sidearm. The lock crumbled easily and fell to the ground. When the tensions between the cops were squelched, Ray and Rich joined them as they entered the historic fort.

~ ~ ~

The White House
The Oval Office

"Sir, we have contact with Farahs! They are waiting on the phone," Barbara Harper said as she barged into the Oval Office. The president's secretary was annoyed that she did not ask permission first.

"Assemble the team now!" Seaborne said.

"They will be here in a moment. Sir, do you want to talk to them?"

Before the president could answer, Don Austin walked in and said, "Sir, if you talk to them, the terrorists will win a small victory. I recommend that Ms. Harper talk to them."

"I just want to get this over with, Don. I want Charlie to come home."

"I understand, Mr. President, but it would be better if Harper talks to them."

Kate Jenner and Adam Royal walked in together and the president asked, "What do you guys think?"

"Go ahead and talk to them, Mr. President," Jenner said.

"I need to agree with Don, let them talk to Harper," Royal answered.

"Okay, Barbara, it is all yours," the president ordered.

Harper cleared her throat and said into the speaker phone, "This is Barbara Harper, the director of the Secret Service. With whom am I speaking?"

"You know who you are talking to. This is Aahil Farah, and I have the first son."

"What do you want?" For all the years she worked with the Secret Service, this was the first time she had ever negotiated making her nervous and thinking that she could not pull it off.

"I insist on speaking to the president. If not, I will kill the girl."

The president stepped forward, prepared to speak, but Royal put out his arm to stop him. Royal mouthed, "Not yet." The president gave in and took a step back.

Harper continued, "Mr. Farah, I am speaking on behalf of the president, and my word is his word. I assure you that I can do everything the president can."

"You know my demands, do you not believe me?"

"I believe you, but that will not be necessary because you and I can work this out."

Bluffing, Aahil said to Taybah, "Go get the girl." Turning his attention back to Harper, he said, "You only have a matter of minutes before the girl is dead."

Ignoring his advisors, Seaborne stepped forward then said, "This is the president. What do you want?"

"Ahhhh, Mr. President. I now have four hostages, your son, his beautiful girlfriend, and two random tourists. If you refuse my threats, I will begin to kill them, starting with Irish tourist. I want fifty million dollars wired to my bank account." Aahil gave him the wiring information before continuing, "I also have some company outside that is waiting to give me some trouble. Once they are called off, Charlie will come with us, and I will release him unharmed provided we are out of the city. My terms are nonnegotiable. You have two hours."

~ ~ ~

St. Augustine, Florida
Castillo de San Marcos

While Aahil was satisfied that the president would comply with his demands, the four Secret Service agents continued to look for them in the fort. They were able to gain access to all the rooms with exception to the powder magazine room, which was barricaded.

"They are in here!" Berry said. The four agents gathered around him. Harper relayed the demands to the agents who were attempting to develop a game plan. Berry continued, "They way I see it, we have two options. The first is to barge through that wooden door or second we wait until the president meets his demands. I'm personally for taking the fuckers out."

"Let's be smart about this," Rich said.

"Oh, this ought to be good," Maul said.

"No, wait a minute. We can pay the man his money and have snipers placed in the corners. This place is perfect for hiding snipers. When they come into view, we take them out. We will be done, and we can all go home."

"What about the money?" Maul asked.

"We try to get it back. If not, we lose fifty million. I'm sure the government spends more than that on toilet paper in a day."

"I'll call Washington," Berry said, impressed that Rich came up with a decent plan.

After a five-minute phone call, Berry returned to the group.

"What'd they say?" Maul asked.

"They are considering it. I told them that snipers can hide just about anywhere here. I think they will go for it."

The fort was now surrounded by St. Augustine cops. The lights on top of their vehicles lit the sky as many onlookers started to appear, including boaters that came close to the shore of the fort to see the action.

"We need to get rid of these cops first," Ray said.

"Good idea, get on it," Rich responded. "Make sure they get those boats out of there too. I will call around and get some sharpshooters in here."

~ ~ ~

The White House
The Oval Office

"I can't believe we are about to pay terrorists. This is against everything the U.S. stands for when dealing with terrorists."

"Mr. President, look at it from the angle that you are paying this money to kill two terrorists," Harper said.

"It still isn't right, there has to be another way."

"The only other option is to break down the door, and that is just too risky."

"If it was anyone else but my son, I would not pay."

"Just be happy to get him back alive," Austin said.

An assistant walked in the room and said, "Ms. Harper, there is a Special Agent Jim Thompson on the phone for you."

"Tell him it can wait," she responded.

"He said that it cannot wait another second."

"I'm sorry, sir, I will be right back." She used a phone in the reception area and said, "What is it, Jim? I am real busy here."

"Ma'am, we have a serious problem. We have been reviewing tapes from Ray's Hot Spot for over an hour now and noticed something awkward. We did some more searching, and we found some activities that support our theory."

"I'm in no mood for games, what is it?"

Thompson told her the name, and Harper was speechless. "My god. You can't be serious."

"I am afraid so."

"Thank you." Harper hung up the phone and spoke to the two agents outside the Oval Office door, "I need ten agents here now and lock down the White House." The agent spoke into his radio, and within seconds ten agents appeared seemingly from nowhere.

Secretary of Homeland Security Matthew Jones joined the group in the Oval Office. He too was convincing the president to go ahead and pay the money; the only dissenter was Adam Royal.

Harper walked into the Oval Office and announced, "Mr. President, the White House is on lockdown. We have an immediate threat. Ms. Jenner has been working with the Farahs."

"That can't be true!" the president barked.

"It is not what it seems!" Jenner shouted. "I can explain!"

Seaborne's shoulders dropped as he felt like the most betrayed man in the world. "I can't believe this Kate. I trusted you with my son's life."

"It is not like that! Please, let me explain!" Jenner pleaded.

"I am sorry, but there is just no time for that. Get her out now." Turning his attention back to the president, Jones continued, "We need to order the money transfer now." The president looked to be in shock as they dragged Jenner out of the office and Jones said, "Mr. President, we need you to make this decision now. We need to stay focused."

Seaborne asked in a determined tone, "How thick is the door?"

"Excuse me?" Jones asked.

"The door at the fort, how thick is it?"

"Not too thick, sir."

"Let's go get their asses. They don't deserve to die by a sniper. They need to see it coming. Go get 'em."

"What about Charlie's safety?"

"Everybody out. Get Maul on the phone."

~ ~ ~

St. Augustine, Florida
Castillo de San Marcos

"Maul."

"Bruce, this is the president. I am tired of waiting. I need you to go in and get my boy." Maul could tell the president was angry by the tone of his voice. "Do you trust Berry?"

Maul had to think about it before he answered. He did not like Berry's style, but he had to admit that the man got results. "Yes, sir, I do."

"Break down the door and make sure they look you in the eye when you kill them."

"It will be my pleasure, sir."

Maul hung up the phone and updated the group. They obtained a small charge from the St. Augustine police. They would use it to blow up the door and raid the room. Maul and Berry would be the first two in, followed by the St. Augustine S.W.A.T. unit. This was the moment that Maul was waiting for.

~ ~ ~

St. Augustine, Florida
Castillo de San Marcos
The Powder Magazine Room

"What is taking so long?" Aahil yelled. He was becoming more anxious by the minute.

"Relax, they will call soon," Taybah said, trying to calm her husband.

"We need to kill the Irishman, hell the Canadian too. We need to prove we are serious."

Bang! The sound and the impact of the explosion knocked both Aahil and Taybah to the floor. Maul cleared the remains of the door, and he and Berry stormed the room careful to avoid the splintered wood. Taybah and Aahil ran toward the dungeon when Berry shot Aahil in the back. Aahil landed on his stomach and was in considerable pain but managed to flip over and return fire, hitting Maul in the thigh. Berry pushed forward, hurdling Maul, and shot Aahil squarely between the eyes, killing him instantly.

Taybah was able to free the dungeon door, and she blindly shot in the room trying to get a lucky hit on Charlie. Berry and Maul both fired three shots a piece, hitting her in the head and in the back.

The entire incident lasted less than forty-five seconds, and all who were involved were stunned. Berry was the first to regain his composure, as he made his way into the dungeon where he heard cries of pain. He stuck his head in the room but was unable to see much.

"We need to get light in here now!" he yelled. A member of the St. Augustine S.W.A.T. unit appeared with a large 1,000-watt work lamp and set it up. When Berry could see into the room, he saw Lindsey holding her abdomen, blood covering her hands. "We need a medic now!"

~ ~ ~

The White House
Holding Cells

The White House installed a series of small holdings cells for situations like these. Kate Jenner sat on the bed with tears rolling down her face. She screwed up, and she knew it, but she felt that she did not have a choice. The Farahs put her in a bind that she could not see a way out of. One of the outer doors clicked open, and Don Austin entered the room.

"The president is very hurt, Kate. He took a lot of heat for moving you up like he did. Even giving you top-secret security clearance." Don Austin looked like he was grieving for the president. "He wants to know why."

"Being down here with nothing but my thoughts made me think about giving my side of the story. I've decided that I will not talk right now. I need to see an attorney. I am not going to make the same mistakes Kosar and Wilder made."

"Okay. Understand that we are going to throw the book at you. We will try you as a terrorist, and you can expect a long time in a maximum-security prison. You hurt the man, and I heard Ann wants to kill you with her bare hands." Austin walked out of the room.

Kate did have a good reason, and her story would be out soon enough. One month before the Farahs met Kinsey, they approached Jenner. She suffered from high anxiety, but she was afraid that if she was prescribed medication, it would risk her job. People would hold secrets from her thinking that she was too risky because most anti-anxiety pills have side effects such as impaired thinking and judgment and hallucinations. Her drug dealer went to prison for possession with the intent to sell illegal prescription drugs. That was when Taybah showed up and offered to supply Jenner for a remarkable price, half of what she paid her old dealer.

Taybah's explanation was that she was trying to grow her business; therefore, she offered low prices to her newest customers in order to expand. With the advantage of hindsight, Jenner now realized that it was too easy to find a dealer so quickly, with the same drug that Jenner needed. It was clear that Taybah had done her homework and tracked Jenner's steps, got her dealer busted, and swooped in for her blackmail scheme. Jenner could not believe she had been so dumb. She should have realized that it was so easy to get her drugs that quickly.

After her first two-week supply, Taybah explained to Jenner that she would get an unlimited supply of the medicine, for free. All she had to do was track some guy named Kinsey. Taybah told her, "Walk in, see if he is there. If he is not, text 'Billy' and leave. If he is, I will meet you in the alley with your supply."

It was that easy. She thought that his envelope contained drugs, just like hers did. In return for her services, Jenner received her monthly supply. She didn't know who Taybah or Kinsey was until she saw both of their pictures in the briefing meetings she attended as an advisor to the president. She should have spoken up, but what good would it do? She would only get herself needlessly in trouble since the connection between Kinsey and the Farahs was already made. She never imagined that they would spot her on the video.

She also wondered why they picked her. Anyone could have completed the job; it did not need to be someone close to the Seaborne family. Her only guess was that the Farahs would use her for information if they did not get enough from Kinsey. They would threaten to turn her in if she did not give up the information she demanded.

Kate would plead with the president to save her once she talked to her attorney, but even Kate knew that it was unlikely that she would get off easy, especially after it involved the Seabornes' son.

CHAPTER 38

Washington DC
The White House

Three days after the rescue of Charlie and Lindsey, they returned to Washington DC. They arrived to a small party waiting for them in the private dining room of the White House. Lindsey's parents flew to St. Augustine to stay with their daughter while she was in the hospital. Soon after the shooting, Lindsey was taken to the emergency room where she received immediate care for her wound. She was lucky that the bullet did not hit any major organs in her abdomen, such as her spleen, liver, or kidneys. While she was still in considerable pain, her injuries were not life threatening, so she was discharged.

Ann had not seen her son, and she was anxiously waiting for him to make his appearance. When he came into view, the first lady ran to her son and hugged him tightly; Charlie swore he felt a rib crack.

"I am so happy you are okay!" she said in a wavering voice. "I missed you so much!"

"I missed you too, Mom. You just need to lighten up a little bit."

Ann let go of Charlie and, while holding his arms, leaned back to have a good look at him. "I wish you would have come home sooner."

"I would not have left Lindsey there while she was in the hospital, I told you that."

"I know, but I just missed you so. I see you decided to shave your beard."

"Well, we do have a big interview coming up, so I figured I should look respectable."

The room was set for lunch, and Ann invited her guests to have a seat. "Mr. and Mrs. Skeffington, welcome, please have a seat."

"Thank you," Mrs. Skeffington responded.

Turning her attention to Lindsey, Ann said, "How are you feeling, sweetheart?"

"I am in a considerable amount of pain, but otherwise I am doing fine," Lindsey said with a grimace.

"We better get you seated then!" Ann helped Lindsey to the table, and everyone took their places, including the president. "I took the liberty of ordering us lunch, I hope no one minds. Since Lindsey is our guest of honor today, I ordered her favorite meal, cheeseburgers and fries. I know it is not very fancy, but I am sure we can relax a little and enjoy ourselves."

The president greeted his guests as they took their seats. The butler emerged out of the back room with two bottles of Debonne wine in buckets of ice. Debonne was a winery near Geneva-on-the-Lake, Ohio, and it was the Skeffingtons' preferred wine. The shores of Lake Erie produced some of the best wine in the country. "I didn't order that," Ann said.

"I did," said the president, speaking for the first time. He and his wife had hardly spoken since Charlie was rescued. "Charlie asked me to."

"What is the occasion, dear?" Ann asked her son, ignoring her husband.

"Mom, Dad, Mr. and Mrs. Skeffington, we have an announcement to make," Charlie said.

Lindsey leaned to Charlie and whispered, "What are you doing?"

Charlie stood and continued, "I wanted to let everyone know, especially you, Mr. Skeffington, that if it is acceptable with the Skeffingtons, I would like to announce that Lindsey and I are now officially engaged."

"Well, of course it is all right, son!" Mr. Skeffington responded. Lindsey's father loved Charlie, and the two got along great, due mostly to their mutual love of Cleveland sports.

"That is great, son, when did this happen?" the president asked, not at all trying to conceal his excitement.

"When we were in Savannah, it just felt right. No one makes me happier than Lindsey."

"And when is this wedding going to take place?" the concerned Ann asked, not trying to conceal her disapproval.

"We are not sure; we went through a lot since my proposal. You know we were kidnapped by terrorists and all."

"I just hope you two can make it through graduate school before getting her pregnant."

"I don't know about everyone else, but I am tickled pink about you two," Mrs. Skeffington said, trying to change the mood. "There are a lot of bad boys out there, and I am just so happy that my daughter found one of the last good ones left."

"Thank you, ma'am. I promise to be a great husband to Lindsey."

"Come on and pour that wine already!" the president said to the butler.

"So when are you going to announce your news to the public?" Ann asked.

"I was thinking about tonight's interview," Charlie said.

"Your father will need to run it by his political team first, I am sure." Ann was expecting her husband to agree and ask Charlie to delay the announcement.

"I think that would be just fine! It might even give me a bump in the race!" the president joked.

"Well, it is settled then! We will let the world know tonight." Charlie held up his glass and toasted, "To my future wife!"

~ ~ ~

The White House
The Oval Office

Vice President Aaron Sewell landed at Joint Base Andrews, formally Andrew's Air Force Base, and headed straight to the Oval Office to meet with President Seaborne. Seaborne was more jolly than normal, largely due to the glass of wine he had at lunch. The president did not drink often because of his responsibilities of being president. That meant that when he did drink, the alcohol affected him more than it used to.

"Aaron, I am glad you are back."

"Thank you, Mr. President, I always love coming back to the United States after going abroad. As you know, the Iranians have agreed to our deal, including aid for schools. I also want to tell you how relieved I am that Charlie and Lindsey are safe. I should have been here with you when the end unfolded."

"Thank you. You know that I would have loved you being here, but the country needed you there. You did good work. How did Iraq go?"

"Iraq is becoming more stable. I met with some leaders of their government, and it seems like things are in order there. Overall, I am confident that Iraq will become a stable country and an ally of the United States." Sewell switched the conversation to domestic issues. "Are Charlie and Lindsey ready to give the interview?"

"I think so. They are rehearsing right now with Lisa. They are going to tell Pinkus that they were on a little vacation, mainly so Charlie could ask her hand in marriage."

"That is great, sir! Lindsey is a sweet girl."

"I need to talk to Don about getting another deputy chief of staff. If you have any names, forward them to him."

"You already have her here, sir. Lisa is a great choice. Press secretaries only last a couple of years before they burn out. This will give her an opportunity to remain in the White House. She can handle a large workload. Plus, two African Americans at the top two spots in the White House will go a long way in a Republican administration."

"I'll run it by Don."

~ ~ ~

The White House
The East Room

The East Room looked its finest for the interview, with beautiful flowers in the background and the lighting situated just right. Charlie and Lindsey were sitting in their chairs when Howard Pinkus walked in. Lisa Campbell thought it would help to disguise Lindsey's injuries. After brief introductions were made, Pinkus, a man known for getting down to business, began the interview.

"How was your little vacation?" Pinkus asked.

"It was great to finally get away by ourselves for once," Charlie responded.

"Why didn't you tell the press?"

"We knew they would follow us. This way, we were able to relax without photos of us in our bathing suits on the beach. The time was just for us."

"Don't you think it was a little strange that you didn't even tell your friends that you were leaving?"

"I love my friends dearly, but you know just as well as I do that someone would have leaked it to the press."

"It seems to me like this was not a planned vacation. I mean you left without turning in assignments. I talked to some of Lindsey's classmates, and they claim that she did not turn in a major history paper about POWs held captive during the Vietnam War. If this was planned, I would think that you would have at least turned your paper in early."

"The paper will be turned in, I have spoken to my professor," Lindsey said for the first time.

"That does not answer my question. This will hurt your grade, will it not?"

"If it does hurt my grade, it will be worth it. I had the time of my life with my new fiancé." Lindsey reflected the question brilliantly.

"Fiancé, huh? It sounds like you had a fantastic vacation. How did you propose, Charlie?"

"We had a great dinner in Savannah, and I asked her over a bottle of wine. It was very romantic. We are both very excited that we will be spending the rest of our lives together."

"I was talking to Mrs. Seaborne before this interview, and she was delighted to tell me you both have the opportunity to go to school together."

"Excuse me?" Charlie asked. He could not help but to give his mother a mean glare as she stood across the room. The move was instinctive, and he hoped the camera did not pick it up. His mother stood next to William, Charlotte, and her new friend, Dr. Kryptoforski, who wore his now-predictable shorts and Hawaiian shirt.

"You have both been accepted to Harvard. Congratulations!" Pinkus knew by their reactions that this interview would be played on every television station all over the country.

"Wow. We didn't expect this," Charlie said with an authentic look of surprise on his face. "It looks like we have some major decisions to make."

Dr. Kryptoforski had an acquaintance that worked in the history department at Harvard, and after reviewing Lindsey's transcripts, he was guaranteed a private tour of the White House. Dr. Kryptoforski thought helping Lindsey get into Harvard would be a good way of getting close to Charlotte. Harvard was impressed with Lindsey's transcripts, and it was an added bonus that the couple would bring so much attention to the school, including the full attention of the president.

"Harvard would definitely be hard to turn down. I will need to get my parents' advice of course," Lindsey said. The Skeffingtons were also in the room watching the interview, and began to cry at the idea of their daughter going to Harvard.

The majority of the interview focused on their engagement and the couple going to school together, until the conversation switched focus to

Dan Seaborne, Charlie's uncle. Pinkus broke the news about Dan soon after Charlie and Lindsey were rescued. The press reported that Dan had a heart attack, and there would be a private funeral for him.

"I didn't get to see my uncle much, and in fact on my way to Florida, I stopped in to see him. I am just glad he was able to meet Lindsey before he died. He was a good man with a big heart, and he will be missed."

When the interview ended, Howard Pinkus was certain that he would have the send-off he wanted. The Seabornes, Skeffingtons, Charlotte, and Dr. Kryptoforski relaxed on the second floor of the residency in the West Sitting Hall.

"What do you think about Harvard, Lindsey?" Mrs. Skeffington asked.

"I don't think I will be able to turn it down," Lindsey said. "I am just worried about the tuition. How in the world am I going to be able to pay for it?"

"I don't think you are going to need to worry about that," the president said. "We read Uncle Dan's Will today, Charlie. He left you a substantial amount of money."

"How much, Dad?"

"Fifty million dollars." The room gasped as William announced the amount. "The rest he gave to charity. He asked that you do the world some good with your portion of the money. I think paying for your fiancée's tuition is a good start."

"I think that is a great idea. I don't know what to say. I never expected to have all of that money." Charlie thought about it for a minute and smiled. "I think the first thing I am going to do is send the Skeffingtons on another cruise since their first one didn't go so well."

"Oh my, that would be lovely," Mrs. Skeffington said.

EPILOGUE

Allen Kinsey and Maali were both sent to a supermax prison in Florence, Colorado. They were sentenced to spend the rest of their days in a tiny cell among some of the most violent prisoners that the country had to offer. Both were locked down for twenty-three hours a day. Maali did not receive any visitors, but Kinsey's grandmother did show up three or four times a year until her death. Kate Jenner gave her side of the story and was sent to Butner medium-security prison in North Carolina.

Gideon Kosar resigned from his post at Freedom Air, just like he promised the president. He spent his time joining boards of directors and running races. Brad Wilder started his own law practice in Chicago and soon made millions.

Thaddeus Klug and the Zeta Force returned to their life in a top-secret military installment and continued to execute their missions flawlessly. The members of Zeta Force enjoyed their week in Aruba, where they ate and drank like kings.

B-Mac and Fleck enjoyed their couple of weeks of fame. They were invited to the White House as guests of the president. At the special event, Fleck asked to become the ambassador to Canada, and the president promised he would consider it.

Mo Berry and Bruce Maul reported to their respective agencies and were soon back to work. Maul spent some time in rehabilitation to get his leg back to normal. Berry still drank on the job but was somehow still able to perform to perfection to everyone's amazement.

William and Ann continued their routine of not talking to each other until they needed to, a routine that both of them expected to last the rest of their lives. William could not forgive his wife for the way she acted, and she could not accept the fact that it was not her husband's fault that Charlie got away.

Charlie and Lindsey graduated from Youngstown State University and prepared for Harvard in the fall. They spent their summer traveling throughout Europe, seeing everything the continent had to offer. Life at Harvard was good, until Charlie joined the most surreptitious association in world.

CPSIA information can be obtained at www.ICGtesting.com
Printed in the USA
LVOW091916270312

275003LV00007B/24/P